The Godmothers

Also by Camille Aubray

Cooking for Picasso

The Godmothers

A NOVEL

Camille Aubray

wm

WILLIAM MORROW

An Imprint of HarperCollinsPublishers

THE GODMOTHERS. Copyright © 2021 by Camille Aubray LLC. All rights reserved. Printed in the United States of America. No part of this book may be used or reproduced in any manner whatsoever without written permission except in the case of brief quotations embodied in critical articles and reviews. For information, address HarperCollins Publishers, 195 Broadway, New York, NY 10007.

HarperCollins books may be purchased for educational, business, or sales promotional use. For information, please e-mail the Special Markets Department at SPsales@harpercollins.com.

FIRST EDITION

Library of Congress Cataloging-in-Publication Data has been applied for.

ISBN 978-0-06-298369-5

21 22 23 24 25 LSC 10 9 8 7 6 5 4 3 2 1

For
Rose

The Godmothers

Prologue

Nicole

New York, April 1980

I never needed to ask my godmother for a favor, until the day that my husband was offered a job at the White House. It was April in 1980, and James and I had been living in New York for only a year. We'd met each other in Paris and gotten married there, but, since both of us were American-born, we always thought of the United States as our home, so we were glad to be back. I thought our lives were pretty settled now, here in Manhattan. I was working as a news researcher for Time Inc., while James practiced law.

But one bright spring day, James announced, "I've just had a very interesting chat with Cyrus Vance. He wants me to come work with him in Washington at the State Department."

"The Secretary of State wants *you*?" I echoed, awed. As with all important decisions, we discussed this over a candlelit dinner at our favorite restaurant.

"It won't be an easy job, with President Carter smack in the middle of this hostage crisis in Iran," James admitted. "Mr. Vance is a good negotiator, but there's a lot of infighting going on right now in the White House. And Vance, poor guy, has got a bad case of gout, so he's gone to Florida to recover. He told me to go home and discuss this job offer with 'the wife.'"

I rolled my eyes. "I suppose I'm lucky that he didn't say 'the *little* wife,'" I groused.

James grinned. "Vance wants my answer when he returns from his vacation. If we say yes, they'll do an FBI background check. It's strictly routine. But they will look into *everything* about you and me—our friends, families, work, everyone who knows us well. Vance says it's best to tell him up front whatever he should know—'just so there are no surprises.'"

"Meaning what?" I asked, not grasping the situation at first.

"Oh, you know. They have to investigate to see if there's anything from our—or our relatives'—pasts that could make me vulnerable to blackmail, that sort of thing. I told him my family are modest folks, and I've never known any people as honest and good as your family!"

There in the flickering candlelight, he kissed me in a husbandly, appreciative way that made me feel especially well loved. "So don't worry, it all looks like smooth sailing ahead," he concluded. Then he contented himself with finishing off his *boeuf bourguignon,* and I nodded.

But all this talk of investigating my family alarmed me, although I couldn't say why. It was just an inexplicably uneasy feeling creeping over me, as if shadowy phantoms lurked in my peripheral vision—but if I turned to see them head-on, they instantly retreated into the dark corners from whence they came. I took a quick gulp of red wine to steady myself.

Not long afterwards, we visited my mother in the Westchester suburbs. When James went out early one morning to play some tennis with a friend who lived nearby, I decided to dispense with the little question that was still nagging at me. I told my mother about the job offer and asked, point-blank, "Does our family have any skeletons in the closet?"

It was the expression on her face, rather than her words, that gave me pause. She blushed and glanced away quickly, looking slightly guilty, before she recovered and said, "Not really. Certainly not in *your* time. But why would your husband want to go to Washington? Your brothers think President Carter is in a real fix with this hostage situation in Iran."

My older brothers were prone to making such dire pronouncements at Thanksgiving dinners. Today I had to agree that the times were not auspicious. But at the moment I wasn't concerned with politics; it was family history that mattered. I tried to learn more, but I knew my mother well enough to realize that I would never really get a detailed answer from her.

Moreover, something in her quick, furtive look stirred that strange feeling of dread in me again. This time I was determined to find out why. So, after Mom hurried off to an appointment with her hairdresser, I decided that the only person who could help me was my godmother. She lived right next door, in this secluded seaside enclave of just four houses on a tiny spit of land overlooking the Long Island Sound. Our extended family had moved here after years of living in Greenwich Village.

I knew every inch of these backyards where I'd played with my cousins, and every corner of the little cove where I'd learned to swim in the salty sea. But over time, such memories had receded like the sea's tide, once I'd gone off to Europe to study and grow up.

Now just crossing the lawns and walking up the pebbled driveway of my godmother's house made them all come rushing back— and I felt like a little girl again, peering into the bay windows of her dining room to glimpse her at the big, old-fashioned formal table, where she'd reigned over mysterious "meetings" with my mother and my two aunts. I can still see the four of them commiserating in low, conspiratorial voices, then falling silent whenever the children came running in.

My cousins and I always referred to our female elders as "the Godmothers." When I was ten years old I'd devoured Greek and Roman mythology, so I went through a phase where I pretended that the Godmothers were really goddesses in disguise.

Even their names sounded mythological to me: *Filomena, Lucy, Amie, Petrina*. Four powerful witches brewing their plots and stirring their pots of magic. The very fact that these sisters-in-law had asked one another to be godmother to their children gives you an idea of how insular my family was. They believed that strangers were dangerous, to be viewed with suspicion. But we cousins, like all young people, outgrew such feelings, for we knew we needed to reach out and make our way into the larger world, despite all its perils.

Today I found my godmother standing on the generous front porch of her Victorian house, her back straight, her head held high. She was in her mid-fifties, her fair skin creamy and smooth, with barely a line on her face; and her hair, worn in a coil at the back of her head, was dark and lustrous. Although she'd lived in America for decades, she still had an old-world, formal manner. Her large, almond-shaped eyes seemed to see right through you, which most people found quite daunting. But she'd always had a soft spot for me, her goddaughter.

"*Buongiorno, cara* Nicole," she said as I kissed her cheek.

Her house had an expansive view of the soft and dreamy blue-grey Long Island Sound. I was glad to discover that the porch still had an old-fashioned glider seat, made of metal in a braided basket-like pattern, big enough for the two of us. We sat there, leaning on cushions, gliding back and forth, chatting about the weather.

Finally, with her finely-tuned instinct, she said quietly, "What can I do for you, Nicole?"

The surge of apprehension I'd felt earlier had now intensified into a bone-deep dread that I still could not identify. Maybe secrecy exists in all families, I don't know. The trouble is, you can't entirely forget something that you don't entirely know. It occurred to me that I might not get another such private, meditative opportunity to finally confront these ghosts with her.

So I told her about James's important job offer and the possibility of a "routine" background investigation. Although her face never changed its expression, I heard her make a quick, soft gasp. That was enough to tell me that I had been right to come here and ask questions. I watched her carefully as she remained silent for several minutes.

"Please, Godmother," I said finally. "Whatever it is, I need to know now."

Gently she warned, "You tug on one thread, you might undo the entire tapestry."

But, oddly enough, she looked as if somehow she'd been waiting all along for me to come to her like this. She said, "All right. Only because it's you, Nicole. But some of what we say to each other today must remain just between us." She added wryly, "At least, wait until I die before you chatter about it. And understand, I am in no hurry to go!"

I nodded, and she said, "Well, then, where shall we begin?"

I took a deep breath. Everything about the four Godmothers was so mysterious. Who had they been before they became our Godmothers? They seldom spoke of their girlhoods, lightly but firmly resisting our questions, until we cousins finally accepted that the past was a brick wall, no point trying to peer over it. Just what *were* these secrets that had united them all this time—and were somehow the source of my childhood fears? I sensed that violence and other bad things lurked in those shadows, yet I, too, had kept them hidden, even from myself.

Well, my godmother was right. It only took one tug on a thread, one question leading to all the others. And that's how I finally got the whole story.

BOOK ONE

The 1930s

1

Filomena

Santa Marinella, Italy, 1934

Filomena's mother held her hand tightly as they stood on the platform watching the train pull into the station.

"Stop dancing, Filomena, or you'll fall down and get hurt!" Mama warned, adjusting her daughter's flat-brimmed hat with a sharp tug.

Filomena tried to be still, but she had never been at a train station before, much less ever boarded a train, and her heart was leaping with excitement, like the fish who jumped out of the water with joy in springtime, making her father sing to them as he cast his nets. "How long will we ride on the train?" she demanded, thrilled.

"Many hours, many, many hours," was all that Mama would say.

She had wakened Filomena early this morning as if it were Christmas, and made her put on her best dress and coat and hat and shoes, saying only, "We are going to visit a very important friend of this family." Not only that, but Mama had given her a boiled egg to eat with her milk and bread, and another boiled egg to slip into her coat pocket.

Filomena had strutted with pride, wishing that her siblings could see her, but her two younger brothers had disappeared early with Papa to help him on his boat. And Filomena's two sisters were old; they were twice her age and all they cared about was finding boys to marry. Filomena was going to be eight years old in September.

Now the train slowed to a complete stop at the platform, belching steam and soot like an ill-tempered dragon. Filomena buried her face in her mother's skirts so that the soot wouldn't hurt her eyes. Her mother jerked her by the hand and said tensely, "Come. We go up the train's stairs. Let's count as we go: One, two, three, up! Up! Up!"

The metal steps clanged loudly as they mounted them. Other people were suddenly pushing to get aboard, but Mama managed to enter a carriage quickly and secure a seat for her and her wide-eyed daughter.

Filomena was a bit overwhelmed by all the strangers, and she saw that a few were staring at her mother, probably because Mama was wearing those dark-tinted eyeglasses. Mama sensed this, too, but lifted her chin defiantly and turned her face to the window.

"Sleep, *figlia mia*," she said. "We have a long way to go."

Filomena would normally have broken away from her mother's grasp and run up and down the carriage, fearlessly asking her fellow passengers any questions that popped into her head, for she'd been born with a natural exuberance. But she *was* tired; she had not slept well last night. Her bed was in a tiny room that had once been a closet, right next to her parents' room, and she could hear their noises. Most nights her parents were so weary that they slept immediately, but sometimes they made fearful sounds that reminded Filomena of the night animals who came skulking under the windows, to fight or make babies; often it was hard to tell the difference.

And sometimes her parents yelled at each other, which they had done last night. Filomena had pressed her pillow to her ears,

but still, she could tell that it was a bad fight. Her parents quarreled endlessly until finally, like a storm, their argument broke
into a crescendo of pure rage. She could not hear the words, just
her father bellowing, her mother screeching defiantly, and terrible
thumps against the wall, and cries of pain from poor Mama—
then, silence.

In the morning her father, scowling, mutely went off to work.
At such times Filomena found it hard to believe that this was the
same man who, in a better mood on a better day, would take her
for walks in the town square and buy her a *gelato,* and then sing
to her all the way home. She loved going down to the sea with
him, where the sky was a wide-open blue and the tide a sparkling
complementary shade of azure, lapping at the soft sands of the
beach dozing under a warm sun. The old stone houses there were
huddled together like something from a fairy tale, dominated by
a big medieval castle, built to protect the town from pirates. The
castle was surrounded by beautiful pine, palm, and olive trees,
and in summertime the sea breeze carried a whiff of the garden's
roses and violets. Filomena always thought that one day a prince
would come out of the castle and invite her to dance with him.

But Filomena was not going with her father to the sea today.
Her mother had emerged from the bedroom with one blackened
eye, looking defeated. That was when she'd announced to Filomena that they were going away to visit some friends of the family.
Filomena was glad to escape the tension that filled the house so
thoroughly and seemed to remain there, even when everyone else
had left it.

"Does Papa know we're going?" Filomena had asked curiously.

"Of course," her mother had said shortly. "It was his idea.
Come, let's put on your good dress. And don't forget your hat! Be
quick and be bright."

They all knew that she was "bright," even though her father had pulled Filomena out of school, over the protests of her
teachers—especially one *professoressa* who'd made a special trip

to their house just to say, "Filomena is a shining star who could make you proud." The teacher had made Filomena demonstrate how she could add up long columns of three-figure numbers in her head, without working it out on paper.

"This would be remarkable in a child of any age," the *professoressa* had tried to explain. "But for such a young girl! Imagine what she could do if you kept her in school."

The teacher's visit had provoked one of those fights between her parents, but it wasn't important enough to blacken an eye. Her parents simply decided that the school was only trying to make Papa waste money on the useless education of a girl, end of discussion.

***

IT WAS NEARLY DUSK WHEN THEIR TRAIN LURCHED INTO A NEW STA-tion and jolted Filomena awake. All the people who'd been in such a hurry to climb aboard were now in just as much of a rush to get off, pushing and shoving. Her mother waited calmly until the steps were clear; then they climbed down, again counting aloud as they went.

"We are in Naples now," Mama declared above the noise of traffic, "a very big and important city. But there's no time to waste. We have a bus we must catch. Let's go!"

In the babble of voices, Filomena heard something familiar. "Here, everyone talks like Papa," she said. It had never struck her as odd that her father spoke a bit differently than the other people in Santa Marinella; Papa was from "the South," rougher in manner and speech than her genteel mother. Filomena had a good ear and was a perfect mimic; sometimes this got her in trouble, such as when people like the mayor or the priest thought she was making fun of them.

"Come," Mama said tersely, steering her through the bustling crowd, until they reached an outdoor terminal where several buses were rumbling as if in a hurry to go. Filomena panted as she climbed up onto a bus. She dropped into a seat between her mother and a very fat lady who was already dozing. Filomena yawned and she dozed, too.

When the bus jolted to a halt at its destination, everyone climbed down sighing with relief. More than one person said, "Uf!" with a note of finality. Mama found an empty bench and told Filomena to sit down and eat the egg that was in her pocket. When she was done, her mother told her to use the bathroom, because they would have to walk the rest of the way.

It was much hotter here. The road was dusty. Mama seemed tireless, walking with the steady gait of a hardworking horse and holding her daughter's hand the whole way.

They were in a strange land. There was no sea. There were only wide fields on both sides of this dirt road, full of amazing things, which Filomena gazed at as she and her mother passed them. There were beautiful dusty-green-leafed vines, which Mama told her produced wine grapes, and then fields of golden grain plowed into neat rows. Next came green pastures dotted with strange animals that Mama pointed to and explained: the cow that gives us milk, the sheep that gives us cheese, the pig that gives us sausages, the chickens that give us eggs.

At first, it was like going to a county fair and seeing remarkable things like clowns and jugglers. But after a while Filomena suddenly and acutely missed the sea; she felt an ache in her heart at being away from the salty air of their little village.

The moon rose suddenly, as if with great hurry, casting a ribbon of light in their path while the shadows darkened around them. At last they arrived at a large, stately farmhouse, built to be impressive.

"Your father was born not far from here," Mama said. "Not in this house; in a smaller one, on a nearby farm. His parents and brothers are all gone. But these people that we are visiting, they own all this farmland we've just seen, and they know Papa."

"Papa came from a farm?" Filomena asked, confused. As long

as she'd lived, her father had always fished, sometimes taking her out with him in his boat full of nets.

"Yes, his family were farmers," Mama said. "But there was not enough work here for him. So he came north to find work, and he found my father, who taught him to fish—and then Papa found me. He worked hard, did well. But times are hard everywhere now."

Filomena had heard the story of her parents' courtship before, and it, too, sounded like a fairy tale, of a more highly born princess courted by a noble but poor youth who had journeyed far to find her; yet, today, there was no romantic sentimentality in her mother's voice. It was the voice of many women like her who had married and had children; it was perpetually weary. Filomena squeezed her mother's hand in sudden sympathy.

They'd reached the front door of the farmhouse, and Mama tugged on a cord that was attached to a bell. A servant girl opened the door; she wore a cap and apron, like the girls who worked in the bakery back home. This girl appeared to be only a year older than Filomena, but she had a wary, knowing look. Filomena was tall for her age, even taller than this skinny serving girl, so she drew herself up and stared back.

The girl opened the door wider and stepped aside so that they could enter a small, dark foyer, which led to a very big room where you had to go down a few steps. This room had a terra-cotta–tiled floor and very formal furnishings: a big sofa and two fat chairs, some smaller tables with lamps, and a sideboard with shelves displaying big china plates with patterns of a shepherdess and her flock. The window curtains were drawn against the sun, but it had already set.

Filomena thought her mother should remove her dark glasses in such a dimly lit room, but Mama did not, for she was probably embarrassed about her black eye. Filomena decided that they had been invited to a tea party of some sort, and she became enchanted with the pictures on the china plates and cups.

Then suddenly a *signora* swept into the room with an impervious, aggressive swish of taffeta skirts. She was a short lady, but this only made her tilt her head and her aquiline nose very high, in a crude attempt at regality.

"Your daughter is skinny," the lady said in a surprisingly blunt, coarse tone for such an important person as she evidently was. She, too, spoke the dialect like Papa.

"She's healthy and smart," Mama said defensively.

The *signora* shrugged. She called out, "Rosamaria!" and after a curt nod, she turned abruptly and swept out of the room.

The hired girl returned, and, since the room had grown darker now that night was falling, the girl began to light tall, fat candles all around the room.

Filomena's mother now turned all her attention to her little daughter and spoke in a measured tone as if telling her to do her chores. But today Mama's voice was so low that Filomena had to put her ear almost to her mother's lips, as if she were being told a secret.

"When your papa left this place, his family owed money to the *signor* who lives here. This Boss even paid for Papa's trip north. Papa has always worked hard to pay him back. We all do, your brothers and sisters and I. But times are hard now, and we have fallen far behind on paying back our debt. Now *you* must do your part to help repay the debt. Be a good girl, Filomena. Do everything you are told to do here. Do not disgrace Papa, or there will be trouble for all of us," she added in a warning voice.

But while she spoke, a brief, tender look had softened her face, and now her lips were quivering as she kissed Filomena. Yet when Filomena hugged her back, suddenly, Mama stiffened her spine, released her, then lifted her chin in a resolute way, indicating there was something difficult and unpleasant that had to be dealt with. Her face seemed to turn to stone in the flickering candlelight. Filomena had never seen Mama quite like *this* before, and it made her speechless, uncomprehendingly anxious. The servant girl stepped forward.

"I am Rosamaria," she said in a neutral tone. "Come with me, Filomena."

Although Filomena's mind could not identify what was wrong, her tummy seemed to know all about it. Suddenly she was seized with a cold, fearful pain that made her feel as if she were sinking to the bottom of a deep well, with no way out. She was still clutching her mother's warm, soothing hand, but now, decisively, Mama let go of her.

"Be good," she said, again in that odd new coldly resolute voice, as if she were trying to convince herself as well as Filomena that this was the way it had to be. Then, with a quick straightening of her shoulders, Mama turned and went out beyond the two pillars. A moment later the front door banged closed.

"Mama!" Filomena shouted suddenly. "Where are you going, Mama?"

"Perhaps someday she'll be back," the servant girl, Rosamaria, said unconvincingly. "For now, you must come with me."

Filomena's thoughts were reeling. She was thoroughly exhausted, and the fingers of her hand—the one her mother had been holding on to all this time—had gone from hot and sweaty to cold little icicles now.

"Mama!" she shouted, running to the window and pushing the curtains aside. In the shaft of moonlight she spied the figure of her mother hurrying down the front path, then climbing into a horse-drawn wagon that a farmhand was driving. The wagon took off quickly, guiltily, raising a cloud of dust as it sped down the road until it made a sharp turn and disappeared.

"Mama!" Filomena shrieked now, running to the front door. The gold knob was too fat for her small hands, but somehow she managed to turn it and drag open the heavy wooden door. She ran down the stone steps, gasping painfully. "Mama! Wait for me, Mama!" she sobbed now, the dust stinging her eyes and blinding her, along with her tears.

A big man in work clothes was coming around from the side of the house, and with a single expert move, he scooped Filomena up under one arm. There was nothing friendly about it. He handled her the same way he'd have picked up a runaway pig.

"*Basta!* Do you want the police to come and take you to the orphanage? That's a bad house where they put bad children, and they'll beat you night and day. Is that where you want to go?" the man boomed in a deep voice. He was very strong, and with a few quick strides he had carried Filomena to the back of the house, where there was a smaller, plainer door that led straight into the kitchen.

A stout woman in a greasy apron was working at a thick wooden table with a meat cleaver. She was chopping up something big and dark and bloody.

"Here's the new girl," the man said, depositing Filomena like a sack of flour on the floor, which was rough stone. The woman glanced up with a sour expression.

"At least she's taller than Rosamaria was when they brought her. But they're always so thin! Thin girls get sick too easily," the fat lady complained.

"Better feed her, then," the man snorted as he went out the back door.

The woman wiped her hands on her greasy apron, reached out, and, without even looking up, handed a bun to Filomena. "Go on. Eat!" the woman ordered.

Filomena brought the stale bun to her lips. She chewed and chewed, because in spite of everything, she was hungry. There were still some salty tears in her eyes and somehow they found their way into her mouth, salting her bread. She swallowed hard.

"Finished? You can sleep over there," the woman said, busy putting the meat into a bowl to marinate. She jerked her head toward an alcove at the far end of the kitchen.

Filomena followed her gaze, then walked toward the tiny alcove. There was a flattish straw mat and a tattered cover. No pillow, no lamp, no candle.

The cook carried the bowl of marinating meat through a swinging door to a pantry. When she re-emerged through the swinging door she had taken off her apron. "Someday, if you work hard, you can sleep upstairs like the rest of us," she said briefly. "And you'd better sleep. We start work at four." She picked up an oil lamp that had been illuminating the room, and out with her went the last of the light.

Faced with such overwhelming darkness, Filomena lay down on the mat. In this windowless place, the night was so engulfing that she pulled the blanket over her head, just so that she couldn't see how wide and endless the darkness was. Her mind was still whirling, but exhaustion took over, and she must have dozed momentarily.

Then she awakened with a terrible start and could not remember where she was. She seemed to be nowhere at all, abandoned by the entire world.

"Am I dead?" she whispered. "Maybe Papa and Mama are dead, too. Maybe Mama's train crashed and killed her and that's why she can't come back for me. Maybe a great tide from the sea came upon Papa's boats and killed him and all my brothers."

Filomena lay there quietly, contemplating this. "Well, if I'm dead, the Virgin Mary will come for me and take me to heaven, where the sun shines all the time."

She closed her eyes and waited for the gentle Madonna to come and take her by the hand, like a mother who would never let go of a child who loved her so ardently. As Filomena waited, her right hand felt so unbearably empty that she clasped it with her left hand as hard as she could, as if to lock herself together so that she would not crumble into a million fragments in the darkness.

It was quiet, at first. Then she heard some rustling sounds on the other side of the wall and was seized with a fear of what it could be. A rat? A snake? A wolf outside? A nasty tramp?

Perhaps it was the choir of angels and saints, whispering about her. What if the saints asked Filomena what sins she had committed in order to cause her parents to cast her out like this? That was what a priest would ask.

So Filomena lay there, reviewing every transgression, large or small, that she had committed. She searched her conscience strenuously but only ended up more bewildered than before, for she could not honestly find anything to explain why Mama and Papa had thrown her away. She decided that when the Virgin came for her, Filomena would only beg her forgiveness for whatever she'd done, and hope for her protection in exchange for the steadfast love of the penitent child that she was.

Then Filomena heard a strange, awful wail, a keening cry. It took her a while to realize that this plaintive sound was coming from her own mouth. This would not do. The Madonna would not come for her if she misbehaved. Filomena quickly took both of her hands, one atop the other, and pressed the palms hard against her mouth, so her sobs had nowhere to go but back down her throat and into the dark blackened depths of her own heart.

2

Lucy

Hell's Kitchen, New York, 1934

Lucy Marie was exhausted when she left Saint Clare's hospital on a cold night in March. The emergency room was especially busy tonight: influenza, polio, rickets, and whooping cough among the children; tuberculosis in the homeless people; head injuries and crushed limbs for men hurt on the job or in a fight; syphilis for the prostitutes. Hell's Kitchen, indeed.

All Lucy wanted to do was get back to the rooming house where unmarried nurses lived, in time to take a warm sponge bath before all the hot water ran out. She'd had her cup of tea at the hospital; she was too tired to eat. She just wanted to bathe and climb into bed. Tomorrow was her day off. She'd eat then, and wash her red hair with a henna rinse.

As she turned the corner, an icy wind blew straight off the Hudson River. Lucy shivered and pulled her coat collar up as far as she could, but there was no top button to keep it closed, so she had to hold it. She was only twenty years old, but when the cold sank into your bones, you felt like an old woman.

"'Hell's Kitchen' should be *hot*," she muttered. "Unless hell is made of ice and wind."

She narrowed her eyes against the next cold gust, and because of this squint, she didn't see an old black car pull up at the curb, until two men jumped out and surrounded her. Both wore wool caps and scarves that covered their faces except for the eyes. Each man took one of her elbows, and the taller assailant pushed a gun against the side of her thin coat.

"Don't scream, Nursie," he said calmly in an Irish brogue that reminded her of the old country, "and it'll be all right." He smelled of gas-station grease and stale beer.

"Who are you? What do you want from me?" she said sharply. She'd learned at an early age never to show fear. People could smell it on you, and it emboldened them.

But they were already shoving her into the back of their car and locking the doors. The shorter man slid behind the wheel. The taller one got in the backseat with her and pushed Lucy onto the floor so that she couldn't see much out the windows.

"If it's money you're after, you're out of luck," she said with more bravado than she felt. "I've got five cents and that's the God's truth. Take it and let me go."

"We don't want your money," he growled. This alarmed her. The river was on their left; that much she had been able to see. They were driving toward the Bronx. She'd read too many news-papers and heard too many lurid tales of bodies that had been found under bridges or in the back lots of these boroughs, and nobody knew nor seemed to care about such corpses.

And no one would care about her, either, come to that. The hospital staff might alert the policemen who hauled people into the emergency room; someone might check their missing persons logs. But there it would end; no family member would seek her body and give her a proper funeral. If these men dumped her in a ditch or the river, and somebody eventually found her, she'd probably end up buried on that pitiful island where prisoners were forced to dig the graves of the poor and the unclaimed. So, she could just say her prayers right now.

All of this went through her head so vividly that she was surprised when the car arrived at their destination—only a run-down brick house in Harlem, on a street where all the houses were dark, not a single light on at this hour, the better not to see nor hear what was going on out on the grimy street.

The shorter man stayed in the car. The other—the one with the gun—opened the door and dragged her out with him. He shoved her toward one of these narrow houses.

The front door was unlocked. It opened on a staircase that smelled musty. He pushed her up the stairs to the top, where there was only one room. He knocked once, and another male voice said, "Come." Her escort opened the door, thrust Lucy forward, then backed out and closed the door. She did not hear his footsteps continue down the stairs, so he must have remained outside the door.

The room had a bed, a washstand, and a tiny lamp that shed weak light. Lucy squinted and saw a woman lying on the bed. A tattered bedspread barely covered her large belly.

"She wasn't supposed to have this baby. Your job is to get rid of it," said the male voice from a chair in a dark corner. Although he was speaking to Lucy and watching her, she could not clearly see his face. But she could make out the shape of him—he was broad shouldered, stocky, and powerfully built. "Get it out and kill it," he said calmly, as if speaking about mice.

Lucy gulped but steeled herself. "Why me? There are others who do this sort of thing."

The girl on the bed spoke pleadingly to her. "Please, Miss. I saw you at the church health clinic once. I know you are good, and you try to help people in trouble."

Lucy assessed the situation quickly. Some gangster evidently wanted to keep this girl alive, or he'd have simply murdered her to get rid of the baby as well. This shred of sentiment might be exploitable. The pregnant girl was fifteen at most, and her hair, plastered to her perspiring face, was the same red color as Lucy's.

With startling force, Lucy was reminded of herself at this age, in circumstances painfully akin to these, back in Ireland. A sweet but weak boy had fathered Lucy's baby but then vanished, pressured by his own family. So Lucy's father and brother had dragged her into a wagon and driven her to a "home for wayward girls," which looked like a prison and operated like a laundry from the previous century. Some very odd nuns were in charge. The first thing they did was shave Lucy's head—to avoid lice, they said—and she joined thirty other girls who scrubbed laundry all day long, until their babies came.

Lucy didn't know what cheap kind of doctor the nuns had called, that terrible night when it was "her turn"; but when it was all over, her baby son was dead and Lucy herself very nearly gone. Somehow she'd survived, even though she hadn't cared to. And somehow, months later, when she did finally wish to live, she'd sweet-talked the man who delivered soap to their laundry into helping her escape to Dublin.

She'd worked in a hospital just long enough to earn the fare to America. She had no possessions, no baggage; all she'd left behind was her heart, as if it were buried in the small grave along with her infant son, resting beneath the weeds that grew over it, in a makeshift cemetery behind the home for wayward girls.

"This baby is stuck, I can't help it," the girl on the bed whimpered now, beseeching Lucy's mercy with the eyes of a terrified animal.

Lucy approached the girl to size up her condition, then concluded that she'd nursed people through worse situations than this—more difficult pregnancies, knife wounds, fatal illnesses. The Catholic hospital had trained her well, for they needed all the help they could get, and the Sisters here were kinder, happier nuns, eager to use a girl like Lucy, recognizing her potential to help them.

Emergencies invigorated Lucy, so now her adrenaline was kicking in, overcoming her fatigue. She turned and squarely faced the man in the corner, speaking in her professionally neutral Nurse's Voice, tinged with bossy authority in an Irish brogue that somehow carried weight in situations like this.

"Look here. This pregnancy has gone too far," she said crisply. "I cannot abort it. If I did, the girl might not survive. And anyway, think of all the fuss of disposing of an infant's body."

"Easy," the man said from the depths of his dark corner. "Just get it out."

Lucy tried again. "The Franciscan Sisters have an orphanage upstate. I know them, so they'd take the baby from me, no questions asked," she said. "No crimes committed, no problem. A much simpler solution," she added meaningfully. "That's the deal, if you want my help. Otherwise, I tell you, the mother could *die* and you'll have two corpses on your hands. Three, if you count me," she said, raising her chin with a defiance she didn't really feel.

In fact, her heart was pounding, and she held her breath now, waiting. She'd taken a gamble, surmising that if he didn't particularly want to kill this girl, then all Lucy needed to do was to convincingly remove the stigma and burden of a child born to an unwed mother.

The man's eyes glittered in the dark as he sized her up. "Where is this place? The nuns will take it, no questions asked?" he repeated as if making her swear it.

"Absolutely," she said stoutly, and explained where the orphanage was.

"No names, no information about where this baby came from. If you ever talk about this to anyone, anytime, anywhere, we will kill you," he said in a dead, colorless tone.

"Understood," Lucy said. "Now please give us some privacy so I can get to work to help this poor girl, yeh?" When he didn't move right away, she said, "Well, I hope you're not squeamish. It's going to be quite a bit messy."

The man rose and went out. She heard him confer with the other tough, who'd waited outside the door. Then their footsteps retreated down the stairs.

"Cowards," Lucy muttered. The girl on the bed had been writhing in pain, but Lucy could see that it was only terror holding the baby back, and already things were improving on their own, now that the man had left. The girl was biting hard on a rolled-up handkerchief.

"Don't you worry." Lucy touched the girl's shoulder, yet she could not resist saying, "What kind of man is that, who'd kill a wee babe so easily? Married man?"

She instantly regretted asking, for the girl seemed to think that she herself might die, and she made a sort of confession, blurting it out in a guilty whisper: the father was not married but he was an important man, a loan shark who shook down the unions. She never said his name, just bit her lip as the pain seized her again, and she rolled her eyes sideways so she could gaze at Lucy directly when she spoke next, in a desperate but conspiratorial tone.

"I knew you could be trusted. You won't kill my baby, will you?"

Lucy fixed her gaze on the washstand to quell her own emotions. She often deliberately worked the night shift, just so that she wouldn't have to be out and about in the daytime—seeing young mothers pushing babies in strollers in the park—and so that when she went home, she'd be too exhausted to think of that windswept graveyard that haunted her undefended hours.

But the girl on the bed was anxiously waiting for an answer.

"No," Lucy repeated briskly as she washed her hands. "This baby will not die."

3

Amie

Troy, New York, 1934

Amie Marie was worried. It was now a whole year since she'd been married, and she still wasn't pregnant. Her husband, Brunon, did not wish to discuss it, and her neighbors in this part of town in upstate New York were mostly German and Irish workers who spoke in languages that a French girl like Amie couldn't understand. She was eighteen years old, and her entire life's experience was largely confined to this tavern that she and Brunon owned.

The tavern had once belonged to Amie's uncle. He and Papa had originally worked in a brewery in France, but the uncle came here first, then convinced Papa that there was more money to be made in America, selling beer and food in his tavern that served the local workingmen. So Amie and her father had left their hometown of Bourg-en-Bresse when she was only four years old, just after her mother died.

At first, her father and uncle had done very well in this city on the Hudson River, which was filled with beautiful, ornate nineteenth-century buildings that coal and steel moguls had built. The old part of town, where the tavern was, looked enchanted, especially on snowy winter evenings. Amie loved the library with its magnificent Tiffany glass windows, the decorative façades of the great mansions of illustrious men who'd built the city, the Gothic arches of St. Paul's Church, and the belle époque streetlamps in front of the old offices of the newspaper whose editors had been the first to print the poem that began "'Twas the night before Christmas . . ." Even her father's tavern was part of the elegant, stately architecture.

But by now it was an old city of fading glory and wisps of ghost stories about Indians and early settlers; and even the dark Victorian mansions seemed haunted with the lost spirits of its now-vanished entrepreneurs.

Amie Marie had managed to learn English with her uncle's help, but apart from that, she hadn't done well in school here in America; one day they would call what she had "dyslexia," but in those earlier years they just said she was stupid. It didn't help that she was nearsighted; this, too, was not discovered until a visiting doctor administered eye tests for children at the school. But by then it had already been decided that Amie should leave school early, because of her poor grades.

Her uncle and father were kind to her but taciturn; they'd put her to work helping them in the tavern. When her uncle died unexpectedly from heart failure, Amie's father came to rely on her more and more.

The pale blond girl with the eyeglasses was at first scarcely noticed at the tavern, scurrying like a mouse to help her father. "You'll get married someday, Amie," he'd said unconvincingly, "and then everything will be all right."

But for years, things were never all right for Amie, even when a young man named Brunon came looking for a job. He was a big fellow, sturdy and dependable, but he was what their neighbors called "a mutt," part Polish, part German, part Irish. He'd told Papa all this, and explained that he'd lost his entire family back in Pennsylvania to the Spanish flu pandemic years ago. Only Brunon had survived.

"I am the strong one," he assured her father. Papa was glad to have someone to do the heavy work. But soon, poor Papa died of meningitis, when Amie was seventeen.

Brunon had been a stalwart presence from the moment he'd arrived, a silent but diligent worker, who helped her through her grief by taking over the tavern and making sure that they could pay the bills on time, so that she could go on waiting on tables at lunch and at night, as if nothing had changed, as if Papa were somehow still there, tending bar and keeping the other men away from her. To make ends meet, Brunon worked an early shift at a factory, then came home to help her at the bar at night. When he proposed, it seemed the most natural thing in the world to say yes.

Neither of them had any money to spend on a honeymoon. Amie had worn a white dress; Brunon had put on his one good suit and tie. A few of the men from the factory dutifully brought their wives and babies to the wedding at the church. Their infants wailed during the entire ceremony. Then everyone ate the reception food at the tavern, and Amie cut the wedding cake. Finally the guests staggered home, and Brunon and Amie went upstairs to the small apartment above the tavern where she'd always lived with Papa.

She had indulged in buying new sheets for the bed, a nightgown for herself, and a bathrobe for Brunon. They'd climbed into bed, and then Brunon climbed on top of her, hitched up her nightgown, and did something that shocked her so profoundly that she could not make a sound. The sheer violence of it, the noise of his animal grunting culminating in one desperate, isolated shout, was a nightmare to her. It seemed to take longer than she'd thought possible. When it was over and he roughly withdrew, she felt as if she'd fallen down the rocky side of a cliff at horrific speed, emerging the next day feeling broken, battered and bleeding.

The blood on the new sheets particularly upset her, and the next morning, when Brunon dressed for work, she hurriedly scrubbed the sheets, sobbing a little to herself. Brunon stayed downstairs, sulking at having to make his own breakfast. Just before going off to work he came upstairs to indignantly inform her that a wife should not only make her husband's breakfast but also pack him a lunch in his bucket.

When he saw her tear-stained face, he blushed and then said roughly, "Don't be a child, Amie. It's what grown-ups do. The blood only proves you're a good girl."

She could hardly walk. It hurt so much to go to the bathroom that she tried all day not to. She wanted a baby; she desperately wanted someone to love who would adore her back. But night after night, as she bit her lip and prayed to God to help her understand this ghastly, bestial act, she wished that she could die now and never have to go through it again. Each night was as much a disaster as their wedding night.

When she finally ventured out into the world because she had to shop for things, she could not escape a feeling of shame. A few people made lighthearted jokes about the fact that she was now a married lady, but something in her look of agonized embarrassment made them back off.

Even if her father had lived to give his daughter away to the boy who worked for him, Amie wouldn't have dreamed of asking Papa about the facts of life. She'd never managed to make friends with the other females from working families here; the married ladies stuck together in their ethnic cliques, gathered on doorsteps or front porches. They didn't like the blond girl who'd suddenly blossomed with "a figure" that all their men liked to talk about.

She watched every woman in the neighborhood and wondered how they could bear it. Sometimes she overheard them as they hung their laundry in their backyards, making cryptic comments to each other about a wife's "duty"; and at night the men in the tavern made bawdy jokes to one another. Everyone acted as if it were all great fun. It didn't surprise her, really, that she didn't feel the same way about it; she had been bad at so many things at school that others did quite easily. Yet she could not imagine how the holy church could sanctify this act.

As time went on, the days were fine and peaceable. The nights were not.

"For God's sake, Amie," her husband said if he caught her crying in the bathroom, "it hurts because you don't relax. You have to relax to enjoy it."

So it was her fault, her failing, as she'd expected. Once again she was deficient. She found herself entertaining strange fantasies: when she picked up a knife she thought of plunging it into her bosom; when she passed a lake she wondered how long it would take to drown; when she crossed the railroad tracks she felt an urge to throw herself in the path of a train. But suicide was a mortal sin, and if this marital act was what God allowed on earth, then existence had to be so much worse in Hell.

By now, the teasing that Brunon got about having a wife who wasn't pregnant annoyed him. He was not a man who'd easily strike a woman, and he always behaved in public, but when they were alone he ridiculed everything she said and did. At first he did it somewhat affectionately, but soon his comments lost even that little tinge of exasperated warmth.

"You're too stupid, Amie," he would say if a glass fell from her trembling hands, or if something burned on the stove, or if she paid a bill twice because she didn't understand the way he kept the books at the tavern. "Where is your head these days?" he'd demand. He was always sneering about her brain, her mind, her head.

She didn't know how to talk back; she'd been raised to be quiet. Brunon came home weary from the factory, yet he worked all night at the tavern, sleeping only a few hours after closing. But he often had just enough energy for that brief, brutal act in bed.

AND THEN, ONE DAY, BRUNON CAME HOME WITH A WIDE GRIN ON his face.

"We're going to New York," he announced as he sat down to eat his dinner.

She said automatically, "But we already live in New York."

"Oh, Amie!" he snorted. "You're so dumb! I mean the city of Manhattan."

She blushed with shame. "Why should we go away?" she asked, confused. "We work here, in Papa's tavern."

Brunon took a long gulp of beer. "I sold it," he said triumphantly. "I got a good price for it, too. But better than that, I met a man who wants us to go into partnership with him in the city. We'll be much richer there than we could ever be in this rotten town, and I won't have to work at the factory anymore. I can run things with you during the day, so you won't have to work so hard, either. You see?"

Amie did not know what to think or say. She had a moment's pang at losing the tavern without even being asked if she minded; her father had polished his mahogany bar so lovingly that it felt as if his spirit were still in it. If she left here, she would not know who she was anymore, and who she might become. But she harbored the hope that if Brunon were happier with his work, he would be happier with her.

A week later, they packed their bags and got on the train to New York City. Amie said a silent prayer to God for enlightenment. *Please don't let me be stupid my entire life. Help me to understand what's happening to me. I understand nothing, except that I want to die.*

Getting aboard the train felt like the end of the world to Amie. But not long afterwards, she discovered that, in a neighborhood called Greenwich Village, her prayers were finally going to be answered.

4

Petrina

Coney Island and Greenwich Village, New York, 1931

One bright spring morning, Petrina Maria was in her dormitory room at Barnard College, studying for her last exam before her graduation with the class of 1931. Then, unexpectedly, she was summoned for a phone call.

"They said it was urgent," the girl at the telephone desk reported.

Filled with trepidation, Petrina picked up the receiver. It was Stella, the cook back home in Greenwich Village, whom Petrina had bribed to alert her if the youngest member of her family, little five-year-old Mario, got into trouble.

"He's run away with some of the bigger boys," the cook whispered. "I went to the schoolyard to pick him up, and a girl there said she saw him go off with them."

"Any idea where?" Petrina asked worriedly.

Stella replied, "She said they were talking about the Cyclone roller coaster."

Petrina groaned. "Where are Johnny and Frankie?" she demanded.

"I don't know where your brothers are, Miss. And your parents aren't home, either."

"I'll find Mario," Petrina said quickly. "Just keep it quiet for now."

"If he's not home by suppertime, I'll have to tell your parents!" the cook warned.

But no one would ever call the police; this family always settled its own problems.

Petrina hung up the telephone, silently cursing herself for making such a rash promise to go off and rescue Mario. Leave Barnard College for Coney Island? Going to Brooklyn from here would be a long and tedious jaunt. She wasn't worried about her exam; she knew that she would pass this one. Art history was her favorite subject, her major. She'd already aced her minor, Italian literature. Having skipped a grade in high school, Petrina had entered college a year early, and she was an honors student. School had always been easy for her; it was life that was so hard.

She didn't want Mario to be punished; her parents could be severe. Petrina calculated the fastest way to get to Brooklyn. She'd have to take a succession of subways, which she hated. Something about being underground made her feel trapped, buried alive. But then she pictured Mario wandering around with a gang of delinquent schoolboys and she shuddered. One of her brothers— Johnny, a boy with a pure heart—had, years ago, stumbled into trouble on the playground and ended up in reform school, which had nearly killed him. She could not let that happen to Mario. He was only five years old. She closed her books and went off.

**

WHEN PETRINA ARRIVED AT CONEY ISLAND, SHE HEADED STRAIGHT for the Cyclone roller coaster. You couldn't miss it, looming above the other rides, roaring like thunder. It was made of wood, and its elegant curves had a certain beauty, if you liked that sort of thing. She felt a bit guilty; Mario had peppered her with eager questions about it when she was home for Easter, only a scant ten days ago.

She'd put him off with vague promises.

"You're too young for that," Petrina had said. "Wait until you get a bit older."

The truth was, she found amusement parks slightly silly. They were always noisy and filled with riffraff. She couldn't see the point of eating a lot of terrible stuff—cotton candy, Cracker Jacks, oversize waffles, sweet sticky soda—and then climbing aboard a wooden contraption that boasted an eighty-five-foot drop to deliberately terrify you. Life already had enough dangerous ups and downs. Mario was so little, he'd probably fall right out of it. Did they let children that young onto such a wild ride?

She could hear the screams of glee even before she arrived at the ticket booth, beneath the tremendous shudder and rumble of the carriages as they swooped on their perilous track. Her throat tightened as she stood there, worriedly scanning the faces of people on line waiting for their turn, and the others who were already on the ride which swooshed by her in a blur. She watched closely when the ride ended and the passengers staggered off, but still, no Mario.

She paced back and forth. Where else would a little boy go? The distractions were endless. She walked on, past the Wonder Wheel, the Steeplechase, and the carousel, with more than one over-excited kid in the crowd banging into her at every turn. Then she doubled back to the Cyclone, becoming truly worried now.

"Hello, Petrina," came a matter-of-fact voice. She whirled around. There was Mario, sitting on a bench all by himself, in his school uniform of white shirt, grey trousers, and navy blazer. He looked pale, his big dark eyes round as saucers, his beautiful soft mahogany-brown hair the same color as hers but slightly mussed. There was a smear of chocolate on his face.

"For God's sake!" Petrina cried out. "Do you have any idea how worried we are back home? How on earth did you even get here?"

"Some big kids from the fourth grade took me with them

'cause their brother drives a truck, and he dropped us off here. They said I could ride the Cyclone with them if I gave them my pocket money," Mario explained. "But I wasn't tall enough. So they left us here."

"Who's 'us'?" Petrina demanded.

"My friends," he said matter-of-factly. "I don't know where they went. I didn't want to follow them anymore. We got candy and frozen custard, and we went on the Wonder Wheel, and then I got sick. I threw up in the bushes," he said proudly, pointing in that direction.

"You're lucky I found you before Mama and Papa realized where you've been!" Petrina exclaimed. "You'd be in big trouble."

"Why?" Mario asked, his little mouth turning down. "I didn't do anything bad."

Petrina sighed mightily, sitting beside him. "Do you know how many subways I took to get here, even though I had to study? Do you know how hot the subways are at this hour?"

For the first time, Mario seemed apprehensive. "I can't go on the subway," he said. "I still feel sick."

"Too many sweets!" Petrina exclaimed.

But Mario looked so woeful at the thought of the subway that Petrina said, "I'll call home and tell them I took you for a walk. A walk is a good idea; it will make you feel better."

Mario tilted his small face up to her and said in a soft voice, "Thanks, Sis." He leaned toward her and she bent down for his sticky kiss on her cheek.

"Rotten little charmer," she replied. "Come on, the boardwalk is this way, and the sea air will do you good. Take some little breaths like this . . ." She showed him how her dance teacher had taught her to carefully breathe, and Mario dutifully imitated it.

When some color came back to his face, they stood up, and he put his small hand in hers. She called home, then found a fountain and got him a drink of water. They went along the boardwalk, past sandy beaches. It was the only part of this place she liked.

The sea seemed to offer limitless possibilities, in contrast to the relentless crowds and noise of this gritty side of town.

It must have been nearly two o'clock when Mario said, "I'm better now."

"Good," Petrina said. "Let's go home this way."

They were walking down Fifteenth Street when Mario suddenly announced, "I have to go to the bathroom."

"For heaven's sake, Mario," she said in exasperation. Why couldn't he have said so when they were closer to the rides? Now they were beyond the public washrooms, and even if they went back, she certainly wouldn't let him go into the men's alone. She hated the ladies' rooms, too; they were all grubby. Petrina, with her long, fine bones and heightened sensitivity, couldn't help having a natural delicacy; her brothers called her *la principessa sul pisello:* the princess who could feel even a pea under her mattress.

She glanced about searchingly. She spotted a seafood restaurant with ornately curved windows and its name spelled out on a grand awning, *Nuova Villa Tammaro.* She'd never been inside; it looked like a serious, sit-down place that might have nice bathrooms, but perhaps it wasn't a spot where you'd bring children.

However, at this hour the lunch service would be nearly ended, so maybe they'd take kindly to a well-behaved little boy needing their washroom while she had a cup of coffee. She wiped his face with her handkerchief.

Petrina pushed the front door open and peered into the fancy dining room. Indeed the tables were empty, except for just one, where a fat man sat with other men in suits, playing cards with the tense concentration of betting men and looking supremely sated after their lunch. One of them stood up now. He was thin and wiry and the most elegantly dressed, but his face was a bit pockmarked, and there was something odd about one of his eyes. He left the table and headed for the men's room.

A woman in a long white apron came out of the kitchen door at the back, spied Petrina and Mario immediately, and hurried over to shoo them out.

"Get on, for your own good," the woman whispered in a low, warning voice, closing the door firmly. Petrina knew that men who played cards so seriously could indeed be ill-tempered if intruded upon. So she stood on the sidewalk wondering if she should search for an empty bottle for Mario to pee in, or just let him do it against that wall in a shady alleyway.

"Come on," she said to him, watching uneasily as a car pulled up to the far curb and dislodged more well-dressed men heading determinedly for the restaurant.

Petrina and Mario retreated into the alleyway. But while she was still searching for a spot where Mario could clandestinely go, the sleepy afternoon hum was shattered by a sudden, shockingly brutal sound that came from inside the restaurant.

Rat-tat-tat—tat-tat! Petrina grabbed Mario and flung him, then herself, on the ground against the wall. She hugged Mario beneath her and kept her head down. They heard somebody scream, and then the front door of the restaurant was banged open.

Petrina raised her head cautiously for a quick look. She wasn't sure how many men came barreling out, but it struck her that now they all had their hats pulled down low to hide their faces. They moved quickly into the waiting car and sped off.

Still holding tightly to Mario, Petrina prayed that no more gunmen would come out. She waited. From a nearby garage, another car, which looked more like a tank, slowly pulled up to the restaurant's curb. Petrina held her breath, but the driver just waited there. She would later read in the newspapers that this car was made of armored steel, and its windows were of inch-thick plate glass; but it was of no use to its owner—Joe "the Boss" Masseria—who had just been murdered here with five bullets, while his driver had gone off to fetch the auto.

When Petrina heard police sirens wailing, this galvanized her into action. She stood up quickly and yanked Mario by the arm.

"Let's go!" she cried. "We've got to get out of here, now!"

Mario understood her tone of voice more than the situation, and he obeyed her without a peep, but his little legs could hardly keep up with her long stride. At one point, Petrina was so frightened that she simply picked him up and slung him under her arm.

It wasn't until they reached the subway that she saw that he'd wet his pants.

"Oh, Mario, poor baby!" she said, and she tied her sweater around his hips. "Come on, we've got to get you home, quickly, quickly!"

When they reached their elegant house on a quiet, leafy street in Greenwich Village, it looked like the safest haven on earth. Petrina smuggled Mario in through the side door and across the kitchen, past Stella the cook, who shook her fist at them but looked enormously relieved. Petrina, with her finger to her lips, guided Mario stealthily upstairs, then bathed him and put him into fresh clothes, combed his hair, and said severely, "We're both going to have to lie about today, which is not a good thing. But nobody must know we were at Coney Island, so don't you dare tell your friends what we saw! We'll tell the family that I took you to the park for the afternoon. I mean it, Mario. Do you understand what happens to stool pigeons?"

Mario nodded mutely, still barely comprehending the situation but taking the message to heart, looking very sober. "I have to go back to my school tonight," Petrina said in a softer tone. "I have to take my test. But I'll be home again soon. All right, Mario?"

"Okay," he whispered trustfully.

It wasn't until the next day, after she'd gone back to Barnard and after she'd taken her exam, that Petrina saw the big headlines on the newsstand:

Racket Chief Slain By Gangster Gunfire

Reprisals Imminent

***

WEEKS LATER, CLUTCHING HER DIPLOMA TIGHTLY IN HER HAND AS the crowd applauded, Petrina scanned the audience hopefully, looking for a sign that her parents had had a change of heart. But she knew better. Nobody from her family had come to see her graduate; her mother had made it clear that this was impossible. In fact, Petrina had barely obtained permission to be here herself—even though she was graduating *magna cum laude* and had made the dean's list every semester.

So she joined the line of lovely young girls in their caps and gowns, who were all soon surrounded by proud parents and family. Petrina smiled and nodded and hugged and kissed her friends, saying goodbye to her favorite classmates.

"Mother, you remember Petrina, don't you?" one bubbly blond girl said to her bubbly blond parent. "Petrina danced next to me at our Greek Games recital in our Isadora Duncan tunics. You said *she* was the only one who looked like a real goddess, with those wonderful long legs!" The girl took Petrina's arm and propelled her to meet a family of bankers and bridge players. With one eye on the clock, Petrina chatted and fended off the questions that everyone was asking everybody else—which parties was she going to tonight, and where was she planning on spending the summer. Maine? Cape Cod? Connecticut? The Hamptons?

She smiled and went into the changing room, to toss off her cap and gown, and smooth her dress and hair. Then she sidled her way out of the room, but not before one of the girls called out, "Petrina, you're not leaving already, are you?"

Petrina whirled around, caught in the act. "I have to find Richard," she said truthfully.

"Woo-ooo! Tall, rich, and handsome!" her friends said

approvingly.

Petrina hurried off to the front gate, where her boyfriend—he was actually her secret fiancé—was waiting for her, leaning against his baby-blue sports car. It crossed her mind that he looked just like a magazine ad for what a young Princeton graduate should be, dressed in spring flannels, with his well-trimmed sandy hair, and his hazel eyes so calm and confident. When he saw her, he held the passenger door open for her, then he jumped behind the wheel.

As they headed downtown, he offered her a cigarette. Petrina held hers out the window between puffs, careful not to let the smoke blow onto her hair and dress.

"I told my parents you couldn't make it to the country club dance tonight," Richard said. "They're at the Plaza right now. Sure you don't want to stop in and have a drink? I want to show you off to all their friends before we head out to Westchester."

He stroked her hair, admiring the many hues of brown shining in the sunlight. "You're like a beautiful violin," he said softly.

Petrina laid her cheek on his hand. "Sweet man. Wish I could go with you. But I promised my folks I'd go to a party downtown with *their* friends. I'm late already."

"I know, baby. You and your mysterious family event. Sure you won't even let me drive you downtown?"

The thought of letting Richard see an old-fashioned ceremony like the opening of a restaurant filled her with dread. These weren't really friends of her parents. More like business associates. It would be too embarrassing. So Petrina smiled her most winning smile, loving Richard for his wholehearted and earnest enthusiasm, but said gently, "Not today, my love."

"Listen, baby, are we on for next week?" Richard asked seriously now, taking her hand in his and kissing her palm in that slow, deliberate way that made her shiver with delight. She nodded. "Are you sure it's the way you want it?" he asked tenderly.

"Yes," she said softly. Elopement, to her, sounded quiet and dignified.

"Good," he said. "I know a minister in Westport who'll marry us without a fuss, and then we'll honeymoon in Vermont. When we come back to my folks in Rye, and it's all a *fait accompli,* our parents can throw whatever parties they want. But they won't be able to run—or ruin—our wedding!" He squeezed her hand and held it, even though he was driving.

They fell silent until they reached the opulent Plaza Hotel, with its beautiful fountain in front.

"I love you, Petrina," Richard said as he pulled over to let her out. He kissed her.

"I love you, too, Richard," she said, and they embraced once more before she left.

***

"YOU'RE LATE," HER MOTHER SAID SEVERELY WHEN PETRINA SLIPPED into the banquet room of the restaurant, which was festooned with paper lanterns and streamers for its grand opening. A band was playing in a corner, and the room was filled to capacity.

"There are so many people here, I'm sure they didn't miss me!" Petrina pleaded.

"You can't count on that. People are touchy, and such resentments last forever. Especially now. These are dangerous times. Bosses being killed by their own *capo*s! Young Turks with their disrespectful ideas! The bloodshed isn't over yet, you mark my words. So, we must, at all costs, avoid insulting *anyone*," Tessa admonished her daughter.

Petrina had already noted that her parents, who always looked dignified, were dressed especially well tonight—her father impeccable in his well-tailored wool suit, her mother regal in a pale blue satin dress. She wished they'd dressed up like this for her graduation today. Perhaps they might have, if it weren't for this "business" event. But her parents always acted oddly about Petrina's scholastic achievements. Each time she received an accolade, they'd be momentarily proud, then wary and resentful, treating it like just another shameful act of rebellion by their willful daughter, which must therefore never be mentioned again.

Petrina brooded over this as she returned from the punch bowl to give her mother a drink. *Imagine if Mom knew what Richard and I were planning to do!* Petrina smiled to herself, enjoying her secret. Her parents had met Richard only once, for tea at the Plaza. Richard thought they were "just great," having completely missed the mistrustful expression in her parents' eyes. But that was enough for Petrina; she knew better than to bring him home again and appear "serious." She'd have to make her escape with Richard next week, as planned, before her parents got the bright idea of finding her some other husband from the neighborhood.

Her father, Gianni, now joined them. "Dance with me, Papa?" Petrina said breathlessly, then noticed that two other men were with him. They looked up from their cigars and smiled.

"Mr. Costello, Mr. Luciano, this is my eldest child," her father said in a formal tone.

Petrina stifled a gasp. Of course she knew the name of Lucky Luciano, for, even though he was only in his mid-thirties, he'd managed to become both a fearsome gangster and yet the toast of New York society. Slender and nattily dressed, he had an undeniable magnetism, despite the fact that his face was a bit pockmarked, with a scar on his chin, and one eye was half-closed, reminding Petrina of battle-scarred alley cats.

But something in the way he moved his head made her realize that this was, in fact, the slender man she'd glimpsed playing cards at that table in the Coney Island restaurant—the one who'd ducked into the men's room just before Joe "the Boss" Masseria was shot dead by mysterious gunmen.

And now, as Lucky Luciano smiled at her, she glanced at him fearfully and wondered, *Does he recognize me?* But if he did, he didn't seem to care.

The other man, Frank Costello, was a bit older. Although she did not know him, she'd overheard her parents discussing him at home in hushed voices, when they thought their children weren't listening. Mr. Costello was what they called a "big earner." From bootlegging to slot machines, he had a Midas touch. Both Mr. Luciano and Mr. Costello were proudly dressed in expensive clothes, known to be good customers of Wanamaker's department store.

And, until recently, these two men had answered to that gangster, Joe "the Boss" Masseria. But because they'd now taken over his operations, it was believed that they, among others, were behind that brazen Coney Island shooting of their Big Boss, thus igniting "the War," a spate of murders that was now threatening to blow the town apart.

Petrina had never uttered a word of what she'd seen at Coney Island to anyone, yet she could still hear the shattering sound of the gunfire from that day.

"Your daughter wants to dance, Gianni," Mr. Costello said genially in a strange, raspy voice. "May I have the honor?"

Petrina saw the faintest flicker of hesitation in her father's eyes as he said, "Of course."

Costello led her out to the dance floor and handled her gently, moving with surprising grace. "So, Petrina, where ya been today?" he asked astutely. "I didn't see you at the ribbon-cutting here earlier, now, did I? You, I would have remembered."

Petrina did not dare lie to a man like this. "I—I graduated from college today." She gulped. He stopped dancing and pulled back to stare at her admiringly.

"Did you? Good for you! You meet all those boys from Yale and Harvard?" he asked as they resumed dancing. She nodded shyly. "It's good to be brought up nice," he said approvingly. "Me? I was brought up like a mushroom," he added plaintively. After a pause, he said, "Your father's a good man. And you're a good girl, I can see that. Say, who are those two young bucks staring at us? How the hell old are they, to stare at you like that?"

"They're my brothers. Johnny's nineteen; Frankie is seventeen," she said, embarrassed.

"Ah! They're watching out for you. Good, that's what brothers should do," he said sagely. The music ended and he commented, "You're a good dancer, College Girl." As he led her back to her father he added, "Don't let anybody break your heart."

***

WHEN PETRINA AND HER FAMILY RETURNED TO THE OASIS OF THEIR town house in Greenwich Village that night, she gave a sigh of relief that this huge day was over. Little Mario had remained at home and was already tucked away in his own bed, but he wasn't asleep. He heard her footsteps in the hallway and he popped up, coming to his doorway to say, "Hi, Petrina. You look beautiful," before he yawned and went back to bed.

"I guess he's all right, then," Petrina murmured. Not long after the shooting, she'd had to explain to Mario about the murder, because the older boys, Johnny and Frankie, had enthusiastically discussed the Coney Island slaying of Joe the Boss, and Mario, overhearing them, had already been putting two and two together.

But Mario had kept his promise to Petrina and hadn't told his brothers what he saw. He only came to her and asked, "Why did they kill that guy who was playing cards?"

"It's like there's a war going on," Petrina told him. "The big fish are fighting with one another, because they all want to be in charge of the pond."

Mario had absorbed this with his usual intelligent seriousness. "Is Pop a big fish?" he asked, a little worried now.

She'd patted his head reassuringly. "No, not that big."

Apparently this had satisfied him, because he seemed fine tonight. Everyone in this house had the ability to forget unpleasant things. So Petrina closed the door to her bedroom, where she could finally think her own thoughts without having her mother watch her face and guess every idea that crossed her mind.

Actually, Petrina had not lived in this bedroom for six years. When she was fifteen, the local teachers had called her "wild and

independent," so her parents sent her away to a strict convent
boarding school in Massachusetts, with no intention of having
Petrina continue her education any further than high school. But
away from the family, she discovered her love of learning. The
teachers liked to get a high percentage of their students accepted
by good colleges; and with Petrina's excellent grades, her adviser
was able to help her obtain a scholarship, making it clear to her
parents that they could not possibly turn it down.

The idea of returning to New York yet still living apart from
her family appealed to the rebellious Petrina. It sounded so sophisticated. Her mother believed that Petrina herself had somehow deliberately engineered this whole feat.

"What did you say to the teachers?" Tessa had asked suspiciously. "Did you tell them we were poor, when your father is one
of the richest men in our neighborhood?"

"No, Mom, of course not! They just like to help their smartest
students get into college."

"Smart," Tessa had muttered. "One day, maybe, you'll wise up
for real."

Indeed, Petrina felt she *had* wised up at college, for it was such
an eye-opener to live among girls who were more privileged and
so easygoing, who expected to get the best out of life. Music, art,
dance, history, literature, languages. These were like the keys to
the kingdom for Petrina. She felt she could go anywhere, be whoever she liked, leave the past behind, escape from her mother's lim-
ited ideas. The art world especially beckoned her, with museums
and galleries full of wisdom and beauty. People treated Petrina as
if she had a bright future.

Thinking about it now, Petrina opened her pocketbook, pulled
out her diploma, and ran her fingers over her name and her de-
gree. "*Magna cum laude,*" she whispered to herself.

She hadn't bothered to show this to her parents, and they didn't
ask to see it. She wondered what you were actually supposed to do
with a diploma; probably frame it and put it on a wall, like doctors

and dentists did. But it felt safer to keep it in a small drawer in her dresser, which had a lock. So she deposited it there, locked it, and hid the key on a chain beneath all her best silk slips and chemises in her lingerie drawer.

"Mom and Pop think I'm just going to climb back into this bed and become their little girl again, until they marry me off," she muttered as she turned off the light and leaned on her windowsill, gazing at the moon above the treetops.

Richard was surely in Rye, New York, by now, dancing at his country club under this same moon. She had played tennis with him and their friends up there in the suburbs. Then they'd eaten especially good hot dogs at a popular stand in Mamaroneck, where the yachting set liked to stop when they were hungry. These were graceful, serene towns by the Long Island Sound in a county called Westchester. Even the beaches there were quieter, less crowded.

"One more week," she whispered to the rustling leaves in the trees. "And then I'll have my own home and my own life, and nobody here can ever boss me around again."

5

Filomena

Capua, Italy, 1935-1943

By the time Filomena was sixteen-about-to-be-seventeen, she had ceased to pray. She still believed in "the other side"—a heavenly place beyond the blue sky and bright sun and stars where God and the saints and angels lived—but she had stopped believing that the poor and the meek and the honest would be invited to join them.

Being forced to do exhausting, dirty work, carrying heavy baskets from the fields and farms, and then cleaning up the kitchen, from four in the morning until eleven o'clock at night, was bad enough, but she was beaten for small transgressions by whoever happened to be bossing her around and given food that wasn't even good enough to feed the pigs. On Sundays she served the *signor* and *signora* and their five spoiled children, who spent their idle hours getting pleasure from crushing their workers under their pampered feet like grapes.

By now, too, Filomena no longer wondered where her parents and siblings were, because it was clear that they did not want her back. When she'd turned twelve, she'd written them a heartfelt letter, asking how much longer she had to stay here to repay Papa's debt, but the letter was returned to her, accompanied by a short note from a neighbor saying that Filomena's family had gone away, farther north, to start a new life. So now she could never find them.

But why? What could she have done, when she was only a child, to make her own parents despise her so much that they never wanted to see her again? Forever?

Then one day, the other servant girl, Rosamaria, finally explained it all to her.

"Your parents sold you, just like my parents sold me. We can never go home. It's not about what you did or didn't do. Good girl or bad, they'd have sold you anyway to pay off their debt. No matter how hard we work, nobody is ever going to come back for us. Everyone has to pay tribute to somebody. We are the payment."

Filomena trusted Rosamaria to tell her the truth because during that awful first week, when Filomena had sobbed herself to sleep every night, Rosamaria had been her savior. One night, Rosamaria had crept downstairs into the kitchen like a phantom in her nightgown, carrying a candle. When Filomena saw the female figure in white approaching her with a light in her hand, she thought it was the Madonna at last, coming to take her away to heaven, and she stretched out her hand imploringly.

But when she saw that it was only the other kitchen girl, Filomena flung herself at Rosamaria's feet and burst into hysterical sobs, begging her to go get a kitchen knife and kill her, tonight, so she could die and go to be with God in his heaven.

Rosamaria said, "Hush, you fool!" and quickly clasped Filomena to her skinny chest, just to smother her cries. "You silly girl. You're exactly the way I was when I came here, and look at me now. Nobody can make me cry! Yes, I was just like you, I even looked like you. We are cousins, didn't they tell you? Now, quiet down."

Filomena whispered, "You are my cousin? But where did you come from?"

"Tropea," Rosamaria said.

"Where is Tropea?" Filomena asked.

Rosamaria stuck out her foot. "Italy is shaped like a boot," she said, running her hand down her right shin, stopping at the top of her foot, "and Tropea is like a button on the boot, here, on the beautiful blue sea. Haven't you heard of Tropea onions? No? They are red, and so sweet that we even have ice cream made of them! Oh, but we were so poor, we had to pick the pockets of the church mice!"

It took Filomena a moment to smile at the joke. "I hate this kitchen," she whimpered. "I lie awake all night listening for the rats. They come right up to my feet."

"I know. This was my bed once. Look, if I let you sleep upstairs with me, you must promise to be quiet and not let Cook know you're there," Rosamaria whispered.

They tiptoed upstairs to an attic room, where they huddled together in one narrow bed, down the hall from the cook and other servants.

"But every morning you must come back downstairs earlier than everyone else," Rosamaria warned, "and you must lie on your mat as if you've been sleeping in the kitchen all night. Work hard, be good, and one day I'll ask her, officially, to let you sleep in my room, and Cook will act as if she is a great lady and say yes."

This was exactly what happened, because Rosamaria was right about everything. She was the only person on earth whom Filomena cared about now, this cousin who shared the same destiny so bravely. Rosamaria had been a good student, too, in her few years of school; and in an act of utter defiance, she had continued to read and learn. Even now, she sneaked off to the library in Naples to read books and then tell Filomena what she found out. She helped Filomena understand that Italy was one country made of the fragments of old kingdoms, which was why there were various regional ways of speaking. When Rosamaria got angry or excited, she slipped back into the dialect of Tropea, which Filomena, fascinated, learned to mimic when teasing her new friend.

"But why are so many families like ours in debt to these Bosses?" Filomena asked.

"Because the Bosses own everything! You can't get work without their favors. And if they do you a favor or make a loan, you have to pay back more than they gave you, every month, whether you caught any fish or not. If you can't pay, you owe them your life and the lives of your children." Rosamaria patiently explained the old feudal system that had started the whole thing, creating a world where a few powerful men reduced everyone else to pawns. Even the *signor* and the *signora* seemed less important than the kings and dukes who had once ruled over everybody.

"But nowadays, it's the big criminals who run the world," she declared. "They pay off the judges, the politicians, even the clergy, to do their bidding."

And just when Filomena thought they'd figured out history and the way the world worked, along came a braggart called Mussolini, who took all the men away to fight for his demented dreams, filling the sky—God's home—with death.

Whenever people talked to one another these days, it was to ask which towns had been bombed yesterday and which were likely to be bombed today. Everyone knew of relatives who'd died, sometimes whole families, even whole villages razed to the ground. So now, when Filomena lifted her eyes to the heavens, it was only with dread.

"What's going to happen to us? If we don't get killed by the bombs, must we work on this farm until we die?" Filomena asked when they were on their way back to the house after a backbreaking day in the fields. The air was buzzing drowsily with flies flitting in the tall grass. Here and there a plow horse led by a barefoot boy tiredly plodded back to his stable.

Watching one, Filomena said dolefully, "I don't want to drop dead here, like an old horse that the *signora* has worn out."

"We'll find a way to get out. Leave it to me," Rosamaria said firmly.

"Think fast," Filomena warned, explaining that just yesterday, the *signor*'s youngest son had grabbed her and fondled her breasts. "So I picked up a kitchen knife and said I'd kill him! He just laughed."

Rosamaria reached into her skirt pocket and pulled out a small but impressive-looking knife. Its handle was black and gold, its blade sheathed in leather. She unsheathed it, revealing a fierce-looking blade.

"My father," she said proudly, "could hit a mark fifty feet away. He showed me how. You should learn, and then the *signora*'s son won't laugh anymore. Never make an empty threat. Here, I'll show you." She held the knife aloft fearlessly, from the blade end, then aimed and hurled it at a tree. The knife flew swiftly in the air before slicing neatly into the tree and remaining there, handle side out. "You try it now," she said, retrieving it.

Filomena took the knife, listened to her friend's instructions, and tried, over and over. Each time it landed either in the grass, or on a rock, or even lodged in the earth, until it finally hit its mark.

"See?" Rosamaria said triumphantly. "When you know you can do it, your threats sound real."

They resumed walking toward the farmhouse. Filomena said apprehensively, "I heard the *signora* say she might 'give us away' soon. What does that mean?"

Rosamaria said darkly, "Hah! The *signora* doesn't want her husband and sons to hunger after us, now that we are getting prettier. She does this all the time when her little kitchen girls grow up. The last girls were sent off to a whorehouse. Too many curves, too much flirting, and that's what happens. Oh, but I'm still so skinny! I wish I had your curves."

"No, you don't," Filomena said. "Men are worse than pigs. I'm glad that so many of the field hands were sent off to the war. What's the point of marrying and having many children if we'll only give our daughters away to pay debts, like our mothers did?"

"It's different in America," Rosamaria declared. "That's the place to go."

"America!" Filomena scoffed. "Aren't they the ones who are bombing us now?"

"Everybody's bombing us. They call themselves the Allies. Don't expect war to make sense. It never has and it never will. But nobody's bombing New York. And that's where I'm going!" Rosamaria said confidently. "I went to a matchmaker in Naples, and she said she would find me a husband. Well, it took her forever, but at last, she did! I had to give her my gold and pearl rosary beads that my grandmother gave me just before she died. But I did it, just to make sure that the matchmaker picked *me* to send to New York. Now she says I must go soon to America, or that family will find someone else for their son to marry."

"Don't they have Italian girls in America?" Filomena asked.

"Yes, but they are too independent, she says," Rosamaria replied, reaching into the bosom of her dress to retrieve a letter from America that the matchmaker had given her. "This lady in New York came from Tropea, like me, so that helped! She wants her son to marry a girl just like her, so she's paying my fare there. It's all arranged. I'm going as soon as they can get me my ticket."

"Wait a minute!" Filomena said. "Who is this boy you're going to marry? Do you know what he looks like? Does he know what *you* look like? Does he love you?"

"He's rich, so I don't care what he looks like. They didn't send a picture, they're not trying to impress *me*! They don't care what I look like, either. It's more important that I'm a good girl who will be loyal to him and obey his parents. Love will come or not, but I'm going."

Filomena, still shocked by all this, gave her a skeptical look. Rosamaria said stoutly, "It's just a way to get me there. If I don't like him, I'll find someone else."

Filomena noticed that Rosamaria had been saying *I* and not *we*. The thought of losing her only friend was too terrifying to bear. "Can I come, too?"

"Yes, but not right away," Rosamaria said. "It's not so easy anymore to get into America. You have to have a sponsor or some such thing, like I do. And you have to be careful, because sometimes these sponsors are bad people who make you their slave until you pay them back, just like here on this farm. But my matchmaker knows who to trust. Do you have anything you can give to her, so you'll be next in line? Everyone wants to get out of Italy, away from the war. So her price is higher now."

Filomena shook her head and gulped back a sob. Rosamaria hugged her fiercely and said, "Listen, when I get to America, I will find you a husband and you won't have to pay anybody for it. I'll be your sponsor and send for you. Don't you worry." She squeezed her hand to calm her. "You have to be brave, Filomena. You have to trust me."

"Promise that you'll get me out of here!" Filomena gasped, for she couldn't allow herself to cry. "Swear to God you won't make me wait so long."

"I promise," Rosamaria said solemnly. "You know I will find a way. And here, just to prove it, look at this book I borrowed. You and I are going to learn to speak English, because that's what they speak in New York."

And so, their English lessons became their shared secret, and when weeks went by and nothing happened, Filomena was secretly glad, having convinced herself that time would provide a way for them to make this journey together.

But one hot August day, Rosamaria pulled her aside and said exultantly, "It's done, I'm going! I have to go to Naples and pick up my ticket and my documents. I have *so* much to tell you! You come with me and meet my matchmaker."

"I have nothing to give her," Filomena said dully.

"She knows that. But I can introduce you to her, and she'll see what a nice girl you are. Then, when I send her the money to get your documents, she will know it's *you* she's supposed to help, because she'll remember you from this visit."

Filomena only dimly recalled the city of Naples, since her mother had rushed her through it when they'd arrived at the train station. "Okay, let's go," she said.

***

NAPLES WAS GIGANTIC, TERRIFYING, YET EXHILARATING AND ENERGETIC. Amid roaring traffic, ancient stone buildings, pushcarts, and bustling shoppers, everyone seemed hell-bent on getting from one place to the next, as if their lives depended on this frenetic pace. Nobody was more determined than Rosamaria, who took Filomena's hand and dragged her through the maze of twisty streets and the crush of people. Overhead, laundry fluttered from intricate clotheslines, and exhausted mothers shouted out the windows at raggedy urchins who were shrieking and scampering in the courtyards below.

But the first thing that went wrong was that the matchmaker wasn't home to meet them and be introduced to Filomena. The woman's grizzled, elderly husband opened the door of their tiny apartment, then shuffled inside and handed Rosamaria a brown envelope with her name on it, and he wished her "*buon viaggio*."

"What's in the envelope?" Filomena asked when they were back on the street.

"My ticket! I don't want to open it out here where someone might snatch it from me. Let's go into that church and we'll look at it there," Rosamaria said, grasping her by the hand again. "Wait until you see the inside of this place. It's the most beautiful church I've ever seen! It's called Santa Chiara. A king built it for his wife."

Filomena suddenly felt overcome, with the heat, the news, the crush of aggressive people. Her heart weighed heavily in her chest, as if it were made of stone; this had happened to her only once before, when her mother abandoned her.

But Rosamaria dragged her off, once again careening around street corners with a jubilant energy that Filomena could not share. When they arrived at the church they were both breathless.

Rosamaria paused on the steps and pointed up, then put a hand under Filomena's chin to make her tilt her head far back.

"Look! See the little statue standing on the very top of that skinny pole? That is the Spire of the Virgin Mary. Isn't she beautiful? She's higher than everyone. Let's go inside and light a candle to her."

There was no service going on inside the church, so the pews were mostly empty. Just a few old ladies in black, praying to their favorite saints. The girls dipped their fingers in the holy water and crossed themselves, then sat down in a pew that smelled of finely-polished wood, and incense. Excitedly Rosamaria tore open her envelope and scanned its contents.

"It's all here!" she whispered triumphantly. "My ticket for the passage to America, some money for the trip, and the documents I need so that they'll let me into New York."

She tucked the packet into the bosom of her dress, then knelt on the padded kneeler, and closed her eyes and clasped her hands to pray.

Filomena knelt beside her but could not pray. She doubted that God had room in his heart for more than one desperate girl. She knew that she was not blessed like Rosamaria was. This church of stained-glass windows and marble pillars was too beautiful for the likes of Filomena; it was more like a cathedral, built for important people. Somehow Rosamaria, with her insistent vitality and courage, had managed to inveigle her way into this gorgeous holy place. But it meant that Filomena would never see her again; of that she was sure.

"WHEN DO YOU LEAVE?" FILOMENA ASKED WHEN THEY EMERGED from the cool, dark church, blinking in the bright sunlight and the stifling heat.

"Early next month," Rosamaria said in a low voice. "No one must know, Filomena. Don't breathe a word of this to anybody. If the *signora* found out, she'd find a way to stop me, I just know it."

"I won't tell," Filomena promised miserably. "You know that."

Rosamaria said, "Come on, then. We have to go back to the farm now."

Filomena felt as if she were finally waking up. "What did you tell the cook? Why did she let us go out today?"

"I told her that one of our uncles died and we had to go to the funeral." Rosamaria paused before a man who was selling *gelato* in cones. "We'll buy one and share it," she said, paying for a pistachio one. They plunked themselves on the stone steps outside the church and took turns eating this cool, creamy treat, watching crowds of remarkably energetic people scurrying by, chattering loudly with broad gestures.

Just as the girls finished their *gelato,* they heard a hum and then a roar that made them gaze upward. It was a fleet of military planes. They shaded their eyes to see where the fliers were headed today. But even before she realized that these were enemy planes, Filomena detected a shrill buzzing sound that quickly intensified into a deafening whine.

A split second later, the bombs fell, and the city simply erupted all around them.

Eventually, Filomena would find out what happened that day. She would learn that the city caught fire when four hundred B-17 airplanes dropped their bombs and killed three thousand people in Naples; and another three thousand were injured when a ship blew up in the harbor. The Santa Maria di Loreto hospital and the very church of Santa Chiara whose steps they had just been sitting on were completely destroyed.

But all Filomena actually remembered was the explosions, louder than thunder, whose very sound hurt her eardrums, her chest, her whole body to its very core, even before a harsh, forceful wind knocked her clear to the ground. It felt like an earthquake, a fire, and a hurricane all rolled into one. She felt Rosamaria clutch her just as the stones of the church began their downward tumble.

Then, just as suddenly, everything went black and silent for a long time.

WHEN FILOMENA OPENED HER EYES, THE ENTIRE CITY WAS LIKE A ghostly skull, emitting an agonized shrieking sound, and she was in the very center of it. The city was so eerily dark from the billowing black smoke that she couldn't see at all. She gasped for air, but the air itself was full of ash and the acrid smell of everything—flesh, metal, oil, tar, wood, bricks—burning in a hellish bonfire. Something was pinning her down, something much heavier than Rosamaria, who lay on top of her.

"Rosa! Rosa! Get up, I can't breathe!" Filomena cried out in panic, wriggling and panting to be free. She staggered to her feet, with the ashy air still blurring her eyes to the chaos all around her. Choking, she fumbled for her kerchief to put over her mouth and nose, but her eyes felt as if a hundred tiny needles were piercing them.

Now she realized that this awful keening sound was coming from the blend of air-raid sirens, fire engines, horns, and crowds of people screaming in a way she'd never heard grown people scream before. She could feel that everyone was running around in panic—but where were they running to? They seemed to be shouting from all directions.

"Rosamaria, we've got to get out of here, before something else falls on us!" Filomena cried. In the rubble at her feet, she spied a hand reaching out to her. For a fleeting moment she thought of her mother's hand—just before her mother let her go. But this one was child-size. Filomena grabbed it and the hand came loose—for it was not flesh, it was made of stone.

Numbly, she put it in her pocket, hardly realizing what she was doing. Now the wind blew away enough smoke to admit a brief shaft of sunlight. She saw that, amid big stones and bricks, the statue of the Virgin Mary, having toppled spectacularly from its spire, had shattered into powdery fragments nearby. Still stunned, Filomena looked upward and finally realized that the entire church was gone. There was only a frightening gap in the sky, and nothing but piles of rubble here on earth below, as if a vicious child had knocked down all the building blocks.

Rosamaria still lay motionless as a discarded doll, face-down near a heap of stones. It was the first time that Filomena was able to actually see her cousin through all the smoke.

"Rosamaria, get *up*!" Filomena cried desperately, dropping back to her knees and turning her over. Rosamaria's face was full of blood, and when Filomena hastily wiped it away with the skirt of her dress, she saw that Rosamaria's nose was crushed.

"Rosa! Rosa!" she sobbed, frantically unbuttoning her cousin's dress to try to hear if her heart was still beating. Filomena had to push aside the matchmaker's brown envelope—full of all Rosamaria's hopes and dreams, still tucked close to her heart—in order to listen to her cousin's chest, which was as silent as the stones around her. No heartbeat, no breathing. Already, Rosamaria's flesh was like cold clay.

"Rosa!" Filomena sobbed. "Please, wake up!"

A man in white hospital garb that was smeared with black dust emerged out of the drifting black smoke like a phantom. A policeman followed, not far behind. Filomena hastily buttoned Rosamaria's dress so that her chest would not be exposed. As the wind tried to snatch up the matchmaker's envelope, Filomena caught it and tucked it inside her own dress, just before the policeman clamped a hand on Filomena's shoulder.

"You can't stay here. Get out while you can," he bellowed.

Filomena pointed at Rosamaria. "Help her," she begged. She could barely hear her own voice; the incessant noise all around her had made her ears go numb, as if they were padded with wool.

The man in hospital whites shouted into her face. "Is she alive?" He signaled to other men in white to bring a stretcher over, motioning toward Rosamaria.

"I don't know," Filomena said, hoping that somehow he could revive her.

"Name?" the policeman demanded, staring at Filomena while the hospital men were bending over Rosamaria's limp body.

"Filomena!" she cried obediently. He asked for the last name and she gave it.

Too late, she realized her mistake. Someone had written Filomena's name down on a tag and tied it to Rosamaria's foot.

"Come back tomorrow," the policeman advised. "Her family can claim the body then, if any of us are still here. Go home, girl. There may be other bombers coming."

* * *

BUT FILOMENA DID NOT RETURN HOME THAT NIGHT. IT WAS impossible—the roads were jammed with wild, fleeing survivors. A short distance from the city, Filomena discovered that tents had been erected to shelter the lost souls and keep them from becoming hordes invading nearby towns. Some people dressed in white were distributing water. Filomena took her place on line.

The next day, she crept back to Naples. The weather was already so hot that people had hurriedly begun to bury the dead. She managed to get there in time to locate Rosamaria's body and sprinkle some holy water on her cousin, which Filomena got from a priest who was making the rounds. An enterprising mason was selling gravestones that he could hastily scratch names onto. Filomena took some of Rosamaria's coins to pay the mason. The gravediggers had so many people to bury that it was all done quickly in the terrible heat. Filomena said nothing, even when she saw that the tombstone she'd paid for had her own name on it, because that was the name on the body tag. The brave girl who'd died too young now slept under the wrong name.

Feeling dazed, Filomena moved slowly, as if she were walking through water.

The priest, seeing her lost, devastated face, touched Filomena's shoulder and told her of a convent on a nearby hilltop that was sheltering orphaned girls.

Filomena heard the sobbing of other mourners at other headstones as she said a silent prayer over Rosamaria's grave, and stared briefly at her own name on the tombstone. She knew now that she was indeed an orphan. Her parents would never come looking for her, of that she was certain; but even if they did, they would find only this marker, telling them that their unwanted daughter had died in the bombing of Naples.

And only a few weeks later, when Naples was finally "liberated" and the harbor was working again, a girl going by the name of Rosamaria got on a ship bound for New York.

6

Lucy

New York City, February 1935-1937

Say, Fred, who's the doll?" Frankie asked, peering out the window of a room that was called the janitor's office. But Fred himself seldom actually occupied this room; it was really an office that Frankie occasionally used to make his mysterious phone calls.

Fred glanced at the pretty redheaded woman walking purposefully toward them, and he shook his head. "Never saw her before in my life, Frankie," he muttered. Fred was almost seventy, so he said "in my life" a lot these days.

As Lucy approached the office, she saw that the door was ajar, but she knocked on it anyway. "Come in," said the younger man, called Frankie.

Lucy pushed the door farther open. She had the distinct impression that both of these fellows had been talking about her. Men were like that. She chose to ignore it. A businesslike attitude was what was called for. She sized them up. The janitor was a slightly wizened older man in overalls, staring at her now. The younger one was a well-dressed buck who looked to be Lucy's age; he was seated at the desk with his head down, reading the newspaper racing results, pretending to be unaware of her.

"I'm here about the apartment for rent," she said.

Old Fred gave her the once-over now and asked, "You live alone?"

"Me and my baby boy," Lucy said crisply. "My husband went missing and they say he's dead. He was in the British navy."

She'd been telling this incredible lie ever since that strange night when she was ordered at gunpoint by an Irish gangster to deliver a baby and "get rid of it." In the wee hours of the morning that followed, a lovely little boy had been born, and the thuggy men had gone away, after repeating their dire warning and extracting a promise that she would take the baby to the orphanage that very day.

Lucy had waited until they were gone, then she asked the girl on the bed if she really wished to give the baby up. The girl wanted to know about the orphanage, so Lucy told her all about the kindly nuns. *Yes, you take him,* the young mother said finally. *I'm a working girl. I can't keep him.* It turned out that the room in Harlem belonged to the girl's cousin, who worked nights as a hat-check clerk, so the young mother would be cared for until she was well enough to go back to Hell's Kitchen.

Quickly, Lucy had bundled up the baby and carried it off to the nearest bus stop. She'd paused to pick up baby formula and other supplies, truly intending to take the infant to the orphanage upstate. But this boy was one of those sweet babies who slept quietly and gurgled gently when awake. He'd reached his little sausage fingers up to her face and cooed at her. People on the bus had smiled at Lucy as she climbed aboard, and a man gave up his seat for her.

"Your first?" asked the lady beside her. Lucy only nodded. The baby nuzzled his warm, sweet head against her chest, gave a tiny, weary yawn, and fell asleep on her bosom.

Over and over Lucy reminded herself that the orphanage was run by good, gentle people, but to her own great astonishment, she simply could not go through the actions of giving up a baby to the nuns, just as she'd once been forced to do back in Ireland when she was only fourteen and they'd shaved her head and made her work in the laundry. Glancing down at this infant when he stirred awake briefly and gazed back at her so trustfully, Lucy's heart swelled with ferocious desire, and she whispered, "No, never again. You're safe now."

She knew it was madness. But she rode the bus past the train terminals and continued on, even past the place where she lived, because it was for single girls only. She went beyond Hell's Kitchen, farther downtown where no one knew her, to a cheap rooming house that took people on a temporary basis, no questions asked. All the while, she peered over her shoulder and, seeing no one suspiciously watching her, she checked into a furnished room.

She called the boy Christopher, registering his birth under her name as the mother, with the father "deceased." An older lady who lived in the room next to Lucy's said that this baby had Irish looks just like "his mama," and a sweet temperament; Lucy paid her to care for little Chris while she was working at the hospital. It all had evolved so miraculously that she was sure God was on her side this time, for doing what she felt in her heart was right.

But Lucy couldn't keep Chris in that rooming house for long. He was getting bigger and needed to play, somewhere safe and clean. In every free moment she had, she walked around town, searching for a good building on a nice street. Finally she spotted a sign in the window of a genteel apartment building on MacDougal Street in Greenwich Village; she calculated that she could catch a subway to work at the hospital.

NOW, WHEN FRANKIE FOLDED HIS NEWSPAPER AND LOOKED UP AT her, Lucy suddenly experienced something she'd never felt before with any man. It was as if her body reacted to his gaze without consulting her mind. Her brain stopped thinking about the apartment and the money, and she found herself wondering what it would feel like to have those strong arms around her, and that chest close to hers, and those lips kissing her. This sensation came over her in a flash, and it was so engulfing that she wondered if her thoughts and feelings were plainly visible to everybody, as if all her clothes had fallen off. She was stunned.

"I—I'd like to see the apartment right now, if possible," she stammered.

Frankie spoke to Fred, without ever taking his eyes off Lucy. "I'll show it to her," he said, holding out his hand. Fred obediently placed the key in Frankie's outstretched palm.

"This way," Frankie said, leading her to the stairs.

They climbed to the second floor and entered a spacious one-bedroom apartment at the back of the building, blissfully quiet, which overlooked a small yard. A bird was singing contentedly in a nearby tree. The apartment had hardwood floors and plenty of windows to let in the sunlight.

"You work around here or something?" Frankie asked casually.

"I'm a nurse," Lucy said, and she told him about St. Clare's hospital. "I can give you references," she assured him.

But Frankie only smiled and shook his head. "Not necessary," he replied.

Taking a deep breath, Lucy asked cautiously, "What is the rent?"

When Frankie answered, her face must have fallen, because she saw his reaction, and then he said quickly, "But for you, I can make it half that."

Lucy gave him a cynical look. "What sort of malarkey is that, eh?" she demanded.

Frankie threw back his head and laughed. "I'm not foolin' with you," he said.

Lucy still wouldn't believe him. "And how on God's green earth are you able to perform such a miracle with this rent?" she asked.

"My family owns the building," he answered with a grin.

LUCY AND CHRISTOPHER MOVED IN THE NEXT DAY, AND SHE FOUND
a girl to look after him while Lucy worked. She didn't see Frankie
again for three weeks but thought of him often; he was unlike anyone she'd ever met. The boy in Ireland had been just that, a callow
youth by comparison. In America, she'd flirted with doctors at the
hospital but was wise enough to avoid dating them; nothing must
jeopardize her job. And none of these men had Frankie's utterly
desirable maleness and confidence in his own power. She could
not help remembering the gaze that had thrilled her, no matter
how resolutely she tried to forget about him.

Then, almost as if she'd summoned him, he turned up at the
emergency room of the hospital, just as Lucy was going off her
shift. It was midnight. There was nobody there, and the doctor
was away on a coffee break.

"Nurse, got a minute?" Frankie asked her. "And a room that's
private?" Against her better judgment, she let him into the doctor's consulting room. Only then did she notice how he was holding his arm against his left side, almost cradling it.

"What's the matter over here, now?" she asked, reaching for
his arm.

"Promise to keep your mouth shut, no matter what," Frankie
said in a tense tone. He refused to take off his coat and shirt until
she promised. He'd wrapped what looked like a small white tablecloth around his arm, over and over. It was drenched in blood.

"I don't want my family to see this," he muttered. "They'd
have fits."

It was a gunshot wound, but mercifully his coat and suit had
slowed the bullet, so it hadn't hit the bone, although his flesh
needed some stitches.

"Can you make it stop bleeding?" he asked. "Maybe close it
up?"

"I really should call the doctor," Lucy answered, cleaning it carefully. She looked up at him, straight in the eye, and said, "You know I'm supposed to report all gunshot wounds to the police, don't you?"

"But you won't report me, right?" he said urgently, leaning closer. She could sense the heat of his body, see his beautifully sculpted chest, and she was once again amazed at the way her own flesh responded; his mere presence nearly knocked the breath out of her. She couldn't believe that she could be so foolish over a man.

"You can stitch this one up yourself, can't you?" he inquired.

"Yes," Lucy responded in a low voice. "But don't ever ask me to do this again."

Frankie grinned. "You think I'll be stupid enough to go out and get shot again?"

"And just what business are you in?" Lucy asked with a challenging tilt to her chin.

"Real estate," Frankie said easily. "We invest in residential and commercial properties, we partner with the owners. Restaurants, nightclubs. You like to dance?"

FROM THEN ON, LUCY SHRUGGED OFF THE DRABNESS OF HER OLD LIFE just as if she'd shrugged off an old coat. Frankie always got a good table in chic restaurants; he was never relegated to a corner near a swinging kitchen door or a drafty hallway. He seemed to know everybody, even famous people, and he took her to fancy supper clubs that she'd heard about on the radio. Only enchanted people went to such places. Now she was one of them.

"Hello there, Frankie!" a glamorous blond woman in a silver satin gown once called out to him while clinging to the arm of a rich movie producer.

And Lucy gasped, "That was Carole Lombard, the actress!"

On another occasion an enormous, powerfully built mountain of a man about six and a half feet tall looked up from the bar and said, "Frankie, whaddaya say?" slapping him on the back and nodding to Lucy. Frankie introduced him as Primo Carnera, the famous heavyweight champion who'd only recently been knocked out by Joe Louis. All kinds of celebrities—singers, socialites, news reporters, and politicians—went out of their way to say hello.

Suddenly Lucy was growing accustomed to the taste of good champagne, and steaks more tender than she'd ever eaten in her life, and lobster thermidor.

"Don't get spoiled," Frankie teased her one night when they were out on the town. "The truth is, I usually eat regular food at home—pasta, trout, veal stew. And lots of vegetables and beans. Pop says beans make you strong, and fat makes you lazy. He also says, 'One meal, one glass' of wine. So that's what you'd really be facing if you ended up with me."

"Then why are you ordering champagne and caviar?" Lucy teased him back.

"To impress you, of course," he said. "To catch you and keep you all to myself."

"Can I have chocolate cake for dessert?" Lucy replied.

"Anytime you want it."

Frankie said he liked Lucy's outspoken way of talking; he told her that she was so different from the girls he met. He was a decisive kind of man, but he also had a sweet, protective side. He and Johnny had a younger brother named Mario, so perhaps that was why Frankie was so patient with Lucy's little Christopher, pushing him on the swings in the park. Lucy realized that Frankie would defend her and Chris from anyone who tried to harm them.

They courted for a year. One year of joy and almost unbearable, deliriously thrilling kissing and petting. Although it was obvious that Lucy had a child and was therefore not a virgin, Frankie never pushed her beyond the limits of propriety, indicating that he was truly serious about her. And Lucy vowed to herself to "do it right" this time, to wait.

They were both soon to turn twenty-three, and were ready to

get married. So they became secretly engaged, at first; Lucy was afraid to meet his formidable family. But then they found that they couldn't wait, and when people saw them together, even his family, it was clear that nobody could stop Frankie. On Valentine's Day he bought her a diamond ring to make it official, and they set their wedding date for October, that same year. Neither of them wanted to wait any longer.

Then one day, shortly after their official engagement, Frankie said, "Listen, it's my big brother's birthday. Do you mind if he comes skating with us?"

"Of course not," Lucy said. She'd met Johnny and liked him.

"Let's go by his bar and pick him up, then," Frankie said.

And that was when Lucy met Amie.

7

Amie

Greenwich Village, 1937

Let me tell you something, Amie Marie," said Johnny-Boy, the tall, dark-haired man who had become Brunon's partner at their new tavern in Greenwich Village, "if it weren't for you, I'd give Brunon a little shaking up for his own good."

Amie looked alarmed. "He doesn't mean to be rude," she said apologetically. "It's just that things aren't working out exactly as he'd hoped."

"They never do." Johnny shrugged, then paused. Amie was rubbing the counter of the bar vigorously, nervously, with a soft cloth, but Johnny reached out and grabbed her forearm with his warm, generous paw.

"Where'd you get a bruise like that?" he demanded, turning her arm upward.

Flushed, Amie pulled her sleeve back over her arm. "Oh, I'm always bumping into doorways around here," she murmured. "I'm so nearsighted."

"Did that fat-head hit you?" Johnny demanded. "You want me to straighten him out for you, Amie? A man who hits a woman isn't a man at all."

Amie shook her head mutely, embarrassed. Brunon wasn't happy in his new surroundings and he wasn't making any friends. Even his elegant "silent partner," Johnny, was becoming impatient with Brunon. Johnny had frightened Amie at first, because he carried an air of danger with him. But he blew into the bar like a gust of fresh air, all male energy and the kind of confidence Brunon wished for but never had.

The deal was that Brunon's bar functioned legitimately out in front, serving a hearty lunch and supper in the main room to the working people of Greenwich Village. But in the back room, at night, the card players showed up in their fancy cars—all well-dressed men in natty wool coats and suits, polished shoes, expensive hats, and silk ties. Lawyers, doctors, politicians, stockbrokers, assorted businessmen all came to play poker here. No one was allowed in the back room unless Johnny said it was okay.

Amie ventured there occasionally, to serve beer and whiskey and sandwiches. Sometimes the card table was piled so high with their bets that she just left the tray on a sideboard and silently hurried out. It was terrifying at times, the amount of money at stake. The air crackled with tension. "High rollers," as Brunon enviously called them. They gambled big, so someone always won big—and someone always lost big.

These men also bet on prizefighters, football games, baseball and basketball players, even college teams. One time Amie actually saw a group of men betting thousands of dollars on which ant would cross the table first. And Johnny profited from it all.

There were other things going on in the back of the bar, in the "office" room that was kept under lock and key, because it had a safe in it. In the daytime Johnny and his men came in and used this back office as a "policy bank" for the numbers game. Their "runners" brought in the bets that had been placed with bookies at local barber and candy shops. Brunon told her that Johnny backed these bookies in a numbers racket, where Johnny's policy bank operated like an insurance company. Since the odds of winning this illicit lottery were so tiny, and there were few winners each time, Johnny's "take" made for an enormous windfall.

"So Johnny cleans up, and you and I make a few dollars' profit off the beer and tips," Brunon said sarcastically. "But you can never tell anybody about this," he warned Amie. "Unless you want us both to end up floating in the river."

She knew that Brunon had imagined that being partners with a big man like Johnny would automatically make Brunon a big man, too. But when it didn't turn out that way, Brunon, ashamed, had turned his rage onto Amie. Nothing she did could please him anymore.

Every year since they'd been here, she'd tried to make a nice Thanksgiving and Christmas for them, as if they were a real family, even if there were only the two of them. She'd decorated a small tree in the bar for the customers, and another one in their tiny apartment upstairs. She only wanted to believe that they were happy and normal people, like everyone else milling around this great city.

But Brunon ridiculed her pitiful attempts to put some beauty in their lives, as if it only served to remind him of what a small man he was in a big town. Whether it was a homemade silver ornament for the tree or a little costume jewelry to brighten herself up, Brunon despised these things for their cheapness. What embarrassed Amie was that other people could see how miserably Brunon treated her. The toughest of men who came into the bar were oddly gentle with her, filled with pity.

Especially Johnny. But he never made her feel pitiful. Every time he saw Amie he had a big smile for her and treated her as if she were one of the glamorous women she sometimes saw on the street, their gloved hands proudly tucked under the elbows of successful men.

Amie loved New York City. "Don't you miss Troy?" her new neighbors asked her. She shook her head. Here she was, in a tiny apartment over the family tavern, just like in Troy. But back there, she'd lived among struggling workers' wives, and their outlook, even on a good day, was soured by the defeat of an old industrial area whose best days were long gone.

By comparison, New York seemed like a young city to Amie, not just because of the modern skyscrapers but because of its people, who had so many interesting things to do that they did not waste time with petty details. Yes, the ladies gossiped here, but they did it with a certain lightness that came from the joy of enterprise and profits. And while Manhattan had slums more terrifying than anything she'd ever seen—and you had to always look over your shoulder no matter what neighborhood you were in—still, so much money was circulating, and there were tantalizing rewards that could make one's efforts worthwhile: restaurants with the country's best food; shops that had the world's best clothes; new buildings with lobbies of marble and gilt. Manhattan was full of energy, a magical promise that if you learned how to navigate around the tricksters and pitfalls, you just might forge your own path toward success.

Today was Sunday, and the bar was closed. Amie had already been to church. Johnny had stopped in to make a few phone calls from the back office. Brunon was out on some errand that he hadn't bothered to explain to her.

Johnny said easily, "Amie, I tell you what. Why don't you come to the ice-skating rink tonight? My brother Frankie and his fiancée and their friends will be there. Bring Brunon if you must. Just come. We'll have fun."

Amie looked up with a smile but said quickly, "I don't think Brunon skates."

"But you do, right? C'mon, it's my birthday," he confided, "and I don't want to spend it with married couples or out drinking with the guys. I gotta have dinner with my family at home, so they can have a birthday cake for me. But after that, I'm going skating just to exercise off the cake!" He patted his stomach, which was flat and firm. "To my folks, I'm still Johnny-Boy, even though, you know how old I am today? Twenty-five!"

Amie smiled. "That's not so old."

He took a cigarette from a silver case embossed with his initials, picked up a matchbook from the bar, lighted his cigarette, and drew on it thoughtfully.

"Yeah? Well, it's too old to be called Johnny-Boy. Know why they call me that? Because my father's name is Gianni. Here's how they spell it in Italy." He wrote it down on a paper coaster on the bar. "See? But in America they spell *Johnny* this way." He wrote that underneath. "It's all pronounced the same way. How old are you, Buttercup?"

"Twenty-one." When Amie said it, she almost cried; she felt so much older. Especially this winter; she'd had a chest cold since Christmas that she couldn't seem to shake, which made her feel weak and even older.

"Your hair looks like gold in this light," Johnny said gallantly. "You always remind me of an angel at the top of a Christmas tree." Amie smiled, feeling momentarily better, as she always did whenever Johnny looked her way.

"Here comes my brother Frankie," he said as a well-dressed man with a woman at his side peered in the plate-glass window. Ignoring the CLOSED sign, they pushed the door open.

The man who entered the bar looked only a couple of years younger than Johnny; but Johnny was tall and wiry, whereas Franco, as he was properly introduced, was more athletic looking. Both men had beautiful dark hair and eyes, pale skin, and sensuous mouths. When they were in a room together, it was like being around two elegant, healthy stallions.

"This is my gal, Lucy Marie," Frankie said, his arm around the redheaded girl.

"These two are getting married in October," Johnny proclaimed.

Lucy blushed. She was thinking that if a Gypsy had read her palm and predicted this, she never would have believed it. Yet, here she was, a bride-to-be.

"I'm trying to talk Amie into coming out with us tonight," Johnny was telling them now. "*You* talk to her, Lucy. Tell her it's my birthday."

"You big baby," Lucy teased him. Amie laughed, but this caused her to cough in a way that Lucy, her nursing skills always alert, recognized. She didn't say anything at first, but when Amie coughed again, Lucy looked at her more keenly.

"I think you should see a doctor," she said briskly. "You want to get rid of that cough before it gets the better of you. Pneumonia is no joke. I know some good doctors who are on call today. We work together. Why don't you and I stop by the hospital?"

When Amie protested, Frankie said, "Better listen to Lucy! She can out-argue anybody."

"Which is saying something, for a hothead like Frankie," Johnny replied. "Amie, go with Lucy," he said, looking concerned now. "I'll watch the bar till Brunon gets here. I've got some business to discuss with him anyway. I'll tell him where you are."

Amie couldn't resist being taken care of. Lucy had such a comforting, nurturing way about her. So Amie put on her coat and they went. The day was sunny and windless. Perhaps spring wasn't too far off.

"So," Lucy said conversationally. "Do you have any children?" It was usually a safe question with married women to break the ice. But to her surprise, Amie burst into tears. Lucy handed her a handkerchief, and Amie apologized, saying that she was sure there was something wrong with her, for she and her husband, Brunon, had relations every night, and yet she could not get pregnant.

"Come now, dry your eyes," Lucy said gently. In any crisis, her take-charge attitude kicked in. "What you need is for the doctor to examine you and see if there is a difficulty."

When Amie looked horrified, Lucy said, "It's the only way to know what to do. You *do* want to have a child of your own, don't you, now?"

"More than anything in the world," Amie whispered.

"Then don't worry. Dr. Arnold is very gentle and very wise. He will know if there's something to be done."

"Will you come with me?" Amie pleaded. Lucy nodded.

AFTER THE DOCTOR EXAMINED AMIE, HE SUMMONED LUCY ALONE into his office. "Your friend is getting dressed," he said. "And now I think you'd better have a little talk with her yourself."

"What's the matter?" Lucy asked, alarmed for the first time. "Is it her chest?"

"What? Oh, no. That's just an infection; she's a bit run-down. I gave her some medicine. What she really needs is rest, and sleep. And probably a different husband."

Lucy said quickly, "Why? Can't they have children?"

In a sudden, embarrassed burst, the doctor said, "I have no business with sodomites, Lucy. You tell her that for me, and explain the facts of life to your friend!"

Still looking both embarrassed and furious, he walked out, leaving Lucy to grasp what he meant. When Amie emerged from the examining room, Lucy at first did not quite know what to say. Then she saw the medical books behind the doctor's desk, and she reached for one, saying nothing until she found the proper page.

"Amie," she said as delicately as possible, "didn't your mama ever tell you the facts of life?"

Amie felt the pang of a lost memory. She could barely remember her mother—just a vague sensation of some softness, some nice warm female scent was all she could recall. She told Lucy this, as if admitting to yet another personal failing.

"I'm sorry," Lucy said gently. "Look at this book, Amie. This is a picture of the inside of a woman. Here is where the baby grows inside you. And here is where a man is supposed to enter you. This is the vagina. It's a lovely thing. It's able to stretch to let a man in, and even to let a baby come out. So, *that's* where a man is supposed to put his penis. Here. *Not* here. This other place, well, that's for your body to use for waste. And you see, if a man puts his penis *there,* you can't possibly get pregnant. That place isn't where you make babies. It can't stretch as much, so it must hurt, if that is what your husband has been doing to you all this time."

Amie had been sitting very still, looking shocked. "But— but—" she gasped. And yet, reality was sinking in. Everything she'd ever heard people say about proper sex, she realized, had absolutely nothing to do with what had been happening between her and Brunon. She had just misunderstood. *A wife's duty. You must learn to relax more. Yes, a virgin will bleed the first time, and keep bleeding if the man's too rough.*

"Are—are you sure?" she whispered.

"Yes," Lucy said firmly. "Yes, Amie. Your husband hasn't been doing it right. That's why you haven't been able to get pregnant. Understand?"

"Yes," Amie whispered, flushed with shame.

Lucy said, "When you go home, look at yourself down there in the mirror. Feel with your fingers where the right place is. And then tell that stupid brute of a husband—I'm sorry, dear, but honestly—tell him the right way to make love to a wife!"

LUCY WENT HOME TO GET DRESSED FOR SKATING. WHEN AMIE RE-turned alone to the bar, Johnny was gone, and Brunon was waiting, seething with fury.

"Don't ever leave this place without my permission!" he thundered. "And stay away from Johnny, do you hear? It's bad enough that I have to put up with his bookies and his card games in the back room. And now this guy Johnny is asking my wife to go skating with him? Well, you're *not* going anywhere tonight, you understand me?"

Amie's throat felt dry. "He wanted both of us to come. But the doctor said I should get some rest, and drink more water," she said, reaching for a glass. Brunon slapped her arm, and the glass shattered to the floor.

"Stay away from that guy, you understand me?" he insisted.

"Brunon," she said quietly, "the doctor told me other things. He told me why I haven't been able to get pregnant. The nurse said I should talk to you—"

In a split second, she saw the truth cross his face, before he had time to hide it. She saw that Brunon was not as ignorant as everyone supposed he must be.

"You knew," she whispered. "You knew all along, that this was the wrong way?"

His eyes took on a cunning look. "You're so damned ignorant," he said shortly. "Get me my dinner."

Mechanically, Amie went into the kitchen to heat up some baked beans and add some sausage pieces to it. She heard Brunon banging around and cursing to himself. She knew what tonight would be like.

The doctor had given her some sleeping powders and recommended rest as the best cure. The more Brunon banged and cursed, the more she knew she simply had to get some sleep tonight. She thought about swallowing all of these powders at once to sleep forever.

But to her surprise, she realized that she did not want to die. All these months, she'd thought she did, but now, she knew she wanted to live. Not only that, but she wanted to feel as young as she was, and not a day older.

So when Brunon's dinner was heated up, Amie, feeling tired and somewhat dazed, took the powders and dumped most of them into the pot and stirred them. She put some powder in his beer, too, and brought it to the table, thinking, *This is the best thing to do. Brunon needs sleep, too. Tomorrow, we can talk, and maybe he'll listen to reason.*

Brunon ate and drank rapidly. Amie was as quiet as a mouse, but everything she did seemed to annoy him; he kept scowling and making impatient faces at her.

"Aren't you going to eat something?" he demanded, so she took a few spoonfuls herself and ate some bread. They would both sleep well tonight.

"Brunon," she said finally, "if you knew the right way—then why all this time have you been doing it the wrong way? You knew this way we couldn't make babies."

He had been eating rapidly and barely looked up. "I hate kids," he said defiantly. "They cost money, and we can't afford them. Not now, and not for a long time. You should be glad I'm not making you have sixteen kids. That's how many my mother had, until she dropped dead. And the babies, some of them died, too. The ones who lived were miserable. You ever try to take a bath in water that five brothers have washed in first? I'd rather raise goats than kids."

He can't really mean that, Amie thought, returning to the kitchen to drink a glass of milk. Milk was good, for mothers and for babies. Now that she knew the right way to do things, she didn't feel so defective. She clung to a small particle of hope that she could still have the life she craved, as a loving wife and the mother of loving children. Why shouldn't she have that?

Brunon finished his dinner and got sleepy while he sat there drinking his beer. He yawned, looking suddenly exhausted, then rose and staggered into the bedroom, calling out over his shoulder, "Amie, come to bed."

She washed the dishes first. Then she followed slowly, praying that by the time she got near the bed he would be fast asleep. *But he's such a big ox,* she thought. *Maybe those powders aren't enough to make a man like him go to sleep.*

He had flung himself down on the bed. "Come on, Amie," he said, sounding drowsy.

She changed into her nightgown slowly, then approached the bed on tiptoe. He was silent at first. But when she slipped under the covers, he turned to her, all in a rush, his eyes blazing, saying,

"I don't want you talking about us to other people anymore, you hear me? Not Johnny or his stupid brother, or some ugly doctor, or even some smart-ass nurse, you hear me, Amie? You're my wife, and you do as I say!"

"No, not that way, Brunon!" she whispered in dismay as he climbed on top of her, regardless of all she'd said about it. He was too heavy and she could not move.

But he kept repeating, "You do as I say!" until his energy was finally spent. And at that point, the sleeping powders had their effect on Brunon. He fell asleep right then and there, with his full weight pinning her down. Disgusted, Amie pushed him off her and crawled out of the bed. Brunon had rolled over on his back, and he lay there undisturbed, snoring loudly, as if he would sleep forever.

But he won't, Amie thought as she went into the bathroom. *He'll wake up and behave like a beast every day of his life—and mine. There will be no peace. Not now, not ever.*

She washed the blood off her nightgown just as she had done so many times before. The sheets would need washing tomorrow morning, and Brunon would pretend he hadn't seen it, and their world would keep turning and turning the same way, over and over again. He would never change, because he didn't want to, and because he simply didn't care how she felt about it. And how would Amie face people, now knowing the sordid truth of her own life? The shame would engulf her until she might as well be dead.

The familiar dull sensation of hopelessness returned to her and was all the more awful after that small spurt of hope she'd just experienced. She went into the kitchen thinking about the skating party she'd missed tonight. They were all so healthy. It was hard even to imagine having the energy to be that happy. She could feel herself growing older by the minute.

And yet, sitting here at the kitchen table, she felt something else. She was hungry. There were still some beans left over. She could heat them up. Brunon had eaten all the sliced meat, but there was more sausage in the icebox, which she could add to the beans for herself. She *must* keep up her strength, the doctor had said, so she could fight off this chest infection and finally get well.

Amie picked up the knife and began to slice the sausage. But she had to stop, seized by a sudden panic. The sausage felt like something else, something familiar, and she didn't want to touch it. She put the knife down, and heard herself wheezing for breath. She could feel her own life ebbing out of her, like blood. She heard Brunon, snoring louder than ever. She remembered countless nights lying beside him, praying he wouldn't wake up again that evening—praying, in fact, that he would never wake up— then asking God to forgive such terrible thoughts. The shame, the hopelessness, the brief flicker of anger, the guilt. It was all so exhausting, like a merry-go-round that would not let her off until she died. One thought remained: She did not want to get into that bed again with Brunon. Not tonight, not ever again.

She tried to resume slicing the sausage. But instead, still holding the knife, her arm simply dropped to her side. Nothing seemed worth any effort. Numbly, she left the kitchen and headed back to bed. She felt woozy. Brunon was lying on his back, stark naked, his penis exposed, smaller and more innocuous now. He was deeply asleep; he'd stopped snoring.

Like a sleepwalker, she moved closer, thinking, *If he doesn't want children, then he doesn't need it. It must be a burden to him.* They would both be so much better off without it. He had turned it into a weapon of hate instead of a tool of love. She was so tired of all the hatred.

Afterwards Amie did not remember exactly how it happened. She only knew that one minute her arm hung limp beside her, still clutching the knife; then, in one swift moment, she made her move. She did not notice if Brunon even stirred. The next thing she knew, she was back in the kitchen with that thing in her hand, where, at last, it could no longer hurt her. She couldn't keep this thing here, where he might find it when he woke.

So she carried it into the bathroom and flushed it down the toilet. She washed out her nightgown and hung it to dry. She washed the dishes, put on a bathrobe, went into the tiny parlor, and sat in the chair where she usually did her sewing. She pulled her shawl around her chest and put a pillow behind her head. Having eaten some spoonfuls of the bean dinner, she dimly understood that it had more sleeping powder in it than she'd realized, which must have been why she felt so distant from her own body. Now she just let herself drift off into slumber.

HOURS LATER, THERE WAS A KNOCK ON THE DOOR. AMIE WOKE WITH a start and could not imagine who would come calling at this hour on a Sunday. Even so, she was prepared for anyone—a policeman, a priest, a neighbor—when she opened the door.

But it was Johnny and Lucy and Frankie, returning from their skating party. They had seen her light on and wanted to say hello, have a drink with her and Brunon. Johnny looked a bit worried and seemed to be checking on Amie.

"Brunon's asleep," Amie said, as if in a trance. Lucy instinctively felt that something was very wrong here. She told the men to go downstairs, so she could speak to Amie alone.

When Lucy asked what was wrong, Amie was in such a fog that her reply sounded as if it came from an eerie other world. "The doctor gave me powders so I could sleep. Brunon ate some, too. And he had beer. Maybe you should see if he's all right."

"How many powders did he take?" Lucy asked, confused.

"I'm not sure," Amie said in her foggy, dazed way. With a certain dread, Lucy forced herself to tiptoe into the bedroom, expecting to have to deal with a hostile drunk.

Lucy didn't stay in that bedroom long. "Who did this to him?" she demanded. Amie didn't answer. "Amie, for God's sake," she began sternly.

But now Amie was shaking uncontrollably, like a stray puppy

on the street in the pouring rain, her eyes looking huge in the way abused animals and children appeared.

"Was it you?" Lucy whispered.

Amie only nodded, still shivering. "I just had to make it stop," she quavered.

If this poor girl goes to prison she won't last a week, Lucy thought. She hurried downstairs, where the men were seated in Amie's bar, pouring drinks and talking in low voices.

"Lucky Luciano is going to jail for at least thirty years," Johnny was saying. "Got railroaded on a trumped-up charge of 'aiding and abetting compulsory prostitution.'"

"Aw, c'mon, that case won't hold up. He'll get off on appeal," Frankie replied.

"Nah. Pop says the D.A.—Tom Dewey—has had it in for Lucky all along, and they'll throw away the key forever," Johnny said. "It's Frank Costello who'll replace Luciano as Boss now. Strollo will still be *capo* of the Greenwich Village Crew, but he'll answer to Costello."

"Costello's all right," Frankie said. "He's a classier act than most, and he's got all the politicians in his pocket. Pop says he won't ask for more of a cut from us than we can bear." They looked up and saw Lucy emerging from the shadowy hallway.

She'd recognized those terrifying names from the newspapers but never knew anyone to drop them so casually. *Well, tonight a gangster is just what I need,* she thought. She walked right in and told them everything. She knew that she could trust these men to help her with a situation like this.

"Amie did *what*?" Frankie asked incredulously.

"I think he was already half-dead from the sleeping powders," Lucy said. "No sign of a struggle. I don't believe she meant to kill him. She just couldn't stand it anymore."

"Serves him right. You don't know just how much abuse that poor girl's been putting up with," Johnny said. He added urgently, "I love her, Frankie. We've got to help her."

Frankie studied him for a long moment. "All right, Johnny," he muttered.

Johnny stepped away to pick up the telephone. Frankie turned to Lucy now. "Babe—we can't ever tell anybody else about this. You understand?"

Lucy's eyes searched Frankie's face, the face of the man she loved, the only man she'd ever trusted.

"I do," she said. "I do understand."

But she was still a little surprised when the person Johnny called was their father.

"We need a clean-up crew here tonight, Pop," she heard him say. "It's got to be done. Otherwise the entire bar and all its operations will be in jeopardy. We can't have cops sniffing around here. Yeah, I understand, Pop. We'll owe somebody a big favor."

It didn't take long. The men who came to remove the body and the bloody mattress were brisk and businesslike.

Incredibly, Amie slept in her chair in the parlor alcove through most of this. Lucy hovered in the kitchen, making coffee, mostly to avoid being around the "clean up" detail.

But she caught a glimpse of the big man who was in charge of these thugs—and once you saw that terrifying face, you never forgot it. He had coal-black eyes, a nose that curved at the tip like a hawk's beak, a jaw like a stone monument, and well-slicked hair. His body was big and broad, as imposing as an icebox. He strode in and surveyed Brunon's body, then his gaze rested on the dead man's bloody crotch. His mouth twisted into an ugly grin of comprehension, and his eyes were alight with such sadistic pleasure that he looked half-mad.

"Where's the missing piece?" he asked. His men shrugged. "This is not a detail you want to leave behind," the big man growled. The other men looked about uneasily.

At that moment, Amie stirred from her chair in the parlor alcove. She'd been so mousy-quiet, the men had barely noticed her. But now she spoke.

"I flushed it," she said in that eerie, faraway voice. The big man gazed at her in fascination, causing Amie to realize that her bathrobe had fallen open slightly, revealing her large, lovely bosom. Like a dreamer, she pulled up her shawl and turned away.

Johnny and Frankie had been helping the crew. But now Johnny went over to Amie, protectively reaching up to close a curtain that shut off the alcove, hiding her.

When the strange men were finally gone, the room looked entirely blameless. Lucy tried not to think about how professionally it had been taken care of. They were more scrupulous, even, than the hospital.

Johnny poured another round of drinks downstairs in the bar. This time, Lucy joined them. Frankie had been on the telephone, but now hung up, swore under his breath, and looked keenly at his brother.

"Christ, Johnny! Do you know who those guys were?" he demanded.

"Strollo's men, right?" Johnny said impatiently. "So what?"

"It only started with Strollo. This had to go higher up, to get it done fast and get it done right. We just had a visit from Murder Inc., man! And the big guy? That was Albert Anastasia! We just raised the devil out of hell."

There was a long pause before Johnny spoke again. "It had to be done. It's in everyone's interest to protect this place. We're good earners now. We can handle whatever comes."

Lucy stifled a gasp and hurried on upstairs. She knew instinctively what she must do, right this second. Amie had not once moved from her chair in the parlor, still looking confused, until finally, in a childlike way she said to Lucy, "Brunon is dead?"

"Yes," Lucy said shortly. "Yes, and you did it, Amie. And Johnny and his family are going out of their way to help you, so that you don't go to jail. So, no matter how you feel tomorrow, or the next day, or month, or years after, you must never, ever speak of this again, or tell anyone, or even say his name to anyone, ever again—even the priest in the confessional—or you will send all of us to jail. Do you understand me, Amie?"

Lucy was speaking sharply now, and she grasped Amie's shoulders so that they would look each other in the eye. "Don't act stupid with me, girl. I need to know that you hear me and understand. We all protected you tonight. Now you must protect us. So *tell me you understand*, *Amie*, and that you will never feel sorry and try to confess to *anyone*. Say it, Amie. You won't betray us. Eh? Or, if you can't keep quiet, then tell us right now, and we'll take you to the police tonight, and you can confess everything." She gave her shoulders a shake. "Answer me, Amie!" Lucy cried.

Amie seemed to suddenly awaken, looking straight at her, clear-eyed. When Amie spoke, it was in a calm voice that was new, even to her, yet it seemed like the voice of someone who'd always been there, simply waiting to come out.

"All right. I won't tell. I won't go to jail for Brunon," Amie said firmly. "And I will never betray you and Johnny's family."

"Swear it on the soul of your father and mother," Lucy insisted.

It seemed to Amie in this moment, with Johnny and Frankie and Lucy circling like pioneer wagons around her, that this was the first time anyone had really tried to protect her. So, this was her real family. She would die for them, if she had to. Yes, this she could do.

"I swear it on their souls, and mine," Amie said.

8

Petrina
Rye, New York, 1937

Petrina loved the terrace of the country club in the summertime. It overlooked a small, private beach. By day, the sea was dotted with sailboats, and the shore was a joyous place to frolic with children. The clubhouse had an especially festive atmosphere at night, when it was festooned with paper lanterns glowing like jars of fireflies.

So when her daughter, Pippa, turned five years old in the summer of '37, Petrina felt lucky to secure the clubhouse during this busy season for a birthday party. Richard's family had pulled strings, as they always did. Richard's father, a prominent lawyer, had been nominated to be a judge, and already, people were happy to curry favor with him ahead of his expected victory this autumn. Petrina understood the power of family connections; her father's name carried the same weight in his neighborhood. But Greenwich Village and Westchester's suburbs were worlds apart, she thought. At least, people here acted as if they were.

And suddenly, the birthday party for Pippa had turned into something much bigger, since Richard's parents insisted on paying for it.

"Look at all the important people who are coming," Richard

marveled as they studied his mother's guest list. Top businessmen, a newspaper publisher here, a politician there; Petrina also recognized the name of a fantastically rich heiress who was the biggest donor to the library and the hospital, and who bossed all the other ladies around during every board meeting and each charity benefit.

"What about my family?" Petrina asked when she reached the bottom of the list and did not see their names. "Aren't they 'important' people, too?"

"Would your parents even come all the way up here?" Richard asked in an evasive way that was new for him, just this year.

"How would we know unless we invited them?" Petrina said tartly. "They invited *your* folks to their party for us."

Her parents had handled the elopement better than she'd expected; while they still thought of her as "Miss Independence," they were relieved to have her married and "settled down." So they'd thrown a party for Petrina and Richard at a good restaurant in Greenwich Village and invited their closest friends, but Richard's family had politely declined, conveniently being at the Cape Cod seashore that month, so they'd sent a cut-glass punch bowl instead.

Petrina and Richard had been married for six years now, yet his family had never reciprocated with a party for the newlyweds; his mother acted as if Petrina were an orphan whom Richard had discovered at the club's tennis match, which was close enough to the truth.

"She's a Barnard girl, you know," his parents assured their friends. That seemed to pass muster, although Petrina noted that the other girls in the suburbs, like her, had apparently hidden away their diplomas to focus solely on being well-bred wives and mothers. Only men had careers; women were allowed to have "projects" but they weren't supposed to take them too seriously.

Petrina had discovered certain charities that allowed her to use her artistic background; it turned out that she had what they called "a good eye" for artwork, which came in handy for assessing donations for the charity auctions. Petrina was beloved by children and the elderly in hospitals, who appreciated her warmhearted efforts. So she threw her energy into making each fund-raiser not merely a social success but a financial one, too.

At home, she loved having a garden to tend, but even here, the suburban conformity surprised her. She could not understand why privileged people restricted their own lives so voluntarily. They actually gossiped about neighbors who didn't mow their lawns exactly like everyone else or plant the same fastidious flower beds. Even wives her own age did things just the same way as the older generation, using the same beauty parlors, joining the same clubs; while their husbands made the same jokes. They all seemed terrified of anything unusual—a red flower, a lamé dress, or a meal that had a speck of spice in it. Petrina had hoped for more freedom and independence with her own generation, so she found this baffling.

"Why does everyone do only what their parents did?" she asked her husband.

Richard said, "It reminds us of when we were kids, but now *we're* the grown-ups, so we get to do this grown-up stuff. Besides," he added, "the old folks still have all the money." The threat of being cut off, apparently, lurked under every raised eyebrow.

Whereas Petrina didn't miss her girlhood at all, it had been so stifling. What she did miss was the energy and verve and warmth of her old neighborhood. But when she went back, everyone treated her like a stranger. She supposed she looked different to her family and their neighbors. They called her "glamorous," a word tinged with disapproval. She managed to get into the city on other, grown-up expeditions, like visiting the museums and galleries and shops, having tea with the ladies, or having drinks with Richard and his colleagues at the Plaza.

In the suburbs, she made friends, but their time together was hardly stimulating. Petrina was invited to play bridge and tennis, which was all right, but she discovered that the real purpose of these get-togethers was to say mean things about other women who were currently being excluded from such gatherings; this was their real sport. Petrina had spent the first few years here holding her breath, wondering what they said about her when she wasn't around. Then, suddenly, she just didn't care anymore. And this, oddly enough, gave her status.

But as she grew to care less, Richard began to care more. Perhaps it was the constant drip of listening to his mother and sister carry on at Sunday dinner, reminding him of all his old girlfriends that he might have married instead of Petrina, deliberately reminiscing about things Petrina couldn't possibly know about or join in on. Every so often she felt a stab of hurt whenever it looked as if Richard's family was getting to him at last. The fact that he tried to conceal this only made it worse.

"Of course, invite your family if you want to," Richard said awkwardly now. "How many of them do you think will come? Mother has to let the caterers know."

"Just my parents," Petrina said. She knew that Gianni and Tessa would be more quiet and dignified than any of the other guests. "My brothers are busy with their wedding plans. And all Mario cares about these days is baseball."

"Only two seats for your family at the party, then?" Richard asked, relieved.

Petrina nodded, wishing he'd at least asked how her brothers were these days. Anyway, she didn't want to parade them all up here for her mother-in-law's merciless scrutiny. Her brothers were still at an age where they resented anyone trying to rein them in. Petrina felt very old and very wise, even if she was only twenty-seven.

So she didn't tell Richard that, according to Tessa, Johnny had fallen for "a barmaid" and Frankie was engaged to a nurse. Petrina, who'd always wistfully wanted sisters, had met them, briefly, but Lucy and Amie, already comrades, had only stared at the elegant Petrina in awe, then whispered when they thought she was out of earshot.

As for little Mario, well, he wasn't so little anymore; at nearly twelve years old he was tall for his age, and eager to break away from the female influence of Tessa and Petrina. He worshipped Johnny and Frankie, just because they were older and exuded such confidence and seemed to know all about the world. But there were still times when he trusted Petrina to tell him the truth, about things the others preferred to brush off.

"Are we 'racketeers'?" Mario had inquired earnestly during her recent visit home.

Petrina said, "No, but sometimes we've been forced to deal with them. See, when Mama and Papa first came to America, they were planning to be wine importers. But their timing was bad. Prohibition—a law against booze—started a year after they got here. Nobody in New York really wanted Prohibition, not even the cops and the judges. Papa had to keep on making a living. He and Mama saved their money and invested well, and they even loaned money to our neighbors to help them. But then the big racketeers noticed how well Papa was doing, and they wanted a piece. They call it 'protection' but mostly they protect you from *them*. So Papa had to keep making more and more money, to stay in business and still pay off the Bosses."

"How come nobody arrests the Bosses?" Mario inquired.

"Once in a while they do. I guess the law can't catch them all red-handed. Maybe they don't really want to catch them, 'cause a lot of cops and judges and lawyers get paid off," she said. "But this family wants something better for you, Mario. We want you to be free to be your own man. Just study and keep doing well in school, like Richard and I did."

Mario absorbed this in his usual meditative way.

"Okay," he said. They were sitting in his room, surrounded by the records he liked to listen to and the guitar he liked to play. He had a beautiful voice, singing alone in his room when he thought nobody else was home. There were so many things Petrina wished she could tell him, but he was still too young to hear it all yet.

Mario said unexpectedly, "Does Richard like baseball? We get good seats at the stadium. How come he never comes with us to the ball games?"

"He likes golf and tennis," Petrina said gently.

AND SO, ON THE AFTERNOON OF PIPPA'S FIFTH-BIRTHDAY PARTY, Petrina was glad that the weather was fine. Pippa made her entrance with perfect posture learned from her ballet classes; she looked "just like her beautiful mother," people said: tall, slender, long-legged, with pale skin and naturally rosy cheeks and lips. Pippa handled the attention with aplomb; she had a knack for making friends, so the other children happily came to her party, enjoying the beachside hamburgers and hot dogs, the pony ride, the glorious birthday cake and ice cream.

Then, after the little ones were sent home to bed in the care of their nannies, the clubhouse bar opened, the kitchen staff cooked up steak and lobster, the band began to play, and the "real fun" began as the adults kicked up their heels.

Petrina floated around in her chiffon dress, like a rose petal sailing on the soft summer night's sea breeze. Her parents had come, and she was proud of them. Tessa looked serene in a lilac silk dress, and her father was impeccable, as always; she'd seen several of the wives gaze admiringly at Gianni's beautiful head of hair and tall stature.

But Petrina realized that her mother-in-law, who'd insisted on supervising the seating arrangements, had placed Gianni and Tessa at an outlying table for the "odds and ends" kind of people. When Petrina indignantly pointed this out to Richard he only said wearily, "I can't stand getting caught between you women."

"I'm not just another woman, I'm your wife! You're a man, you're in the driver's seat, your mother will respect you if you stand up for me," she said, exasperated, and momentarily despised him for turning out to be weak, just standing there shrugging help-lessly.

Well, it was no use now to make a scene. If Petrina's parents had noticed the seating arrangements, they didn't let on.

"Did you have a good time, Pop?" Petrina asked anxiously to-ward the end of the evening, when she found him standing in a corner smoking his cigar while waiting for the cloakroom girl to find her mother's wrap.

"Very nice," Gianni said calmly, watching the other guests drifting about. He glanced at his daughter and added softly, "I know these people."

"You do?" Petrina asked in surprise. "Which ones?"

Her father paused, then said in his deep, rich voice, "Your father-in-law was one of my best customers, years ago, during Prohibition, when he was younger. He pretended he didn't rec-ognize me tonight, to be polite. He was one of those college boys who insisted that I meet him out at sea, on his boat, several miles offshore, to supply him his gin and whiskey. You see, *possessing* li-quor was not a crime, only buying and selling it." Petrina blushed, glancing around to make sure nobody was listening as Gianni continued, "And, that man over there?"

"Richard says he's the editor of some big newspaper," she of-fered.

"Yes, he is. But he likes to bet on the horses and he's rather unlucky; he now owes seven hundred thousand dollars to the Bosses."

Petrina gasped, first at the sum, then to say quickly, "Are you sure it's him?"

"Oh, yes," her father replied, still careful to speak low so that no one else heard. "Now, those two over there—the judge and the politician—they always need campaign financing, no matter where it comes from. And they rely on those lawyers standing at the bar as middlemen; their job is to 'fix' things, especially when their clients get in trouble, with prostitutes, or unlawful stock trades, or shady real estate deals. And that lady over there?" He nodded toward the heiress whom Petrina thought of as the Queen Bee. "On her high school graduation day she was drunk and got behind the wheel of her father's car, and killed a classmate in a crash. That required a large payoff to silence a family—and therefore a large loan."

Petrina whispered, "Papa, why are you telling me this now, on my daughter's birthday?"

Gianni said rather sorrowfully, "Because I can see that today is the day you need to know. Bear these people no ill will, but never let anybody make you feel as if you are not good enough for them. And remember, there are good people and bad people, honest and dishonest, everywhere, both here and at home."

He took her mother's cape from the cloakroom girl, to whom he gave a tip, then he draped the cape around Tessa's shoulders as she emerged from the ladies' room.

"Our grandchild Pippa is very beautiful," Tessa said as they all kissed goodbye. "Please bring her to see us as often as you can. And Richard, too."

There was a note of finality in her voice, and as their car was brought to the front door by a valet and they waved, Petrina knew that they would never come up here again.

THAT NIGHT, SHE LAY IN BED WIDE AWAKE, FRETTING, WHILE RICH- ard snored. She missed her friends from college; there were only three girls that she'd really gotten close to, but they had been scattered like autumn leaves across the country, following their husbands' careers to Seattle, Chicago, and Los Angeles. They'd exchanged letters, tried to keep up, but husbands and children took up time and priority, so, little by little, they'd drifted apart, until they'd become only polite strangers to one another by now, exchanging Christmas cards in the mail.

She couldn't talk to her mother about loneliness; Tessa's only advice was to have more children. But Petrina was exulting in the freedom of not having babies year after year until you dropped from exhaustion. She and Richard had agreed to have another child someday, but not yet.

Petrina still wished she had sisters. She thought of her brothers' upcoming weddings, and it made her sad. She wasn't sorry that she and Richard had evaded the whole formal wedding-and-white-dress ceremony; she was only sorry that the world didn't give young lovers more of a fighting chance to stay sweetly in love. There was talk of another big war coming, although everyone seemed to agree that America would stay out of it this time.

Richard stirred sleepily and awoke. "What's the matter? Can't you sleep?"

"I'm okay," Petrina said. "Richard, what happened to your idea of moving to Boston to work in your father's Massachusetts branch? You used to say it would be better for us to be away from our families, on our own."

"Mmm, Dad wants us to stay put, at least another five or six years. More opportunities here for me." Richard yawned. "You're too serious, baby. Try to relax and have fun." He took her in his arms, holding her against his chest like a boy with a teddy bear as he fell back asleep.

Petrina felt slightly better against the warmth of his body. She wished it could always be like this, just the two of them, and little Pippa, in a cozy, private world of their own. She wondered why it couldn't be, even if they stayed here. All it would take was a firm word from Richard to his mother and sister, letting them know that his wife was to be respected, and that there would be no more talk of old girlfriends, and that from now on Petrina would handle the seating arrangements for her daughter's parties.

She thought of all the people at the party and their shameful secrets, which her father had revealed to her. She'd never look at them the same way again, but she would also never hold it against them. Everyone had secrets; Petrina did, too.

Five or six more years here, Richard had said. She tried to imagine where they'd all be by then. Richard had agreed that they could have another child once they were more "settled."

The days went by more quickly than she expected. Other things changed, too.

BOOK TWO

The 1940s

9

The Family

Greenwich Village, September 1943

Filomena's ship arrived in New York Harbor on a bright, cloudless September day. She felt as if she'd been hurtled into not just another country but another universe. The pier and processing center were a deafening hubbub of noise and confusion. At first she stood alone with her small suitcase, anxiously peering at the long lines that were quickly forming in every direction; then she shuffled on with the others. Everyone talked so rapidly that Filomena gave up trying to follow it all; she simply went where they flagged her to go, in a blur of customs and immigration.

But soon, on the other side of the cordon, she saw two men holding up a handwritten sign with Rosamaria's name on it. She waved to them, and the pair strode confidently toward her. They spoke in English and Italian, and introduced themselves as Johnny and Frankie, the sons of the lady who'd arranged her passage. These two cheerful, well-groomed men seemed to know how to do everything, including getting her through the throng of other new arrivals and helping her with the immigration officials.

She was already used to being called by her cousin's name, first on the boat, and now here. It was on all her papers. So she was ready to forever call herself Rosamaria, to think of herself as Rosamaria might, and to do whatever Rosamaria would do to survive. She held her breath until she was told that her papers were in order and she was free to enter this great city.

The two brothers showed her to a fancy black car that apparently belonged to them but whose door was opened by a hulking man wearing a cap and gloves. They called him Sal, and he was evidently their driver—and something more, because when he reached out to take her suitcase, Filomena saw a gun in a holster under his coat.

For a brief moment she wondered if either of these young men was the one she was supposed to marry; they looked older than she'd expected. But then the taller one, Johnny, said to her reassuringly in Italian, "You'll meet our younger brother, Mario, tonight."

"You'll like Mario. *Tutte le ragazze lo chiamò* a 'dreamboat,'" Frankie could not resist saying teasingly. She had no idea why "all the girls" called Mario that, but she understood the playfulness of Frankie's tone. Then, in Italian he said more soberly, "You'll keep him out of the army, so Ma doesn't get a heart attack, okay? We must get you married before his birthday."

Johnny nudged him. "Ease up," he advised.

Mentally Filomena reviewed everything that Rosamaria had said about her arrangement with the matriarch of this family, via the matchmaker in Naples. The son, Mario, was seventeen, about to be eighteen at the end of this month, so he'd been born in the same month as Filomena. Was that a good omen? Filomena had already become seventeen a week ago, but then she remembered that, since she was supposed to be Rosamaria, she must pretend that she had actually turned eighteen, in the month of May. She must not make an error out of fatigue or confusion.

Based on what Frankie had just said, there was a connection between Mario's age and the army. America had entered the war, and Filomena comprehended the anguish of families who didn't want to lose their sons to this madness. Perhaps being married would protect Mario? Now she thought she understood more about why she was here.

They drove through Manhattan amid cars honking their horns incessantly while swooping expertly and daringly around one another. Filomena had never seen such towering buildings, so tall that she could not see the tops unless she ducked down in her seat and craned her neck for a glimpse. In this slanting light, it was like driving through gilded, man-made canyons.

Then, unexpectedly, they entered a leafy area of town houses that were only three or four stories high. Frankie told her they were in a place called Greenwich Village, which was a relatively quieter and cozier part of this roaring city. They passed a lovely green park ringed with mature trees, called Washington Square, and soon, they turned down an attractive street where, at last, they came to a stop in front of a row of three attached, red brick homes set off by wrought-iron fencing.

"Number One is where Frankie and I live with our families," Johnny told her, pointing to the town house on the left. "Number Two is where our parents live." This was clearly the biggest of the three houses. "And Number Three is for our guests, like you," he concluded, gesturing toward the smallest of the houses, which was on the corner.

The men now left her in the care of Donna, a young maid with a long braid down her back, who said, "*Buongiorno,* come with me," and led Filomena up a staircase to a small guest room. Donna explained that the driver, the cook, and Donna herself had rooms in this "guest" house, so they could help her if she needed assistance. Filomena could not help wondering if she was really a guest, as the brothers said, or if this family simply thought of her as just another servant. Well, she'd soon find out.

The maid showed her a tiled bathroom at the end of the hallway, a miraculous place with astonishing indoor plumbing, a bathtub, and a basin with a spout for water that ran hot and cold with a mere turn of the faucets. Donna said, "Dinner is at eight, in the main house. All three houses are connected by corridors. I'll be around to show you." She smiled and shut the door behind her as she went away.

Alone at last, Filomena breathed a sigh of relief. Even now she could feel, in all the cells of her body, the relentless vibration of the ship that had carried her here. She opened a window to breathe in the fresh air and to feel the setting sun, which made the brightly-colored trees dazzling. September in New York was cooler, crisper than in southern Italy. Her room had two windows, one of which overlooked a well-tended garden. She noticed a stone fountain in its center, and she was unexpectedly touched by this; for the first time, she felt a kinship with this family, sensing that they'd poignantly re-created what they loved and missed of Italy.

Overwhelmingly fatigued now, she undressed, washed, and collapsed gratefully on the bed—which was small but so comfortable, with a four-poster frame and heavenly soft bedding that even the *signora* back home would have coveted. As soon as Filomena closed her eyes, sleep settled on her like a warm blanket.

MEANWHILE, FILOMENA'S ARRIVAL IN AMERICA WAS HERALDED AS A major event in the family.

"Mario's girl is here!" Lucy's daughter, Gemma, announced excitedly as everyone congregated before dinner in the big parlor of the main house. "That lady wore a funny-looking scarf on her head, tied under her chin!"

"Gemma, be quiet, she'll hear you!" Lucy admonished. Her daughter had been born a year after Lucy and Frankie got married, so now the little girl was a precocious five-year-old. Gemma had Frankie's dark eyes and pale peachy complexion without a single dot of Lucy's freckles, but her hair was strawberry blond, a paler version of Lucy's red color.

Nine-year-old Christopher enjoyed having a little sister to

protect and boss around, but they were so rambunctious today, chasing Amie's twin boys around the room and coming perilously close to tipping over fragile vases and lamps. They were behaving like dogs who sensed something festive and foreign in the air, aware that the adults were more distracted than usual, so the young ones were ready to take advantage of the situation.

"Ahoy, mateys!" Chris intoned to the twins, swaggering like a pirate, coercing them into sliding along the floor behind the sofa, as if rowing a boat in unison.

"Chris, Gemma, you be nice to your cousins," Lucy scolded.

Amie looked up alertly at her twin boys. "Vinnie! Paulie! Get off the floor, you'll get all full of dust," she admonished. She could not believe that these little wild creatures were hers. Vinnie and Paulie didn't have a shred of Amie's innate shyness; they looked a lot like Johnny, but they had not yet acquired their father's calm gracefulness. Well, they were only four years old. Amie wished that she had a daughter, too, as Lucy did. Surely there was still time for that. Amie felt like Cinderella, whisked off by a noble prince and brought into this mysterious kingdom of his family.

Johnny had waited only a month before courting her. *Until I met you, I didn't care if I got married or not,* he'd confided. *I see now, I was just looking for you to come into my life.*

Amie had tried to resist him at first, but it was impossible to refuse a man like Johnny. From the beginning he'd always acted as if she were a fair maiden who needed to be freed from her prison with Brunon. After "the accident," as she preferred to think of it, Johnny had taken charge of the bar and hired people he trusted to help her manage it. Amie had only a supervisory role there now, watching the income, no longer having to do the backbreaking work of waiting tables double-shift and cleaning up.

There were times when Amie thought she saw Brunon out of the corner of her eye—coming up from the basement with a box, or sweeping up in a corner—but when she turned her head, startled, she realized it was just one of the men that Johnny had hired.

Even in church, sitting in the pew, she closed her eyes resolutely, and silently told Brunon she felt sorry for him, as if indeed he'd been hit by a truck and it had nothing to do with her. But she simply could not deny that she felt relieved to be freed from all the fear and mind-numbing dread.

It helped that Johnny had made their courtship seem so natural—bringing her to meet his parents, and then, after their wedding day, to come and live in his beautiful town house, next door to his parents. He and Amie now occupied the spacious first-floor apartment. Frankie and Lucy had a separate entrance that led them directly upstairs to their equally spacious second-floor apartment in the same house. The walls were thick and sound-proof, so everyone had their privacy. The furniture, inherited from Johnny's parents, was all handmade, solid, high quality, especially the beautiful rosewood armoire with beveled-mirror doors.

For the first time in her life, Amie felt like a cherished wife. And Johnny's lovemaking was a revelation. He was tender and pa-tient, leading her into a crescendo of easy pleasure that struck her as a warm, inevitable wave from a playful sea. Once, after Johnny left to make his rounds of work, Amie was folding their clothes, and upon remembering their night of lovemaking, she burst into tears, thinking of all the time she'd lost being miserable; she had nearly missed out on love entirely, and might have spent a whole lifetime never knowing this natural joy.

But she still found his family rather daunting. The parents ruled supremely and seemed to tolerate their non-Italian daughters-in-law, Lucy and Amie, with a wary air of resignation. Yet, when Tessa spoke to Johnny in Italian, Amie could never know for sure if Tessa was talking about her. Also, the strong bond among these three brothers was so vital that it was as if they believed they could not exist without one another. Lucy understood this, too, so she and Amie had become natural allies, helping each other adjust to living so closely with their in-laws. They'd even taken classes in Italian together, to better understand their husbands' family.

"I'm hungry," Frankie said now. "What's for dinner?"

"Your mother and Cook kicked me out of the kitchen this morning," Lucy confessed. Turning to Amie, she murmured ruefully, "They both say I can't cook to save my life, so they think my opinions are useless. But I *do* know what Frankie likes to eat!"

"At least you can sew straight," Amie whispered. "I'm too nearsighted. I keep sticking myself." She sighed, then whispered, "Why do we have to know these chores, when the servants do such a good job? Tessa is *so* old-fashioned." Lucy nodded conspiratorially.

"Are we waiting for Mario?" Frankie asked impatiently. "He isn't going to try to skip this dinner, is he? Bet he's halfway to Frisco by now," he joked.

"He'll show up," Johnny said calmly. "In his good time. You know how he is."

"It's because all the girls chase him," Lucy volunteered. She'd noticed that Mario, who was contemplative and solitary by nature, did not like to be the center of attention, and the more people pushed him, the more he retreated like a turtle into his shell.

"What's this girl from Italy like?" Lucy couldn't resist asking her husband.

Frankie shrugged. "She's nice. Kinda mysterious. Big eyes, like almonds," he said. "Like a cat, watching and thinking." They were all drinking small glasses of an *aperitivo*, a ruby-colored vermouth homemade by Tessa, with a touch of good bourbon in it and a dash of bitter orange. "Where's Mom and Pop?" he asked.

"Tessa and Gianni have been in their study all morning," Lucy answered.

Amie whispered to Lucy, "Wonder what *they'll* say about this new girl?"

"We're about to find out," Lucy replied as Tessa and Gianni finally emerged from their study, beckoning the others to join them in the large formal dining room.

When Filomena awoke, at first she couldn't remember where she was, what day it was, even who she was. Then it all came flooding back, along with a certain measure of panic. But, just as she'd done throughout her voyage, she thought of the real Rosamaria, lying in a grave in Naples marked with Filomena's name on it, and asked herself, *What would Rosa do? What would Rosa say?* and then she knew how to behave.

Rosamaria would have put on a good but sober dress, and combed her hair and pinched her cheeks, so this was what Filomena did. She'd bought a dress in Naples, just before she set sail. It was a soft navy with white piping that flattered her pale skin. Reaching under the pile of clothes in her suitcase, she paused to momentarily clasp the stone Madonna's hand that she'd kept from the church in Naples. Somehow it felt like her last link to Rosamaria.

"Protect me, guide me," Filomena chanted, as if holding a talisman. She realized that this was the first time in a long while that she'd uttered anything resembling a prayer. So perhaps some faith and hope were returning at last. She went to the mirror to give her hair one final smoothing. Then she descended the staircase.

The maid, Donna, was waiting at the foot of the stairs, to show her an indoor passageway that led straight into the bigger, main town house. Here they passed the swinging door of a kitchen, where a busy, pie-faced cook named Stella was visible. To their left was a small cloakroom and hallway that led to the front door.

They walked on, past a large parlor with cut-crystal doorknobs that glittered with refracted light. Filomena could not help thinking that Rosamaria would have considered this home a triumph. The parlor had built-in bookcases, a fine fireplace, and mahogany furniture covered with delicate lace runners. The chairs were upholstered in a lush claret color, with embroidered and fringed gold antimacassars on their backs. There were round, glass-topped marble tables holding lamps with gold-fringed, rose-colored shades, some of which had glass teardrops dangling from them. There was nobody here, but she heard voices in the next room.

Sure enough, the entire family was assembling in a large dining room that had gilded light sconces on the walls, a polished sideboard, and a formal table ringed by ornately carved, high-backed chairs. "Please take a seat," the maid murmured.

The men politely rose to their feet upon her entrance, and Filomena shyly sat down in the chair that the patriarch gallantly pulled out for her at his left. At the opposite end of the table, the dark-eyed matriarch was staring at her intently, without smiling. From the matchmaker's notes Filomena knew that this woman's name was Tessa. Her expression declared that this was her brood and she meant to protect it.

So this is the one who will tell me if I can stay or go, Filomena thought. Her pulse quickened as she made a rapid assessment. Tessa appeared to be in her early fifties, with abundant black hair threaded with silver, drawn into an elegantly arranged bun. She wore a dove-grey silk dress and a large gold and pearl brooch.

The handsome older man who'd invited Filomena to sit beside him had to be Tessa's husband, who, according to the matchmaker, was named Gianni. His hair was more silver than black, indicating that he could be as much as a decade older than his wife.

Gianni and Tessa's sons were arranged around the table with their wives and children. But Filomena noticed that there was one empty chair directly across from her, and also, two more empty chairs at the far side of the table, near the mother, Tessa.

Now the patriarch turned to Filomena and, like his sons, spoke in a mixture of English and Italian; when others spoke, he politely provided an Italian translation where he thought it might be helpful to her. "So," Gianni said in a courtly way, as if announcing the arrival of a great lady to the group, as he passed her a glass of *prosecco,* "this is Rosamaria. We now have three Maries at our table: Amie Marie, Lucy Marie, and now Rosamaria." He nodded toward each daughter-in-law as he introduced her, and they nodded deferentially back at him, allowing themselves only a flicker of a curious glance at Filomena.

But a little girl with reddish-blond hair was staring at her with undisguised fascination. When Filomena smiled, the girl looked suddenly self-conscious, as if she thought she ought to say something. "I'm Gemma. My mama is a nurse!" she offered.

"*Un'infermiera*," the patriarch murmured for her benefit.

"*Ah, bene.* How old are you?" Filomena asked politely in English, feeling the eyes of the girl's parents, Lucy and Frankie, upon her as they watched their daughter respond.

"I'm five years old," Gemma declared stoutly, "and my brother, Chris, is nine," she added, indicating a quiet blue-eyed boy with deeper red hair like his mother, Lucy. Filomena nodded, and calculated that Lucy and Frankie looked as if they were in their late twenties.

Across the table was the eldest brother, Johnny, who, Filomena saw, was married to the shy blond woman named Amie. They had two identical little boys beside them.

Seeing her gaze, Johnny introduced his sons. "*Ecco i miei figli,* Vincenzo and Paolo."

"They're only *four* years old," Gemma added, as if that made them babies compared to her. "Vinnie and Paulie are twins!" she declared, happy to announce the obvious.

"*Sono gemelli,*" Gianni translated helpfully.

Someone new had just entered the room: a handsome young man who had an easy way about him as he moved toward the chair directly across the table from Filomena.

"And now," Gianni said with a twinkle in his eye and a low voice, as if confiding something important in his introduction, "Rosamaria, *ecco mio figlio* Mario."

Everyone around the table fell silent, and stared straight at Mario as if they could hardly bear the tension of seeing him finally meet the girl his parents had brought over from Italy for him to marry. Mario, with admirable self-possession, seemed aware of this and yet calm.

"*Buonasera,* Rosamaria," he said in a formal tone to Filomena as he sat down. The roomful of relatives breathlessly awaited her reaction.

"*Buonasera,* Mario," Filomena answered shyly.

"I hope that you had *un piacevole viaggio,*" he continued.

"*Si, grazie,*" she murmured, although one could hardly call the journey here peaceful.

By now she understood the meaning of the American word *dreamboat,* which his brothers had used to describe him on the car ride over here. All these sons were tall, fair skinned, dark eyed, with beautiful dark hair, but Mario had a certain delicacy of feature, something perfect in the balance of his finely-chiseled nose, chin, high forehead, and those soulful brown eyes. He was not as skinny as Johnny nor muscular like Frankie; he was just tall and lean and lovely to look at, the kind of man that made a woman want to run her fingers through his soft hair, or feel the touch of his elegant hands upon her face.

"Mario wanted to be a priest!" Gemma burst out, unable any longer to bear the silent suspense in the hush that had fallen over the family.

Mario murmured, "Ah, that was Mama's idea, but it didn't last long."

The others chuckled, released from the spell, and soon everyone resumed their relaxed chatter as the maid came in bearing a tray of *antipasto,* which was composed of olives and finely-roasted vegetables served in beautiful flowered bowls, and *prosciutto* wrapped around pieces of melon. There were murmurs that the war was affecting what food was available in the market this week, but Filomena was awed by the plentiful meal. Moreover, she could see that beneath this innocuous talk, the adults often glanced at Gianni and Tessa, as if already trying to gauge what the verdict would be, but the parents' faces remained inscrutable.

From the head of the table, Gianni said the prayer of grace over the meal. Then the family ate, passing bowls of food to one another with the ease of much practice. The adults had a refined, unhurried attitude at table, and the children were astonishingly obedient and quiet as they ate. The grown-ups spoke of the weather, the war, the neighbors.

Mario said very little. Sometimes when Filomena looked up she caught him watching her, but he did not look away guiltily, he only nodded politely and smiled.

They had finished the *antipasto* and were just beginning to eat the pasta course of ravioli stuffed with ricotta cheese, sun-dried tomatoes, and delicate herbs when the eldest child of Tessa and Gianni entered the house.

"Ah," said Gianni with a trace of annoyance, "the fourth Marie arrives at last. This is my eldest child, *mia figlia* Petrina Maria, and *her* daughter, Pippa."

Filomena instantly admired Petrina—a tall, slim, long-legged woman in her early thirties, wearing an expensive, fitted red dress and extraordinarily high-heeled shoes. Her hair, well styled, was especially beautiful, with many shades of brown that had hints of other hues—caramel, burgundy, plum—perfectly dazzling when she turned her head and caught the light. Her skin was a delicate pale pink. She had the effect of a stunningly attractive celebrity, like an actress. Lucy and Amie took in all of Petrina's fashion choices like students memorizing a lesson, as Petrina proudly and a bit defiantly slid into one of the empty chairs.

Her daughter, Pippa, took the chair next to Petrina with the same proud, regal expression. "Good evening, Grandmother and Grandfather," Pippa said with impressive natural ease. She was a tall, slender girl of eleven, with similar features to her mother's, and a long, dark ponytail. Pippa was too old to play with the other children but too young to chat with the adults. There was something touching, almost painful, in her reserve. Filomena instantly felt sympathy for her.

"Is that a flower on your arm?" Gemma asked her cousin, awed.

"It's a wrist corsage with a real rose on it. See? Elastic. Here, you can have it," Pippa answered generously, slipping it off and looping it onto her younger cousin.

"Traffic was terrible after we left Westchester," Petrina murmured as her one and only concession to being late. "Richard's away for the whole weekend, in Boston, on business. Give me some wine, Mario," she added with sudden and surprising authority.

Mario rose easily, with an indulgent smile, carrying the carafe of red wine that had been placed on the table before him and his father. He poured Petrina a glass, then deposited the carafe on the table near her, returning to his seat without saying a word the entire time.

Petrina seemed indifferent to her other brothers, but she gave Mario a smile of gratitude. Filomena was still admiring the movie-star quality that clung to this woman, but then Petrina looked directly at her with a fierce expression, as if she'd registered some grim thought that made her delicately beautiful face harden, revealing feelings even more antagonistic than Tessa's.

Uf! Filomena thought. *This woman truly hates the very idea of me; this, she decided even before she laid eyes on me, even before my feet set foot upon this country's earth.* Filomena glanced away, and once again caught Mario's eye.

Ever so slightly, Mario gave the smallest of shrugs and shook his head, as if to say quite plainly about his sister's attitude, *This does not matter.*

The father, Gianni, spoke in a low murmur to the children as the main course was served—delicate veal cutlets with a finely-made mushroom sauce. Gianni had the attitude of a king who reigns over his subjects with a certain quality of emotional detachment.

"Our guest, Rosa, comes to us from Italy, a great and beautiful old country," Tessa interjected, as if instructing her grandchildren on a history lesson. They sat up straight and listened dutifully as she continued in Italian and English. "In Italy, all the sons and daughters understand that nothing matters more than loyalty to one's family. *Fedeltà alla famiglia.*"

From the reactions Filomena could see that this remark was meant to welcome her and yet, at the same time, to chide Petrina for arriving late, judging by Petrina's sudden scowl.

And then, one by one, each of Tessa's family members seemed to know exactly when a particular comment of Tessa's was meant for them. The men bowed their heads as if in church when she spoke to them; the women looked resigned. So when Tessa mentioned a neighbor who gossiped too much, Filomena noticed that Amie blushed; when Tessa said that only a wife who was a good cook could create a happy household, it was Lucy's turn to look uncomfortable; when Tessa expounded on the need for discipline with children, the eldest son, Johnny, shushed his sons; and when Tessa said that the measure of a man was his ability to rule over his own temper, Frankie looked away impatiently.

The only one whom Tessa did not chide was Mario. When he spoke, she listened closely, with narrowed eyes, but Mario said very little. He seemed to know how to achieve something unusual in large families—how to preserve his own privacy.

Just as the meal was ending with bowls of fresh fruit and nuts, the telephone rang and the maid came and whispered in the father's ear. A sudden irritated look passed over Gianni's face as he excused himself. Tessa registered this with a brief, hardened expression. The others seemed unaffected, and Gianni returned with a smile and a nod.

After the children had eaten sweet little pastries for dessert, Petrina said, "Well, Pippa and I have a long drive ahead. We must go now."

For a moment, as she rose to leave, she seemed to teeter perilously on those extravagant high heels, which gave Filomena an unexpected sense of pity for her, because it made Petrina seem vulnerable, despite her hauteur, like someone walking on a tightrope over a dangerous chasm.

"Mario, walk me out," Petrina said, and he obligingly followed her. Gianni rose, too, but went into the parlor, and this seemed a signal, for the others got up and stretched, and the children began to chatter again, as they all filed into the parlor. Under this chatter, as Petrina slipped into a sable coat, Filomena distinctly heard her hiss to Mario, "You can't be serious! Why do you let Mama and her ideas go this far?"

"Nothing has been decided," Mario said quietly. They'd moved into the vestibule, so Filomena could no longer hear them. Petrina seized on this moment alone with Mario.

"What's this I hear about you going to gemology school?" Petrina demanded.

"Yes, it's done. I'll have my certificate by next week. Pop wouldn't pay to send me to college. He wanted me to study a trade instead. It's good. I like working with gems. They're beautiful," Mario explained, looking genuinely happy.

"But you *should* go to college, like Richard and I did!" Petrina exclaimed. "You could study to be someone important. A doctor or a lawyer or a financier."

"I don't like any of those businesses," Mario answered reasonably. "And I can't see that college has made you or Richard any happier."

Petrina was momentarily taken aback, then said, "We'll talk about this again." Mario only kissed her cheek and opened the front door to let her and Pippa out.

The others were already settled in the parlor, chattering with contentment, looking up only when the front door closed behind Petrina. Amie turned to Lucy and said quietly, "Petrina drinks too much," and Lucy answered rather tartly, "She'll get home all right. Her chauffeur's been sitting out there in the car the whole time, waiting for her."

Filomena stood there uncertainly. She only wanted to go back to her little room and sleep again. But rather unexpectedly, Tessa took her by the arm and steered her down a back hallway and outdoors into the small backyard, whose garden was rimmed by a stone wall. In the center was a patio, with the fountain that gurgled meditatively.

Tessa did not waste time. "Why did your parents allow you to go away?" she asked, staring at Filomena intently, as if daring her to lie. Filomena had a bad moment of wondering if Rosamaria or the matchmaker had already provided Tessa with this information, and perhaps the lady was just testing her for her honesty. Tessa spoke in Italian exactly as Rosamaria did, which made sense, for they both came from the same town. Filomena had always been able to mimic Rosamaria's inflections and speech, so she'd been doing just that today.

She framed her answer carefully. "My parents let me come here because of the war. These days, Italy cannot offer me the better life that they hope I can find in America."

Tessa's expression was inscrutable. "The good life does not come without a price. When times are bad, will you cry and want to run back home to your parents? You can't. They all think the streets are paved in gold here, so they'll only pick your pockets. I won't allow that. If you want to marry my son, you must leave the old country behind, never look back."

Clearly Tessa was protecting her family's wealth from being siphoned off by a daughter-in-law's greedy relatives. Well, Filomena would show her just how unsentimental she could be. She couldn't afford to let herself even *think* or *feel* any longing for her lost family; if she opened that door in her heart, she might never be able to close it again, and it could imperil her very survival. "I will never go back," she said flatly. "I will never even *look* back."

"Yes. That is the fate of we women from Italy. What do you think of these American women?" Tessa inquired, clearly referring to her daughter and her daughters-in-law.

This could be another trap. Filomena thought quickly. "All wives share the same destiny, no matter where they live." She herself wasn't even sure what she meant by this.

But it brought a small smile to Tessa's face. "American women are too independent," Tessa declared. "My daughter, Petrina, wants to stay young and glamorous forever, because she believes this is the source of a woman's power, but if you live only for a man's admiration, you will forever be a slave. As for the girls who married my sons—that Lucy is too hardheaded; she refuses to give up her job at the hospital where she bosses her assistants around, so when she comes home she still thinks she ought to be in charge, and she argues with her husband. Whereas the other one, Amie, rules by weakness. Men always feel that they must defend her, but she doesn't need their protection half so much as they imagine. Either way, my two sons work hard to make their wives happy. It should be the other way around. *Capisci?*"

In a flash, Filomena understood what was underneath all this. Tessa's sons were accustomed to obeying their formidable mother, so, ironically, they were susceptible to their wives in a way that Tessa found threatening to her own authority. That was no doubt why she'd sent for a nice, obedient girl from the old country. To ensure control over Mario.

"*Si, si,*" Filomena murmured, lowering her lashes in a show of modesty and deference.

Tessa observed this silently, then moved on.

"And Mario?" she asked. "Does he please you?"

Filomena could not suppress a genuine smile, allowing herself to reveal her own true feelings of admiration for what she had seen of Mario so far. "It would be an honor to be with him," she said, careful not to use the word *wife* yet.

"And babies?" Tessa prompted. "These days, with the war, we can take nothing for granted. There is no time to wait. If you want babies, you must have them right away. Do you?" she asked, peering sharply into Filomena's face.

"Yes," Filomena said, slightly embarrassed. She could see that there would be no half measures with this destiny, once embraced.

Tessa nodded in approval. She put a hand under a blood-red rose from a tall climbing shrub that was still blooming even as autumn approached.

"Children are like flowers in a garden," Tessa said in a surprisingly hard voice, considering what she was saying. "They need constant attention and care. As do husbands. I hope, Rosamaria, that you are capable of that."

Filomena said nothing. This petite lady's grip on her arm was remarkably strong, and she wished that Tessa would let go of her now. But it was a signal that Tessa intended to keep her close. *She wants to get the smell of me,* Filomena thought. *This is a woman who operates on her instincts, and she behaves as if they have never failed her.*

"You must go to bed now," Tessa said abruptly. "Travel can weaken a woman, and a woman must stay strong."

Filomena, who felt like a horse that had just had its legs and teeth checked, was only too glad to finally go back up the staircase and into her room.

But that night she lay awake for some time, unable to sleep. Perhaps it was the food; she was not accustomed to having that much to eat at one sitting. It wasn't that this family over-indulged; they ate slowly, carefully, small portions of many things. But Filomena hadn't realized, until now, that she had been underfed for years.

She turned over in bed and sighed. A scary mother, gossipy wives, a bossy older sister. *If I'm going to survive here, I've got to*

marry this boy as soon as possible, she thought.
Rosamaria would have said the same thing.

10

New York City, Autumn 1943

Not long after the conversation in the garden with Tessa, Filomena found herself being courted by Mario. It was the oddest thing Filomena could have imagined, because she was living under his parents' roof, in the servants' section, yet each time Mario took her out, he behaved as if he were picking her up at a king's castle.

At first, they only went for a decorous stroll in the park, then a cup of coffee at a local café, and then a movie. As innocent as these excursions were, Filomena found them profoundly shocking, because the young couple was permitted to be alone. In the villages of the old country, there would have been a flock of vigilant aunts accompanying them, and behind the aunts, the watchful uncles.

But even more surprising was that, unlike most men, Mario asked her opinion on everything—from small things like what foods she liked and what movie she wanted to see, to larger issues, like the war. Moreover, he listened without interrupting. They spoke in a combination of Italian and English as he helped her learn the local language better.

Mario's courtship went on every night for two weeks, at the end of which, on a Saturday night, they had dinner in a very fine restaurant, at a candlelit corner table.

"*Buonasera*, Mario!" the proprietor greeted them in person, immediately ushering them to a prime spot with the utmost privacy. The waiters were in strict but unobtrusive attendance.

Filomena noticed this great show of respect, then caught Mario observing her.

"My father is a part-owner of this place," he said briefly.

Alone in their private corner, he spoke to her in a low, pleasant voice. He acted like a man who was expected to explain his own reliable prospects to a princess. "My family has done well in this great country," he said in a modest tone. "We have many businesses that will not only support all of us but our children, and our children's children."

"Your father is a great   " She searched for the English word and said, "Boss, *si*?"

But apparently this word meant something more to him, for Mario's expression darkened. He said, "No, not a Boss. I can't discuss everything my family does; it's really their business, not mine. But I can tell you what we *don't* do: we don't shake down the unions, or rig bids for building jobs, or ask for kickbacks from anybody; we don't extort 'protection' or tribute from neighbors, partners, tenants, and shopkeepers; we don't have anything to do with narcotics or prostitution; we don't fix elections or ball games, or rob trucks or break heads or break legs. We *do* invest in bars, shops, and restaurants as silent partners; we loan money, take bets, own buildings, and collect rent."

He'd spoken in his usual mixture of English and Italian, and, although Filomena wasn't sure of all the American expressions, she understood the tone and tenor. He seemed to be both defending his family and yet distancing himself from them at the same time, which left an obvious question.

"But—what do *you* yourself do, exactly?" she asked tentatively.

Mario glanced away and was quiet for a few moments. Then he said, "I worked for my father and brothers for a while. But then I told them I wanted to go out on my own, be independent. Papa is old-fashioned, but finally he made some suggestions for having my own business; I didn't like any of them, except the jewelry trade."

Filomena said, "Ah! This work makes you happy, *è vero*?"

He looked up appreciatively, as if no one had ever really asked him this. "Yes! I *like* working with stones." He raised his hands in a carving motion, as if shaping something. "It's like catching stars as they fall to earth. But one must truly have 'the touch' to discover where the firelight resides in a gem, like a beating heart, a dancing flame; you don't want to cut the heart and fire out of it. This is something I can do well, where I won't have to answer to Papa, Mama, or anyone else. I'm opening my own shop; it's being fixed up already. Soon I'll be able to show it to you, if you like."

Filomena unexpectedly felt a profound sense of peace descend on her. It had to do with his voice. It was so utterly melodic, even more beautiful than his looks, with such a warm musical quality that she was mesmerized, like sitting before a fireplace and falling into a trance while gazing into the flickering flames.

"Yes, I'd love to see it," she said softly. The pleasure that his work gave him was so plain on his face that she found it touching.

"So that is who I am," Mario said simply. "What do you think? Would you like to be a part of this family?"

She nodded shyly. Her thoughts were so intense that she feared they might show on her face. *Yes, you are beautiful, and with you, I can make it to the other side of life, where the happy people are. So I will do whatever it takes—marry, make babies, steal, or kill—as long as I can sleep in a good bed, live in a warm house, eat decent food, keep my children safe from the harm of this brutal world.*

He continued in that calm, musical voice, but now there was an added depth to his tone. "Then, if you think you might like to marry me, there is one thing I would like to know before I propose. All I ask is an honest answer. Who are you, really?"

Filomena suppressed a gasp. Her heart began to beat rapidly

in anticipation of fight or flight. She was in trouble, and she knew it. Trouble was the one thing that her past experiences had taught her to instantly know the scent of.

"You see," Mario said thoughtfully, "Mama didn't care what you looked like, but I did. Not that I had to have a beauty; I just needed to see your face, to see your soul. I didn't tell my mother that I found the matchmaker's address on her letters, so I wrote and asked for a picture of Rosamaria. I've told no one about this. Just you."

Calmly he reached into his wallet and pulled out a photo. Filomena saw Rosamaria's face staring back at her. She was wearing a dress that she'd purchased for the trip, so the matchmaker must have asked for a picture around that same time. In all the excitement, Rosa had failed to tell Filomena that her prospective bridegroom had finally wanted a glimpse of her, after all. Perhaps this was what Rosamaria had meant on that last day when she'd whispered, *I have so much to tell you,* and they'd gone to Naples and shared a *gelato,* sitting there on the stone steps of the church.

For a moment, the pain of remembering the joyful Rosamaria was almost too much to bear. Filomena gulped and sat absolutely still.

"Are you all right?" Mario asked, looking concerned.

Filomena's eyes were bright with tears. "That is my cousin Rosamaria," she said. "She died before she could come to meet you. I didn't mean to take her place, but it seemed as if fate insisted upon it." Taking a deep breath, she told him all about that day near the church, when the bombing of Naples changed everything, and the fateful mix-up of the names—one on a grave, the other on a ticket to America.

Mario listened closely, in that attentive but unrevealing way of his. Filomena said finally, "Now you know the truth. What will you do with it? Will you expose me to your family? If you want me to go, I'll go, but please give me time to run away."

She had only the barest of contingency plans, because, after the bombing of Naples, when she'd sheltered briefly at the convent as the priest had suggested, she'd assured them that she would be leaving soon for America; and an older nun had given her the name of an employment agency in New York that Filomena might contact if she needed help. If she couldn't find it, she simply planned to walk uptown and knock on the doors of great houses to offer herself as a servant to anyone who'd take her.

"I won't tell anyone about this," Mario answered. "But I have another question."

Filomena waited, still filled with dread.

"What is your real name?" Mario asked. "I won't say it to anyone else. It is just something I myself want to know."

When she told him, he repeated it with a smile. "Filomena. Yes, that suits you better. But in my family, I will still call you our Rosa. All right?"

She wasn't prepared for the way she felt when he said *Filomena*. He seemed to caress it, with genuine warmth. What a relief, to hear her own name spoken again, even if only this once. She surely should leave well enough alone, but there was something else she had to know.

"It doesn't matter to you, whether you marry me or my cousin?" she asked warily. "Why don't you care about which girl you marry?"

"I do care," he said, looking amused. "But when it comes to my mother, it's best not to fight her, just let her idea run its course. Then, I can make *my* choice. I suppose I was curious, too, to see a girl who would come across an ocean to meet me. Why would she do such a thing? It sounded like a fairy tale. I thought I must at least meet you. If we didn't hit it off, well, I could always allow *you* to be the one to call it off."

Filomena comprehended that if she had not appealed to Mario, possibly he would have threatened to reveal the truth about her, unless she agreed to go away.

"Why does your mother want you to marry so quickly?" she

asked.

Mario sighed deeply. "You and I are so young, but the world is so old. Now the world is having yet another big war. But maybe you and I can gain by this insanity. If it weren't for the war, my mother might *not* be in such a hurry to marry me off and let me run my own business. But in wartime, she is superstitious. She thinks the Angel of Death passed her first two sons in this war, so it will surely come for me if I'm not protected. She knows the law better than a lawyer, and she says a man must have a wife dependent on him, and children as soon as possible, to claim an exemption. Well, that's fine with me. I don't want to go off and kill people in the country that my ancestors came from. I don't want to kill anyone. Well, I'd kill Hitler."

He added ruefully, "Maybe I'm just a peasant after all. Because I only want to be left alone to do my own work and live my own life. It's been impossible, being the youngest; everyone wants to tell you how to live. My mother is possessive with us all—you've seen that—yet, she thinks I'm different than my brothers, so she watches over me more closely."

"Your sister, too, watches over you," Filomena murmured.

Mario seemed glad that someone else understood this. "Yes! It's a good thing that I have only one sister, because Petrina treats me like a pet dog! As for my brothers, they like to boss me around. My father just expects his sons to toe the line. They all have opinions about me, and all of them believe that a son remains a boy, and belongs to his family, and doesn't become a man—until he takes a wife. So, the sooner the better." Clearly he was warning her about the possessive family she'd be dealing with; they might be even more difficult than they appeared.

Perhaps this had discouraged other women. "Have you loved anyone else?" she asked tentatively. She didn't want to find out later that he was longing for some girl he'd lost.

"Oh, there were girls I liked in school, but they all seemed to have nothing in their heads except shopping and gossip. My mother would make toast out of all of them," he said frankly. Then he smiled slyly. "She thinks if she brings over a girl from the old country, this bride will be grateful and intimidated and become her handmaiden. But as soon as I looked at the face of your cousin in the picture she sent me, I saw a woman who could say no to my mother, when necessary. I see it in your face, too. Also, you are not easily fooled."

Filomena grasped that he was hoping she'd be an ally, his ticket out as much as she had such hopes for him. Mario said, "The day you arrived, at dinner, I could tell that you see everything. I think perhaps you see it correctly, yet you are kind to everyone. And, I think you have the passion for living. It's what I want—to be really alive, not just doing what everybody else does. No matter how bad a day is, to wake up the next day still glad to be alive."

Filomena gulped. No one had ever credited her with much before. Mario's tone was seductive now, undeniably hinting at a physical chemistry that was possible between them. She felt a strong pull toward him and hoped that she was not somehow being tricked or deceived.

"So," he said, watching the candle on the table flickering, "what is it that *you* want most of all from marriage?"

"I want to be safe from harm," she whispered. "And to never, ever be indebted to someone who could take my children away from me or hurt the ones I love."

"*Certo!* Then, do you think you could be happy if we tried to have a real marriage—not just one of convenience? I think that would be so much better, don't you? But, is it even possible for you and I, do you think, Filomena?" Mario asked earnestly.

She was surprised to hear herself say, "Yes, I think that is possible."

Mario smiled. "Then, let's be good to each other, all right? Because with or without the war, life is too short to be miserable. I want to be happy. Don't you?"

"Yes," she said, feeling the first strong, bold surge of hope she'd ever really had.

Mario signaled the waiter to bring them a small bottle of an anise liqueur called *sambuca*. Then, he reached into his pocket and pulled out a small jewel box.

"I worked on this myself," he said. "For my imaginary girl-friend. Even before my mother started talking about marriage, I thought, *There must be someone out there who is looking for me, as I am looking for her. One day I will want to give her this.*"

Filomena's hands trembled slightly as she opened the box. The ring inside had an antique gold setting, in which nestled three small but beautiful stones, and he told her their names: a blue sapphire, a red ruby, and a yellow diamond.

"These are the only colors a painter needs," Mario said. "Let's paint a life. Will you marry me, Filomena?"

His hand lay outstretched on the table, and although he was not expecting her to take it, she put her hand in his. "Yes, Mario," she said. "I will be happy to marry you."

***

As soon as the family heard that Mario and his girl had agreed to marry, the household sprang into action, to do in a matter of weeks what normally would have taken months: plan a wedding. Tessa of course took charge, delegating roles to each family member. It was clear that Filomena was expected to simply stay out of the way, still like a servant.

She didn't care. It made her nervous to be involved; when they visited a dressmaker to do a fitting for a white dress, Filomena found that being with Tessa, Lucy, and Amie was completely terrifying. New Yorkers seemed to talk so much faster than people did back home, even in Naples. These American women were much more forthright, too; they said whatever they thought, without fear of causing offense. It ought to have been liberating, but Filomena found it overwhelming. Even when the women commented on Filomena's lovely height and curves, she felt apprehensive, as if under their admiration the "evil eye" of envy might be at work.

Then, just when Filomena breathed a sigh of relief that things were under control and her role was done, Mario's big sister stepped in.

"For God's sake," Petrina said to Tessa, "this girl still looks like she just came off the boat. Give me a day with her to make her look like a normal person, all right?"

Tessa waved a hand in the air, too busy to fully listen. "Do what you want," she said distractedly.

"Fine," Petrina said triumphantly, turning to Filomena. "*You,* come with me."

PETRINA HAD SIZED UP MARIO'S GIRL AS ONE OF THOSE COMPLIANT creatures that parents and men approved of, and which she, Petrina, would never be. She felt jealous, too, whenever her mother and Filomena commiserated in a version of Italian that was different from the fancy Italian that Petrina had learned in school. Listening closely, Petrina could grasp most of what they were saying, but she noted wistfully that Tessa seemed soothed by her exchanges with Filomena, revealing an almost girlish side that Petrina had never seen in her mother before.

Filomena was polite and respectful to Petrina; apparently the girl had no idea of the battle that Petrina had waged to change Mario's mind about this ridiculous wedding. In fact, Petrina had called a conference with Johnny and Frankie about it but got nowhere.

"Mario's in love, can't you tell?" Frankie had said. "Good for him."

"Love? We are all too young when we fall in love," Petrina responded bitterly.

"It's not just love. Mario wants to be left alone. But he's a sly fox," Johnny explained with a sage nod. "He saw that open rebellion didn't work for you, Petrina; Pop just sent you away to a tough school. Mario has figured out that the best way to be left alone is to marry this girl that Ma found for him, because Rosa is so grateful that she won't give him any grief."

Petrina had left that meeting in disgust, but she'd fared no better when she confronted Mario directly and he turned unexpectedly vehement.

"*Basta!*" he'd exclaimed, his eyes blazing with passion. "I tell you, this is the only girl my age I've met who is capable of thinking her own thoughts. Not her mama's thoughts, not her girlfriend's thoughts, not some magazine's ideas. So back off, Petrina, and you'd better be nice to her." He absolutely meant it, she could tell.

Petrina could not help being impressed, and wished that her own husband had said exactly that to *his* family. So she decided that if she couldn't put a stop to it, she could at least mold this girl into a proper wife for Mario.

Now, having obtained permission from Tessa to do so, Petrina marched Filomena off into her own automobile, driven by her own chauffeur. "Where are we going?" Filomena asked apprehensively, feeling trapped, as Petrina's driver steered the car away.

"Uptown, of course!" Petrina exclaimed. "First stop, Bergdorf's."

HOURS LATER, WHEN THEY EMERGED FROM THE DEPARTMENT STORE onto Fifth Avenue in the late afternoon sunlight, Filomena felt as if she'd been kidnapped and sold into some kind of white slavery. Her fingernails and toenails were painted a blood-red. Her face had been scrubbed, polished, and painted, and her lips were the same blood-red. The spa woman had even shaved off the hair on Filomena's legs, to her acute embarrassment. Apparently American men preferred their women to look like skinned rabbits. Back home, only prostitutes did such a strange thing.

Meanwhile, the hair on her head had been cut shorter—not as short as Petrina wanted, because Filomena had put her foot down here; so her hair still hung below her shoulders, but now it was shaped so that it swung like a bell, with a deep side part, making a long curtain of hair that fell over one eye.

"Not bad, she looks like a brunette Veronica Lake," the hairdresser had told Petrina. At first Filomena thought they were saying that she looked like she'd drowned in a lake, until it was explained to her that they were talking about a movie actress.

Lightheaded from all the perfumes and spritzes and sprays, Filomena had trailed after Petrina to more dizzying experiences— like boarding a terrifying cage with noisy doors called an "elevator," piloted by a uniformed person who briskly yanked levers and pressed buttons, to send his passengers rattling up and down a shaft. When the elevators got too crowded, Petrina dragged Filomena over to a moving staircase called an "escalator." At first, she balked like a mule, refusing to go forward, to the exasperation of everyone behind her. Sternly, Petrina counted aloud, "One, two, three, *step*!" And Filomena leapt as if her life depended on it.

From store to store, Petrina supervised the purchase of an extensive wardrobe, right down to the stockings, nightgowns, and silk underwear. She was dressing Filomena the way a little girl dresses a doll, allowing salesladies with their sharply manicured talons to button and unbutton Filomena into and out of various outfits, while Petrina stood back and assessed the effect, accepting or rejecting their offerings with a firm, curt yes or no.

With each purchase Filomena wondered how they could possibly fit another shopping box into the car. But Petrina's driver expertly packed the trunk and piloted them through fearsome traffic, then sat behind the wheel impassively waiting throughout each escapade, until Petrina finally declared, "One last stop. We're going for drinks at the Copa."

The Copacabana turned out to be a nightclub, outfitted, as Petrina told her, in Brazilian decor, yet inexplicably serving Chinese food. The cocktail crowd was very glamorous: women in furs and men in silk suits, all being very clever and making one another laugh. Petrina waved to various people at bar stools and tables as a waiter led her to a prized booth. She slid into a curved leather seat, pulled Filomena in with her, and tossed their coats on the other side.

"Two champagne cocktails," Petrina ordered the waiter.

Filomena had taken only two cautious sips when a nattily dressed man in a three-piece suit, every hair in place, and with the face of a Roman emperor, entered the room and began an impressive round of hand-shaking, back-patting, and chatting until he reached Petrina's table.

"Hello, College Girl! How's your father?" he asked. He looked to be in his early fifties.

Petrina smiled enigmatically. "Fine, thank you. This is the girl who's going to marry my baby brother Mario. Rosamaria, say hello to Mr. Frank Costello."

For once, Filomena was glad she'd endured all the beautifying today, because the man gave her a sharp once-over and then said approvingly, "Is that so?"

"She just came here from Italy," Petrina added significantly.

The man's expression instantly softened, and he addressed himself to Filomena for the first and only time, speaking in Italian. "Ah! I was only a little kid when I came over. There wasn't much room in steerage, so you know where I slept? In a cooking pot! How 'bout that? Well, congratulations! My regards to Mario." He turned to Petrina with a nod and said, "Your money is no good here tonight." He kissed her hand in a debonair way and moved on.

"Did he say your money was bad?" Filomena asked worryingly.

Petrina laughed. "It means we drink for free tonight!" Then she whispered, "They say he's the 'silent partner' of the Copacabana! It means he's a part-owner," she explained impatiently at Filomena's baffled attempt to keep up. Really, this girl was like a lost lamb. It brought out Petrina's protective urge, akin to the way she felt about Mario—that if she didn't explain the world to these innocent souls, they'd get eaten alive.

A waiter appeared carrying a bucket filled with ice and a whole bottle of champagne, which he expertly popped open and then poured into tall glasses. Petrina lifted her champagne glass, took a satisfied sip, and sighed.

"Now, *that*," she said, "is the good stuff. Taste and learn, kid."

Filomena's head was already spinning from this whirlwind day. They watched as Mr. Costello's passage through the crowd elicited fawning respect from many people, not merely the ones who worked there but the elegant customers as well. Filomena whispered, "He is very important, yes?"

Petrina said in a low, conspiratorial tone, "You bet! Frank Costello is the man they call the 'Prime Minister.'" At Filomena's puzzled look, Petrina added, "Because he's got all the *uomini importante*—every politician, judge, and cop worth knowing—*in tasca*—in his pocket. He's the Big Boss of our neck of the woods. But he started out *un povero immigrato*, like everybody else. He knows my father from the Prohibition days. He's always been fair, Pa says."

Filomena had been nodding, but at the word *Prohibition* her blank look caused Petrina to say impatiently, "Prohibition—it was a stupid law, years ago, that made it illegal to sell drinks! Then, after that, Mr. Costello made a *ton* of money on slot machines. Oh, for heaven's sake, you know, machines you put coins into, to gamble, like candy machines. You never saw one? Well, anyway, now he lives in a beautiful penthouse at the tippy-top of the Majestic apartments—I'll show you on the way home."

Petrina had adopted the tone of a schoolteacher, and somehow it reminded Filomena of Rosamaria. For, despite Petrina's hauteur, there seemed to be an earnest sincerity lurking in her efforts to educate her future sister-in-law, so Filomena made a valiant effort to understand.

"People pay tribute to this man?" she asked, finally catching on, and remembering something that Rosamaria had told her. *Everyone has to pay tribute to somebody.*

Petrina nodded. "Let's drive past his apartment building—the Majestic—on the way home. They say Costello even keeps slot machines in his penthouse, for his dinner guests to use. But they're rigged—to make sure that his guests *never* lose!"

II

Greenwich Village, Autumn 1943

Early the next morning, Filomena was roused out of her bed by
Tessa herself.

"Get dressed, hurry! You are coming with *me* now. It's market
day," Tessa said. She waited, silently at first, watching Filomena
dress, observing her new clothes from yesterday's expedition with
Petrina. "Yes, it's nice for a wife to look pretty," Tessa said dryly,
"but there are more important things in life. Come, I'll show you."

They set out on foot, passing through the cozy part of Greenwich Village, with its graceful old houses built around quiet,
sedate parks, sometimes tucked into eccentric, twisty cobbled
streets. Tessa, dressed in a light wool suit and veiled hat, held
herself proudly erect, not speaking, except for moments when she
nodded to other well-dressed neighbors. Silence seemed the rule
on these well-to-do streets. But not very far from these genteel
residences were the busy market streets, teeming with enterprise
and life.

Amid shops, stalls, and pushcarts, Filomena quickly saw that
this was much more than an ordinary grocery expedition. Tessa
moved briskly through the neighborhood like a serious business-
woman, stopping at each specialty vendor to assess what to order,
and to teach Filomena by pointedly saying, "This is what Mario

likes to eat." But Tessa put only some fruit and a few other things in her basket; she ordered everything else to be delivered to her house.

Sometimes she would demand of Filomena, "Do you know how to tell if this is fresh?" as she selected the ripest melon or a box of the best tomatoes. But when they reached the fishmonger, Filomena put up a hand, and it was she who selected the fish. She came from a family of fishermen, after all. "*Bene!*" Tessa said approvingly. They moved on.

Tessa never had to stand on line. All the merchants were so deferential to her. No matter how busy they were, they dropped whatever they were doing to come and take Tessa's hand, to greet and serve her personally. The balding, rotund baker came around his glass counter to personally put a warm loaf of bread into her basket. The tall, mustachioed butcher went into the back room and cut his freshest meat for her, then sent his boy to deliver it to Tessa's cook so that it would be there before they got home. At a time when everyone else was using ration coupons to pay for their restricted shares of everything from gasoline and shoes to meat, butter, and sugar, Tessa seemed to have limitless credit. Filomena could not help admiring Tessa, and she felt her own prestige rising as the shopkeepers smiled at her with courtesy.

"Respect," Tessa said as they left the markets, "is what separates us from the animals. Remember that you must never do anything to lose respect for this family."

They turned a corner and were nearly home when something emerged from an alleyway and blocked their path. It was a stray mastiff, his muddied fur mottled and matted. He planted himself on four strong, tall legs, growling through heavy, drooling lips, as if daring them to pass. When Tessa took a small step, he snarled, baring sharp teeth, and he emitted a vicious bark. Tessa froze. A taut moment of dread seemed suspended in the very air, as the wild, angry creature was evidently trying to decide which one of them to attack first.

The decision rumbled in his throat as he sprang toward Tessa. But she managed to sidestep him, so he ended up butting his powerful head against her basket. This momentarily distracted the creature, as oranges and lemons bounced at him like missiles.

In that brief confusion, Filomena made a swift calculation. As a girl, she'd seen a pack of wild dogs maul a boy. But this beast was alone, a stranger in the neighborhood. This wasn't his territory. It was hers. "Go home!" she shouted loudly, firm and decisive. "Now! Go home!"

The dog turned his reddened, furious eyes to her, his nostrils flaring as he bared his long, ugly teeth. She straightened up taller but stayed in place. "Go home!" she shouted in a clear, fearless voice that rang through the street like a bell. The dog, still growling, paused, sizing her up; then, dropping his head, he turned and trotted away.

"*Brava,*" Tessa said quietly, as if seeing Filomena for the first time.

WHILE TESSA WAS OUT SHOPPING WITH FILOMENA, THE BROTHERS were in charge of other preparations.

"Look, Mario," Johnny said early that evening, lighting a cigarette, "Frankie and I just want to have a little talk with you, okay?"

Mario had been summoned to a place he scarcely ever went to—the town house where Johnny lived with Amie and their kids on the first floor. Tonight, all of the children were upstairs at Lucy and Frankie's place, being fed an early dinner by the maid. The wives were over at Tessa's. So this meeting was clearly for men only.

"What's up?" Mario asked with mild suspicion.

"First of all, understand that we support your ideas," Johnny continued. "Pop says you want to start your own business; that's fine."

Mario eyed his brothers with some amusement. He surely

hadn't been summoned here to discuss business; they'd never do that without having their father present. Yet they'd taken time out of their busy day to team up for this meeting, playing their usual roles: Johnny, the measured "thinker" of the family, and Frankie, the "charmer" and dealmaker.

"Secondly," said Frankie, as if the two of them had rehearsed this among themselves before inviting Mario here, "we want to be sure that you are getting married because you want to, not just because Ma set this up, you know?"

Again, this struck Mario as a formality, and he replied, "Yes, it *is* what I want."

The brothers exchanged a significant look.

Frankie said, "Christ, Johnny, put that cigarette out, will ya? You smoke too much." Then he took the plunge. "Look, kid," Frankie said awkwardly, "we took you out for your sixteenth birthday, so we know that you know the *basic* facts of life."

Mario, who preferred not to think too much about his one and only excursion with prostitutes, waved his hand without comment. "But marriage," Johnny began, "with somebody you love, I mean, it's different from all that."

Frankie said quickly, "What Johnny means is, most young girls like your Rosa don't know anything about it. So, you can't just charge in like a bull in a china shop, as they say."

Mario suppressed a smile. "Right," he said soberly. He decided this wasn't the time to tell them he'd also had a brief fling with the widowed art teacher at school, until she married the music teacher and ran off with him to Philadelphia. Mario had not been sorry to see them go; he'd learned plenty but was glad to have it end on a lighthearted note.

"So, just take it easy," Johnny said. "Don't expect a lot from your bride on the wedding day; everybody's exhausted by the time you go to bed, you know? Getting to know each other takes a while. And speaking of time, even if *she* starts worrying about when the babies will come, don't worry. They'll come, soon enough."

"Okay? You got that?" Frankie asked briskly.

"Got it. Thanks," Mario said. Both of his brothers breathed a sigh of relief. Frankie went over to the sideboard and poured them all a drink.

"*Salute!*" Frankie said.

"Amen," Johnny replied, giving Mario a slap on the back.

WHEN LUCY CAME HOME FROM HER HOSPITAL SHIFT THAT DAY, SHE went to Tessa's house first; it was customary for her to do so before going to her own house. She found Amie alone in the parlor.

"No Tessa today," Amie reported. "She's taken Mario's girl to the market, then to the dressmaker for the final fitting. Johnny says you and I must stay away from our house till dinnertime, 'cause he and Frankie are having 'a little talk' with Mario. Isn't that sweet?"

Lucy knew that Amie had gotten into the habit of sipping a little sherry at this hour. Today, what Lucy herself wanted was a whiskey, badly. Not just because the hospital had been busy; by now, Lucy was accustomed to handling all kinds of crises: patient distress, staff nerves, the assorted catastrophes of blood and flesh that she always did her best to put right.

But today, just as her shift was about to end, she'd been in the emergency room to make a last check on a staff issue there when an ambulance arrived with the police behind it, and Lucy received a small shock. A girl had apparently drowned in the Hudson River.

Lucy was standing right by the hospital's door when the stretcher arrived, and as the sheet was pulled back from the corpse, Lucy recognized that poor bloated face as belonging to the girl who'd given birth to Christopher, nearly a decade ago. Lucy had never even learned her name.

"Another Jane Doe. I think I've seen her before; she's a hooker from the West Side," the policeman told the doctor who was on call.

"Looks like a suicide," said the doctor after examining the body. The policeman nodded.

"I'll ask around and see if she had any family, but these girls never do."

Lucy had felt herself going lightheaded, and she actually had to sit down and pretend to be going through charts to regain her composure. Even after she'd roused herself and hurried home, she still felt shaky, glancing over her shoulder as if she were guilty of murder.

What does it mean? she asked herself. *Did the girl really jump, or did someone throw her in? If so, why, poor thing?* Girls like that got "used up" fast, ageing before their time. Lucy knew that she herself could have ended up on the streets if her luck had run out.

It was a relief to be home now, sipping her whiskey, quietly brooding.

But Amie was in the mood to chat. "Mario's girl is getting very glamorous," she commented. "Petrina's got her all gussied up. Nail polish!" She paused. "Well?" she asked. "What do you think of this new girl that Mario is going to marry?"

"Hmm? Oh, she's all right, I guess." Lucy nodded thoughtfully, resolutely trying to forget the bloated face of that drowned woman. In the warm, sheltering lamplit glow of this parlor, Frankie's family had always felt like a fortress, where she and Christopher would forever be protected. But tonight was a reminder that there was still a nasty world out there that might come tapping at her windowpane like the tree branches on a windy night. Lucy reflected that by now she should be used to life's little shocks.

Even the shocks that occurred *inside* her own home. Once, she'd found guns hidden under the bed. Frankie swore it would never happen again, and it didn't. Still, there were times when she'd discovered an astonishing amount of money, in cash, hidden in empty coffee cans or stashed in an old steamer trunk in the closet, even a hatbox. But that had been a while ago.

"The cook's son is in trouble. He's a dope addict," Amie volunteered. "I felt so sorry for her. She had to send him away to stay with friends in New Jersey. They know a priest who helps dopers kick the habit." Amie sighed. "Boys are harder to control than girls. You're lucky you have a daughter like Gemma. I hope I have a girl one day."

Lucy felt a familiar pang. After the birth of her daughter, Gemma, the doctors had said that Lucy couldn't have any more babies, because she'd had a uterine rupture, caused by bad scarring from the previous birth in Ireland. Lucy suspected it had to do with the pitiful medical care she'd gotten back at that girls' home; the nuns there always sought the cheapest doctors they could find, who acted as if they had been called into slums and couldn't wait to do the job and get out.

Lucy thought it was an unfair punishment, that she couldn't give Frankie any sons. She'd sobbed on his shoulder, but he assured her that he didn't care, saying he loved Gemma and Chris and it was enough. Still, she made him promise not to tell his family of her "defect."

"I'd love to have a little girl to dress up," Amie was saying dreamily.

"Why don't you?" Lucy asked curiously.

Amie blushed. "Johnny was so amorous when we met. But once the twins were born, I don't know, he's still very loving, but he acts as if I'm the Madonna now. Is Frankie like that?"

Lucy was embarrassed. "No, Frankie is insatiable," she admitted. "Honestly he wears me out sometimes. But I can't resist him. It's like I just have no control over it."

Amie felt a stab of envy, for Johnny had once been that way, too. Such handsome men, so full of life and joy, and yet, there was something elusive about all of them. This new girl and Mario seemed so in love. What might interfere with *their* marital harmony?

"Men are too complicated." Amie sighed.

"No," said Lucy ruefully, "men are too simple."

WHEN FILOMENA AND TESSA RETURNED HOME, TESSA WENT straight to her private study at the back of the house. Filomena found Lucy and Amie chatting amiably in the family parlor, but they fell silent when they saw her and did not resume talking until she went upstairs. *Perhaps they think I'm a spy for Tessa,* Filomena thought wistfully.

At suppertime, Lucy and Amie went back to their house to dine with their husbands. Filomena ate with Mario and his parents, mostly in silence, which was a relief, after such whirlwind days. Then Gianni spoke. "Mario, we've arranged for you and your new wife to live with us, here in this house," he said with a certain formality.

Mario, unperturbed, turned to Filomena and explained, "This house is the biggest, and my parents' bedroom is on the first floor. Ours will be upstairs, so we'll have privacy. With the war on, we think this is the best way."

Filomena nodded. But when his parents had retreated to their bedroom, Mario said to her in a low voice, "I will save our money, and as soon as we're able, I'll buy a house for us that will be all our own, if that's what we decide we want. All right?"

Filomena again consented. Mario put his arms around her, and kissed her on the lips, for the first time. She liked this unexpected intimacy and felt herself kissing him back, and since he was still a bit of a stranger, this was a new, somewhat illicit thrill.

"I'll say good night now," he whispered. Mario's bedroom, she learned, was a third, smaller room upstairs that he'd lived in all his life, since childhood; right down the hall was another, much bigger bedroom that had once been Petrina's but would soon be theirs.

Filomena turned away and followed the corridor that led to

the guesthouse. She climbed the stairs to her little bedroom with a sigh of relief, eager to sleep. But through the window on the street side, the lamplight was so bright that she went to close the curtains.

Then she saw, in the light of the streetlamps, two heavyset men below, standing in the road at the corner, their faces in half-shadow. They were staring at this house, or staring at nothing; she couldn't tell. She saw the red-tipped glow of a cigarette that one of them was smoking. Instinctively she drew back from the window, not wanting to be seen in her nightgown. Cautiously she peeped out from the side. The men seemed to confer with each other awhile, then finally they moved away and disappeared around a corner.

Feeling unsettled, Filomena closed the curtains, returned to bed, and pulled the covers over her, shivering a bit. But soon she felt warm and safe again, and she drifted off to sleep.

12

Greenwich Village and Candlewood Lake, Connecticut, Autumn 1943

Filomena's wedding day dawned bright, cool, and sunny.

"You look so pretty, Miss," whispered Donna, the maid, as she helped the bride dress. The guest room was already empty of Filomena's things, for she was no longer a guest. After today, she would be family.

Mario's father, Gianni, was going to give her away, so he was waiting downstairs in the parlor. The house was eerily quiet; everyone else was already at the church.

When Filomena descended the stairs, the maid picked up her train and put it over Filomena's arm, then left her alone in the parlor with Gianni. He had dressed up proudly for the occasion in a dark suit, and his elegant head of hair, so full for a man of his age, made him look like a regal lion today.

Filomena waited nervously as he rose to his feet, for he deliberately lingered there, even though Sal the driver waited outside with the car running. "Dear girl," Gianni said, peering into her face before she covered it with her veil, "I know that everyone in this family has talked to you, welcomed you. I myself am not a man of many words and speeches. But I want you to know that I am happy you are here, and I can see that you make Mario happy."

He paused. "I would just like to say, that if you have any reason not to want to do this thing today, it will be all right. I will
still sponsor you if you wish to stay in this country and go off on
your own. So please, if you would rather not go forward, do not
be afraid to say so, at least to me." Filomena saw that he meant it.
She was touched and stunned. Such genuine consideration for *her*
needs and desires made her feel like a real person, not just a pawn.
Her heart swelled with a gratitude that only deepened her loyalty
to this remarkable family.

"I thank you for your kindness. But yes, I do want to marry
Mario," she said simply.

Gianni nodded appreciatively; then he said something that Filomena could not truly comprehend until much later. "There are
things that happen in life that can't be helped," he said quietly.
"Mario's life has not been without its complications. He does not
fully understand this yet. But whatever happens, please, always be
there to remind him how important it is to have his family near,
for they only want to love and protect him."

Filomena had no idea what to say, so she just nodded. Gianni
said, "All right, then. We must go now. Quietly and calmly. It is a
great day."

Sal opened the car door for her and waited, and for the first
time he gave her a brief smile and a nod. Seated there surrounded
by yards and yards of her precious dress, Filomena felt as if she
were being whisked off on a cloud of tulle.

When they arrived at the church, with its lovely columns and
bell tower, the doors were wide open. On the sidewalk, a few little girls were playing hopscotch amid the fallen leaves. As they
paused in admiration of a bride, Filomena recalled doing that as a
girl. But she felt a moment of panic; she'd been fearful of entering
a church ever since the bombing of Naples had literally brought
down a church on her. She paused involuntarily, trembling, causing Gianni to look up inquiringly. Filomena could almost hear Rosamaria hissing at her, *He thinks you are having second thoughts*

about his family. So, in a silent prayer to Rosamaria, Filomena forced herself to straighten up and smile, certain that her cousin was with her, right now, giving her a shove to go on.

Determinedly, Filomena climbed the stone steps and peered inside. The aisles were decorated with white and pink roses and white satin ribbons. The pews were filled with many people who were complete strangers to Filomena but whom Mario's family obviously knew well. The guests craned their necks to get a first look. Filomena hastily ducked out of sight.

Petrina, initially irritable and impatient that morning, had rallied now and was waiting at the back of the church, insisting on checking Filomena's dress, hair, veil. Lucy and Amie were the attendants, and Lucy unexpectedly stepped forward to squeeze Filomena's hand.

"Don't be afraid," she whispered. "It's a piece of cake."

"She means it's a cinch," Amie offered, not to be outdone. Filomena didn't recognize either slang expression, but the looks on their faces were reassuring.

At the first startling notes of the organ, the children went forward: Pippa and Gemma scattered pale pink rose petals from little baskets onto the white satin runner laid at Filomena's feet. Christopher followed, carrying the rings pinned to a white satin pillow. Next, the matrons of honor, Amie and Lucy, with Mario's brothers as the ushers. Gianni offered his arm to Filomena, and as they moved forward, she heard the crowd rise in response.

With all these people staring at her, she was glad to have Gianni's calm and steady guidance down the aisle. Through her gauzy veil, she saw Tessa poised like a queen in a front pew. Mario was waiting at the altar, his intelligent face aglow but looking slightly nervous.

When Filomena reached Mario, she gave her bouquet to Amie, then placed her hand on the prayer book that Tessa had given her, and Mario put his hand on hers. His reassuring touch melted the chill in her fingers, which had felt like icicles. The priest spoke, and Filomena and Mario began to murmur their pledges of love to each other. Then suddenly, Mario was kissing her, the organ burst into music, and as they left the church its bell began to peal.

THE BRIDAL RECEPTION WAS HELD IN A NEW, PRETTY RESTAURANT IN Greenwich Village, whose trees and shrubs were strung with tiny lights. Inside, the banquet tables were dotted with flowers, and from a corner, a string quartet was playing. Mario's brothers danced with Filomena; they were graceful and dignified.

When Mario reclaimed her, Frankie said in a quiet, congratulatory tone, "Your doll's a doll, Mario." This seemed to please Mario immensely.

"He never says that unless he means it," Mario told her.

Even Petrina's husband was there—a tall, dapper man named Richard, who was dragged onto the dance floor by his daughter, Pippa. The wedding banquet lasted all day. Amie had let slip that the cake alone cost a princely sum, for it was made with the finest ingredients, despite the rationing of butter, sugar, and flour. Filomena didn't dare calculate the entire expense the family had gone to for their youngest son, the last to marry, but she had a few spells of panic at the unthinkable cost of this single event.

Mario was always at her side now, steering her from one ritual to the next, until it was time for them to change into traveling clothes and escape. The faithful Sal was ready and waiting to drive them to their destination, where they would finally be alone.

"Well," said Mario as they settled into the backseat of the car, "we did it!"

***

THE HONEYMOON COTTAGE ON CANDLEWOOD LAKE HAD AN ENchanted look in the slanted autumn light. There weren't many guests here on weekdays, which gave the newlyweds the quiet and privacy that they craved. Nature, too, was good to them, with days of unseasonably warm weather, so that they could take a canoe and paddle out across the lake, which sparkled under a bright blue autumnal sky. Leisure was still an amazing luxury to her—to be outdoors all day solely for fun, not to do farm chores. They picnicked, then drifted lazily along; and in the evening they sat on the porch after dinner and finished their wine. Instinctively their bodies followed the rhythm of the sun, so they went to bed early. In those spicy-scented, cool nights, they lay there in the soft darkness, making plans, making love.

That first night, when Filomena went into the bathroom to put on her nightgown, she had a moment's panic, even though Rosamaria had long ago explained the facts of life to her, and, indeed, told her how to "tame" a man so that he didn't rush things.

But when Filomena slipped into bed, Mario murmured sweet things to her, and took his time caressing her body, exploring her desire; and Filomena, at first shy, was utterly surprised to discover her own pleasure from a hunger that she no longer had to repress. Afterwards, she slept so deeply, in a contented way that seemed like a memory of a primordial past.

It was easy to fall into a routine of waking early with the delicate rising sun, sharing a quick breakfast, going out on the lake with a canoe to watch nature frolicking. Ducks paddled companionably alongside them; other birds went flying over their heads in a V-shaped hurry, and little frogs leapt out of their way while making odd pinging sounds.

Sometimes Filomena and Mario hardly spoke out on the lake, exchanging happy looks whenever they spotted something unexpected and miraculous—a swan taking sudden flight with a great noise of wings, a fish leaping in an arc of grace. Mario was an expert fisherman, and they cooked what he caught. Filomena hadn't been out in a boat to go fishing for years; she'd missed it without realizing it. But it was also a painful reminder of her father. And one evening, a chance remark by Mario prompted her to reveal more than she'd ever intended.

She was lying in bed in the dark, pleasantly exhausted from a day spent outdoors. Mario stood at the window, gazing at the stars, and said reflectively, "When I was a boy, I used to pretend I didn't really belong to this family. I'd read a lot of books, you see, about orphans who turned out to be princes or warriors. I was certain that someday, I'd leave home and pull a sword out of a stone, or sail across the high seas to my true father's magic kingdom."

As he came to the bed and lay beside her, Filomena said in a sudden burst, "You don't know what you're talking about! It's no joy to be an orphan. It's horrible. You ought to get down on your knees and pray to God to forgive you for your ingratitude."

Mario turned to her in astonishment as, under the cover of the darkness, she burst into tears. He instinctively cradled her in his arms, uttering soothing sounds, until finally he asked, "What is it, *cara mia*? What makes you so sad?"

And in a sudden rush, she told him all about how her parents had quarreled, and how her mother had taken her away and then let go of her hand to give her away to strangers. He was silent, the way a horse listens in mute but palpable sympathy, till her tears subsided. "Poor baby," he whispered, still rocking her as if she were a child. "I can't imagine such a thing, done to such a sweet, loving girl as you! They must have been horribly desperate. No one will ever abandon you or hurt you again, I swear it."

"You won't tell anyone, will you?" she whispered anxiously. She had been unwanted long enough to know that if people found out that you'd been abandoned, it made the whole world think of you as undesirable.

"Of course not. The past is gone," he said firmly. "You are one of us now."

He paused. "I didn't mean to be ungrateful to my family," he said haltingly, as if he owed her an explanation. "But you see, when I was born, my mother was at an age when she didn't want to have any more babies. She had already lost two infants at birth.

So when I came along, she didn't have much patience, at first. I was always too slow. Took too long to tie my shoes, to change my clothes, even to eat—she told the maid to take away my plate from the table when I wasn't even finished. She got angry at me, a lot. I couldn't see why. She wanted to send me off to a seminary, to get rid of me. So, that's when I thought of running away."

Filomena understood now and said quietly, "But she seems so fond of you."

Mario sighed. "Now, yes. But she used to get a lot of headaches, after working in her study doing the bookkeeping. She would lie on a little sofa in there and just moan to herself. The doctors couldn't help. One day, when I was six, and no one else was home, I made her some 'sunshine tea.' You put nice verbena herbs in a jar with water, and let the sun infuse it. I brought her a cup. Then I put a washcloth in a bowl of ice water, and wrung it out and put the nice cool cloth on her forehead. And I sang her a little song that Petrina taught me. Mama was so surprised, she cried. Things got much better for me after that."

Filomena, watching his face as moonlight peeped through the window, could see his genuine sorrow. She understood why Mario struck a careful balance between pleasing himself and pleasing his mother. Childhood terrors were part of one's blood and flesh. Even now, as an adult, he did not want the loving Tessa to revert to being angry and impatient with him. Perhaps, Filomena thought, this family was a bit more complicated than she'd realized.

AND THEN, ONE DAY THE PHONE RANG IN THE VILLAGE STORE, AND the man who owned their cabin and the little store across the lake took his motorboat out to tell them to call home. They went back with him, across a lake so calm in the morning sun. An elderly couple was fishing in a nearby cove, looking as if they'd been there since time began. A few people who lived year-round along the lake called out to one another cheerily on this day that seemed meant to be savored. When they saw Mario and Filomena puttering by, everyone smiled knowingly and said, "Honeymooners," as if all the world loved this couple, because they loved each other.

When the boat docked, they climbed out and went into the shop, which had a long soda fountain on one side and a single phone booth at the far end. Mario telephoned home—and Filomena saw the glow in his face extinguish, as if someone had turned off a lamp within him. She knew that there was only one thing that had such awful power.

"What did you say?" Mario asked, holding out the phone so that she could hear.

"Mario, it's Pop," Frankie answered urgently. "He's dead. He was walking home with a box of pastries from the bakery on Sunday. I saw him coming up the front walk. He said, 'I don't feel so good,' and then he fell like an apple off a tree. Doc says it was probably a stroke. Ma is a wreck. Johnny's been crying like a baby when he thinks nobody can hear him. Mario, you gotta come home." He paused. "Ma says Pop was getting strange phone calls in the middle of the night that upset him, but he never said who it was. Petrina is sending her own driver up there to get you. We gotta keep Sal here." The call ended on this ominous note.

"Mario, I'm so sorry," Filomena said, hugging him.

He let her hold him close for a while. "We have to go," he said finally, looking stunned.

"Of course we do," she answered. "I'll pack up our things." She knew immediately that it was her turn to take care of him. Until now, it was Mario who'd paid the bills, ordered dinner, and talked to people, but in the first shock of mourning, her husband could not be expected to take on the world; every little movement would feel like a major effort, she knew.

So she spoke quickly to the man behind the soda counter and ordered some sandwiches to be wrapped up—egg and bacon for Mario's breakfast, with a thermos of hot coffee, and some roast beef sandwiches for the drive home. The proprietor's wife, who made the sandwiches, clucked her tongue in sympathy and did thoughtful extra things, like adding some sugar cookies and chocolates for them to have with their coffee.

The man who owned the store let them take his motorboat back across the lake. When they reached their cabin, Filomena made Mario sit down at the wooden picnic table with the coffee and the egg sandwich, while she quickly packed their clothes.

"Eat, because you must be strong for your mama, and for us," she urged.

Mario ate mechanically, staring out over the lake without seeming to be aware of what he was doing, as if he could not muster the energy to resist her instructions. When he shivered once, Filomena put his jacket over his shoulders and snuggled closer to him, to keep her sweet young husband warm—just as the world was turning colder.

13

New York City, Autumn 1943

Gianni's wake was attended by more people than had come to Mario's wedding, but it did not escape Filomena's notice that many of the guests were men who'd come alone, sober and well dressed, to pay their respects.

Even now, lying here in his coffin surrounded by flowers, Gianni still looked handsome, his beautiful hair in place, his clothes impeccable, as he'd dressed in life. Filomena kept expecting him to rise up and resume his role as the wise anchor of this family, to tell them what they should do.

Mario stood like a sentinel near the coffin, at his father's head, and did not speak much when people shuffled by and took turns telling him how sorry they were; he only nodded.

Tessa, who at home had seemed unexpectedly frail to Filomena—almost as if a gust of wind might reduce her to powder—had now risen to the occasion, putting on her black satin dress and veil, and a necklace of gold. She sat in the front row before her husband's coffin, holding herself erect and never once shedding a tear nor showing any signs of her devastation. She was like a statue, immovable, for the benefit of the crowd, as if to say, "I am still here, and I am in charge now." Filomena was more in awe of her than ever.

Johnny sat on one side of his mother and Frankie on the other. Their wives were behind them, with the children, who were all dressed formally, too, and dared not fidget. Filomena sat with the wives and watched as each youngster was led to kiss their grandfather goodbye and then returned to their seat. They looked solemn, scared, but determined to act like the grown-ups.

At one point, Johnny went to the back of the room to smoke, looking devastated, his tall frame stooped, as if he literally had the weight of his family on his shoulders; he stood there immobilized, lost in thought.

In contrast, Frankie, always filled with vital energy, seemed unable to contain himself today, pacing, watching, speaking to people, ever in motion. Lucy gave up trying to placate him. She had seen enough of death at the hospital to know that she must let her husband expel his grief energy, and then just be there when he suddenly ran out of it.

Petrina wore a dark veil over her tear-streaked face, once again without her husband's comfort, for although Richard had come with her to briefly pay his respects, he had taken their car back to the suburbs, leaving Petrina and Pippa with her family. Dressed in black silk, Petrina looked stunning without even trying—so tall on her high heels, a faint scent of some perfume that evoked deep-purple flowers. Her daughter, Pippa, looked sad and anxious in her first black dress, holding her mother's hand before she took a seat among the other children sitting in a straight, hushed line like a row of little birds.

Tessa had insisted on only one morning for the wake, so that the funeral Mass could be the same day and the burial late that afternoon. The young wives sensed that it was as if Tessa were protecting Gianni somehow.

"Watch out," Lucy whispered suddenly when, in the last hour of the wake, there was a sudden stir among the remaining visitors at the back of the room. A slender man had walked in. The entire room came to attention, like soldiers snapping into place when a general arrives for inspection. Everyone watched silently as the newcomer moved forward.

Filomena studied him covertly. He was in his mid-forties, of medium height and weight, with sandy brown hair, but he had a "tall head," she thought—a high forehead with hawkish eyebrows angled sharply over his dark, brooding eyes—and he had a rather long nose and full, sensuous lips. Quietly and respectfully he approached Tessa without once relinquishing an ounce of his own authority. He bent slightly to murmur something consoling to her, then he spoke in a low voice to her sons.

When he straightened up, the man's glance darted swiftly once around the room, taking it all in. For a fraction of a second, his gaze rested on Filomena like a wasp on a bloom, as if she were a new plant in the garden. It didn't last long; he'd evidently dismissed her as unimportant. But it was enough to send a chill through her.

Filomena glanced inquiringly at the other women. Lucy shook her head warningly, but Amie could not resist whispering in her ear, "That's Anthony Strollo. They call him 'Tony Bender.' He runs the crew of Greenwich Village. He's the man we all have to deal with."

Petrina leaned forward meaningfully and whispered to Filomena, "But he's just a *capo* for Mr. Costello, the 'Prime Minister' of the underworld. Remember?"

"For the love of God, ladies, pipe down!" Lucy hissed in disbelief. "Do you want him to hear what we magpies think of him?"

But Strollo had already moved up to the coffin. He paused, took a white flower out of his buttonhole, and placed it on Gianni's chest.

Filomena saw Mario wince, almost imperceptibly, for no one else noticed. But when Strollo turned, nodded to the family again, and walked out, she saw Mario unobtrusively reach over and pluck the flower off his father, just before the coffin was finally closed.

LATER THAT DAY, EMERGING FROM THE CHURCH, AND STILL FEELING slightly sick from the copious amounts of incense that the priest had distributed at the funeral with an impressive gold censer on a thick gold chain, Filomena followed the wives and children into a car that bore them to the cemetery. She was surprised that Tessa had chosen to bury her husband far outside of town, in a suburb in Westchester County. The cemetery had a large, arched black iron gate.

As they walked across this bucolic, peaceful place, Filomena saw that an entire section had been set off for this family, encircled by its own smaller iron gate. Tessa must have paid mightily for this prime spot, shaded by a big tree. An enormous mausoleum reigned here; Gianni was going to be buried aboveground, like a pope. The door to the structure yawned open, and Filomena could see a number of stone alcoves, with statues of patron saints in them, standing above various stone sarcophagi, many of which bore no engravings yet. Filomena gasped when she understood the plan.

"We're all going to end up here," Lucy whispered, as if she was having the same thought at the same time. Amie shuddered. Petrina passed them a small silver flask of gin.

The funeral director and his attendants moved expertly, placing Gianni's coffin on a narrow temporary platform before the door of the crypt, so that the priest could say the prayers and make the final blessings.

Rows of folding chairs were arranged outside the crypt, waiting for the family to be seated. None of the neighbors from the city had been invited to the burial; this part of the ceremony was only for family members, who sat there exhaustedly listening to the priest as he intoned his words about a life hereafter, in a weary manner that was strangely unconvincing, even to the devoted listeners who believed in it.

Then a black car came rolling down the road that snaked around this peaceful, remote cemetery. Filomena saw Johnny,

Frankie, and Mario exchange a dubious glance, shaking their heads to indicate that they had no recognition of the odd trio that emerged—an older woman and two young men, who came marching purposely toward them.

The strangers sat down somewhat defiantly, in empty chairs on the other side of the coffin. Everyone stared. The woman was not much younger than Tessa, but her bleached blond hair and garish, heavily made-up face could not disguise the puffy look of a woman who had indulged in heavy drinking in her youth and was now suffering from the results. Her clothes, once formal, seemed shiny with wear.

Her escorts were around Mario's age, and evidently the woman's sons, since they looked like her, except they had spiky, dark hair, well oiled; one son seemed slightly older than the other, but both were chunky and resembled overfed pets. A gust of combined synthetic cologne wafted from the entire group and caused Pippa to sneeze.

Filomena was studying the young men. Something about their girth and gestures seemed oddly familiar. "Oh!" she said under her breath. No one heard her. But she was fairly certain that they were the two men she'd seen out on the street beneath her window on that moonlit night, not so long ago, loitering under the streetlamp and gazing up at the house. She would have to tell Mario, as soon as the service was over.

The priest had paused momentarily, then concluded his farewell sermon. But when he mentioned Gianni's name, the frowsy woman began sniffling, then moaning. Her sons, one on each side of her, remained impassive, but occasionally the woman put out both hands dramatically, as if to steady herself and prevent a swoon.

"For God's sake," Petrina muttered. "Who is that ghastly woman, and why is she here, making such a racket?" The others shrugged in bewilderment.

"Ma, you want me to chuck them out?" Frankie whispered.

Tessa shook her head. "Don't give her the pleasure of feeling that important."

Now the funeral attendants handed a white rose each to Tessa and her children, so that they could take turns placing a flower on the coffin. Filomena was proud of Petrina, Johnny, Frankie, and Mario, who rose to the occasion with grace as they placed their flowers.

Tessa went last. She laid down her rose, then hesitated only momentarily to touch her fingers to her lips, and then to touch the coffin. This small gesture moved Filomena and the other wives to tears, which they hastily brushed away.

The funeral attendants stepped forward, one to escort the family back to their cars, the others to tend to the coffin. The ceremony was over; it was time to go.

But now the blond woman, as if on cue, sprang from her chair and lunged forward, flinging herself across the coffin, scattering the roses so carefully placed there.

"No!" she sobbed loudly, clutching at the sides. "Don't go, Gianni, don't go!"

Frankie stepped up immediately as if to pry the woman off his father's casket, but her two escorts moved to stop him. Johnny stepped in to assist Frankie, but the funeral director, seeing men mobilizing for a fight, quickly intervened and took the strange woman's arm as if to comfort her.

"So sorry," he said soothingly, skillfully handing her off to her sons, to direct them away from Frankie.

The woman, still howling, now whirled around, eyes blazing with fury, aiming her gaze directly at Tessa, and when she spoke, Filomena thought, it was like an actress in a melodrama, eager to deliver a carefully rehearsed line.

"Gianni belongs to *me* as well as you!" she shouted. "These are *his* sons!"

14

Family Council, Greenwich Village, 1943

As soon as the family returned home, a conference was convened in Tessa's study, which was a smaller, secondary parlor on the first floor at the back of her town house. But Filomena discovered that "family" meant only Tessa, Johnny, Frankie, Mario, and Petrina. The wives and children were not invited.

Lucy and Amie resignedly took the kids into Tessa's big dining room, where Stella, the cook, had left a sideboard of food for everyone. After they ate, Christopher, Gemma, and Amie's twin boys, Vinnie and Paulie, were already droopy with fatigue from the long day, so they offered no objections when their mothers finally announced that it was bedtime, and Lucy and Amie took them off to their town house.

Therefore Filomena found herself alone in Tessa's parlor with Petrina's daughter, Pippa, who was staying overnight in the guesthouse with her mother. In all the hubbub, Pippa had managed to wander unnoticed from the dining room to the door outside Tessa's private study, shamelessly eavesdropping until she got bored.

Filomena herself was wondering what was going on in that family meeting. Before leaving the cemetery, Tessa had spoken briefly to the strange woman, standing with her apart from the others, under a tree. Filomena had told Mario that she thought she recognized the men. He absorbed this silently. Then, abruptly, everyone had gotten into their own cars and departed.

"The fat lady is from Staten Island!" Pippa reported slyly to Filomena now, twirling, as if practicing a ballet move, to steady her nerves. "Uncle Johnny made some phone calls, and now he's going to give Grandma a full report." She wrinkled her nose. "Those weird people at the cemetery stank of perfume!"

"Yes, they did," Filomena admitted.

Pippa sighed deeply, as if wise beyond her eleven years. "Well, I'm off to bed," she said nonchalantly, cocking her head defiantly, as her mother might have. "We're going back to Rye tomorrow, because I have ballet class." She kissed Filomena on the cheek, as if paying homage to an old auntie, then went off to the guesthouse, to sleep in the bed that Filomena had once occupied when she'd first arrived.

Filomena finished her last sip of wine. Donna, the maid, had gone with Lucy and Amie to help them with the kids, so Filomena carried the dishes into the kitchen. She filled the basin with soapy hot water and let the dishes soak a little. Then she went to the pantry to fetch a dishcloth.

Standing there in the pantry, she heard the distinct voices of Tessa and her children, conversing on the other side of the wall. Filomena paused. She knew what Rosamaria would say. *Survival is more important than manners.*

Johnny was speaking, as if reporting to a committee. "Their name is Pericolo. The woman is called Alonza. The sons are Sergio and Ruffio. She told Ma at the cemetery that her sons have birth certificates with our last name and Pop's signature."

"Oh, come on! Any jackass could have forged that," Frankie burst out.

"Those boys have criminal records, which is why they aren't in the war overseas; they were tagged 4F, 'unfit for duty due to antisocial behavior,'" Johnny went on.

"What were they in jail for?" Frankie demanded.

"Ruffio, the younger one, got caught purse-snatching, stealing cars. Stupid things. But the older one, Sergio, he's violent—knife fights, beating people up for fun, you know, like a mental case. Too touchy, too emotional, his own worst enemy. As for the mother, people who've known her say she spent her whole life trying to latch on to one man after another who dumped her. Used sex to get them, when she was young, but now she just depends on these useless sons that she can't control anymore."

"Ma," Petrina said in a gentle tone, "you haven't told us what *you* think."

There was a silence, and then Tessa said, "I think that woman killed Gianni."

There was a chorus of exclamations and then Tessa continued, "Your father received a number of telephone calls that he never explained to me, usually at night. He said not to worry, but he always seemed upset after those calls. I think it was her."

Petrina said in a shocked tone, "Do you believe it's even possible that this woman's sons really are—?" She couldn't bring herself to finish the thought.

Tessa said in an even, steely voice, "No. Why wouldn't she have contacted him sooner, when they were younger and needed support? I do the accounts, and I saw nothing to indicate that Gianni ever gave money to her. Also, your father, in all this time, did not see fit to take these boys into any of his businesses. You all know your father is an honorable man. What do you think he would have done if he really believed those boys were his?"

Johnny said reflectively, "Ma's right. Even if he wanted to keep all this from us, Pop would have tried to help those guys, without causing our family any real pain."

"This Alonza may have met your father sometime in the past. But I suspect she just recently learned that he's become a man of wealth and respect," Tessa continued in her measured tone. "From what you've said, she sounds like the kind of weak woman who seeks to attach herself, at all costs, to the most successful man she meets, any way she can, including lies and threats. Like a drowning woman who thinks she sees a life preserver."

Petrina, who'd been listening closely, thought it entirely possible that Gianni had had a brief fling with that promiscuous woman, perhaps had even been seen in public having a drink with her, and this alone, in the tangled world of racketeers, could be problematic if a fuss were made about it. But Petrina was also convinced that such an affair had not produced those sons. She sensed this, viscerally and utterly. "That Alonza has the face of a liar who doesn't even believe her own lie," she noted aloud.

"She won't stop," Johnny warned. "She told Ma she'd take us to court."

"How does this woman dare to threaten us?" Frankie demanded, outraged. "Take us to court, is she kidding? Pop didn't leave them anything in his will. What does she think she's going to do in court?"

"She isn't really going to court," Johnny surmised. "It's just blackmail. She's threatening to put Pop's businesses under scrutiny."

"She's stupid, then," Frankie retorted. "Doesn't she know that people disappear every day for a lot less than that?"

"She might be missed," Johnny warned. "She's well-known in that little neighborhood of hers in Staten Island. Look, we don't want her running around making noise about us to anybody. It would bring us too much attention, and we can't have that, not now, when there's so much money coming in."

"Why don't we go to Strollo?" Frankie objected impatiently. "Strollo showed up at the wake for Pop, didn't he?"

"Strollo will tell us we have to settle it ourselves," Mario said unexpectedly.

"How do you know that?" Frankie said testily. "We can ask him, can't we?"

"No." It was Tessa's voice, cold and firm. "When you ask such a man for a favor, you are in debt to him, and what he asks in return will always be something that you don't want to do. You boys already received a favor not so long ago, have you forgotten? You can be sure that *they* have not forgotten. One day that favor will come due. Do you want to remind them about it now and awaken the sleeping dogs?"

"What's she talking about?" Petrina asked, sounding baffled.

"Never mind," Johnny said swiftly, not wanting to tell her what had happened on that night when Amie's first husband had to be disposed of.

Mario spoke in his calm, deliberate way. "What exactly does she want from us?"

"She wants to be *me*," Tessa said. "She can't ever be me. But we can make her feel she's won something from me. We can make her feel that her boys are almost as important as you. She said she wants us to let them 'in' on our business."

"Why should we do that?" Frankie said in disbelief. "You give them an inch, they'll ask for a yard. When people who aren't used to money get some, it goes to their heads. And somehow, they'll bring us all down with them. Termites always do."

"*Silenzio,* Franco," Tessa commanded with more force now. "Do you think for one moment I would give away anything important to those people? Do you think I'd give her the pebble from the bottom of my shoe? Tell him, Johnny. Tell him what we can do."

Johnny cleared his throat. "We can set up Alonza in a better house. A nice one on Staten Island, to impress her friends. We will own it, but she'll live there rent-free."

"Also, we'll give the sons something," Tessa said. "Not in any of our businesses; you know your father has been working to move us into more legitimate work, away from the Bosses. We cannot let anyone jeopardize our plans. So we must steer Alonza's sons to some other enterprise that will keep them busy, and away from us. Set them up in respectable enough work as a test, to see if they are dependable, hardworking, honest—or not. If not, well, a lazy man can always find trouble, like cheese in a mousetrap."

Frankie whistled admiringly at this strategy. "Give 'em enough rope to climb, or else to hang themselves with. Fine. Where do we send them? Chicago? New Orleans?"

Johnny said quickly, "Florida. Let 'em work for Stewie, he owes Pop a favor. He's looking for people to run his ice-cream parlors and souvenir shops. They're mostly legit. If those boys save their money, they'll do well. It'll keep 'em a thousand miles away from us. But if the Pericolo brothers are looking for a big, easy score, they'll go astray—with the racetracks, the bookies, the truck hijackers who steal cigarettes, booze, electronics. It's their choice."

"You saw their faces. Those morons haven't worked hard at anything in their lives. I bet they can't even tie their shoes straight. Any bets?" Frankie responded.

"But we'll give them a shot at making something of themselves," Johnny said.

"It might work," Mario admitted. "It just might work."

"All right, then. We agree," Tessa said in a tone of finality. "Solve it without blood. Set them up in business with that man in Florida. If they are honorable, they will become independent and thrive. But if they squander this opportunity—well, debt is something most people fall into without ever noticing it."

"Yeah, Florida's waters are swimming with bait," Frankie observed. "But if the Pericolos don't play straight with the alligators down there, they won't live to bother us anymore." A silence settled on the group. Tessa pushed back her chair and rose.

"It's time for sleep," she said firmly. "Tomorrow there will be much to do."

Filomena, who'd been holding her breath, now scurried to the kitchen sink to resume washing the dishes. Tessa went directly to her bedroom. The brothers emerged with Petrina, just as the maid returned from helping Lucy and Amie with their kids.

"For God's sake," Petrina said impatiently to Filomena. "You don't have to do dishes around here! Mario, tell your wife she's the lady of the house now."

Petrina's voice had an exhausted, bitter edge to it. The maid stepped forward to take the dishcloth from Filomena. The others went into the dining room, grateful for something to drink and eat from the sideboard, with its platters of sandwiches, olives, and salads, and carafes of water and wine, and coffee on the warmer. Filomena filled a plate for Mario.

"Ma looked exhausted," Johnny said as he sat down tiredly. "She doesn't need these clowns popping into her life. She was pretty cool about it, though."

"You think Ma knew about this Alonza woman all along?" Frankie asked curiously.

"I couldn't tell, from her face," Johnny admitted.

Petrina said quickly, "Maybe she sensed it, and didn't really want to know."

"What does it matter, anyway?" Mario asked, looking weary, too.

"I wish I'd realized Pop needed our help. I'd have dispensed with that bitch and her bastards once and for all," Frankie said darkly.

"Stop it, Frankie!" Petrina said. "That's just *why* he didn't discuss it with you." She jerked her head at Filomena. "And don't talk that way in front of Mario's blushing bride."

"Ma's right, we all need sleep before we say anything stupid," Mario said, calm as ever. "Go to bed, Petrina. It's been a long day."

He spoke gently; at first Petrina balked at being ordered to go to bed like a naughty child. But when Mario touched her arm with his fingertips, her expression softened immediately. Mario's voice had taken on that resonant, caressing quality, which Filomena loved; but now it irritated her to hear him use that same tone as a tool to placate his possessive, mercurial sister.

Is that all it is? Filomena wondered. *A voice meant to tame a horse or a woman?*

For the first time, she wished they could get away from this lively, possibly dangerous family that had brought her to this strange new world—which, perhaps, wasn't so very new or different from the old world, after all.

15

Greenwich Village, November-December 1943

The holiday season began with a burst of energy in New York City, for there was money to be both made and spent, in a frenzy that could not be matched at any other time of the year. Gianni's family had to really rally to help one another cope with their loss and carry on their business. Tessa was clearly in charge now, and her sons were determined to make it as painless as possible for her. It was important, too, that the rest of the world understood that Gianni's sons were here—ready, willing, able, and determined to protect their various enterprises.

Filomena was touched by the courage they all exhibited in spite of their palpable grief. Her loyalty deepened, and she wanted to help in every way that she could. She sensed that she must get closer to the other wives, so she got Mario to find her an English-language class, which met twice a week. It helped. And Amie advised her, "Work with Mario. It will keep you close."

Filomena took this advice to heart. Mario's jewelry shop on Thompson Street filled her with pride. He had some of his own designs and other exquisite pieces to sell, and he excelled at altering a setting if a customer wished it. This first year would be critical to his success. They'd opened in October and were now doing brisk business as the Christmas gift-buying spree commenced.

Filomena had assisted him in all phases of the opening, including decorating the front windows with silver, gold, and red stars, and real pine boughs.

Every day Mario unlocked their shop and took the jewelry out of the safe, and Filomena arranged it all in the elegant wood-and-glass display cases. At closing time, they locked everything up again and retreated to their back room to go over the orders, invoices, payments, and profits. They sat with their heads together, tallying everything up.

Tessa let the whole neighborhood know about Mario's new shop, which proved to be excellent publicity. One evening Tessa surprised Filomena by appearing at the store, promptly pulling up a chair in the back room, and ensconcing herself in front of the adding machine, looking ready to do serious work as she produced a brand-new ledger.

Mario said patiently, "Mama, we already have an account book. I'll show you."

He disappeared into a closet to get his records. Tessa turned to Filomena and hissed under her breath, "Why are you here? You should be at home. Why aren't you pregnant yet? Your job is to have babies and keep my son out of this war."

"Well, I can't make babies at home alone," Filomena responded lightly, taken aback but trying not to feel hurt. Tessa eyed her resentfully as Mario returned with his records.

"Mario, read me today's numbers," Tessa commanded. "I will add them up." She glanced dismissively at Filomena. "Go home, and help cook your husband's dinner."

Seeing Filomena's outraged expression, Mario opened the ledger and said quickly, "No, Mama, look! My wife has a gift. She can add whole columns of three-figure numbers in her head. She is better than any machine—and faster, too! She did all this."

Now Tessa looked skeptical. "Show me," she said.

Mario turned the page to one of today's lists, which had not yet been added up, and handed it to Filomena. "This one needs a total," he said, smiling.

Filomena studied the page raptly. Then, after a moment, she picked up the pencil that Mario gave her, drew a line at the bottom of the column, and wrote the total that was in her head. Numbers had individual personalities to her, and when grouped together in hundred-number combinations they seemed to dance and sing in tidy choruses, all at a glance.

"Go ahead, Mama, check it on your machine," Mario said proudly. "It will take you three times as long as she does it! I tell you, she has a gift." Then, sensing that diplomacy was needed, he added, "You were so smart to find me this wife!"

Tessa took the book and stolidly inputted the figures on the machine. When she reached the end, Mario peered at it. "You see?" he said triumphantly. "I told you so!"

Tessa said abruptly, "You have forgotten something, Mario." But he'd already reached into his breast pocket and pulled out an envelope, thick with cash.

"No, I haven't." He stooped down to kiss Tessa's cheek. "How could I forget?"

Tessa took the envelope and put it in her black silk purse with the gold frame, which made a snap of satisfaction. She rose and smiled now, cupping his face in her hands before kissing him. But as soon as Mario stepped away to answer the telephone, Tessa stared hard at Filomena and said, "Remember what your *real* job is."

As Tessa swept out majestically, her long black skirts and coat billowing like a regal bird's plumage, Filomena thought of all she'd heard about the evil eye; it was the gaze of envy, when people coveted your good fortune—love or health or youth or money—and wished you harm. Such a gaze, the superstition went, could cause bodily injury unless you warded it off quickly. So Filomena crossed herself, and then did the same across her belly.

When Mario returned from the phone, Filomena said, "What was in that envelope? Did you give your mother our money?"

"I didn't *give* her money," Mario said carefully. "I repaid her."

"What does that mean?" Filomena asked unflinchingly.

"She financed the opening of this shop," Mario explained. "You don't think gemstones grow on trees, do you? Or these jewelry cases? Or the shop's rent?"

"I don't understand. You buy gems and gold from the dealers, don't you?"

"They sell them to my mother," Mario said, correcting her. "Because most of them owe Ma money, so they give her a much better rate for our supplies than we'd get on the open market. You see, my family helped a lot of our neighbors start their businesses, when no bank would give them a loan. Pop was a silent partner for many of them, for years, until they were able to pay us back."

Filomena studied his face, which was calm and unrevealing. Yet she sensed that there was more he wasn't telling her. "And the rent?" she asked. "Does the landlord of this building owe your family money, too? Is that why we got a good price for the rent?"

"No," he said. "That's not why."

Filomena felt herself growing irritated. "Then—how *did* we get it?" she persisted.

"She owns this building," Mario said simply.

"Your mother is our *landlady*?" Filomena asked.

For the first time, Mario looked annoyed. "Why should any of this matter to you? You know nothing of the world. Do you have any idea what the rent on this place would be if our landlord were a stranger? This is New York City, my dear!"

As they locked up and went outside to walk home, Filomena thought of all the merchants who bowed and flattered and deferred to Tessa. It had made Filomena feel like an important lady, too. Now she felt like just another one of the merchants. Indebted, too!

"Mario, I thought you wanted us to be independent," she objected.

"I do, of course." There were dark warning clouds hovering

over his expression now.

"But how can we be—?" she persisted.

"When we make our profits, we'll be able to open more stores, maybe even buy our own buildings," Mario explained with more than a trace of impatience. "Really, you don't need to think about these things. I will take care of all of this." Then he said more gently, "Let's go home now. I'm hungry!"

A WEEK LATER, TESSA CALLED FILOMENA INTO HER INNER SANCTUM— her little study at the back of the house—where she sat at a rolltop desk. Filomena had never been in this room before. She took the chair beside the desk. For a moment, Tessa said nothing as she sorted some papers.

Then she rose and stepped inside a closet. Filomena happened to glance up at the window, which at this hour was shaded by a tree outside, so it acted as a mirror reflecting Tessa in her closet. Fascinated, Filomena watched as Tessa extracted a key from the pocket of an apron that hung in the closet and used it to unlock a drawer in her desk. She reached in and took out a book. It was a thick, red-and-black ledger.

"Mario and I have had a little talk," Tessa said in a slightly guarded tone. "He explained that you are a lot like me, in the way that you work to protect your husband. When I was a young wife, I, too, worked by my husband's side. In work and at home, a good wife should know what her husband's needs are, even before *he* knows."

Filomena remained silent, waiting to see if, indeed, Mario had charmed his mother into accepting his wife's work. Tessa opened the ledger, but then she put another book on top of the left-side page of the ledger to obscure it. She pointed only to the right-side page and said, "Go ahead. Add up these numbers, and write down your total."

Filomena took a deep breath and did as she was told.

"Very good." Tessa wrote it down, then turned the page, again covering the left pages and revealing only the right. "Add these now." They continued for a couple of pages. When they were done, Tessa closed the book and locked it away.

She had timed it perfectly, because now they could hear Frankie and Sal the chauffeur arriving via a side door that opened into the large kitchen, where most supplies were carried in. Sal was evidently making multiple trips to unload the car with crates of supplies for the cook. But Frankie came into Tessa's study.

Casually he placed on the desk a rubber-banded wad of envelopes that looked like the one Mario had given Tessa, so Filomena understood that these, too, were stuffed with cash payments.

"It's all there," Frankie said briefly, waiting.

"You may go," Tessa said to Filomena. As soon as she rose from the chair, Frankie sat there. On her way out the door, Filomena saw that Frankie was reporting each total that was written on each envelope so that Tessa could record it in her ledger.

Filomena heard Tessa ask her son, "Any problems?"

Frankie said, "No, Ma. I've been collecting our rent ever since I could walk. But, we must make extra cash payouts this week— holiday 'gifts' to the cops, you know?"

As Filomena passed the kitchen, Johnny and Amie arrived. Johnny was nonchalantly carrying canvas sacks that he, too, brought into Tessa's study.

Amie saw Filomena's gaze following Johnny. All month, the gamblers in the back room of the bar had been roaring loudly with special holiday cheer, so jocular that they didn't care who heard them—for the pot of money that they bet was terrifyingly high at this time of year. All of this was written on Amie's face, and Filomena sensed it.

"People will bet on anything," Amie said quietly. "Especially around Christmastime. Even the little old ladies. They love their lottery numbers, and their saints' days, and they believe in the big score just as much as the high rollers do."

AS THE YEAR DREW EVEN CLOSER TO ITS FESTIVE END, WITH FROST ON the windowpanes and wisps of snowflakes in the air, the city became even more aglow and lively, humming like a beehive in anticipation of Christmas. Men dressed as Santa Claus rang loud bells, asking for contributions; pushcart peddlers madly and perilously trundled their wares while dodging the overwhelming, honking traffic; and the brisk wind made pedestrians shriek and scurry.

Filomena had never known such cold weather before, and yet, she'd never had such luxurious clothes to keep her warm: skirts of fine wool lined with silk; soft cashmere sweaters and wool stockings; sumptuously shaped coats and hats trimmed with real fur. Even her feet and fingers were kept snuggly in wool-lined, buttersoft leather. Such high-quality goods were all the more precious in wartime.

"We have partners in the garment district," Mario said laconically when Filomena asked how all this was possible.

Enormous, beribboned gift baskets and wrapped packages began to appear at the house, sometimes delivered personally by the tradesmen who were paying special holiday tribute to Tessa and her family. Often, Sal and the "boys"—Johnny, Frankie, and Mario—received these gifts at work, enough to fill up the backseat and trunk of the car, which had to be unloaded at the house. The packages were deposited inside the kitchen pantry or placed under the enormous Christmas tree in the parlor, which wasn't even decorated yet.

"The whole family must wait until Christmas Eve to trim the tree together," Lucy explained. "It's a sacred tradition, like everything else around here!"

Indeed, this was the season when Johnny and Frankie made the rounds of giving generous donations to the family's charities—the church, the school, a ladies' club that fed the elderly, a war-widows-and-orphans' fund.

Meanwhile, Filomena and Mario continued to do a very brisk business at the jewelry store, staying open late even on Christmas

Eve, when last-minute shoppers rushed in, made quick purchases, and happily departed with their shiny wrapped parcels, which Filomena had tied with ribbons of red and blue and gold and silver.

"That's the last customer!" she gasped finally, after the front door closed with a jingle behind the departing shopper.

"Good!" said Mario, pulling her close to kiss her. Filomena hugged him, wishing that she could give him one special gift—the child that he and his family desired. And yet, not yet. But soon, it must come! She buried her face in his neck.

Mario, with his uncanny way of sensing exactly what she was thinking, said, "I know my mother's been pressing you about babies. You've been so patient with her."

"Every week, when I go to help her with her 'book,' she asks me if I have any 'news,'" Filomena confessed. "Oh, how I wish I did!"

"What a world we live in, eh? Everyone thinks they can talk out loud about something we must do so privately in our bedroom! Very well," Mario said teasingly, "we'll just have to spend a lot more time in bed together, è vero?" He kissed her again.

Filomena sighed contentedly and glanced out the plate-glass window, just in time to see two stout figures emerging from a café across the street, and, even before she figured out who they were, she felt a cold shudder ripple through her, beneath her warm wool clothing.

"It's the Pericolo brothers," Mario said, following her gaze.

"I thought you said they went to Florida," Filomena said in a low voice.

"They did. We set them up nicely."

"Quick, lock the door before they see us!" she whispered.

"No, you never hide," Mario said abruptly, straightening up. His jaw tightened as the bell on the front door jingled when the men entered the shop.

"Ciao, Mario!" said the older one, Sergio, in an insultingly familiar tone.

"*Ciao!*" echoed the younger one, Ruffio, jutting out his chin.

Filomena could not help noticing Sergio's shirt cuffs, sticking out from his coat sleeves with the buttons in the wrong holes. Both men smelled of coffee, hair oil, and cologne.

Disgusted, she busied herself by getting her coat and hat off the hooks and handing Mario his, as an obvious hint that the store was closed and she wanted to go home. But she kept her eyes averted. She was remembering what she'd overheard Johnny telling the family, about how Sergio in particular was a violent man.

Sergio was gesturing at the nearly empty jewelry cases. "Only a few pieces left! Do you make all that jewelry yourself? *Bella!*" he said in an ugly tone.

"Nah, I wish I could," Mario said modestly.

Ruffio's gaze traveled around the shop as if lusting after the space, the fixtures, the holiday decor. "We saw from our table in the window that you had so many customers in this candy shop of yours," he said with a smirk. "You must be making a nice profit! *Ti saluto!*"

"I'm sure you are also doing well in Florida," Mario said indifferently.

"Ah, not as well as you, my friend!" Sergio said, spreading his palms.

"Nice and warm there this season," Mario replied. "You'll have better luck in the New Year." The brothers had wandered to the back room, where customers weren't allowed.

"No. Things didn't work out too good for us there. We can't go back," Sergio said firmly, somewhat threateningly. "But we got something that should interest you."

The younger man, Ruffio, reached into his pocket and pulled out a black cloth, which he now laid on Mario's work-table. Ruffio unfolded its four corners to reveal an irreverent tangle of jewelry, none of it in boxes—gold watches, various rings, sterling belt buckles, an assortment of chains and bracelets, all mixed together.

"You see," said Sergio, "we were inspired by your example

here, Mario. We're willing to cut you in. We just need a man like you to get these stones out of the settings. Melt down the gold and silver, too. You know what I'm talking about, eh? Then, we all make a nice profit," he said with a broad gesture that included Filomena.

Very calmly, Mario refolded the four cloth corners back over the stolen loot. "I'm not a fence," he said firmly.

Sergio opened his coat to show his gun in a holster. "Get started," he said.

"Easy, easy!" Ruffio said in a false voice, as if they'd rehearsed the whole scene.

Mario, still unruffled, said, "So, you showed me your gun. Then, I and my brothers will show you ours. What good is that? If you were really my father's sons, you'd remember what he always said: 'Tough guys die young.'"

"Yeah, sure, he told us," Sergio said unconvincingly. "Get to work on the swag."

"I tell you, I'm not very good at this." But to Filomena's astonishment, Mario switched on his table-lamp, sat down in his chair, and picked up a ring. He studied the piece, held it under his magnifier, then reached for a tool. He began to narrate how a stone must be removed from its setting, but then in mid-sentence he exclaimed, "Ay!" just as his tool made a terrible scratching sound.

"Hey, watch it!" Sergio exclaimed.

Mario handed him back the damaged piece with an apologetic shrug. "I'm only a shopkeeper," he said with feigned helplessness. "You need someone with more talent to do this job." Filomena was impressed by the convincingly hapless look Mario wore.

"You can say that again," Ruffio said in disgust.

Sergio appeared mistrustful but said impatiently, "We're wasting our time. Let's get out of here." But he gave Mario a look of warning, saying meaningfully, "You can't let your mama run your life." He jerked his head at Filomena before returning his gaze to Mario to add, "Women are nice for some things, cooking and making babies. But you and I need to talk business, man to man. And then, we come to a better arrangement."

Filomena could not help a gasp of indignation at this obvious slight to Tessa as well as herself. Resolutely, she put on her coat. Mario shrugged into his, then switched off his lamp. They both moved purposefully toward the front door, so the Pericolo brothers, looking annoyed, had to follow. Mario turned out the showroom lights.

"Good night, gentlemen," he said firmly, holding the door open to let them out.

A policeman on his beat strolled by, looked up, and touched the tip of his baton to the tip of his hat at Mario, who nodded back at him. Filomena had seen that policeman collect his Christmas payment from Mario only just yesterday.

The presence of the police seemed to clinch the evening for the two visitors.

"We'll see you again," Ruffio promised hurriedly.

"*Buon Natale* to your family, especially your mother," Sergio said meaningfully as he sauntered out.

Mario's fingers clenched around his keys, and for a moment Filomena thought he might actually strike the man who'd mentioned his mother so insolently. But he paused in his doorway, watching as they disappeared around the corner.

Filomena, barely waiting until they were gone, spluttered, "Who do they think they are? How dare they come here and insult us all!" Mario didn't answer, just pulled her back into the shop, pushed the front door closed, and locked it, pulling down the shade. "Aren't we going home?" Filomena asked anxiously.

"Not yet," he said decisively. "I want to bring the strongbox of our jewels to Ma's safe at home. We'll take all the money with us, too. The banks aren't open tomorrow for deposits, and neither is our shop. I don't want to leave anything valuable here tonight. Let's call Sal to come and pick us up with the car."

Filomena muttered, "The whole shop reeks of their cologne!

We all noticed it at the cemetery because it made Pippa sneeze so. But I thought it was the mother who wore it. Such vanity for such unimpressive men!"

Mario observed, "They are too desperate to be successful businessmen, and too hotheaded to be successful criminals. They were jittery; they must have someone pretty bad chasing them, most likely for money they owe somebody."

"What are we going to do if they come back?" Filomena demanded. "We can't have them hanging around us here."

"I'll talk to my brothers. We'll have to handle this," Mario agreed.

Filomena helped him gather their valuables. She did not relax until Sal arrived and they were safely ensconced in the car, and driving off in the frosty night.

16

Christmas 1943

When Filomena and Mario returned home on Christmas Eve, the family was already gathered in the big parlor to decorate the gigantic Christmas tree, which towered over everyone, even the adults. There was a crackling fire in the fireplace, and its mantel was decorated with boughs of balsam and gilded pine cones. Gianni's favorite chair in the corner was decorated with his best scarf, as if he'd just gotten up to get a newspaper and would soon return. Somehow this was comforting.

"Come in, and have some Christmas cheer!" young Christopher intoned to Filomena and Mario while standing at the front door, pretending to be the host and imitating Frankie's swagger, despite the fact that Chris looked like a little drummer boy in his new blue suit.

Lucy said meaningfully to Frankie, "This boy thinks strutting like a gangster makes him a man. Hmm, I guess he's seen too many tough guys . . . in the movies!"

Frankie, who was pouring drinks for the grown-ups at a round table covered with a snowy white lace tablecloth, said to Christopher, "Hey, kid. Tough guys chase fast money, fast cars, fast women—and a fast trip to the cemetery. Got that?"

Mario grinned as Filomena heard that familiar warning of

Gianni's again tonight. Chris, undeterred, stuck his thumbs in his red holiday suspenders and said, "Got it, pal!"

"Come over here and I'll 'pal' you," Frankie said affectionately. "And I'll tell Saint Nick to take all your Christmas presents back to the North Pole."

"Am I getting a baseball bat?" Chris demanded.

"Depends. Go get me some more ice," Frankie replied. Chris bounded obediently to the kitchen. Frankie said, "Where's our pitcher and our shortstop? Vinnie, how's your pitching arm? Lemme see. Paulie, let's see how you catch."

He tossed a cloth reindeer ornament and watched Paulie catch it. "Attaboy!"

Lucy observed their camaraderie wistfully. Frankie loved all three boys and had enjoyed picking out their holiday gifts. But she knew he'd like to have a son of his own, no matter how he assured her that they had "enough kids in this family."

Amie was watching, too, but she was concerned that her normally rambunctious sons seemed a little subdued, speaking only to each other in low murmurs, and halfheartedly pushing their little trucks across the floor under the tree.

"I hope the twins aren't coming down with something," she fretted to Johnny.

"Nah," he said, eyeing his sons as he handed them strands of silver tinsel for the tree, "they're just used to too many gifts. We spoil them rotten."

"Hey!" said Lucy's daughter, Gemma, who was sitting in a corner counting the contents of a green-and-red holiday envelope. Gemma's brow was furrowed in earnest confusion. "How come Grandma gave all the boys twice as much money as I got?"

"Shh, she'll hear you," Lucy chided. Catching Filomena's eye, Lucy told her daughter apologetically, "It's because they're boys, honey. Grandma is old-fashioned."

"Well, that stinks!" Gemma said disconsolately. "I'm older than the twins."

"Watch your language, little girl," Frankie commented.

Lucy confided to Filomena, "Tessa never gives them toys for Christmas. Only money. She says she wants to teach them to be 'serious.'"

"Where is Ma?" Mario asked.

"In her study, where else?" Frankie answered.

Filomena and Mario went to deposit their treasures from the shop into Tessa's safe. But in the hallway, they saw a silky-voiced, silky-haired man in a camel-hair coat standing by Tessa's desk. Mario signaled to Filomena to back up and discreetly wait for the visitor to leave, but not before Filomena saw Tessa hand over an impressive bundle of thickly-filled envelopes to this man, who placed them into a briefcase. "You'll take it to Strollo tonight, yes, Domenico?" Tessa was saying to the man.

"Of course—right now, in fact," he replied with a bow.

So, it's Tessa's turn to pay tribute, Filomena thought, remembering the name of Strollo. He was the *capo* who ran Greenwich Village; he'd walked into Gianni's wake and placed a flower on him. Tessa now poured Domenico a drink in a crystal cordial glass, and she politely drank one herself as they said *"Buon Natale."* Then Domenico left, nodding to Mario on his way out.

"Who is *he*?" Filomena asked Mario as they moved toward Tessa's parlor.

"Pop's lawyer," he said quietly. He gave Tessa a kiss and told her, "I need to put a few things in the safe tonight. Didn't want to leave them in the shop while it's closed." He handed her the jewelry sacks and strongbox of cash, which she put in the big safe in her closet. When she re-emerged, Mario said, "The Pericolos are back in town," and he explained what had happened at the shop. "They talked like they screwed up in Florida."

Tessa looked unsurprised. "I had Johnny make inquiries, and his friend in Florida says that those boys are incapable of taking orders from anybody. The Pericolos refused to keep working for our friend down there, and they gambled what they earned, lost more than they had, and borrowed money from someone else, which they must now repay."

Tessa glanced at the items on her desk and continued, "I received a Christmas card from their mother, Alonza. It was just an excuse to make more demands." She picked up the card and read the handwritten message aloud. "She says, *Every year at Christmas, Gianni gave us gifts and money. I hope you will do the same, in his memory.*" She put the card down. "I have no records of your father ever doing such a thing. But I have arranged to meet with Alonza after Christmas, for tea. She and those boys need a firmer hand. We'll talk about it with your brothers, before I go to see her."

OUTSIDE THE HOUSE, PETRINA SAID TO HER DRIVER, "THANKS, Charlie," as she and Pippa alighted from their car, and her chauffeur drove off. Petrina noticed the lawyer Domenico just getting into his own auto, and she waved at him to wait.

"Pippa, take the presents inside. I'll be right there," she said to her daughter.

Then Petrina hurried down the sidewalk, still slippery from the falling snow, to catch up with the family lawyer. "Can we talk inside your car?" she asked.

Domenico opened the passenger door for her and she slipped inside. He went around the auto to take his seat, and he turned on the engine to warm it up. He was a handsome man, older than Petrina but younger than her mother. "What can I do for you?" he asked.

Petrina took a deep breath. "Richard just gave me a big Christmas present today. He wanted to surprise me, so he had it delivered to my house early this morning, when I was the only one at home. I thought it was a florist when the bell rang. But no, it was a man to 'serve' me with these papers. Does it mean what I think? He wants to divorce me?"

Domenico took a quick glance at the pages. "Yes," he said. He paused. "I have to ask you this. Did you do anything—have an affair, neglect your child—?"

"*Me?* Of course not!" Petrina said, outraged. She'd expected this man to be professional, but he sounded as old-fashioned as her parents, blaming *her,* the wife. Indignantly she said, "If anyone's to blame, it's Richard. *He's* the one having the affair! With a girl who's twenty-two years old, the daughter of a judge. Richard's family is behind this, they all want him to divorce *me* so he can marry *her.* These two fathers expect him to run for the Senate someday! They say she's 'more suitable' to be a politician's wife. You can't be around his family for more than five minutes before they have to let you know that they all came over on the godforsaken *Mayflower.* All I can say is, that *Mayflower* must have been some gigantic boat—*everybody* claims they came on there. Richard used to be more modest and say that his ancestors were all horse thieves. Not anymore! He's ambitious now. He says it's not *me* who's the problem, it's just that he can't have even a hint of criminal connections with *a family like mine.*"

Domenico had waited patiently for Petrina to run out of steam. Now he said, "Fine. Then you can accuse him of infidelity. They know this, so I expect they'll want to make a settlement and keep it as quiet as possible. That may work to your advantage."

"But I don't want a divorce!" Petrina exclaimed. "This is just his mother and sister's idea. They peck away like hens at both of us. They criticize me and praise *her,* over and over again, and it gets to him. If we could just get away from his family, be on our own . . ." Her words trailed off at the obvious impossibility of this. Then she said in a small voice, "Nobody's ever gotten a divorce in my family's parish. The priest won't let me take communion."

Domenico patted her hand awkwardly. "As your lawyer, and as your friend, I advise you not to try to force a man who no longer wishes to be your husband to stay with you. From what you have told me of Richard's family, they would not have gone ahead with these documents unless they were prepared to fight—and win. I will read this more closely and handle it for you. But you must help me. I want you to write down everything you can about whatever wrongs your husband has done you. If there is evidence of his affair, I want whatever you've got—receipts for gifts he gave this girl he's seeing, for example. Let me know if you have any influential friends who might testify against your husband, give evidence of his bad behavior—and your good behavior. Give me anything that makes him look bad, anything that might embarrass him if it were made public."

Petrina whispered, "But I don't *hate* him. Richard and I—it's not like we were ever *enemies*."

"You are now," Domenico said bluntly. "Put aside your heartache and treat it like business. You are in the business of protecting yourself and your daughter financially. Collect all the evidence you have. I don't expect to have to use it in court. But if they know we have it, they might be more inclined to be—more reasonable."

WHEN PETRINA ENTERED THE PARLOR, SHE SAW THAT HER DAUGHTER had caused a small commotion. After depositing several packages under the tree, Pippa had shrugged out of her coat and danced around in her green velvet dress, showing off her new pink satin ballet shoes that were specially built to make it possible for her to dance *en pointe.* All the children were impressed with the sound the toe shoes made on the wooden floor.

"I never heard the Sugar Plum Fairy clomp onstage like that," Gemma said.

"That's because the orchestra drowns her out," Pippa informed her haughtily.

Then she turned to her male cousins and announced, "My father took me to his club and taught me how to shoot skeet." At their blank looks she said, "Don't you *know?*" She mimed the shooting process while saying, "You tell a servant to 'pull' and he releases a kind of little cannon that fires a round clay target up into the air, and you have to shoot it to bits. It's called a clay pigeon."

"That's dumb," Christopher said. "Why would you shoot a piece of clay?"

"So you don't kill *real* birds, dumbo yourself," Pippa retorted.

"I'd rather shoot bears," Chris replied, shrugging.

"I'd rather shoot Richard," Petrina grumbled under her breath. Aloud she said to the maid, "Don't bother to set a plate for my husband, Donna, he's celebrating Christmas at home with his folks." The maid was carrying a tray of filled champagne glasses. Petrina picked up one gratefully and took a deep gulp.

"Stop yakking, folks, and pitch in," Johnny said to everyone. "Otherwise we won't get this tree trimmed before midnight, and Saint Nick will fly right by us."

Filomena had noticed instantly that Petrina appeared distressed, even though she looked like a Renaissance queen in her deep-red velvet dress and a stunning necklace of gold fan-shaped objects that were like the rays of the sun, emanating from beneath her beautiful but troubled-looking face. Petrina's mouth looked sad, despite its cheerful, cherry-colored lipstick. Her gaze swept the room and settled on Filomena, who was standing arm-in-arm with Mario, her head on his shoulder.

Petrina said spitefully, "Mario, isn't your wife drinking? Or does she just like to watch? She watches everything, you know."

"Pull in those claws, kitty cat," Frankie said, putting a hand on her shoulder.

"I'm tired from the traffic. I need to freshen up," Petrina said abruptly, finishing her drink. As if refusing to go all the way to the guesthouse, she stalked up the stairs to the bedroom that had once been hers but now belonged to Filomena and Mario.

Mario pulled his wife aside and said in a low voice, "Petrina can be a pain, but she's only trying to hide the fact that she's got a soft heart. And she's brave. I'll tell you a secret which you must keep between us. Once, when I was a kid, there was a shooting of a Big Boss in a restaurant on Coney Island. We were there. Bullets were flying. Know what she did? She threw herself on top of me. She would have taken a bullet for me. That's Petrina."

Filomena murmured, "I understand. Did you tell your brothers that the Pericolos came to our shop today?" Mario nodded. "What do they think?" she asked.

"We've agreed to let Ma see if she can reason with Alonza, since it's already arranged," he said. "But we are prepared for a fight."

There was a sudden scuffle behind the sofa. Frankie had caught Christopher teaching the twins how to shoot dice, or "craps," and then demanding that four-year-old Vinnie "pay up" what he owed. Chris had held up a threatening index finger and, in a perfect parody of Frankie, fixed Vinnie with a meaningful gaze, saying, "Fork it over, or else you'll get a little visit from my man Sal." Vinnie laughed, but Frankie, seeing this, went white with embarrassment, then seized Chris by the shoulders.

"Hey!" Frankie said severely. "Don't *you* try to be a big shot. It is *not* who *you* are. You get me?" Chris looked utterly startled, his ears red with shame. Filomena comprehended that Frankie was horrified to see this child emulating the very life Frankie was trying to protect him from, but Chris misunderstood, hearing only that, as a stepchild, he was not, and never would be, accepted as a real member of this family.

"Gather 'round, everyone!" Amie said quickly, going to a brand-new player piano that had been delivered just this morning, as Johnny's gift to her. They'd decided to place it here in Tessa's house for family celebrations. Amie now demonstrated how the rolls of music were inserted, to make the piano keys move on their own, magically, as if a ghost were playing a tune. This fascinated the children.

The adults stopped what they were doing to cluster around the piano and sing Christmas favorites that they all knew. They sang song after song, and Tessa finally emerged from her study.

"Where's Petrina?" Tessa asked, slightly irritated. "I thought I heard her voice."

"She's upstairs, Ma," Mario said. "I'll tell her you're looking for her."

"I'll do it," Filomena offered. She was the only one who didn't know the English words to these Yuletide carols, which made her feel slightly alienated. Besides, Petrina's slumped shoulders had seemed pitiful to her, and she could almost hear Rosamaria's voice advising, *Go help her. You need a female friend in this family. So does Petrina.*

So Filomena slipped quietly upstairs. Petrina's clothes were lying on the bed that Filomena shared with Mario. A pair of red high heels had been kicked into a corner, near silk stockings dropped in a coil, like snakes. A beautiful beaded handbag was spilled open on the glass-topped dresser. The door to the adjoining bathroom was ajar, and someone was splashing in Mario's tub. In the stillness, Filomena heard a woman softly sobbing. Filomena hesitated, then knocked on the partially open bathroom door.

Petrina leaned forward to peer around it. She looked like a little girl, her hair tied haphazardly atop her head with a ribbon, and her face bobbing above a sea of violet-scented bubbles from a bottle that Mario had given Filomena. When Petrina saw Filomena, she didn't speak. She only covered her face with her hands.

"To hell with Christmas," she said in a muffled voice.

Filomena silently reached for the biggest, fluffiest towel and held it open for her. Petrina sighed and stood up from the billowing bubble bath, her body so beautifully sculpted that she resembled images of the birth of Venus, arriving on the foam of the sea. Regal but disconsolate, she allowed Filomena to wrap the towel around as a servant might. But Filomena automatically did something she vaguely remembered from her childhood: she patted Petrina's back and gave her a brief hug, as one would do with a baby after a bath.

Petrina said in surprise, "Mama used to do that."

"Mine, too," Filomena said as she stepped back into the bedroom. Petrina stood there, clutching her towel, her mouth trembling. "*Che successe?*" Filomena asked softly.

"What happened? Oh, nothing much," Petrina said bitterly as she toweled off and slipped back into her clothes. But her next words ended up in a plaintive wail. "My husband doesn't want me anymore. He wants to marry another woman. He says she makes him feel younger, like he can start all over again."

Filomena said, "*Bella ragazza! Meritate un principe, non un animale di un uomo!*"

The familiar saying, spoken so maternally, struck Petrina deeply. But her own mother would probably not say so under these circumstances; Tessa would no doubt be as stern as Domenico. "Yes, you're exactly right!" Petrina cried. "I *am* a beautiful girl and I *do* deserve a prince, not that *animal* of a husband." She started to laugh but then, with a gulp, burst into tears and sank onto the side of the bed.

Filomena sat beside her. "Speak, so your heart doesn't break trying to hold it in," she suggested. And in fact, Petrina *was* feeling such an unbearable ache in her chest and throat.

Unable to hold it back any longer, Petrina spat out, "Oh, God, I've been so *tired* of the strain. What a torturer Richard has been! I knew something was wrong. When I thought it might be an affair, I tried to talk to him, but he kept telling me I was imagining it."

Filomena said quietly, "That is a slap in the face."

"Yeah, I should challenge him to a duel. That's what men would do. Women, we just get all the pain and the blame when somebody hurts *us*. How can I tell my family that Richard wants a divorce? Ma will say I must have done something wrong, been a bad wife. Johnny and Frankie will treat me like a fallen woman. They won't believe me, no matter what I say. They're all talkers in this family. None of them are good listeners. Except for you. You see it all, don't you, with those big eyes of yours? I've watched you, watching us. I see that you really love Mario. I wish someone truly loved me like that."

Filomena asked tentatively, "Do you still love Richard?"

Petrina sighed gustily. "I thought he was beautiful. He said he wanted to share his world with me. He told me I was like a movie star, and I would be *his* guiding star. I thought, *Here at last is my chance, I'll be safe with him.* How stupid I was, after all."

"Do you want to fight for him, for your marriage?" Filomena asked.

Petrina shook her head. "I've tried. I lost. Now all I have left is my pride."

"And Pippa?" Filomena asked. "Will she be all right if her parents are no longer together in the same house anymore?"

"Pippa is an old, wise soul, and she's like you—she sees it all," Petrina said wryly. "Anyway, for the last few weeks my husband and I have hardly been together in that house. So for Pippa, having me and her father live apart will be nothing new. No, I don't think it will harm her any more than it's already harmed her."

"Then," Filomena said, "perhaps it's for the best. Now you will be free to love another man, someone who loves *you* even more than you could imagine possible."

Petrina fell silent for a while, before saying in a low voice, "I already had that love, but I was only a girl. His name was Bobby. He used to sing in a band. He could have been a big star, but I heard he went off to military school. I never saw him again."

"Then you'll find someone else to love. Three is a lucky number," Filomena suggested. Petrina laughed with genuine appreciation.

"Oh, Rosa!" she exclaimed. "Maybe you can be the sister I never had. I always wanted a sister." She looked keenly at Filomena now. "How is it with you and Mario?" she asked delicately. "Are things—all right between you, as they should be with a husband and wife? Will you have children?"

Although she'd been worrying about this, Filomena said

resolutely, "*Certo*. And when the first baby comes—will you be godmother to my child?"

Petrina gasped, then seized Filomena's hand. Filomena could feel her long, sharp nails, painted blood-red, as Petrina said, "You know, Lucy and Amie asked each other to be godmother to their children. Nobody ever asked me. And they really should have. I'm the oldest. But it's understandable, I guess; they're afraid of me and Ma."

"The children will bring us all together, all in good time," Filomena declared.

"*Brava!*" Petrina said, taking a deep breath. "Let's go have a merry Christmas—and a better New Year."

Filomena smiled, but she harbored a slight superstition from the old country. You would never wish someone a happy New Year until the actual first day of January. Otherwise, you might take some of your old troubles from this year into the next.

17

Winter-Spring 1944

Tessa was a woman of her word, and so she arranged to meet Alonza in a fine tea shop on Fifth Avenue, which was decorated with swaths of pink and white draperies, and marble-topped tables set with fragile china vases and teacups, and a platform where a woman was playing a harp for ladies in large hats and furs—all to discourage men from entering.

Tessa chose a table in the center of this decorous world, where the murmurs of well-bred patrons were punctuated only by the delicate clink of their teaspoons, thus inducing newcomers to keep their voices low in thoughtful conversation.

However, Alonza was late, so she came blowing into the restaurant, oblivious to its atmosphere, and she gave her name, loudly and indignantly, to the hostess, who signaled the waiter to hurriedly escort Alonza to Tessa's table.

Alonza wore a small fur-piece of an indeterminate animal biting its own tail, and an overblown hat, but no gloves. When she threw back her coat and haughtily handed it to the waiter, Alonza proudly revealed that she was wearing a big, expensive silver necklace with real turquoise stones. "A Christmas present from my loving sons," she announced, by way of greeting Tessa. "They spent their last dollar on it."

Tessa had been feeling genuinely sorry for her, but at the mention of the necklace, she said, "According to my sources, your boys stole quite a bit of jewelry. This might not be the place to parade such a piece. You may run into its original owner."

Alonza's worried expression revealed that she hadn't considered this possibility. But she recovered and insisted, "All the more reason why my boys need your help and guidance."

Tessa said calmly, "We introduced your sons to the best help they can get in the nice, sunny climate of Florida, yet, from what I hear, they failed to appreciate this favor and take advantage of it."

"It's not their fault! Those people in Florida were too tough for my sweet boys," Alonza whined. "They belong here in New York, and are entitled to be treated just as Gianni's other sons are." Reaching for a cream pastry from the gold, three-tiered tray, Alonza demanded, "You must do right by Gianni and take his two sons into your family businesses here in New York, to give my boys a fair share."

"No," Tessa said firmly, "that is simply not possible. I've heard that your sons are already going around town telling bookies that our family will back their bets and debts. I want you to know that I have now put out the word that we absolutely *will not* support them financially, or vouch for them."

Alonza, still chewing mightily, sputtered furiously, "You loan money every day to people you don't know. To criminals! Why not to your husband's sons? You act so high and mighty. Gianni never treated us like that."

Tessa said slowly, "My husband always made a point of being present at the hospital for the birth of all his sons. I doubt that *you* can make the same claim."

"Oh, yes, Gianni *was* with me!" Alonza pounced on this bit of catnip. "He stayed at the hospital for the entire day that Sergio was born. And he did the same for Ruffio, a year later. He came to my house and drove me to the hospital, both times."

Tessa leaned forward. "Sergio was born in July, wasn't he?

And Ruffio was born a year later, that August. Those are the dates on the copies of the documents you gave me. They were signed in New York. But my husband was out of town, with me, at a summer cottage in Maine, during both of those times. This I can absolutely prove."

Alonza stopped chewing, and in panic, she hastily gulped her tea. "But he *would* have been by my side, if he could have," she cried. "He *wanted* to be. And he told me to put his name on the birth certificates for him!" Then she recovered her wrath and exclaimed, "If you don't help Gianni's sons, you might as well put a bullet in their heads!" Her voice was so loud that the other ladies in furs at nearby tables looked up, startled, and for a moment, even the harp player stopped plucking her strings.

Tessa said quietly, "My husband never, ever *gave* any of my sons money to burn. If they needed our help, they had to pay it back, in installments, just like anyone else. No doubt, Gianni told you this when you harassed him on the telephone."

Alonza's guilty glance revealed that she had indeed made such calls, and then, having no other recourse, she burst into tears. "You are *not* a good woman!" she wailed.

Undeterred, Tessa said, "You must be an unfortunate woman, to tell such lies to a grieving family. Yet, in memory of my husband, I will give your sons the guidance you asked for, but only in the way that Gianni would do it. I will make one last loan to *you*—but understand that this is the last one, and that it is indeed a loan, which must be repaid. I myself will not put this money into your sons' hands. That will be *your* task. I suggest you give it to them in installments and make sure they understand that it is a loan, not a gift, and that they will have to find good, honest work so they can pay *you* back, Alonza; so that you, in turn, can repay me in monthly installments, with interest. Now, understand—this is the last time. If they get into trouble again, they are on their own. You must believe me when I tell you that I mean this. If you ever again try to contact my family, or make any trouble, I will demand the full payment immediately, and if I don't get it, you will all pay the consequences."

Alonza had been theatrically dabbing her eyes with her crumpled handkerchief. Now she watched in undisguised fascination as Tessa reached into her purse, pulled out an envelope, and slid it across the table. Alonza pounced on the envelope as if it were raw meat.

"How much is it?" she whispered, drawing it into her lap.

Tessa signaled the waiter for the check. The waiter arrived promptly, poured the last of the tea into their cups, and cleared away the empty pot. While Tessa paid the bill, Alonza counted her money. She could not resist a smile of satisfaction.

"Remember," Tessa said, "this is a loan. You must repay it."

The note of finality in Tessa's voice seemed to awaken Alonza to the reality. First, she looked panicked. Then, quite deliberately, she spit into Tessa's teacup before she could drink the last of it.

WHEN TESSA RETURNED HOME THAT DAY, SHE UNPINNED HER HAT wearily and went into her study. After dinner, she told her children to join her in there. She explained what had happened and how she had tricked Alonza into revealing the truth.

"I *knew* she was lying about the sons. But, Mom," Petrina said softly, "we only went to Maine one summer, you and I—and Pop did *not* come with us."

"That's right," Johnny agreed. "I remember, Ma couldn't stand the heat of the city, so she took Petrina to the seashore to visit relatives up there. You two were away from May until late September, because Ma helped Petrina get started in that fancy New England boarding school. But Frankie and I stayed in town with Pop, and he took us to all the great ball games."

"That is correct," Tessa said shortly. "But Alonza didn't know this. So she confessed that Gianni wasn't with her for the birth of her sons. I now believe she's lied about everything."

"Then those idiots aren't Pop's kids," Frankie chortled.

Tessa said, "It no longer matters. It's late. Time for bed."

Mario went upstairs and relayed this information to Filomena, and he concluded, "The point is, we're done with the Pericolos. They'll get no more from us."

Filomena asked tentatively, "These loans Alonza says your family makes to other people—is that how your father built his business? And now that he's gone, your mother has taken over it?"

Mario said, "No. It's the one part of the business that my mother was always in charge of. She's had that loan book as long as I can remember."

Filomena said nothing as they turned out the light. But she lay there recalling how Tessa always covered the left side of her ledger to conceal those pages. Whatever its secrets, that valuable book was always kept under lock and key, and, evidently, nobody but Tessa knew the whole story of what it contained.

***

ONE AFTERNOON, AS LUCY WAS HURRYING HOME FROM WORK, SHE passed the local candy store, and the proprietor, a jolly man in an apron, rushed out to speak to her.

But today he looked stern. "It's about your son, Christopher," he said in a low voice, pulling her aside so that others could not hear what he had to say. Lucy's heart fluttered apprehensively. "That kid's been passing counterfeit money," the man continued.

"*What?*" Lucy said, then added sharply, "You must be mistaken."

The man shook his head regretfully. "No mistake," he replied. "I've been watching Chris, after the first time. He comes in with a fake twenty-dollar bill, buys five cents' worth of candy, and makes off with the change. That way, he gets some real money in return. I'm not the only one to get hit; other kids have done it to the cigar shop. We think some racketeer gets these kids to make the change for him, and then he pays the kids a little pocket money for it." He paused. "I haven't told the police this, Lucy. I know your family and they've been good to me. But you need to speak to your boy."

Lucy reached into her purse to repay him, then mumbled her thanks and rushed off in a blur of first confusion, then fury. When she got home, she yanked Chris by the shoulder and hauled him into their kitchen. He always looked so angelic, with those bright blue eyes and the sprinkling of freckles across his button nose.

"Now, what's this I hear about you passing funny money at the candy store, eh, laddie?" she demanded. Chris looked surprised, then he had the grace to blush.

"I only did a man a favor," he said with a broad gesture, in a pint-size imitation of Frankie.

Lucy took him by both shoulders and shook him slightly. "A favor! Since when do you do what strange, bad men ask you to do? Don't you know it's against the law to pass off phony bills as real? You could go to jail!"

"He didn't say it was fake. He said he knew our family. He said he just wanted some small change to play the numbers," Chris objected.

Lucy said severely, "And you expect me to believe that you didn't know how fishy that sounds? Even if you believed him, gambling is illegal, too."

Now Chris gave her a knowing look. "Well, if it's so bad, how come Pop and Uncle Johnny run numbers?" he countered. "How come it's only bad when kids do it?" Lucy was taken aback when Chris added slyly, "*You have to take a chance in life if you're going to get anywhere.* I heard you say that to Godmother Amie."

Lucy felt her own ears burning now. She *had* said exactly that, when Amie once voiced concerns about Johnny's betting operations at the bar. Furthermore, Lucy could not deny that part of the thrill of her own courtship with Frankie had been the aura of danger and risk that accompanied the glamorous whirl of being seen with an influential man. But until now, she hadn't realized how much Chris had observed and absorbed.

More gently she said, "You got lucky, because the man at the candy shop likes us. But you can't depend on luck to hold out forever. That's why Frankie wants you to have a better childhood than he did. If I were to tell him what you'd done, he'd thrash you for it. So I won't bother him with this. I have big dreams for you, too. But for now, my lad, all you have to do is be a good boy and walk the straight and narrow."

"Okay," Chris muttered, but as he went off, although he was chastened, the look on his face indicated that he was not entirely convinced.

***

THE WAR NEWS THAT WINTER WAS GRIM; EUROPE SEEMED HELL-BENT on destroying itself, with vicious bombardments across the continent—including an ancient site near Rome called Monte Cassino, where a historical Benedictine monastery was blasted to ruin. The fighting was especially fierce in a town called Anzio, where American soldiers were trapped in caves and attacked by the Nazi army.

Filomena felt an acute sympathy, remembering how awful it was to watch the skies and think of who would die next. It pained her to wonder if her family in Italy had survived. She forced herself to push away such feelings. She could hear Rosamaria speaking from the grave: *Your family didn't care if you lived or died. The world you left behind is gone. So do as Tessa said. Live the life you chose, and give your love only to those here who love you.*

So when Tessa enlisted her daughters-in-law to collect clothes, food, and Easter toys for Italian war orphans, and for American families whose mothers were war widows, Filomena pitched in. They made packages of cakes and sweets to send to soldiers overseas, too. Tessa's grandchildren, eager to help, had heard about the war in school, in church, and in the movies.

Tessa was also determined to make the hopeful season of Easter beautiful for her grandchildren, so she marched them off to a department store called Best & Company to get the youngsters completely outfitted for Easter. She chose peony pink for Pippa, butter yellow for Gemma, and navy suits with dark velvet collars for Chris, Vinnie, and Paulie. Everyone got a haircut. And their mothers received pastel scarves and stylish new Easter hats.

The grand finale, of course, was the food. Tessa insisted that all the ladies accompany her on a shopping trip for *la domenica di Pasqua*.

"She does this every year," Amie explained to Filomena as the wives assembled in the vestibule of Tessa's town house, buttoning their coats. "She's old-fashioned; she says that when *she* was a girl, Easter was a much bigger deal than Christmas."

Petrina's daughter, Pippa, was going along with them; her school term ended a little earlier than the younger children's, so she and Petrina were spending their Easter holiday in the guesthouse.

"Where do things stand with Richard?" Filomena whispered to Petrina after Amie got into the car, since nobody else knew about the impending divorce.

"The lawyers are still hashing it out," Petrina said gloomily.

"Come, ladies!" Tessa called out as Sal opened the car doors for them.

The last one on board was Lucy, who came hurrying down the street to join them, having just returned from the early shift at the hospital. "Listen," she said breathlessly, "guess who just got admitted to the coronary ward? Alonza! She had a heart attack. The doctors don't think she's going to make it."

Tessa paused. "Then we must say a prayer for her at the Good Friday service."

They piled into the car, and Sal drove them to Tessa's favorite shops. They filled their baskets with spring's first and freshest vegetables and fruit, then moved on to the butcher to order lamb for their holiday roast. The next stop was the baker's shop for a sweet Easter bread made into a braid with a whole egg baked into its center, the bread dotted with currants, orange peel, and sliv-ered almonds, all glazed lightly with honey. Then, cookies for the children, cut into rabbits and chicks. The baker's brisk assistants put everything into white boxes tied with red string that came from dispensers that resembled golden beehives hanging on chains overhead.

The ladies deposited their purchases in the car and collapsed in their seats, ready to go home. Then Tessa said, "Oh, look at the florist's new shipment! I just want to see the tulips. Wait for me here. Pippa, you come with me."

"I don't know where she gets her energy," Petrina groaned from the back of the car, slipping her feet out of her shoes and rubbing her heels.

When Tessa finally emerged from this last stop, Pippa was carrying her tulips for her. "You go ahead," Tessa said, pausing at the sidewalk to admire the outdoor display of baby trees and shrubs—azalea, lilac, magnolia.

Pippa was halfway to their car when an unmarked black deliv-ery van, which had been parked at the far end of the street, sud-denly pulled out speedily with tires screeching, causing people to pause, startled by its recklessness. Tessa, still at the floral display, glanced up and frowned, because the van squealed to a stop right next to her.

Two men, wearing sunglasses, with hats pulled low and scarves wrapped high, jumped out of the van. In a flash, they raised their guns and fired away. Then, as quickly as they had come, they jumped back into the van and drove off. One of them knocked Pippa to the ground as he escaped.

Tessa had only enough time to register a look of surprise be-fore she fell to the sidewalk, crumpled like an abandoned doll.

"*Nonna!*" Pippa cried out.

"Pippa! Mama!" Petrina screamed, running out of the car without bothering to retrieve her shoes. Sal had jumped out and rushed to Tessa's side. Lucy emerged and, after looking about cautiously, hurried over to check Tessa's vital signs.

"For God's sake, call an ambulance!" Lucy shouted to the horrified bystanders who had come running out of the shops. "Somebody call an ambulance!"

Filomena had already gone into the florist's shop to telephone for help.

Petrina was cradling her mother in her arms, so they were both covered with blood. Amie had run over to Pippa and was trying to drag her back into the car. Pippa scrambled to her feet but could only stand there on the sidewalk and scream and scream. Finally they all heard the wail of an ambulance and the police sirens.

Tessa had not regained consciousness. "*Nonna, Nonna!*" Pippa was still crying as her grandmother was carried on a stretcher into the ambulance, with Petrina still clinging to her mother's hand as she climbed into the ambulance beside her.

"I called Mario at the shop," Filomena said to Amie. "He and his brothers will meet Petrina at the hospital." Gently they managed to guide Pippa back into the car.

"Ladies, I've got to take you straight home," Sal said to the wives. "Then I'll go to the police station. But please, keep everybody indoors—and away from the windows. We don't know who those savages were—and whether they might come back."

18

April 1944

In the days that followed Tessa's death, her house was engulfed in a terrible, heavy silence, broken only by the occasional whispers of her family as they struggled to overcome their shock. After the exhausting ordeal of hospital, police, funeral parlor, and burial, the family discussed the question that still remained unanswered but which Amie articulated: "Who would *do* such a horrible thing?"

They tallied the possible suspects, saying to one another what they could not tell the police: it might have been any number of people—those who owed Tessa money and could not repay it, or those who had been refused a loan, or those, like the Pericolos, who coveted the family's operations.

"My sources tell me that this hit definitely didn't come from the Bosses; we're still good with them," Johnny explained, lighting up a cigarette as he emerged from Tessa's study. All the ashtrays in the house were filling up with his spent cigarette stubs faster than the maid could clear them away. "So, I doubt that this came from anyone else we've been doing business with. They'd know better, they just wouldn't dare."

But one evening, after a silent, mournful family dinner, when the women and children had gone into the parlor, and the men once again retreated into Tessa's study, it was Pippa—who'd been

sobbing in her sleep with terrible nightmares for days on end—
who finally made a definitive statement.

"We all *know* who did it. Those two fat men who came to
Grandpa's funeral," she said furiously. "I smelled their rotten cologne on the street *again,* that day they killed poor *Nonna.*"

"That could have just been the scent of the florist shop,"
Petrina cautioned.

Pippa stamped her foot and shouted, "NO, it *wasn't* the flowers. I tell you, it was those big fat bad men!" And she ran off to her
bedroom and slammed the door. Lucy signaled the maid to put
the other children to bed before they got too upset.

"The gunmen *did* look like the Pericolos, size-wise," Amie recalled as Johnny, Frankie, and Mario entered the parlor. Petrina
told the men what Pippa had said.

"Yeah, we figured it had to be the Pericolos," Frankie said bitterly.

"But it's stupid," said Lucy. "Why would they do this, so pub-
licly, so brutally? What can they hope to gain from it?"

Johnny said shortly, "Revenge. Because of their mother. I bet
those mama's boys blamed Ma for Alonza's heart attack and were
afraid that their mother was going to die." But, as Lucy had found
out at the hospital, Alonza had recovered and was sent home.

"Maybe they imagine they can do business with us—
with
men—better than they could with an old-fashioned woman like
Ma," Mario said, reminding them of what Sergio had said as he
left the jewelry shop at Christmastime: *You can't let your mama
run your life . . . you and I need to talk business, man to man.
And then, we come to a better arrangement.*

"We can ask Strollo to dispense with the Pericolos, tell him
they're trying to muscle in on the business," Frankie said impatiently.

"No, that could backfire," Mario said quickly. "If the Bosses
think there's money to be made in getting me to fence stolen jewels, *they* may want me to fence for *them.* They haven't noticed my

business yet, it's so small. I'd like to keep it that way."

"Then let's handle this ourselves," Frankie retorted. "Let's just do it."

"We could arrange a meeting with the Pericolos at Mario's store," Johnny suggested. "Get them to show up after hours for a 'business conference.' It might flatter them enough to make them come. Then, we finish them off."

The women, who'd been silent, now looked utterly horrified.

"Are you all *crazy*?" Petrina said in a sudden burst of scorn. "Do you know how hard Mom and Pop worked to keep you all from becoming murdering thugs?"

"Right, and you see what came of trying to settle this problem without bloodshed. Ma shed *her* blood!" Frankie shouted.

"Stop it, Frankie," Lucy said to her volatile husband. "Don't yell at Petrina. She's only trying to keep all of her hotheaded brothers out of jail."

"We won't get caught," Johnny assured her. "The cops couldn't care less about the Pericolos, can't you see that? They don't even care to find out who killed Ma."

Petrina reached for a cigarette. "Well, Johnny and Frankie, you can do what you want," she said furiously. "But, Mario, *you* are not to get involved, do you hear me?"

"I'm already involved," Mario said in his reasonable tone. "They came into my shop and said they'd return. Rosamaria can't work there with those creeps showing up."

"Then close your shop and take your wife out of here!" Petrina retorted. "And go as far away from this family as you possibly can. They'll only ruin you, Mario! You'll never get to 'the other side' and be free and safe and happy." Petrina's face was streaming with tears now.

Her brothers looked stunned. "You're just upset over Ma," Johnny said reasonably.

"That's not it," Petrina snapped. She turned to Mario. "For once in your life," she insisted, "you are going to *listen* to me. Pack up that shop of yours, get on a train with your wife, and go make a life for yourself somewhere far away from this mess."

"Stop it, Petrina!" Mario said firmly. "I'm not your baby brother anymore. I can fight for myself. So please, mind your own business."

Petrina visibly flinched, then raised her long red talons as if she wanted to claw his face. "You don't know *what* you're talking about!" she shouted. "I'm sick of this family and all its secrets and lies. There is only *one* thing you're right about, Mario—you are *not* my brother. You never were. But you *are* my baby—you always will be!"

"What the hell is she talking about?" Frankie demanded. "She's lost her mind."

"I tell you, she's hysterical over Ma," Johnny suggested.

Petrina said furiously, "You all make me sick! I am the sanest person in this family. Mama was a liar. Papa was a liar. And they made *me* lie! I was only fifteen years old, what was I supposed to do? You dumb fools," she said, turning on Johnny and Frankie with her eyes blazing, "you were too stupid to see what was going on, right in front of your own eyes. You say you remember that summer that Mama took me to Maine, but you forget that was the year she said she was pregnant with Mario. That was why she said the city was too hot for her and she needed to rest by the ocean. She took me up to Maine with her, all right, and none of you noticed or cared why, because Papa took you to all the baseball games and introduced you to the famous ball players. And when Mama and I came home with the new baby, they made me say that little Mario was her son. Well, he wasn't! He was *mine*, mine!"

The room was filled with a stunned silence. Amie reached out a comforting hand to Petrina, who waved it away, her cigarette making a trail of smoke.

Frankie spoke first. "*You* are the liar," he exclaimed. "Pop would never—"

"Oh, yes, he would!" Petrina cried. "They put their own names on Mario's birth certificate. Then they sent me off to that strict boarding school in Massachusetts. They made me live there, sleep there, away from my baby, so I wouldn't break down and tell the truth. They only let me come home to see him on my school holidays—"

She broke off, sobbing. For a while, nobody dared speak.

Finally Mario, horrified, said, "But—Petrina—then—who is my father?"

Petrina glanced at Filomena before saying, "Bobby. A boy I loved. A sweet boy, as sweet as you, Mario. A good boy, but not good enough for us! Mama said he was 'beneath us' because he came from 'the wrong side' of town. Papa said he would 'kill the boy.' He meant it. It was all about his pride. Not once did he or Mama think of *me,* what I wanted. They said *they* knew what was best for me. They said if I dared to defy them and speak of this, they'd send me to a mental hospital, for crazy girls, where I would live like a prisoner, a madwoman that nobody listens to, for the rest of my life."

"Oh, God, Petrina!" Lucy said in shocked sympathy, recalling her own girlhood fate.

"Did they kill that boy?" Mario asked in disbelief.

Petrina seemed to be gathering energy from the giddy pleasure of telling the truth at last. "Bobby was my age. He had no father, no one to help us. I told Bobby to run. Run, run! He said he'd come back for me. He never did. He had a beautiful voice, he could have been a great singer, but he had to run, run as far away from here as he could. I got a letter from him, months later, to assure me he was safe. He joined the army. I only heard from him one more time after that, to thank me. He's an important man in the army now. He married an English girl. So, I say to you, Mario, what I said to him. Run, run! Get as far away from this family, this life in New York, as you possibly can!"

Johnny and Frankie, still dumbfounded, were looking at each

other as if rapidly revisiting their own past with all this new information.

And suddenly, Filomena remembered what Gianni had said to her on her wedding day, in the parlor, just before they left the house to go to the church: *There are things that happen in life that can't be helped. Mario's life has not been without its complications. He does not fully understand this yet. But whatever happens, please, always be there to remind him how important it is to have his family near, for they only want to love and protect him.*

"Mario, this *is* still your family," Filomena said softly. "These people love you."

Mario, still reeling, said slowly, "Petrina, if what you say is really true—"

"Of course it's true," Petrina snapped. "Why would I make this up? Just so you could all call me a crazy liar? Think about it, Mario. Did any sister ever love her brother as much as I've loved you? What sister worries so much about what her kid brother wears when it's cold outside? When you had measles that year, who sang you to sleep? What girl gives up her Easter vacation to take care of her stupid little brother?"

"*Basta!*" Mario shouted suddenly, trembling. He had been drinking a whiskey but now he hurled the empty glass into the fireplace, and the shattering sound made Amie flinch. Apparently no one had ever heard Mario raise his voice before, because they all looked awed. "All right, then," he said, as if throwing down a gauntlet. "If this is true, then take me to my father. Right now!"

Petrina said, "All I have is his name. The last I heard, he was living in Washington, D.C. I don't have his address. I haven't heard from him in years."

"That's all I need. I'll find him," Mario said bitterly. "Give me his name. And then I'll find out if you're just a liar, Petrina, or if this man's name is really *my* name."

19

April-May 1944

The situation with the Pericolos required decisive action, so, the next day, Johnny sent a message to Alonza's house, and she replied that her sons would meet with Mario at his shop. A date and a time were arranged. Frankie secured weapons.

"Isn't there some way we can stop our husbands?" Amie exclaimed.

"Sure," Lucy said. "We can go to the police. Short of that, no."

At six o'clock on the appointed night, Johnny, Frankie, and Mario calmly ate their dinner together, at Tessa's table. Then they left the house. They looked so grim that the women didn't even dare to kiss them goodbye. Amie jumped every time she heard a siren wail outside.

"What's the plan, they're just going to kill them?" Lucy asked Petrina, remembering what a big deal it was to dispose of a body. "What if somebody sees or hears?"

"They'll have to pay them off," Petrina said shortly. She realized that all her life she'd feared exactly this—that her brothers would be forced to cross that line and become mobsters.

What does that make me, then? she wondered. Were they all doomed, unable to escape fate?

"What if they shoot back? It's just not worth it!" Amie cried.

"To lose one of our men."

Filomena, in utter agony, imagined Mario unlocking the door of the shop he loved, meeting with those awful men. Sergio had shown that he carried a gun. He was known to be violent, vengeful, so dangerous that the U.S. Army didn't even want him. She imagined a shoot-out, with the unbearable image of sweet Mario falling to the ground, mortally wounded.

And yet, she heard herself say, "Our men are doing what they think they must, to protect us and our children. We all know that they can't allow the Pericolos to keep threatening this family forever. Life would be impossible that way."

The others nodded but were as startled by her steely tone as by the words she spoke.

At eight o'clock, the children were sent to bed. At nine, the women assembled in the parlor to halfheartedly listen to the radio. Amie tried to do some needlepoint. Lucy and Petrina nursed their whiskeys. Filomena closed her eyes and prayed to the Madonna.

"*What* is taking so long?" Amie cried. "They could be lying in a ditch somewhere. We'd never even know—until it's too late!"

At midnight, they heard the car pull up. The men came inside. Filomena counted rapidly—Johnny, Frankie, Mario. They were all here, appearing strangely jocular as they went directly to the sideboard and poured themselves drinks.

"Well?" Amie demanded. "What happened?"

Johnny took a long swig. "Absolutely nothing," he said. The others were incredulous.

In the unbearable tension, Lucy punched Frankie in the arm. "What's going on?"

"Those clowns didn't show up," Frankie announced, shrugging out of his coat.

"And, so . . . ?" Petrina prodded. "Do we have to do this all over again some other night?"

"Nope. The Pericolo brothers just got themselves arrested," Johnny announced. Unable to control himself, he guffawed, then had a fit of coughing.

The women looked on in amazement. "What on *earth* are you talking about?" Amie demanded. "You think this is funny? I don't find it funny. *What* is going on?"

"Those jerks," Johnny said, gasping for breath, "had a big fight with Alonza after she ordered them to meet with us. They told their mama they don't need us anymore, because they found a better fence for their loot—in Hell's Kitchen. They just walked up to an Irish fence they heard about and acted like big shots. So of course, the fence tells his buddies that some idiots were hanging around *their* neighborhood, trying to muscle in on their turf."

"How do you know this?" Petrina demanded.

"Because we've had some of our guys tailing them all week," Johnny said. "And we've got a contact at this bar where they hang out. So, this afternoon, when the Irish were drinking together and getting more and more pissed off, our guy heard the Irish say that they gotta run those jerks out of their neighborhood, before they attract the cops. So the fence calls up the Pericolos, tells 'em to bring their stuff to be fenced—and the Pericolos walked right into a firestorm in Hell's Kitchen."

Filomena spoke for the first time. "Then—where have *you* been all night?"

Mario looked at Filomena a bit apologetically. "When the Pericolos didn't show up at the jewelry store, we had Sal drive us to the Irish hangout. We laid low in the parked car, just waiting to hear from our contact and watching. And what a show that turned out to be."

Frankie broke in. "Imagine those dumb-asses in a fight—even with a bunch of drunks? They all smashed up the bar, and while we're sitting outside there, some lady walks by and sees the whole fracas and shouts for a cop. We hightailed it out. But our spy stayed in the bar. He said that when the cops came, the fence points to the Pericolos and says, 'These guys tried to coerce me into fencing their loot, but hey, I'm just an honest jeweler.' The Pericolos denied it. So the cops go out and find the goddamned jewels in the *trunk* of the Pericolos' car, which, by the way, was a *stolen* car!"

Frankie collapsed into laughter, having to lean on Johnny's shoulder for support. Mario, who'd been circumspect until now, allowed himself a rueful grin. Lucy and Amie exchanged an uneasy look. Petrina threw up her hands. Filomena understood that the brothers were simply releasing all the pent-up energy that they no longer needed tonight.

"So," Johnny said with a wry shake of his head, "our best-laid plans were called off. From what our contacts at the police station told us, the Pericolo brothers, with their previous arrest records, are going to jail for a long time."

"I'm still sorry we didn't get a chance to kill them," Frankie admitted. "For Ma's sake."

"No, this is better," Mario said. "She would have preferred that the Pericolos end up in jail, rather than have us get mixed up in murder."

At the mention of Tessa, the men grew quiet and poured themselves another drink. Finally, they turned off the lights and everyone went to bed. For the first time that week, Filomena fell asleep instantly.

NOT LONG AFTERWARDS, MARIO LOCATED THE MAN THAT PETRINA claimed was his father and telephoned him. When Mario got off the phone, he looked visibly calmer.

"This man says Petrina is telling the truth about everything," Mario told Filomena. "Bobby—I mean, Roberto—is a general in the army now. He was very kind. He asked if Petrina is well these days. Then he invited me to come meet him in Washington, on Monday."

"Don't you want me to go with you?" she asked softly.

Mario shook his head. "I have to do this alone. Petrina offered to come, too. I just don't want any women around. I hope you understand."

"All right," Filomena said worriedly, taking his hand. "Try not to expect too much from this man, Mario. You are still *you*, no matter what happened in the past."

"I know," he said quietly, still looking vulnerable.

So that weekend, she helped him pack his suitcase. Then, on Monday, just as she was giving Mario his breakfast, there was a knock at the door.

The adults had gotten into the habit of having a quick breakfast together in Tessa's parlor, after the children had been fed and Sal had taken them to school. Only Petrina was missing; she had brought Pippa back to Rye, so that the girl could finish her school term.

It was just the postman at the door. "For Mario," he said, looking stricken, as if he recognized the kind of envelope he was delivering. He tipped his hat and departed quickly.

Mario tore it open and then laughed without mirth. "Perfect," he said, throwing it on the table. Filomena picked it up.

"What is it?" she asked, afraid to read it from the look on his face.

"My draft notice," he announced.

"But—you are married," she said in panic. "They're not supposed to draft you!"

"We don't have kids," Mario said. "I don't know, maybe that's why."

"It's a mistake," Frankie said quickly. "You've got to straighten it out, that's all."

"That's not so easy to do," Johnny warned. "We tried it for Sal's kid, remember?"

"Mario, you said this Roberto guy's kind of a big noise in the military, right? See if he can fix this draft notice for you," Frankie suggested.

"I'll talk to him about it," Mario said, shrugging. "Maybe he can advise me."

Filomena walked him to the door. He looked so serious, so susceptible, that she was moved to kiss him and hold him close. "I love you very much," she murmured.

"*Ti amo anch'io*," he answered, kissing her again.

After he was gone, Filomena brooded over how she had failed to do the one thing Tessa had told her she must. She wasn't pregnant yet. Perhaps if she was, Mario would have an easier time dealing with that draft notice. She hoped that Frankie was right and that Mario's father would help him.

BUT WHEN MARIO RETURNED FROM WASHINGTON, FILOMENA HAD her first big fight with him. He came in late at night, smelling of trains, cigar smoke, and leather. Filomena heard him moving about, so she came downstairs in her robe and slippers. He took off his coat and hat and methodically placed them on the hooks in the vestibule.

"Are you hungry?" she asked. "There is veal stew; I can heat it up."

"Something warm to eat would be good," Mario said, following her to the dining room and pouring himself, and her, a glass of red wine. They sat together at the enormous table, which had seemed so reassuringly permanent when Filomena first saw it, as if the furnishings, and this family, could never be uprooted. Now the two big chairs at either end of the table were always empty. Nobody wanted to take the places of Tessa and Gianni.

"How did it go?" she asked gently.

"This man Roberto—my father—he's a good man," Mario said haltingly as he ate. "He told me how much he'd loved my—I mean, Petrina." Mario looked pained, as if he still could not bear to think of Petrina as anything but his sister.

"They call him Bobby, just like Petrina said. Anyway, he built a whole career around the service," Mario explained. "He wears his uniform with pride. He trains men for battle, and he says that this terrible world war must be won, or our children will have hell for a future, if Hitler is victorious. Bobby has provided well for his own family; he and his wife have two daughters, and both of *their* husbands are in the war now."

Filomena, sensing that she would not like what was coming, asked, "Will he help you explain to the draft board that you have a wife, and will soon have a baby? You know we will someday soon, Mario."

Mario drank some wine before he spoke. "Filomena," he said gently. "I see now that I can't turn my back on this war. I've decided I want to follow my father's example, do my duty, serve my country, just as he did."

Filomena felt a mounting sense of panic. Was she doomed always to be abandoned by people who claimed they loved her? First, her parents. Then even Rosamaria had abandoned her, because of this crazy idea of coming to America, which had caused them to go to Naples that awful day, and which had driven Filomena to flee here, to this man, who was now going to abandon her for his pride. So her answer came out as anger instead of love.

"Don't lie to yourself," she said harshly. "You just want to run away from your troubles, your family, and leave me to fend for myself, because you think you no longer care for us."

"That's not true! I only want to stand on my own two feet. Filomena, that night in Hell's Kitchen, sitting there in a dark car, staking out the bar and ready to kill the Pericolos—that's the first time in my life I ever felt like a gangster."

Filomena fell silent. Then she said, "So you'll leave *me* alone here, in this dangerous town?"

"You won't be unprotected. I know that my brothers will look after you like a sister," Mario said quickly. "Until I get back from the war."

"*If* you get back!" she shouted. "*If* you don't get your head blown off! And *if* you come back in one piece—and not all crippled or blind or God knows what!"

"I *will* come back in one piece, and meanwhile, you will get my soldier's pay," Mario said firmly. "You'll have honest money that you'll never have to be ashamed of."

"And what of your shop?" she demanded. "You don't care anymore? Maybe you won't care about *me* anymore, either!"

"That shop of mine was where all our troubles began," Mario said bitterly. "I was fooling myself. I thought I could have independence while staying right here in my own backyard, where Petrina and my big brothers could catch me if I stumbled." He paused. "Brothers! They aren't even that. Apparently, they are my uncles!"

"Stop it. It's only words," Filomena said sharply. "Men's words, men's rigid ideas. Who cares which one of the loving women who raised you is named 'Mama'? Who cares if the boys that grew up with you and loved you are not 'officially' called your brothers?"

"I guess I care. But no matter what, I'm doing this for you, for us, for our children," Mario said, looking troubled now.

"Don't try to tell me you're going off to kill people for me and our children!" Filomena shouted. "Don't tell me you're going to get *yourself* killed for my sake."

He took her by the shoulders. "I promise, I'll come back. And when I return, I'll get paid properly, don't you see? I can build an honest life that our children will never be ashamed of."

They quarreled more, each trying to convince the other. Then they both apologized, and made up, and made love, and cried in each other's arms. The next day, nobody could talk Mario out of his plans, not his brothers, not Petrina, not Filomena.

Before he left her again, Mario told Filomena that it was her choice to close the jewelry store or not; Johnny and Frankie would help her, either way. He paused. "One more thing. Do you know where Mama kept her book? Can you get it, if you need to?"

Startled, Filomena said, "Her ledger? Yes, I do."

"The others may ask you about it," Mario said. "If they do, you tell them that I said it's your book now. I have written a letter, saying so. Here it is—but don't give it to them, unless they ask you for Ma's book." He handed her a sealed envelope. "She trusted only you to work on her book. So it's yours now. You do with it as you see fit."

He went to the closet, reached for a shoebox, and withdrew something wrapped in shoe-shine cloth. It was a gun. He showed her how to use it, and how to keep it safe when it was not in use. He said steadily, "It was for me to use on the Pericolos. It can't be traced, which is good. So, just keep it in the shop to protect yourself. If you need to, get close, and aim straight."

Mario left home the next day.

20

May 1944

One Sunday afternoon, when Amie's twins were at the movies with their cousins, she found Johnny still lying in bed, listening to the radio, his cigarette poised on an ashtray, only half-smoked. She sat beside him, snuggling close, and as she began kissing him, she felt not only her own arousal but his. And yet, he gently but maddeningly pushed her away.

"Whoa, girl," he chided. "Kids will be home soon. Don't make trouble, now."

"It's a double feature, and Frankie's taking them out for pizza afterwards," Amie murmured. "I'm not making trouble. But maybe we'll make a sweet little baby. Don't you want me to have a little girl to dress up in pretty clothes, like Lucy and Petrina do?"

"Sorry, babe. I'm too tired."

Amie decided it was time to have a little talk with her husband.

"Johnny, it's been a long while since we've made love," she said bluntly.

"Ah, c'mon, not that long," he said, staring out the window. "Aren't you sick of me, anyway?" he teased.

Amie was all the more irritated by this useless denial of his. "It has *so* been a long time," she persevered, "but maybe it's *you* who's sick of *me*!"

She hadn't intended to let her voice end in a pathetic wail, but it did. Johnny turned to her in astonishment, then raised himself on an elbow and said soothingly, "Aw, honey, of course I'm not sick of you! I'm just plain old sick, that's all."

"And don't hide behind that flu of yours," she retorted, refusing to be mollified. "Either go to the doctor or shut up about it!"

He was silent a moment, then said more roughly, "It's not flu, okay?"

"Then what is it?" Amie demanded.

Johnny sat up completely now and threw back his covers. "Just forget about it," he said brusquely. Amie sat up, too, and reached a hand up to his forehead.

"You don't have a fever," she said accusingly.

"No, I don't. I'm just coughing up blood again, that's all!" he exclaimed. "Are you happy now?"

Amie looked at him in astonishment. "Coughing *blood*? What do you mean, *again*?" He had been coughing all winter, it was true, but she hadn't seen blood and she assumed it was the flu that was going around. "Johnny, answer me!" she demanded.

"Forget it," he said shortly, reaching for the smoldering cigarette.

"Stop that!" she exclaimed, snatching it away. "You answer me, right now. I'm your wife. I have a right to know."

He stared at her a long time, then said in a rush, "It's the TB again. I had it as a kid. I beat it, a long time ago. Now it's back, I guess."

Amie took a good, hard look at her husband, which, she realized, she hadn't done in a while. Johnny had always been lanky, but now he looked a bit gaunt and pale, with dark shadows under his eyes. She'd put it down to grief over his parents, to stress, to winter's chill. Now she was seeing, at last. "Oh, Johnny," she said softly, going to him. "Why didn't you ever *tell* me you got so terribly sick when you were a child?" But even now, he held her off.

"I thought I beat it! I don't want *you* to catch it. I couldn't bear it if I gave it to you." His voice was a bit unsteady with emotion. Amie suddenly comprehended his standoffishness.

"I'm going to have the doctor come right away," she said quickly.

He looked as if he wanted to object, but when he coughed again and cursed the cough, he said resignedly, "All right, Amie."

Amie called the doctor, then, while waiting, fussed over Johnny, heating up some chicken soup, putting him to bed with warm brandy, hushing the children when they came home. She told them that their father was feeling "under the weather," and she sent them to bed early.

Johnny surrendered gratefully to her comforting, maternal ministrations. The doctor came, and Amie exchanged a few words with him to explain. Then, while the doctor was still with her husband, Amie, for the first time in her life, called a family meeting of all the adults, in Tessa's house, so they would not be overheard by the kids.

Frankie immediately demanded, "What's up? Why isn't Johnny here?"

"Johnny is very sick," Amie said, trembling. "The doctor is with him now. Johnny says it's the tuberculosis returning. Please tell me—what tuberculosis?"

Filomena, Lucy, and Amie could see by Frankie's expression that this did not entirely shock him. "Yeah, Johnny caught it when he was a kid," Frankie mumbled.

"What happened?" Lucy asked, sensing there was more to this story.

Frankie glanced at Amie, then said, "Johnny got in trouble when he was ten. A fight on the playground with a kid bigger than him. The guy beat up Johnny pretty bad, but then Johnny managed to give him one good shove, and the kid hit the ground and got knocked out cold. He was in the hospital for months, and they say he never 'got right' after that, but I think he just shut up and got scared, like bullies do. Anyway, the family pressed charges, and Johnny was sent to reform school. That was a bad place. It almost killed him. He came back real thin, and sick with TB. But, he *did* get well. Until now."

"He smokes too much," Amie said worriedly.

"Just can't stop. Another habit he picked up in reform school," Frankie replied.

"Sometimes TB patients self-medicate," Lucy said, her nursing instincts alert. "Usually it's drink." But these brothers, she knew, had been raised to avoid drinking except at mealtime, where it was all moderate and carefully calibrated.

Amie blurted out in panic, "The doctor said he doesn't expect Johnny to live to the end of the year!" They all gasped. "I told him not to tell Johnny that. You know how he is. But I must go back and make sure the doctor doesn't tell Johnny all the dire things he said to me. How can you tell a man he hasn't got even a chance to recover?"

Lucy said quickly, "Amie, there's a good sanitarium upstate—a place up in the mountains, where they've had success with people who were terribly ill. It's hard to get into, because their beds are always full. But I know some people there; I think I can get him in. He'd have to stay for a long while, probably. But it just might save his life."

Frankie's eyes were bright, but he blinked away the threat of tears. "You really think so, Lucy? I don't want to sell my brother a pipe dream."

"Yes, I'm sure," Lucy said firmly. "Johnny should go there, as soon as he can."

Filomena said, "Why don't you talk to the doctor, Lucy?"

"Yes," Amie said, rising. "He'll listen to you. It's your business to know these things. Hurry, before that doctor starts measuring Johnny for his shroud."

AT FIRST, JOHNNY VIOLENTLY RESISTED THE IDEA OF A SANITARIUM.

The thought of another institution reminded him of reform school, and he shuddered.

"I'm not going someplace where they make you sleep on the porch in the freezing cold," he said after the doctor left and the adults had gathered at his bedside. "Fuck that. Think I'd leave my work and my wife and my kids to go live with other sickies I don't know? I once beat this TB on my own. I can do it again."

"You were younger then, you dope," Frankie said with brutal affection. "You fool around this time and it'll be curtains for you, unless you do exactly what Lucy says."

"Think of the children," Amie reminded him. "Do you want them to catch TB?"

Johnny turned his head away for several moments and then said, "No," in a barely audible voice. Then, "What if the food is rotten?" he objected. "Which it will be. You get ten miles outta New York, and the bread is inedible."

"I'll bring you something good to eat, every week," Amie promised.

"Yeah?" Johnny said skeptically. "How are you going to get there? Fly?"

"Sal will drive me," Amie said resolutely.

"I'll take her up there," Frankie offered. "We'll both come and see you. We'll play poker. You'll get sick of us. You'll get fat, too, with all the food we bring you."

"And who the hell will run my business, eh?" Johnny demanded.

"I will," Amie said unexpectedly. They all turned to her in astonishment. "I always was your silent partner, remember? Well, now I'm your *talking* partner. And I say, you are going where Lucy tells you to go, Johnny. You are not going to make a widow out of me, because I look awful in black." She bit her lip so that he wouldn't have to see her cry.

"Aw, I'll think about it," Johnny grumbled. "Now beat it, all of you. You're all standing around making me feel like I'm already lying in a coffin, instead of a bed."

"Don't think too long," Frankie said over his shoulder as he went out.

A FEW DAYS LATER, AMIE WAS SURPRISED WHEN JOHNNY CALLED HER to his bedside and said, "We have to talk shop, you and I."

She sat beside him and took his hand. "Talking makes you cough," she warned.

"Well, this you have to hear, while I still have some breath. I want you to understand my share of the business. Yeah, yeah, you think you know, but hear me out. I know you can run the bar itself; our staff is good. But right from day one, you have to let them know you aren't some gullible dame. You can probably handle the gamblers most of the time, but I already told Frankie to show up and let them know there's still a wolf guarding the place. Still, you gotta keep your eyes on every single one of them—everybody who works for you—to make sure they don't start stealing; everyone from the busboys to the bartender." He did cough now, but he drank some water, and it stopped.

"I understand all this," Amie said. "I wish you'd save your strength."

"Listen to me. Someday soon we won't have to take the bets anymore. So we won't have to answer to the Bosses who grease the wheels that make this city run. But for now, we take the bets, and the Bosses and the cops still want *their* take. And we give it to them, to keep the peace, so there won't be trouble. If I hadn't gotten sick, you would never have to care about this. But now, you must do what I'd do if I were here."

Amie wished she didn't have to hear it. She'd long ago learned to simply push unpleasant things out of her mind. But this was serious; she could see that. She said quietly, "I'm not clever like Petrina, or as tough as Lucy, or as brave as Mario's wife."

Johnny drank more water. "You're smarter and stronger than

you think. Look, here's how it works. The runners collect the bets from the bookies and shopkeepers. When Mario was a kid, he used to be my runner. But Petrina put a stop to it. Anyway, we don't use family as runners anymore, so no matter what anyone tells you, don't let our twins do any of it. Keep them in school, and make them do their homework."

"Of course," Amie murmured.

"Meanwhile, keep strict accounts of what comes in and what goes out of the betting operation. We used to report it all to Ma, who arranged to pay all our tributes to the Bosses, with her lawyer Domenico as our courier and fixer. Frankie does all the collecting of money, so he will probably take over Ma's book. I'll talk to him. Sal will provide the muscle. But you, Amie, you must be my eyes and ears. I'll show you how the numbers work. Sure, you can rely on Frankie, even to help you with our kids. But in the end, trust nobody," Johnny warned, staring at her hard. "Not even the family. And don't go blabbing to the other wives about it. This is not gossip. This is survival."

SAL DROVE JOHNNY UPSTATE, WITH AMIE AND LUCY GOING ALONG, to make sure that Johnny got settled in properly. They decided to stay overnight at a local inn.

Meanwhile, back home, after the maid put all the children to bed, Frankie went to the main house, where Filomena was now living alone most of the time, except when Petrina visited for an overnight or weekend stay. Frankie wondered how Mario's wife could bear being in that big house by herself on most nights.

He walked into the dining room, where Filomena was drinking coffee. She was surprised to see him. "Would you like something to eat?" she asked, thinking that perhaps he was lonely, with Johnny and the wives gone.

Frankie shook his head. "I ate at Johnny's bar. I'm fine." But he sat down and accepted a cup of espresso. Filomena sat in the chair beside him. He said, "Lucy's got a birthday coming. Think you have anything in your shop she'd like?"

"Oh, yes," Filomena said. "A lovely pair of emerald earrings, perfect for her!"

Frankie said, "I don't know. Lucy *é unica—una ragazza bellissima acqua e sapone*. So, you really think a gal like that would go for earrings?"

Filomena smiled at a man who thought his wife was one in a million, a true "soap and water" beauty whose very naturalness might actually make her resist adornment. "Of *course* she'd like earrings," she replied. "These emeralds are special—they have that rare blue flame in their center, which go with her Irish eyes!"

"Okay, I'll stop by tomorrow to pick 'em up." Then Frankie said casually, "Did you figure out what you want to do with Mario's shop? I can sell it for you, if you like."

"No, thanks. I've decided to keep it, Frankie," she said. "This is Mario's business, and I know it well, since I am his partner."

But Frankie shook his head warningly. "It's a lot to take on, alone." His tone implied, *For a woman*.

Hearing this patriarchal message, Filomena thought wryly, *You don't know the half of it*. For she had been to a doctor recently, who had confirmed what she'd guessed. Mario's baby was due in September. Soon it would be impossible to keep this a secret from the brothers, but she wanted to write the news to Mario first. Especially since here was Frankie, already telling her just what a woman could, and couldn't, do.

"I won't actually be running my business alone," Filomena said, smiling at him with a clear, direct gaze. "Petrina is going to work with me at the shop." She did not add, *Because your sister is getting a divorce, and she says she wants to make her own money*. This, too, had not been announced yet.

"Petrina! She knows how to buy things, not sell them," Frankie scoffed.

Unruffled, Filomena said, "She's actually a very good

saleswoman. The female customers want to be beautiful, like her, so they ask her advice. And the male customers like to show off that they can spend big, to impress her. We'll do just fine, Frankie."

"Until Petrina gets bored," Frankie countered. "She will, you know. At least you can depend on me and Johnny."

"I only get bored by boring people," said a female voice in the corridor. Petrina had emerged from the study and stood in the doorway with a triumphant glint in her eye at having caught out her brother. "But gems are never boring! And yes, Frankie, I *do* know how to buy jewels. I'm taking that course at the gemology institute where Mario studied, so I can make sure our suppliers don't swindle us. As for me not being dependable, well, I'm a college graduate, Frankie dear. With honors. I know how to buckle down and work. And my partner here is as sharp as they come with numbers."

Petrina beamed at Filomena. Tonight they'd had dinner together, and Petrina had confided all her divorce woes, then asked about Mario. So Filomena had decided to tell only Petrina that she was pregnant, saying, *I have good news. You are going to be a godmother at last.*

Frankie now sensed this new camaraderie between his sister and Mario's wife, and he looked uneasy. He cleared his throat and spoke to Filomena. "Okay. That's fine. Keep your shop. But you know, this family reports all our profits together, so that we can make our payoffs together. We reported to Ma, but now, I have to be in charge of the family, until Johnny and Mario come home again. So, there's something else I need. Maybe you know where it is?"

Petrina raised her head alertly. Filomena said warily, "Yes?"

"Ma's book," Frankie said. "You can still help me with the numbers, just as you helped my mother," he said with a wave of his hand, as if he were being generous.

Filomena took a deep breath and said, "Wait here." She went into Tessa's parlor and unlocked the desk drawer. When she returned without Tessa's book and handed him only an envelope instead, Frankie looked perplexed.

"I said, I want Ma's *book*," he repeated, impatient now.

"No, Frankie," Filomena said firmly, giving him Mario's sealed letter. "Mario thought you might ask me about this, so he wrote a letter to you and Johnny."

Frankie tore it open and read the letter quickly, then shoved it back into the envelope in irritation. When he spoke, it was in the voice of a man warning her that he could lose his temper, which was a threat most people instinctively heeded. "Like I said, you can keep doing the numbers, but you still have to answer to someone in this family. Mario's not here now, and neither is Johnny, but Johnny agrees that I should take over."

Petrina lit a cigarette. "I'm the eldest member of this family," she said, exhaling a ring of smoke and watching it tremble on an air current. "So she can answer to *me*."

"You're crazy!" Frankie snapped. Petrina stiffened at this familiar insult. Heedless, Frankie went on. "You just don't get it. The Bosses know that Pop and Ma are gone. They'll be watching us to see if this family can still keep earning, still keep things running smoothly. If we slip up just once, they'll move in on our entire operation."

Petrina said evenly, "And since this was Ma's job, it's more fitting that I, as her daughter, take it over. Therefore, you and Johnny will report to *me*."

With a nod toward Petrina, Filomena said firmly, "So, you can tell Johnny that Tessa's book belongs to us now."

21

May-June 1944

I don't know who the hell that wife of Mario's thinks she is,"
Frankie groused to Lucy a few weeks later, after he'd spoken to
Johnny about the situation. "What gives her the right to take over
Ma's book, Ma's house—everything?"

"Come, now, m'love," Lucy said reasonably. "You don't really
want to sleep in your parents' old bedroom, do you? And who
wants to be the family bookkeeper, anyway? Tessa said that Mario's wife is good at numbers, so let her help the family."

Lucy was more concerned about Frankie's temper. He was
holding on to his troubles too long, like a dog gnawing on the
same old bone. Also, he'd bought a car of his own and had a bad
habit of "going for a drive" when he wanted to let off steam.

"You don't understand," he fumed. "She should be answering
to *us*! Instead, Petrina actually says *she's* going to take over Ma's
job—her and Mario's wife. Can ya beat that?"

Lucy paused. She'd always been close to Amie; and Petrina,
though ultra-glamorous, was an American, after all, and easy
enough to relate to. But Mario's wife, calm and loving and generous as she could be, was more daunting, with a core of steel that
reminded Lucy of the formidable Tessa. If this girl from Italy was
now teaming up with Petrina, it could change the balance among

the wives. "How come you didn't tell me this before?" she asked.

"Because I didn't believe Petrina would actually take charge!" Frankie said. "I thought she'd get one look at all that math and go right back to her country-club set."

"What does Johnny say about it?" Lucy responded.

"He says humor them, and we'll check up on them next month," he muttered. "He says at the first sign of trouble, Petrina will come crying to us anyway. Just wait till somebody fails to make a payment! Just wait till she has a bad month of earnings and then has to face our lawyer Domenico when he shows up to collect for Strollo, who will want his same amount of tribute no matter what." Lucy shivered at the cold tone of these possibilities.

Frankie was silently wondering why Lucy still hadn't worn the earrings he'd given her. She insisted that she loved them, but she never put them on. He blamed this on Mario's wife and Petrina, too. Today, he was tallying up all his grievances. "Meanwhile," he said, "Johnny's leading the life of Riley. He lies there all bundled up on his balcony, with people waiting on him hand and foot; then he goes to bed and just reads all day long."

"What does he read?" Lucy asked, amused. She knew what life was like at the sanitarium, how hard the struggle was simply to breathe, much less have the energy for anything else. And yet, miraculously, suffering people found a way to hang on to hope. But oddly, the invalids' relatives—and sometimes even the nursing staff—envied the unwell, as if they were luxuriating indolently, instead of fighting for their lives.

"What does Johnny read?" Frankie repeated incredulously. "Christ, everything! History, geography, art, science, and all those writers—Dickens, Hardy, Shakespeare, the works. He thinks he's finally figuring out the secrets of the universe from 'all the great minds.'"

Lucy smiled. "That's *great* for his morale. But how does he *look*, how's his color?"

"I don't know," Frankie said wearily. "I can't tell anymore.

Amie is convinced he's going to drop dead any day now. But that's because the first doctor—the one here in town—spooked her, right from the beginning." Frankie sighed heavily. "Maybe you should come with Amie and me on one of these trips, to look Johnny over yourself."

"I will. But for now, I don't want to scare him," Lucy said softly. "Bringing in the family nurse is like bringing in a priest."

FILOMENA FINALLY NERVED HERSELF TO GO INTO TESSA'S CLOSET. She took the key from the pocket of the apron that still hung on a peg, as if it were awaiting Tessa's return. She felt like a thief, and half expected Tessa's ghost to rise up in outrage. But the house was silent as Filomena went to the desk and unlocked the drawer that held the red-and-black ledger.

Petrina arrived a few minutes later, looking glamorous in a cream-colored linen suit. "Ready for business?" she said briskly.

"Yes. Now we will see what's on those left-side pages of this book," Filomena confided. Sitting in Tessa's chair at the desk, she opened it up. Petrina peered over her shoulder.

"Whoa!" Petrina said. "Names. *Lots* of people's names."

They both gasped as Filomena turned the pages. It really did seem as if the whole town owed Tessa money. It began with local shopkeepers and neighbors, as Filomena had guessed from the royal treatment that Tessa got when those merchants gave her the best fish or loaf of bread or cut of beef. But this list of debtors also included teachers and plumbers, bartenders and carpenters, housewives and elderly widows, taxi drivers and small-time gamblers, even clergymen.

Petrina, stunned, said, "It's like seeing the whole neighborhood in their underwear. It's awful! Like being a doctor with a stethoscope, or a priest in a confessional."

As Filomena turned more pages, they saw bigger debtors, from farther afield now: Merchants in the garment district who had to cover bills for fabrics, truckers, and staff. Nightclub owners and restauranteurs who had high rent. Big card players from uptown who came to Johnny's back room at the bar and sometimes needed help covering their losses. Judges and lawyers, doctors, politicians, cops. There were also bookies who couldn't always pay out to their bettors when a boxing match or horse race took an unexpected turn. Even other loan sharks who'd gotten stiffed and couldn't turn to the police to force restitution for illegal lending; they all came to Tessa to cover them with loans. Big fish, little fish. All in debt.

The whole thing horrified Filomena so much that her breath was coming out in gasps now, because it reminded her of what her parents, and Rosamaria's parents, had been forced to do when they could no longer repay their debts.

Petrina had grown very quiet. She'd had no idea of the scope of this operation and it scared her a little. How naive she'd been, whiling away her hours studying and playing tennis, in a life of comparative ease. Imagine if her school chums knew! She felt simultaneous pride in her parents' power and shame at how they'd gotten it. Then she recalled Pippa's birthday party, when her father had pointed out all the "respectable" guests who'd secretly come to him—or to the Big Bosses—for help, and she thought wryly, *Pop's loan and investment operations might have been perfectly respectable if his name was So-and-So National Bank.*

Petrina said hesitantly, "I guess these folks *have* to have someone like Ma to turn to, because the banks won't lend them money to finance a small business or cover a gambling debt. Look—even my brothers are borrowers, sometimes!" She ran her finger down the page.

Filomena followed her and saw that Frankie's real estate ventures, Johnny's partnerships with nightclubs, and even Mario's jewelry shop occasionally forced them to borrow from Tessa to pay their suppliers on time. The ledger indicated that they usually repaid the loans within a month or so. But it made Tessa's sons three of her most consistent debtors.

Tessa had painstakingly kept track of it all. Her clients not only had to repay what they'd borrowed; they also paid something called "interest" for the privilege of being a debtor. And that, Filomena saw, was how lenders made their big profits. "Ah," she said when, at last, they came to pages of red ink instead of black, indicating hefty expenses paid out by Tessa.

"That's the tribute she pays for the Bosses, isn't it?" Petrina said in a low voice. "It goes to Strollo, but it really goes to Mr. Costello—the Prime Minister of the underworld, the one we met at the Copacabana, remember?"

"Yes." Filomena pointed to figures in blue ink. "These are Johnny and Frankie and Mario's contributions, to cover our tributes for the Bosses, and the policemen's 'benefit fund.'"

Petrina nodded, with a new respect for her brothers. "They've managed it well, because they understand each other's strengths, and accept their own role," she confided. "See, Johnny was always closer to my father, more like him—clearheaded, a good decision-maker, sees the big picture. Frankie goes by his guts; he's instinctive and quick to action, and people are attracted to that, so he's a great dealmaker, gets others on board. And Mario—well, *you* know, he's smart and creative, he's a good strategist, knows how to quietly maneuver into a position of strength without causing a ruckus."

Listening to Petrina's assessment of the men, Filomena stared at the pages full of figures. She'd always found solace in numbers; they were her friends with distinct personalities. Now they even seemed to embody the members of this family: Johnny and his father, she felt, both had the personality of a 7, wise and thoughtful; Frankie's charisma was captured in the dramatic swoop of a 6; Mario had the artistry of a 5.

It was not the first time that her mind had worked in this way. Even as a girl, she'd seen Rosamaria as an inspiring number 1; later, when Filomena arrived in New York and was faced with a household of lively women, she'd figured Tessa to be a powerful 8, Lucy a hardworking 4, Petrina an adventurous 3, and Amie a sensitive 2. Oddly, Filomena couldn't see a number for herself, but since she was supposed to be Rosa, it was a number 1 to which she must aspire.

Somehow these images steadied her emotions. For she deeply loved not only Mario but every single troublesome and vulnerable member of his family, so she had an urge to protect them, even from themselves. This surprising tide of maternal love sometimes threatened to overwhelm her. But these numbers could help to keep it under control. By guarding the family's ledger, she could help her loved ones avoid the shoals, and reach safe harbors. *Whoever controls the debt controls the fate,* she thought.

As they worked together Petrina observed, "Our men are like ducks—gliding along serenely, on the surface making it look easy to do business; but underneath, they're all paddling like hell to stay afloat." She even understood the socialites at the country club; they, too, didn't want to know what *their* husbands had to do to stay in the swim. Suddenly she felt much more compassion for everyone. She sighed. "I'll make us lunch. It's Cook's day off."

"Yes, I can finish up here," Filomena said. She remained absorbed in the book all morning until she heard the postman drop mail through the slot. She locked the book away and hurried to pick up the mail. And there it was, the letter they'd both been waiting for.

A message from Mario. "Everything all right with him?" Petrina asked, trying not to be overbearing. But all she could think of was Mario as a little boy, ducking bullets with her at Coney Island. Only this time, that sweet creature was out there all on his own.

"This letter must have crossed with the one I sent him," Filomena said, misty eyed, as she scanned it. "He doesn't seem to know about the baby yet." She was frowning because at first, what Mario had written made no sense. *I am going to Amie's home to say hello to the folks.* Then she realized he'd made a kind of code, because of military censorship. He was saying that he was shipping out to France, the land where Amie came from. An ocean away—where so much of the fighting and killing was going on.

"He's all right. But they're sending him to France," she said. "I'll write him the news again, in case my earlier letter doesn't reach him." Her hand shook as she picked up her pen and wrote back, *Keep your head low. You are going to be a father in September.*

***

ON THE LAST DAY OF SCHOOL IN JUNE, AMIE'S BOYS CAME HOME with strange news. They had walked home alone, for the first time since Tessa's death.

"Where's Christopher?" Amie demanded. "Why didn't he walk with you?"

Two sets of shoulders went up and down as the twins shrugged. "Dunno. He just didn't come for us," Vinnie said, sitting down to devour his milk and cookies.

"But where is he?" Amie demanded. "He knows it's his job to look after you."

"His friends said he got in a swanky car with a redheaded man who had big rings on all of his fingers, and shiny shoes," Paulie reported.

Amie, who was godmother to Chris and Gemma and felt responsible, telephoned Lucy at the hospital immediately. "Have you seen Christopher?" she asked.

Lucy felt the question land like a rock in her chest. And when Amie described the man who'd enticed Chris into his car, Lucy left the hospital at such a hard run that the heel of her shoe broke off. On the subway she thought of every horrible thing that could happen to boys who got abducted—they could end up in the hospital, or the morgue.

Walking home, she stopped at the school and found one of the administrators, who was locking up the building. "We thought the man was an uncle, come to take him home for the summer," the woman explained. "He looked so much like Chris, who seemed to know him."

Lucy began to shake. When she got home, Amie told her that she'd asked Frankie and Sal to go out looking. "They said if we didn't hear from them by now, you should talk to the cop who walks the beat around that apartment building Frankie owns—that place where you used to live when you weren't married," Amie said worriedly. Lucy knew who Frankie meant.

So she ran out to find Pete, the stocky policeman with the round, cheerful face and alert green eyes. He was making his usual rounds. She told him about the strange man in the car.

"What did he look like?" Pete asked. Lucy repeated the description she'd heard. "Sounds like Eddie Rings," he said instantly. "From Hell's Kitchen. Uses those rings like brass knuckles. Shakes down unions, sells 'discount' cigarettes, dabbles in the black market, and murders for hire, on the side. Covers his tracks pretty well, so nobody can pin it on him."

Lucy knew this officer well enough to plead, "Please find my son. You know what can happen to boys in this city."

"I'll do my best," he promised. "Never heard of Rings in the kidnapping business, so maybe he just wanted the boy to do some errand for him, you know, like pass some phony money. Some of these gangsters groom kids, a little at a time, to be their front line, so if they get caught, they keep quiet, and it's not the big shots who get arrested."

Lucy gulped at those words, remembering the incident with the candy-store owner. Hurrying home, she chided herself for not telling Frankie about it. "It might have been better if Frankie *had* thrashed Chris back then," she muttered worriedly.

When Frankie came home, Lucy didn't know how to tell him her worst fears. They were all having dinner together at Filomena's house, where Petrina and Pippa were now staying for part of the summer. "Don't worry, Lucy, we'll find him," Petrina said, but she looked helplessly at Frankie, as if signaling him to assuage their fears.

"I don't think it's kidnapping. Nobody called for a ransom, did they?" Frankie said. Lucy shook her head mutely. Apart from her "adoption" of Chris, she had never shirked from telling the truth, gently delivering bad news to patients at the hospital or telling off doctors, if necessary. But today she was absolutely terrified to speak.

Finally, Filomena asked the right question. "Do you know why this man would pick Christopher, instead of any of the other children in the playground?" She gazed clear-eyed at Lucy, not without sympathy, but sensing that she was holding something back.

Lucy blurted out the whole story of the man who'd asked Chris to go into the candy store with phony money. Frankie was, predictably, furious, but Petrina said, "You see? Lucy knew you'd lose your temper. Calm down, Frankie. This is good information, and it will help Sal find Chris. Let's stay focused on that!"

Later that evening, Sal showed up at Lucy's town house, having made the kinds of phone calls and inquiries on the street that Johnny normally would have, to their contacts in the underworld of bar gossip and racketeer talk. Sal reported to her and Frankie.

"It *was* Eddie Rings. He operates in Hell's Kitchen, and it was *his* gang that the Pericolo brothers ran into trouble with, when they tried to fence the stolen jewelry there," Sal explained. "Turns out, those Pericolos had bragged that they had an 'in' with Tessa, said they had her financial backing. So back then, Eddie decided to check out this family and send one of his crew around here to find out about our operations."

Frankie said impatiently, "What does this guy want with us now, then? Is he holding Chris for ransom or something? Like, a kidnapping? Or does he think we've got some of the jewels that those stupid Pericolo brothers showed to his fence?"

"No. Eddie knows that the cops found the swag in the Pericolos' car and impounded it all. But ever since Eddie's crew got into that big bar fight with the Pericolos, the cops have been giving them hell. It's hard to do business when you're under surveillance! Eddie blames *us* for his troubles—he still believes we sent the Pericolos into his territory; maybe he thinks we're making a move to take over his operations. You might have been spotted that night of the bar fight, cruising his area, Frankie, when you, Johnny, and Mario went after the Pericolos."

"Those Pericolos!" Lucy exclaimed. "For every stunt they pull, *we* pay the price."

Sal said, "Anyway, Eddie's got bigger troubles now. See, a few weeks ago, Eddie killed a guy in the unions who stiffed him, and now a witness has turned up. So the cops are ready to arrest Eddie. But someone must have tipped him off, because word on the street is that Eddie's gone on the lam. Maybe forever."

"Find out where he's hiding and what he wants from us," Frankie said tersely.

"Working on it."

It was a terrible night. Gemma had heard from Amie's twins that her brother, Chris, had gone "truant," but Lucy could only tell her that Frankie would straighten everything out.

The next day was ominously quiet until the late afternoon, when Sal finally returned. Amie had taken Gemma along with her boys to Filomena's house, so that the young ones could play together before dinner and not overhear anything terrible when the men returned to Lucy. Frankie was out collecting rent from the bars and nightclubs, and using the opportunity to see if anybody knew anything. Sal and his men had fanned out farther afield. So when Sal showed up at Lucy's house to report what he'd learned, he found her alone there, just returning from work.

Looking a bit uncomfortable, Sal asked, "Where's Frankie?"

"He'll be home any minute. Sal, tell me, what is it?" she asked urgently.

Sal said carefully, "Lucy, I don't know what to make of this.

Back when Eddie sent those guys from his crew to check out this family, apparently they spotted *you* walking around with a little boy who looked a lot like Eddie. They recognized you as the nurse they'd brought to Harlem to . . . deal with . . . a girl that Eddie got pregnant."

Lucy, already a bit dizzy from a fairly sleepless night, clutched the back of a chair to steady herself. Sal was watching her searchingly, and evidently the look on her face confirmed that he was on the right track. She said slowly, "How do you know this?"

"One of the cops on our payroll made some inquiries. There's a priest in Hell's Kitchen who's actually Eddie's cousin. He said that after Eddie's men spotted you and Chris, they got worried that they screwed up, so they asked this priest to talk to the nuns in the orphanage where you said you'd bring the baby. The priest asked the mother superior if a baby boy was brought there back in March of '34. She checked her records and said that no baby was left there at that time. So, the priest got the job of telling Eddie that he might have a son walking around Greenwich Village; the priest even tried to convince Eddie that it was a sign from God, to repent and change his ways. Fat chance of that!"

Lucy flinched, just remembering the thugs she'd had to deal with that night in Harlem; her own role sounded so terribly sordid, too. Sal said, "So Eddie went to the schoolyard to check it out for himself. He told his priest cousin that seeing Chris was like looking in a mirror. Eddie's got a big ego. But Chris *really* does look like the guy, Lucy. Our cop friend filched a photo from Eddie's arrest file, to give us a face we can search for. I have to give this photo back today, but I thought you'd want to see it. This was taken nearly ten years ago, but—you get the picture."

Lucy peered at it, and her heart sank. Eddie was a dead ringer for Christopher, all the more so because the photo had been taken when the gangster was a very young man.

"I guess Eddie enjoyed getting back at us," Sal said. "I don't think we've heard the last of him, because just before he blew town, he said, *A man in my position can't let strangers—especially a woman—get the better of him.*"

"Meaning, me?" Lucy gasped. If this man wanted revenge on her and the family, he could have it easily, by harming—or killing—poor Chris.

Frankie was at the front door now, letting himself in. Sal said, "Want me to tell him?"

"No," Lucy said in a whisper, "I'll do it. I need to talk to him alone."

"Sure. I'll step out for a smoke." After a pause Sal said, "Holler if you need me."

Frankie saw Sal hastily go out the back door. "What's the matter with him?" he said.

"We need to talk, just you and I," Lucy said tremulously.

"What for?" Frankie demanded. "Did something else happen?"

Lucy cut straight to the point. "We think that man Eddie is Christopher's father."

"But—but—you said his father died," Frankie said, looking so trusting that Lucy burst into tears, right then and there, and told him that Chris was not her son.

Frankie sank onto a chair, looking so confused and devastated that Lucy wished with all her heart that she could die, right now, if it meant that Frankie wouldn't have to look like that anymore.

But when he raised his head as if in a dream and said, "What are you saying, Lucy?" she knew she must tell him everything as directly as possible—starting with the infant she'd lost in Ireland, which had caused her to give all her love to a baby she'd rescued who looked up at her so innocently when she held him in her arms and whom she simply could not give away.

Frankie was silent for a long time. Finally, he said quietly, "You know, Lucy, you didn't have to play me for a sap. I would have still loved you and Chris anyway."

"Oh, Frankie, I played *myself* for a sap," she cried. "I actually thought Chris was a gift from God. That he *was* mine. Can you believe it? I thought God loved me because he knew how much I suffered when I was just a young girl myself."

Frankie fell silent again, sitting very still. Then he said in a choked voice, "If only you'd told me all this a long time ago, I could have protected Chris better. You lied to me, Lucy—not just once, but over and over, all this time!"

"Don't you see—by then, Chris really was *ours*," she whispered.

Frankie said more brusquely, "Apparently Eddie Rings didn't like being lied to, either."

Lucy said in a burst, "Oh, Frankie, I don't care if you hate me for the rest of my life, but we've *got* to find Chris, before that horrible man kills him, just to get back at us."

"Stop it. I don't hate you. He won't kill Chris, because he'd lose his leverage over us. And the boy is his own flesh and blood. That matters. Now, Eddie's in trouble with the cops and has to lay low until he figures it's safe to resurface. So, I'll find Chris. I've got our best people looking. All men have enemies, even on their own crew. We'll find out who Eddie's enemies are."

Resolutely, Frankie stood up and, without another word, went to join Sal. Lucy watched them go off in the car. She knew they'd be out all night, combing the city.

Unable to move, Lucy just sat there at the kitchen table, until Amie came home with the kids and put them to bed. After telling Amie the whole story, Lucy, for the first time in her life, took a sedative and went to bed, waiting for a sleep that felt like death.

22

June-July 1944

I don't see why I have to go to a doctor," Pippa objected, swinging her long, dark ponytail. "I'm not sick. This is a lousy way to spend the summer. And how come it's such a big secret that I come here to see Dr. Nora?"

"It's not a secret, exactly," Petrina said as they alighted from their cab on the Upper East Side. "It's just private. It's *your* time, to tell the doctor anything you want, without worrying about other people hearing what you have to say."

"This is worse than all the homework the tutor makes me do," Pippa complained as they rode up in the elevator. "I'd rather go to dance camp."

"Okay, you can go to dance camp next month," Petrina promised as they entered the reception room. "Just finish out these sessions with the doctor first, okay?"

Pippa shrugged and followed Dr. Nora into her conference room. Petrina, alone in the waiting room, wondered if these visits with the child psychiatrist were really doing any good. Pippa still suffered from nightmares, which she'd been having ever since Tessa's death. Pippa's grades had slipped, which was why Petrina hired a tutor for her. And the normally diplomatic Pippa was now snappish with everyone, adults and kids.

"I wonder what she actually tells that doctor, behind those closed doors," Petrina murmured as she waited.

Richard and his mother would have kittens if they found out about these visits; they thought only the mentally ill, and Jewish intellectuals, went to psychiatrists to spill their personal problems. If Richard's lawyer knew, he'd no doubt use it as evidence against Petrina, in what was amounting to a pitched battle for the divorce settlement.

"Everything's always my fault," Petrina mused gloomily. She'd been treated as an incorrigible and a delinquent by her own family, just because she'd gotten pregnant with Mario when she was fifteen. No other reason; she'd been so obedient the whole rest of her life, but nobody ever noticed. So she didn't want Pippa labeled as "troubled."

"I'll bet Mario's wife blames me for making him trot off to war," Petrina fretted. If Mario got killed, even Petrina would never forgive herself. Yet, to be honest, it had been a huge relief to let go of that damned secret, which had weighed her down for so long. Perhaps, she mused, her parents had done her a favor, after all, by claiming Mario as *their* son, for she'd never had to tell Richard about the child she'd had with another man. Imagine what her in-laws could make of *that* now, if they ever found out! "But they won't," Petrina vowed.

Forty-five minutes later, Pippa emerged from the consulting room looking as inscrutable as ever, and Dr. Nora asked Petrina if she could "have a word." Pippa sighed mightily, flopped into a chair in the waiting room, and perused the magazines.

"Is she very sick?" Petrina asked the instant the door closed behind her.

Dr. Nora said gently, "I'd say she's wounded, but she's a brave girl, a strong one." Petrina exhaled in relief, until the doctor said, "I think it's the impending divorce that's bothering her now. She thinks her father doesn't want her."

"He doesn't," Petrina said bluntly. "It's all because his fiancée doesn't want Pippa around. And Richard's mother and sister don't, either; Pippa reminds them all of me, you see. Even in the best of times, they all treated her like a pet poodle who might win them a trophy at the dog show. Now they couldn't care less. But that doesn't stop their lawyer from holding this custody thing over my head. They use it to make me toe the line about the money, which is all they really care about."

"And your family?" Dr. Nora asked delicately. "How do they feel about Pippa?"

"They adore her," Petrina said softly. "Her cousins especially."

The doctor smiled. "Yes, she loves them, too. She told me quite firmly that she wants to stay with you. But—do you think that you and your family can provide a stable, secure environment for your beautiful daughter?"

Petrina's eyes were bright. "Look, I know what you're asking. My family has its flaws. But they're good-hearted people. There's warmth in that house. Whereas, Richard's parents' house—it's like an ice palace. Ever seen one of those?"

Dr. Nora shook her head, looking intrigued. Petrina explained, "I once visited a friend in Minnesota, where the rich in town built a big ice palace in the winter, for fun—like we New Yorkers make snowmen. Anyway, that's how it is with Richard and his family. They live in an ice palace. You don't notice how cold it is right away. Because from the outside, it glitters in the sun and dazzles you. But inside—it's pitch dark, and cold as hell."

Dr. Nora nodded as if she comprehended everything that Petrina was trying to say. Gently, the doctor concluded, "I do think Pippa would be better off with you. But a twelve-year-old needs an environment where she feels confident that things will be all right. She can't live on a roller coaster, wondering if there's a big drop around the next corner. You see, I think she can survive this shock she's suffered. I'm not so sure she can endure another one."

Petrina absorbed this, but looked the doctor straight in the eye when she said, "I think you underestimate my daughter. Her heart is full of courage. And one thing I've learned is that life *is* a roller coaster. You have to figure out how to handle the downs as well as the ups. When the ride is nice and flat—you're dead."

***

LUCY'S DAUGHTER, GEMMA, WAS SITTING ON THE FRONT STOOP OF her town house, waiting for Pippa to show up. Gemma loved it when she had a girl cousin to play with, one who could teach her all the fun games and popular songs. Gemma didn't mind playing boy games with her twin cousins, but boys got upset when you played better than them.

Just last week, her father had taken Gemma and Vinnie and Paulie to the park, where they all took turns as Frankie pitched a baseball at them, so they could practice their batting swings. And Gemma had hit the ball right past the outfield and over the fence. A home run! So what reaction did she get from her father and cousins? Dead silence, as if she'd disgraced herself.

Then Vinnie said, "You'll have to go chase that ball." So she did, and when she returned, they all resumed playing, but her father didn't give her another turn at bat.

"Your swing is good enough," Frankie had said. "You don't need more practice."

Gemma sighed now, tossing her strawberry-blond hair like a dog shaking itself off. She glanced back at the house and saw Donna, the maid, worriedly peering at her from the window. Gemma groaned. Ever since her brother, Chris, had "gone on a trip" somewhere without the family's permission, now everybody was keeping an eagle eye on Gemma, as if she might wander off, too. So, although she was nearly six years old, she couldn't do anything alone, not even sit here on the front stoop without being watched.

"How come when Chris does something wrong, *I* get punished?" she'd objected.

"Don't get smart with me, missy," Lucy had retorted. "It's for your own good."

Gemma had managed to convince her parents to buy her a pair of shiny ball-bearing roller skates, but nobody had time to teach her how to use them. The maid, Donna, had tried to help, but she was useless, since she'd never owned a pair and had no idea how to skate. So here Gemma sat, with her brand-new skates, hoping against hope that Pippa would teach her. Pippa was twelve, and knew everything about everything.

"Hi, Pippa!" Gemma shouted when her cousin arrived. Aunt Petrina immediately went off to talk to Filomena, so the girls had a blissful time where they could play and talk openly. Pippa had brought her own skates with her, and now she taught Gemma how to find her balance and how to make beautiful turns.

"See, a turn is not like making a squared corner. You go in on a curve, sideways, like this," Pippa said, gliding into something like a ballet second position, "then make a backward semicircle to go out of the turn," she said, guiding Gemma. It made all the difference.

Gemma was thrilled with this new power, and they skated back and forth awhile.

"Sidewalks are bumpy," Pippa said, wrinkling her nose in distaste. "It's better in a skating rink. It's all smooth. Lots of other people at rinks, though."

When they were tired of skating, they sat down on the front stoop. Donna, reassured to see the savvy Pippa in charge, gave them a bowl of grapes to eat, then went back inside.

The two girls sat there spitting out the pits from fat purple grapes, until a pair of ladies carrying shopping bags walked by and one woman said to the other, "Aren't those girls cute? This one here looks like little Elizabeth Taylor," and she pointed to Pippa, who gave them a restrained, tolerant smile at being compared to a child movie actress.

"And the other one looks just like Shirley Temple," said the companion. "Do you sing and tap-dance, little girl?"

"No," Gemma said bluntly, "but I can skate."

"Isn't she a doll?" The ladies laughed and went away.

"Too bad you're too young for dance camp, Gemma," Pippa said thoughtfully. "That's where I'm going, when I'm done with this doctor stuff."

"Why do you keep going to a doctor? Are you very sick?" Gemma asked.

"Nope." Pippa shook her ponytail decisively. "I just go because it makes the grown-ups feel better. The doctor asks me about my dreams and stuff, that's all."

"I had a dream last night," Gemma volunteered. "I saw *Nonna*."

Pippa looked startled. "You saw Grandma?"

Gemma nodded vigorously. "Yes, she told me to tell you she's all right."

Pippa sat so stone still that at first Gemma thought her cousin had swallowed a pit. But then Pippa spoke in a hushed voice. "She said to tell *me* that?"

"Yes," said Gemma matter-of-factly. "She said, 'Tell Pippa I'm doing just fine, so she should stop crying, and tell Pippa to take care of you all, now that I'm in heaven.' But then she said that Aunt Rosamaria can still hand out those money gifts to us at Christmas."

Pippa gave Gemma a sideways look. "Hey, Gemma," she said respectfully, "don't let anybody tell you that you're not smart. You're as sharp as they come."

"I know." Gemma sighed. "But nobody likes me when I'm smart."

"I HAVE TO FIND A NEW PLACE TO LIVE," PETRINA ANNOUNCED TO Filomena with more bravado than she felt, as she entered Tessa's study. "Richard and I don't own our house. His parents do. Now they want it back!"

Filomena looked up from her book of figures. "Our guest-house here is available."

Petrina shook her head ruefully. "Pippa's doctor thinks I should keep her in her private school in the suburbs; less disruption. Plus, Dr. Nora thinks the city has too many 'traumatic memories' for Pippa, even though she loves visiting with her cousins. So, I have to go house hunting in Westchester, and the nice homes don't come cheap."

"All right, we'll find a way," Filomena said thoughtfully.

"It has to be close enough so I can keep commuting into the city, to work with you," Petrina said.

She'd been riding the train along with all those bankers and brokers who were her neighbors. Except for the smoking-car passengers, these men rode to work in silence, punctuated only by the rustle of their newspapers; even then, they seemed to turn the same page at the same time. But she liked being a commuter. Making money was more challenging than gossiping at the ladies' clubs and endless rounds of bridge games.

"Even with the alimony, I'm going to have to sell a lot of jewelry to pay for my new life. But I will," Petrina said resolutely. "I'm done with Richard and his family."

Filomena, seeing that Petrina was truly worried about Pippa, said, "We must all carve out a new kind of life for all our children. It's the only thing that matters now." She knew that this could not be accomplished without risk of more trouble ahead. But she did not say aloud what else she was thinking: *Whatever happens, I am not going to die like Tessa did.*

***

"JOHNNY'S GETTING SO THIN," AMIE WHISPERED TO FRANKIE AS they were driving back from the sanitarium one Sunday afternoon.

"I know," Frankie said quietly. "But he was always kinda lanky. Don't worry, Amie. He's tougher than you know. He beat the TB once. He can do it again."

Amie stole a glance at Frankie's profile—so handsome, like Johnny and Mario and Gianni, but Frankie had become so dispirited ever since Christopher disappeared.

Frankie had managed to weather all the other family tragedies, but this one seemed to be too much for him. On the surface, he'd accepted the situation, forgiven Lucy and was affectionate with her; in fact, because he was so circumspect these days, he was unusually patient with them all. Yet, as stoic as Lucy and Frankie were, the strain of worrying was plain to see, as the weeks went by and there were still no new leads.

"Don't worry. Chris will be returned to us. And Lucy loves *you* so much," Amie said consolingly, reaching out to pat his shoulder.

"I know that Sal and my men will find Chris," he said broodingly. Then in a burst he added, "And I *do* understand why Lucy didn't tell me the whole story at first. I really do. But, hell! I gotta say, once we were married, she could have trusted me. It bothers me. I mean, if Lucy could lie to me once, and then keep that lie going, I can't help thinking that she could lie to me again, anytime. How would I ever know?"

"She won't," Amie assured him. "She feels so awful about it. Secrets hurt the one who keeps them. So do grudges. They chew away at your insides. You must forgive her."

Their car was winding around narrow mountain roads, and Frankie stopped talking so that he could concentrate; this was a tricky spot even on a sunny day, but the sky had suddenly blackened and the wind was picking up. An ominous rumble of thunder seemed to be rolling toward them.

"This looks bad," Frankie said just as a shaft of lightning split the sky and flashed violently ahead of the next, even louder thunderclap. "We aren't going to make it to the highway," he shouted as the rain came down—sudden, loud, and hard.

"There's a little inn at the bottom of the hill," Amie shouted back.

The road had become muddy and slippery, and they skittered perilously with each zig and zag of the descent. Amie held her breath the whole way down, crouching in her seat and flinching at the rain that was pelting hard against the windshield. She wondered how Frankie could possibly see ahead of him through this watery veil. But he plowed on determinedly and managed to steer down the slippery slope, until finally he swerved into the parking lot of the local inn.

A deafening crash of thunder directly over their heads made Amie shriek. Frankie turned off the car, jumped out, and ran around to her side, holding his jacket aloft so that he could make a canopy over them both as they dashed into the inn. The road was flooding already. They just made it into the lobby before another flash of lightning created a sudden white light, like a giant flashbulb popping as if God had snapped a picture of them.

"Care for a room, mister?" asked the short, balding man behind the desk.

"Just a summer storm, right?" Frankie asked hopefully.

The man shook his head grimly. "This is mountain weather, son. Radio says that trees and power lines are down everywhere. Police closed the highway, and the trains ain't running tonight."

"We'd better call home while we can," Frankie said to Amie. "Is there a phone I can use to call Manhattan, sir?"

"You getting a room?"

"Sure," Frankie said, then added, "Two rooms."

The man nodded toward a phone on a desk. "Then be my guest."

AMIE WAS AWAKENED IN THE MIDDLE OF THE NIGHT BY A KEENING noise that terrified her. It was the wind, sounding like it was coiling around itself and picking up speed. Instinctively she jumped out of bed and stood by the closet, searching for her shoes. A moment later, there was a shattering sound as the window glass broke and fell right on her bed, just where she'd been sleeping only moments ago.

Stumbling in the dark, she found the wall switch, but the lights didn't go on. The rain was blowing sideways, right into the room. She felt her way to the door, yanked it open, and scurried across the carpeted hall, then knocked timidly on Frankie's door. If he was asleep, he wouldn't hear her, with all the noise of the storm.

But Frankie opened his door, looking sleepy and disheveled, wearing only his shorts. "Amie, what's wrong?" he asked.

"My window blew in!" she exclaimed, shivering. "There's glass everywhere, even on the bed! The lights are out, too." Frankie pulled her into his room and sat her down on a chair.

"You're soaked," he said. "I'll get you a towel."

Amie buried her head in her hands. She wondered if Johnny was scared, up there at the sanitarium in this storm. He'd looked nearly skeletal, his face so pale, with dark circles under his eyes. He wasn't eating enough. Did he want to die? Was he suffering that much? Was he really going to leave her, alone with their boys, in this terrible world where thugs took kids away from their mothers, as they had done to poor Lucy?

"Oh, Frankie!" she exclaimed, filled with emotion, as he returned with a big towel and a bathrobe, then politely stepped aside so she could change in the bathroom. When she returned, she said, "I'm so worried. What's going to happen to us all?" She had started to cry. Frankie, looking faintly alarmed at her tears, got a flask from his pocket and offered her a sip, putting his arm around her to stop her shivering and reassure her.

"Don't you worry," he said soothingly. "We're all survivors."

"You've been so good to Vinnie and Paulie," she whispered. "I can't tell you how much you mean to those boys. They absolutely worship you."

"Yeah, they're good little ball players," he said. "They remind me of me and Johnny when we were little—" When he broke off, choked with emotion, she saw that these visits to his dying brother were taking their toll on him, too. Perhaps that was why this trouble with Lucy was just too much for Frankie. Fate seemed against them these days, especially tonight, with the wind still howling around them like a pack of menacing wolves.

"I really miss Chris," Frankie confessed. "This is all my fault."

Amie was astonished. "How can you say that?"

"I keep seeing his face, at Christmastime. Remember? When he was playing dice with your twins, and I yelled at him. Did you see the look on his face? Chris just wanted to be a man; he thinks being a tough guy is the only way to prove he's really one of us. Why can't I make him understand, he's got nothing to prove? I always wanted a son. I always thought—he was mine, you know? And damn it, he *was* my boy, too. Is!" he corrected himself, horrified.

"Of *course* he is!" Amie touched his handsome cheek. She was unprepared for the way he turned to her, like an animal grateful for a kind hand.

Before she knew it, they were both reaching for each other— for love, for comfort, for the instinct to stay alive, when sorrow and sickness and death have come too close. Her passion was reawakening like a glowing ember in a dying fire that could be reignited by this spark, even if it *had* been such a long time since a man had reached for her and made her flesh respond to his touch. It was as if she'd been fasting and was now being nourished again; you didn't miss it until it came back to you, and then you found out you'd been truly starving, for far too long.

THE NEXT MORNING, THE SUN WAS SHINING BRIGHTLY, AS IF NOTHing had happened, as if the night before had nothing to do with the new day. Amie and Frankie slept until nearly noon—when there was a sudden brisk knock on the door.

"It's probably the maid," he said as Amie scurried into the bathroom to hide.

But it was Sal. He must have set out quite early that morning, to deliver more bad news. "Frankie," he said bluntly, "you can't go home."

"What the hell are you talking about?" Frankie demanded. "What's wrong *now*? What happened? Is it Lucy?"

"No, it's you," Sal said, looking worried. "The police got a 'tip' and raided your office at the apartment building on MacDougal Street. They found some of that stolen jewelry from the goddamn Pericolo brothers in your desk."

From her hiding place in the bathroom, Amie stifled a gasp and pressed her ear closer to the door to hear.

"*What?*" Frankie exclaimed.

"The Pericolo brothers are making like canaries, singing to the cops and the D.A., telling them the kinds of lies they like to hear, you know, to curry favor. They're saying that *you* put them up to that jewel theft, that you were their Boss and made them do it because they owed you money. They told the cops they'd find the last of the loot stashed in that little office of yours, and, surprise surprise, when the cops raided it, they found a big, expensive necklace. Those jerks had stolen it, and some of the other swag, from some dowager's town house on the Upper East Side; rumor is, the lady's hairdresser was in on the scheme."

"What necklace?" Frankie demanded, bewildered.

"Some big silver thing with giant turquoises on it. That's not all. The cops found a shitload of counterfeit ration coupons in your desk, to boot. So now, Frankie, the police are looking everywhere for *you*," Sal repeated emphatically. "A detective came to the house and asked Lucy where you were. She said she had no idea. Everybody covered up for you. So now you gotta leave that car of yours in a ditch somewhere up here, make it look like you had an accident. That shouldn't be hard to do. Smash a fender and make it look bad. I can drive Amie home. I can say I had to go pick her up after she visited Johnny."

Sal looked around. "Where the hell is Amie, anyway? The guy

at the front desk said she was in the room across the hall, but that place is a wreck."

Amie emerged, blushing, from the bathroom. Sal registered this briefly and recovered, but it was enough to make Frankie feel ashamed. Sal kept pretending he wasn't fazed, which was worse, in a way. Frankie said tensely, "The Pericolos are in jail. How the hell did they get a necklace into my office?"

Amie spoke up now. "Alonza," she ventured. "When Tessa met with her at the tea shop, she said that Alonza was wearing a big, expensive turquoise necklace. Tessa figured that it was part of the jewelry that Alonza's sons stole, remember?"

Sal agreed. "The Pericolos probably got Alonza to plant it in your office, along with those phony ration coupons."

Frankie said bitterly, "I knew we should have killed those guys."

"Frankie, peddling counterfeit ration coupons in wartime is serious," Sal warned. "We have to get you out of the country, *now*. Normally we'd send you to Italy, but Italy's a shambles, with Mussolini and all."

"No, not Italy," Frankie said slowly. "Did you hear anything more about Chris—and Eddie?"

"Yeah, I did," Sal said hurriedly. "They say Eddie Rings has family in Ireland, where he can trust people to hide him. Our cop friend found out what town Eddie's from, in farm country outside Dublin. Best word is, he went back there with the kid."

"Ireland," Frankie said resolutely, as if doing penance. "Then that's where I'm going, Sal. Tell Lucy I've gone to get Christopher back."

***

"I hope Sal got to Frankie before the police did," Filomena said in a low voice.

"He did. Sal phoned to say he's bringing Amie home," Petrina said. She sighed. "But isn't it just like Amie to go off and leave us with *this* crowd? Never thought I'd work in a pub!"

For, although Johnny's bar was usually closed on Sunday, a large group of men had rented out the back room for a private afternoon of card playing that had stretched well into the night.

Twelve men sat around the table, betting, eating and drinking heavily, chortling when they won and swearing loudly when they lost a hand. The room was choked with smoke. The bartender told Filomena that the man who'd set up the card game had been polite enough but he'd given no indication of the roughness of this crowd.

"Why don't they just go *home*?" Petrina moaned.

"Yes, I don't like the look of this group," Filomena agreed in a low voice. She had sensed that these people were trouble from the moment they'd entered. They were nothing like the regulars, the successful, well-dressed men who normally used this room.

No, tonight's customers were coarse and uncouth, hardened to the point where they disrespected everyone, especially women. They had brutish faces and even uglier attitudes, casually abusive; they were the kind of group who thought it was funny to trip the busboy and watch him fall, shattering a tray of glasses and then having to sweep it all up, while they kept jeering.

"These aren't big gangsters," Petrina said under her breath with contempt, confirming Filomena's opinion. "They're a dime a dozen; that's what makes them so mean. They know they'll never be the boss of anybody, except the wives and kids they beat up and the poor slobs who work for them. But *our* bartender isn't their foot soldier!"

As the evening wore on, it became clear that these customers considered Petrina and Filomena their servants, too. They summoned more and more platefuls of food, which they ate rapidly with the table manners of bears. But worse than the mounting dirty dishes and overflowing ashtrays and empty beer bottles was the rising tension that filled the air in a heavier way than the smoke from their cheap cigars. One man even tore up his cards in an infantile fit of pique at the bad hand he'd been dealt.

"This can't possibly end well," Petrina said, voicing the dread that everyone working here tonight felt in their bones.

And sure enough, when some of the men finally threw in their cards, rose to their feet, stretched, and headed out, the nervous, perspiring waiter took this as a signal to deposit their bill on their table—and the storm finally broke.

"Put it on my tab, my good man," said one of the remaining card players.

"You don't have a tab, sir," the waiter said anxiously.

"I *don't*?" The man gave him a murderous glare. Then he burst out into an ugly laugh and turned to his companions. "Anybody got a tab here?" he shouted.

One man pulled his pockets inside out, feigning destitution. Another called out, "Sure, I got a tab, but I left it in Cincinnati," and guffawed uproariously. The entire group began asking one another, "You got a tab? He's got a tab? Who's got a tab?"

Petrina and Filomena, watching from the waiter's station, were ostentatiously polishing the clean glasses and the silverware, as a signal that the bar was about to close.

"Hey, toots!" called out one of the three men who remained seated, counting his winnings, looking at the women. "We'll pay you next month, you cap-eesh?"

Petrina winced, then shook her head. "No tabs here," she said. "You pay now."

"Me pay now?" the man echoed, giving her the same murderous glare. "Me *no* pay now. Me thinks me no pay until your husband comes home. What do you think of that, you dumb bitch?"

Whoosh. The answer to his question came so sharply and swiftly that the whole roomful of people gasped in unison—as a steak knife sliced through the air and only barely missed cutting off the nose of the offensive blowhard. As it was, the knife landed in the wall so close to the man's face that for a moment he didn't dare move his head.

Petrina turned in amazement to Filomena, whose face remained impassive. Before anyone could say a word, she hurled another one, which landed on the opposite side of the man's head, having the psychological effect of pinning him in place for fear of where a third one might land.

"You pay now," Filomena said in a clear, hard voice, "or I'll cut more than those cards for you."

The other men didn't move, either. But the bartender reached under his bar for the baseball bat that he kept there yet seldom had to use.

"You want to play like the big boys?" Petrina said scornfully to the customers. "Know what happens in this neighborhood to a man who's too poor to pay his bills?"

The word *poor* hit its mark as effectively as the knife. The loudmouth scooped up a large handful of his winnings and threw down the cash on an empty table with a show of contempt, before collecting the rest of his profit and then stalking out the back door. The other men followed quickly now, muttering to one another but careful this time not to be overheard.

The terrified busboy hurriedly locked the door behind them.

In the silence that followed, Filomena gathered her and Petrina's coats. Finally, she said, "We're going to have to make some changes around here."

"Right," Petrina agreed. "We've never had trouble from the big fish. But these goddamned guppies have to go. We'll tell Amie that from now on, no more hosting any amateur Sunday card games. These little jerks want to gamble, let them play bingo at church."

Glancing at Filomena, she added respectfully, "But it's a mighty good thing that *one* of us knows how to throw a blade and pin an enemy to the wall!"

23

July 1944

The knife-throwing incident gave Filomena a legendary status for a while. It inspired Lucy, who, still struggling to comprehend the disappearances of both Chris and Frankie, found an outlet for her fears by telling the others that they should all take up boxing, for self-defense.

"I mean it!" she insisted. "Pete the cop knows an ex-fighter who's willing to give us lessons. I'm not saying we ever have to get in a ring with anybody. But if we know we can throw a good punch, people will hear that in our voices. My theory is that men bully women and children because they know we won't punch them in the face like a guy would. So, let's learn how. Then we'll teach the kids, all of them!"

"We'd better humor her," Petrina observed to the others. "She's on the edge."

So they all cautiously agreed and took eight lessons from a very tall, quiet teenage light-heavyweight fighter who'd lied about his age in order to get into the ring. He'd done well for himself and was still living in the neighborhood with his mother, who'd known and admired Tessa. The fighter's name was Vincent Gigante, and he was polite and encouraging, teaching them early in the morning when there were no men around.

"Just remember, ladies," he advised, "watch your opponent's eyes, not only his fists. And don't forget to roll with the punches. That means, don't get caught standing still, 'cuz you'll absorb the whole force of his punch. When a punch comes your way, move ahead of it, so even if he hits you, it won't be so hard when it lands."

ONE AFTERNOON, WHEN LUCY FINISHED WORK AT THE HOSPITAL and returned to her town house, she was surprised to find Petrina there, waiting for her. Amie was still at Johnny's bar. Petrina said cautiously, "Lucy, I was at the jewelry shop with Mario's wife today and we were just wondering—how come you never wear the earrings that Frankie gave you?"

Lucy bit her lip, then said in a burst, "Because my earlobes are too big and fat for the darned post! I'm not all slender and delicate like you with your wee kitten ears."

Petrina said gently, "No, no! It's not that your ears are too big. The posts are too short, that's all. Happens all the time. We can fix that! We just solder on a longer post."

"You can do that?" Lucy said. "Great! I didn't want to tell Frankie I had chubby ears."

Her voice stopped abruptly at the thought of her missing husband. This was not lost on Petrina; it was the real reason she was here, to lend support. She'd seen that the normally stoic Lucy was visibly worn down with guilt and worry, but, as always, Lucy avoided discussing her feelings about Chris. They'd heard nothing from Frankie, because he was a fugitive and could not risk contacting them yet. The plan was that, as soon as he was able, Frankie would send a message via Sal's network of contacts. Lucy hated this helpless waiting.

"Come with me, Lucy dear," Petrina said briskly and decisively. "You and I are going out to hunt for a witness. And, possibly, a traitor in our midst."

"What's that mean, eh?" Lucy asked, taken aback. "Just what are you up to now?"

"Let's find out who planted that necklace in Frankie's office!" Petrina said boldly.

"I'd bet it was Alonza," Lucy said, following her. "But of course I can't prove it."

Petrina made a skeptical face. "Don't you remember what Alonza looks like?"

"Of course." Lucy shuddered. "Who could forget? That garish makeup. I've seen Halloween masks less frightening."

"Exactly. If a stranger like Alonza showed up in that close-knit apartment house to plant the stuff in Frankie's office, she could hardly slip in and out unnoticed. The whole building would be chattering. Her sons were already in jail, so *they* couldn't have planted it. So maybe Alonza paid someone who lives here to do it for her," Petrina said.

Lucy sighed. "Oh, Lordy, these days, anyone is susceptible to a bribe. Johnny told Amie it could be someone we 'know and trust,' like Sal, or Domenico, or the cook's drug-addicted son. Or even the janitor—I suppose he's an obvious suspect. He has all the keys at his disposal. Poor old Fred. He's been working there forever. His wife died three years ago, and his living room is still a shrine to her, bless him. You should see it. He's kept the framed pictures of her patron saints, and he lights the candles beneath them every Friday, just as she used to do. But one thing Fred *doesn't* do is dust that place!"

"Let's talk to him," Petrina said as she pulled up to the apartment building.

When they knocked on the door of his flat, Fred obligingly let them in. He allowed them to make him a cup of coffee and even do a bit of cleaning up in his dusty lair, but he would not let them touch his wife's dressing table, with her silver-backed hairbrush, comb, and mirror—the only real things of value she'd ever owned. They'd never had any children. But Fred was a cheerful man who listened patiently and answered all their questions.

"Did you lock up Frankie's office that day, before the police raided it?" Lucy asked with her best bedside manner. "It's all right if you forgot to lock it, Fred."

"Yes, I locked it," Fred replied. "I only went in there once that afternoon, to use the telephone. But I locked it up again. When the police came to search, they said the window was unlocked. I don't know who did that. I sure didn't."

"Let's go take a look," Petrina suggested. They followed Fred's shuffling gait to the office at the back of the building where Frankie conducted his business calls. Lucy was unprepared for the wave of emotion that engulfed her upon entering the place where she'd first met Frankie. The room was spare: just a coat rack, a phone, a lamp, an adding machine, a desk with a scattering of supplies like pens and paper. He never left anything important here, yet she could feel his presence lingering like a ghost.

This must be what it's like when your spouse dies, Lucy thought with a stab of pain. *Am I going to end up like old Fred, forever mourning the loss of my mate?* Men in this neighborhood routinely disappeared; if the war didn't take them, they might go off to jail, or to the hospital like Johnny, or simply vanish under suspicious but never-investigated circumstances.

That was the price of being in "the business." Whatever the cause, the results were pretty much the same. Wives around here knew it, hoped for better but seldom complained; yet, they carried around this burden in the lines on their faces and the slope of their shoulders, and it aged them.

Frankie, where are you? Where have I driven you to? Are you all alone out there? And, Christopher, my darling lad—can you survive without me and this family to protect you?

Petrina had drifted over to the office window, opened it, and stuck her head out, gazing upward. "Hmm. Let's you and I go talk to the tenants, Lucy."

"I already spoke to 'em. And they all say the same thing," Fred said morosely. "Nobody saw anything."

Undeterred, Petrina kept gazing upward.

"Which apartments are right above this office?" she asked.

"Numbers 15, 17, and 19," Fred replied.

Lucy said, "I've been here with Sal to collect the rent. They're all good tenants."

"Fine. Let's go chat," Petrina said determinedly, closing and locking the window.

Fred handed them his key ring. "Don't know what good it'll do, but here you go. Always knock first."

As she and Lucy climbed the stairs, Petrina confided, "I don't think it was Fred who planted the necklace."

"Neither do I," Lucy agreed. "But they all look innocent to me. You'll see."

They started with number 15, a young woman and her mother-in-law, who lived together since the girl's husband was overseas in the war. Both women worked and were home only in the evenings. They had just started making their dinner. The girl had a framed picture of her soldier husband. These women looked too cautious to be susceptible to strangers like Alonza and her ilk.

The elderly couple in number 17 were so devout that they went to Mass every morning. They could not recall anything unusual about that day, either, but this was hardly surprising; the man was hard of hearing, and the woman wore thick glasses.

The seamstress on the top floor in number 19—a tiny apartment just big enough for a birdlike lady like her—spent all day hunched over a small table covered with her sewing and lace piecework, so she couldn't hear much over the rumble of her sewing machine, which had a foot pedal and a knee brace to make it run. She was running the machine right now, so Lucy had to knock several times at the door before the lady opened it.

"Yes?" she inquired, removing a few pins from her mouth. Her name was Gloria.

"Can we talk?" Lucy began, as she had with all the others. The woman had a halo of delicate, curly light-brown hair. She looked to be in her late fifties. She let them in and offered them some lemonade. They sat at her kitchen table.

Petrina said admiringly, "What lovely work you do. Do you think you could make a lace collar for my daughter? She'd love it." They chatted on about lace swatches, much to Lucy's utter boredom. She glanced out the open window, which did little to relieve the stuffiness of the apartment.

"Nice backyard down there," Lucy ventured, gazing at the small courtyard below. "You have a good view of it. Bet you see everybody who comes and goes."

"Yes, in the summertime people like to sit in the shade of that big tree," Gloria replied, taking a measuring tape from around her neck and using chalk to mark out a collar pattern for Petrina to see. "I like to go there myself to cool off. I bring a whole pitcher of lemonade down there," Gloria said, as if she liked the company of neighbors. "Goodness, this heat is so hard on little kids. And dogs and cats. I put out water for the animals. They need it, with all that fur!"

Gloria took a bolt of lace and began pinning the pattern on it. "And I feel especially sorry for the nuns in this weather. They wear such heavy gowns. And those wimples on their heads! You'd never see a priest wearing that tight thing across his forehead. The priests can always take off their hats. The nuns can't, at least not in public."

Lucy looked mystified. Petrina asked curiously, "Have you seen a nun recently?"

"Yes, there was that Sister of Charity, collecting for the war widows. I saw her out in the yard when I came back from shopping, and I gave her some money, though Lord knows I haven't much left to give. She was a young thing—too young to decide to give up marriage that early, if you ask me. I gave her some lemonade."

"Which Sister was that?" Lucy inquired. "I know the ones who teach at school."

Gloria shook her head. "No, she wasn't one of those. Her gown and wimple were all black, not white like the teachers'. I don't know her. She said the other tenants weren't as friendly as me. I felt sorry for her, being so young and alone."

Petrina stood up decisively. "Thanks. Please let us know when my daughter's collar is ready, and we'll come back. Until then, I think it's best if you don't talk about this chat we've just had. Especially with strangers. Okay?"

Gloria nodded, and Petrina hustled the bewildered Lucy out the door and back to the car. "What's the big deal?" Lucy asked. "I see strange nuns on the street collecting for charity all the time now, with the war on."

"I do, too. Nuns, *plural*. Think about it. Have you ever seen them go out alone to solicit money? They never do. They are always sent in pairs," Petrina said triumphantly. "When I was a Girl Scout, our nuns told us to go in twos to sell our cookies, like they do. In case a 'bad man' tried to attack one of us, the other could call for help."

"You think we've got a rogue nun working for the Pericolos?" Lucy said skeptically.

"She may work for the Pericolos, but I'll lay odds she's not a real nun," Petrina replied decisively. "We now have at least one witness who saw her. We've got to find this phony nun, and then we'll see if Gloria can identify her. I've got some ideas, but I have to go and help Pippa pack up for dance camp. I'll let you know if I turn up anything. Meanwhile, just keep your eyes open, Lucy."

FRESH FOOD WAS AT A PREMIUM THAT SUMMER, SO FILOMENA LIKED to do her marketing early. She especially loved to go to the seafood stall, where rows of glistening fish had silvery skins with shimmering rainbow reflections; it reminded her of the happier days of her childhood. The fishwife sensed Filomena's appreciation and discerning eye, so she saved her best for her.

Filomena was just turning away from the crowded stall when a tall, heavyset man came up behind her and spoke into her ear so that only she could hear. His voice was instantly chilling. "So, the hens are in charge of the roost now, eh? People say you're pretty good with a knife. But somebody can always come along with a bigger knife."

Startled, Filomena glanced up. The brim of his hat was tilted over his face, but when the stranger briefly raised his head to look her in the eye, one glimpse was enough to leave an indelible impression: black, staring eyes that looked coldly dispassionate, yet, strangely, somewhat sad; a hawklike nose; a belligerent chin. His body was big and broad and menacing, like an impending freight train as he moved purposefully forward.

Even before he spoke again, his mere presence made Filomena feel sick inside. She trusted this gut instinct absolutely, for it had never failed her yet.

"Nice kids you all got," he said under his breath as he lowered his head again so that others would not notice him. His tone remained distinctly threatening as he added, "And I hear you ladies are taking in more money these days. So, Johnny's little wife might want to pay for more protection. Just remind her, *I know where the body is buried*."

He picked up a fish with its dead eyes and gaping mouth. He patted its head, then set it back down. Filomena scanned the street, looking for Sal's parked car, where he was awaiting her signal to come help with packages; with relief, she spotted him and waved. But when she turned back to the stranger, he was no longer there, having vanished as quickly as he came.

"Sal, who was that man who just spoke to me?" she asked, feeling shaky.

"I didn't see a man, *Signora*." But when Filomena described him, Sal actually blanched and gave an apprehensive look up and down the street. Satisfied that whoever it was had gone, Sal hustled her away. He waited until they were safely in the car before he said slowly, "I hope I'm wrong. But it sounds like you just had a visit from the Lord High Executioner."

"*Who?*" Filomena asked.

"Albert Anastasia, head of Murder Inc. He's been away in the U.S. Army for a coupla years, but I hear he's back in town now. What did he want?"

"I'm not sure," Filomena hedged, thinking, *But I'm going to find out.*

Sal studied her a moment. Then his eyes narrowed. "*Signora,* we have to talk," he said.

LATER THAT DAY, FILOMENA WENT TO AMIE'S BAR. A THRONG OF people was clustered around the radio Amie kept at the bar, which was loudly broadcasting the horse-racing results.

"Amie, I must ask you something," Filomena began, but everyone shushed her.

"Not now," Amie said tensely. "We've got a lot riding on this one." After her most recent visit to Johnny—after that thunderstorm, after being in Frankie's room and behaving as if Johnny were dead and buried already—Amie had been filled with remorse, and now she was determined to make it up to Johnny, by doing what he'd asked, by looking after his business so carefully that he'd be proud when he came back home to her.

"*A-a-a-and, they're off!*" intoned the radio announcer. "*It's Carolina Quickstep in the lead, with Shadow Boxer close behind, and Blue Daydreamer on the outside.*"

Filomena watched as everyone at the bar collectively held their breath. She saw Amie's expression darken when the droning announcer suddenly broke out of his patter to exclaim incredulously, "*But here's Wrecking Ball moving up on the inside!*"

"Who's Wrecking Ball?" Filomena asked with foreboding.

A young man clutching the racing form said ruefully, "A long shot—but maybe not so long, after all."

"*Carolina Quickstep still ahead, Shadow Boxer at her tail, and Blue Daydreamer now running neck-and-neck with Wrecking Ball,*" the announcer exclaimed. "*And, coming 'round the turn, it's Quickstep and Boxer . . . with Wrecking Ball charging ahead of Blue Daydreamer.*"

"Oh my God," Amie said under her breath. "This never happens. But every one of our bookies took big bets on this race for Wrecking Ball to place. So if that horse actually does come in first or second, we're cooked."

"*And now it's Wrecking Ball closing in on Shadow Boxer,*" the announcer chortled, sounding beside himself with disbelief. Amie clutched Filomena's hand so hard that her knuckles were white.

"*Coming down the final stretch, Carolina Quickstep opening up her lead, with Wrecking Ball falling back . . . a-a-a-and, across the finish line, it's Carolina Quickstep, followed by Shadow Boxer second, and Blue Daydreamer third!*"

There was a communal sigh of relief. Amie sagged against the counter. "That Wrecking Ball could have broken us."

Filomena took this all in. "But—how often can something like this happen?"

"Hardly ever—and yet, anytime," Amie replied. "Even though we're dealing with the most 'professional' bookies, and even though the odds are always staggeringly in our favor, there's always a chance that things can go wrong. Badly wrong, with the stakes this high. Because in the end, a gamble is always a gamble."

The boisterous crowd was now demanding drinks, so Filomena said in a low voice, "We can't talk here. We need to sit down with Lucy and Petrina, at my house. At dinner, tonight."

24

July 1944

When Lucy returned home, Amie was there, and she said gently, "Gemma is upstairs with my boys. They've all had their dinner and they're playing cards together."

Lucy appreciated that Amie was being especially kind to Gemma. On Sundays Amie took all the kids out for summer pleasures: sometimes to Jones Beach for fresh air and a dip in the Atlantic Ocean's tumultuous waves, or to a fancy city ice-cream parlor, or on a picnic in leafy Central Park with all its walking trails.

But always, once every week, Amie instructed Donna to take the kids to the library, so that they could find good storybooks to practice their reading skills. Gemma was diligent and earnest, but her questioning mind chafed under the rigid restrictions of schoolwork.

"Thanks for taking such good care of my little lassie," Lucy said gratefully.

"Well, she's my goddaughter, after all!" Amie replied happily, but she blushed. She *had* been making a special effort to be nice to Lucy and Gemma, partly to assuage her guilt about that stormy night at the inn upstate that had driven Amie into Frankie's bedroom.

Resolutely she pushed it from her mind. The truth was, Amie *did* find Gemma's cheerful company a relief, compared to being with her own sons. Vinnie and Paulie turned sullen so easily these days, especially when told to practice their arithmetic and reading, since their teachers had said they "could, and should, do better." Amie supposed that they were moody because they knew that their father was gravely ill, too ill to see them. They missed him, yet they resisted turning to her, as if it were sissyish to rely on a mother, even at their ripe old age of five years.

"Mario's wife has called a special meeting tonight with you, me, and Petrina," Amie announced now. "She came down to my bar just to tell me. So something's up."

"We just went over the books a couple of days ago," Lucy said apprehensively. "What does she want?" She couldn't help admiring Mario's young wife, whose steely self-control was almost spooky, and whose sharp gaze saw through any ruse. But Lucy had what she herself called "a fighting Irish spirit" that kept her on the alert for anyone trying to push her around.

Amie said in a low voice, "That girl is tough as nails."

"Tough? Well, so are we," Lucy said stoutly, and Amie felt better.

"Maybe when her baby is born, she'll ease up with that ledger of hers!" Amie said hopefully, since Mario's wife had recently announced that she was pregnant.

"Come on, let's get this meeting over with," Lucy said briskly.

AT FIRST, THE FOUR WOMEN SPOKE ONLY OF THEIR CHILDREN, WHILE eating their dinner of *pasta fagioli* soup followed by a pan-seared trout with lemon and pine nuts. But after Stella, the cook, had cleared away the plates from the dining table and gone to her room, Filomena asked the others to update their earnings so she could record it all in Tessa's book. Then Filomena reported the finances of Mario's jewelry store. All seemed well.

"Any questions?" Petrina asked, as she always did, being the head of the family.

Lucy glanced uneasily at Filomena and then said, "I had a complaint from one of our restaurant partners about *you*. He says that you're making the big borrowers pay right on time, but you're giving some of the little borrowers more leniency. He wants to know if we're a bunch of socialists. You haven't told us much about Tessa's loan book."

"Tell that man we're doing our bit for the war against Hitler. These 'little borrowers' are people whose sons or husbands were drafted, so the families can't always make ends meet," Filomena explained. "They make all their payments, just a bit late."

"I have to say, I, too, don't much like the idea of collecting rent from poor folk," Lucy admitted. "But I do feel that some of them are testing us. They know *our* men are away. I had one tenant tell me I ought to be more 'tenderhearted.' They'd never have said that to Frankie!"

"So what do *you* do with people who don't pay?" Petrina asked.

Lucy looked uncomfortable. "I let Sal talk to them. Fortunately, all he has to do is talk, not break any legs. So far."

Amie confessed, "I had to get Sal's help, too. One of our biggest bettors told me he'd pay his debts when Johnny comes back! Sal did have to get a little rough with him, I heard." The women exchanged a troubled look. Amie said quickly, "I don't feel sorry for him! He can afford to pay up. He got so nasty with me, he should have expected to hear from Sal."

Filomena remained calm. Lucy, too, understood the laws of the streets. But Petrina wondered just how far her parents and brothers had had to go to protect their interests. They'd never spoken of it to her. But she knew that there were certain men on the payroll who occasionally "straightened people out" for them—quietly, efficiently. Usually such episodes served as warnings to others—a store burned down, a car found with its tires slashed. Had the

family ever had to make good on a threat and actually hurt people? She'd never thought so, given all the genuine goodwill toward
Gianni's family—yet, Petrina couldn't really be sure.

Amie, with a fearful glance at Filomena, continued, "I also received a complaint about you, like Lucy did. Mine was from Gus,
one of the bookies who owe us. He said that you wrote off one
guy's debt when he agreed to strong-arm Gus to pay up."

"Yes, I did," Filomena said calmly. "It was an exchange of services. We can't over-rely on Sal and his men to be the enforcers.
I'll tell you why. When I returned from the market today, Sal had a
little talk with me. He says business is good, but since we're dealing with people who think they can take advantage of women, we
depend more on Sal for 'muscle' than our husbands did. So, Sal
now wants, in addition to his salary, a cut of our operation."

"The nerve!" Amie said indignantly. "He'd never try that with
Johnny."

"How much does he want?" Petrina asked warily.

"I got him down to two percent of new business. He wanted
ten!" Filomena said.

Lucy whistled. "Strong-arming *us*, now, is he?"

Filomena said matter-of-factly, "Sal is preparing for trouble.
Because, today, a strange man approached me at the market. Albert Anastasia. He seemed to want a cut from us, too."

There was a collective gasp. "Oh, Lordy! You'd better pay him
whatever he wants," Lucy said hurriedly, remembering that big,
terrifying man who'd supervised the disposal of Brunon's body.
Just the way he'd grinned at the corpse made her shudder.

But she couldn't say this aloud without exposing Amie's secret, so Lucy explained, "He's been the mob's head assassin for
years. Whenever they want somebody murdered, the five Bosses
go to Anastasia, and he assigns one of his killers to do the job.
But sometimes he does the killing himself—just for the pleasure
of torturing people. They say he likes to hear his victims scream."

"How come he never gets caught?" Amie ventured, curious in

spite of herself.

Lucy said, "Don't you read the papers? He does sometimes, but he always manages to get off, like, on a technicality. He even beat the electric chair! But that's because Lucky Luciano and the Bosses paid for a fancy lawyer." Lucy's blue eyes widened as she leaned forward and whispered, "The last witness against Anastasia was under police protection at the Half Moon Hotel on Coney Island. Round-the-clock police guards, and still, he went right out a window. They called him 'the canary that could sing but could not fly.'"

"Coney Island again," Petrina muttered. "What *is* it about that place?"

"Anastasia's men don't just kill people," Amie said darkly. "Johnny told me they do horrible murders, to send signals. Like, if someone is going to be a witness, they shoot out his eyes. If somebody steals, they cut off his hands. That sort of thing."

"You forgot the ice picks," Lucy said, glancing at Filomena. "They use an ice pick in the ear to make it look like a cerebral hemorrhage so it could be a 'normal cause of death.' I've seen those death certificates at the hospital. That's Anastasia. You see?"

Filomena had been listening attentively with such mounting horror that she could scarcely breathe. But now she felt the surge of a fierce instinct to protect her loved ones.

"How much does Anastasia want?" Petrina asked worriedly.

"I'm not sure," Filomena answered. "I didn't understand something he said. He mentioned you, Amie," she continued, looking searchingly at her. "He says *you're* doing well, so you might need more 'protection.' Now, we already pay Strollo for protection. But Anastasia said, *Just remind her, I know where the body is buried.* What did he mean, Amie?"

Amie had turned so pale that she looked ghostlike. Lucy glanced knowingly at her and said, "We have to tell them now." Amie closed her eyes and shook her head.

Petrina said briskly, "Listen, when men do business, they have to know that they can trust each other. Well, so do we. Frankie told me that the Big Bosses are very careful about who they let in on their team, and they make each man take an oath of loyalty and silence. *Omertà,* they call it. They even have a ceremony. They are the keepers of each other's secrets. So that's what we must do. You all already know my deepest secret, that Mario is my son."

She heard her voice wobble with emotion, but Petrina pushed on resolutely. "We all know that Lucy stole Chris—yes, you did, Lucy, you rescued him, but you stole him, too."

"Right," Lucy said, her eyes bright with tears now, "and I may lose both my laddie *and* Frankie because of what I did. So, you've got my worst secret. Are you satisfied?"

Filomena had fallen silent, thinking first about Chris and whatever terrors he was facing, and then she thought of her unborn child slumbering peacefully in her womb. Being pregnant had somehow made her extremely sensitive to the suffering of children, as if she'd lost a layer of skin and could feel both the sweetness and the pain of this dangerous world more acutely than ever. She simply could not imagine bringing a newborn child into this arena of treachery. Anastasia had said, *Nice kids you all got.* So, they were all at risk.

Petrina said, "Now it's your turn, Amie. What's this big secret that Anastasia knows about? You'd better tell us, before you get us all killed."

But Amie only looked at Lucy and whispered imploringly, "Sometimes I see Brunon, out of the corner of my eye. Does it mean he's still here, or am I just crazy?"

Lucy said gently, "Maybe it's because I told you never to speak of what happened, so I deprived you of confession. But here—just among us—if you say the words, and you can forgive yourself, Brunon might disappear for good."

Amie gasped, "It was an accident! I can hardly remember that awful night. *You* tell them, Lucy, I don't want to hear it." She clapped her hands over her ears, quivering.

So in her no-nonsense Nurse's Voice, Lucy told the others about Brunon, but even so, they were all gaping in astonishment when she was done. "He really was an utter beast," Lucy concluded. "He drove Amie to it. He gave her no other way out."

Amie, her eyes streaming with tears, could now tell from their faces that they all knew. Cautiously she removed her hands from her ears. "Are you done?" she asked.

Lucy said warningly, "That night, Frankie predicted that dealing with Anastasia meant trouble. The way he put it was, *We just raised the devil out of hell.*"

"Well, it's not hell, exactly," Petrina said wryly. "It's just New Jersey. Anastasia lives in a mansion surrounded by bodyguards and Dobermans to protect him."

Filomena said calmly, "So, this man did our family a favor that night, yes? But Sal tells me that Anastasia is not actually a Boss. He has to answer to the Commission of all the Bosses." The others looked baffled until she said, "So, if he's asking us for a cut, he may be crossing a line, stepping on Costello's toes."

Lucy said, "You know, Frankie *did* tell me that they paid Anastasia for his services that night; it was done through Strollo. So, I think you're right. Anastasia can't cut into our business without ruffling some big feathers. Maybe we should complain to Strollo?"

"No," Filomena said, "we should go directly to Costello."

"But it isn't done that way," Amie said tremulously. "There's a protocol, I heard the men say so. You never go directly to the Boss. You follow the chain of command."

Petrina said, "Nuts to that. For all we know, Strollo could be in cahoots with Anastasia. Wouldn't that be stupid, if that were the case and we unwittingly complained to him? This threat doesn't sound like it came from Costello—if it had, I bet Anastasia would have said so outright. So, I agree that we should go to Costello about this. I've met him; he likes me. And he can bring Anastasia to heel." Amie and the others looked up hopefully.

"Do we all agree?" Filomena asked. They nodded solemnly.

"That's all, then."

Lucy spoke up. "Not so fast. You said we have to trust one another, by revealing our deepest secrets. Well, we've all done that, except for you." She nodded boldly to Filomena. Fair was fair, after all. She'd just bet this self-possessed girl had a secret or two.

Petrina glanced at Filomena. "Well, that's true, Rosamaria."

Filomena was accustomed to being called by her cousin's name, but now, as they all turned to her expectantly, she realized she'd always known that, one day, this moment of truth would come. *I can trust them about as far as I can throw them, I suppose. But oh, Rosamaria, I am so tired of answering to your poor name. You are with the angels, and you have always been my guardian angel. So, I think I will tell them the truth, if only because a secret starts out weighing no more than a pebble, but ends up being a boulder on one's heart.*

"All right," she said. They all leaned forward. She almost smiled at their eagerness, then said quietly, "My name is not Rosamaria. That was my cousin; *she* was the girl Tessa sent for. She was brave and loving. We grew up together, treated like slaves in a cruel household. Rosa kept me alive when all I wanted to do was die. Yet in the end, it was Rosamaria who died."

She heard them gasp. Then she spoke of how she had been abandoned to pay a debt; and of the bombing of Naples, when the church was reduced to rubble; and how she ended up taking Rosa's place. "My real name is Filomena. Now you know my secret. Mario knows, too. No one else. When our men return from the war, and when the children are old enough to understand, we'll tell them, and say that 'Rosa' was just my nickname. All right?" she said softly.

The others, sympathetic now, murmured their assent. Lucy was especially moved, and, grasping Filomena's hand, she said in a low voice, "My mother let my dad kick me out of the house. Just when I needed Ma most! I was only a girl. I couldn't *ever* do that to my girl!"

Petrina squeezed Lucy's hand and said with feeling, "Me too. Mom hid me far away from home, as if I'd committed a terrible crime! What's more natural than having a baby?"

Amie's eyes were already bright with sympathetic tears, but now she grasped Petrina's hand and whispered, "I lost my mother when I was four years old. I think I remember her softness near me—but Papa only had a blurry photo of her, so I can never really see her face."

They fell silent for quite some time, having automatically formed a circle, holding hands to bear the unbearable. But something fortifying had happened on its own; the shared pain was giving them a new feeling of the power that lay within this circle.

"I always wanted sisters," Petrina said finally, looking around the table. "And here I have them. Can you *feel* how strong we are? We should never break this circle. Let's swear it!"

Lucy nodded vigorously and tilted her chin up. "Okay, then! If we're going to pledge our loyalty, let's have an official ceremony. We need a name for this secret society of ours."

"The Godmothers," Amie suggested shyly. Petrina went to a sideboard and picked up a small, sharp knife; a candlestick; a pen; one of Tessa's calling cards; and matches.

"I heard that the men use holy cards," Amie said. "Tessa had ones of the Madonna."

"No. I can't burn a holy card! Especially not the Madonna," Petrina objected. "The nuns told us we'd burn in hell. This will have to do. Lucy, you're a nurse. You sterilize the knife."

Petrina took the pen and wrote a large G on the back of the card. "We are each going to put our blood onto my mother's card," she declared, "and pledge our loyalty to her and each other." The others watched in horrified fascination as Lucy dutifully prepared the knife, and Petrina used the tip to draw blood from her finger and trace it over the top of the G.

"You others," she said, "finish tracing the letter." Lucy cleaned the knife and smeared her blood halfway down the G. Then it was Filomena's turn to prick her finger and trace her blood on the bottom of the G. Amie, looking pale, insisted that Lucy prick her finger for her, then Amie hastily completed the task of tracing the final tip of the G.

"We solemnly swear to never reveal the family secrets and stand by one another, no matter what comes," Lucy intoned. The others repeated the words in hushed voices.

Petrina lit the candle and instructed each woman to hold a corner of the card. Together they guided the card over the flame. They watched in silence as the blood-smeared G sizzled and burned, until the card shriveled into ashes. Now holding one another's hands again, they blew out the flame, and felt the strength of each other's grasp.

25

August 1944

When Petrina got an appointment to see Mr. Costello, she insisted that Filomena come along. "He wouldn't talk on the phone. So I have to go to *him*. Maybe he'll be nicer with a pregnant woman like you there. The meeting's at his penthouse at the Majestic. It's on Central Park West, remember? We saw it when we shopped for your wedding."

"Yes, I'll go with you," Filomena said. She put on a blue linen summer dress, which had a matching jacket. Petrina wore a fitted black silk suit. They both wore hats and gloves.

When they stepped outside on this lively summer day, men and women alike paused on the sidewalk to look up admiringly at the proud, well-dressed Petrina and Filomena.

Their cab dropped them off at Seventy-Second Street. The Majestic was a tasteful art deco skyscraper with two towers of exclusive and expensive apartments that were home to what Petrina called "the movers and the shakers" of New York City.

A uniformed doorman sprang into action to let them in. Filomena was amazed at the stunning opulence of the lobby. Beneath soaring ceilings, the floor was tiled in white, gold, and black diamond shapes. There was a dramatic, sweeping carpeted staircase with elaborate wrought-iron railings and, at its landing, three enormous, arched windows that made it seem like a temple of wealth.

"I feel like Dorothy, going to see the Wizard of Oz," Petrina muttered as they entered one of the soundless elevators that sped upward to the very top. "*The Wizard of Oz*," she repeated. "It's a movie. Oh, never mind," Petrina sighed at Filomena's blank look.

"Petrina—what if it *was* Mr. Costello who told Anastasia to 'shake us down,' as you say?" Filomena whispered, feeling suddenly doubtful for the first time.

"Then we're doomed," Petrina hissed.

A butler showed them into the penthouse, a plush dwelling also decorated with art deco furnishings, very tastefully appointed, except, as Petrina said later, for the gold-plated baby grand piano in one corner. The famed slot machines, supposedly rigged so that guests couldn't lose, must have been kept in another room.

"College Girl!" Costello exclaimed in that strangely raspy voice, emerging from his study, cigar in hand. "You know, I only made it to third grade myself. But I graduated from ten universities of hard knocks. Can I get you a drink? No?" He nodded politely to Filomena. "What can I do for you ladies?" he inquired. In his well-tailored suit and tie, he looked like any powerful businessman who spent the day glad-handing politicians and other worthies.

"We've had a visit from Mr. Anastasia," Petrina began. Costello, with a frown of displeasure, put down his cigar in a big crystal ashtray, then raised a finger to his lips.

"Come see my view," he said abruptly. Fearfully, they followed him out a French door that opened onto a private terrace with breathtaking views of the New York skyline.

Petrina and Filomena exchanged an apprehensive glance. From this lofty vantage point, one would certainly feel like king of the hill. The city of toil lay spread out far below, its noise hushed by the distance, and Central Park's trees and lake looked like a verdant garden of the gods. Above, the sky was a soft, lustrous pinky blue, the clouds a luminous pearly grey-and-white. Yet, it crossed Filomena's mind that you could throw somebody off this terrace and it would be a long, long way down.

Costello closed the door behind him. With a sharp look and a stern tone he warned, "I don't discuss business at home. To-day I made an exception for you, out of respect for your father." He looked at Petrina keenly. At their frightened expressions, he explained shortly, "Wiretaps. There's a new D.A. downtown. Bugged my home phone here, you believe that? Now, what's so important that you couldn't go to Strollo?"

Petrina suddenly felt so lightheaded with terror that she put a hand on Filomena's arm. So Filomena told Costello what Anastasia had said at the marketplace. "Since Mr. Anastasia was paid years ago for his—er—services, we thought we should check with you first," she finished softly. "And we believe that you should hear directly from us about this, to avoid any confusion. We only want to know if you yourself gave this order."

"I did *not*. Say no more, I'll straighten this out," Costello said firmly. "Don't worry, ladies. It's in the bag." He allowed a smile. "Just keep that dough rolling in."

Filomena tried not to imagine this genial, urbane man instructing the terrible Anastasia to dispense with her if she failed to make the payments. He opened the terrace door and they stepped back into his apartment, then he showed them out to the hallway. To their surprise, he entered the elevator with them.

They rode in silence, until a rather sour-faced man with dark, heavy eyebrows got into the elevator. He didn't remove his hat, even upon seeing the ladies.

The stranger said briskly, "How-are-ya, Frankie? Is it true Lucky Luciano is running the war from his prison cell? Heard he's helping the U.S. Navy outfox Mussolini. Are they gonna spring Lucky from jail, for being a good boy?" He barked his questions like a cop.

But Costello grinned genially and said, "You tell me! Maybe

they'll give our boy a medal of honor, too." The man chuckled.

When they reached the lobby and walked out to the street, the doorman swiftly hailed a cab for Costello, who stepped aside and said, "Ladies, can I drop you somewhere downtown?" And he got into the cab with them.

"Wasn't that Walter Winchell, the gossip columnist?" Petrina asked as they drove off.

Costello nodded. "Never tell that man anything you don't want to read in the papers over breakfast," he advised.

They sailed down the avenue until they turned into a side street and the cab stopped at the Copacabana. "Here's where I get off," he told the cabbie. "Take the ladies home. This should cover it," he said, peeling bills from a fat, neat wad of cash. But before he could open his door, a pale, wiry man rushed up to their cab. "This guy's a William Morris agent," Costello muttered, lowering his window. "They never know how to wear a suit."

"Frankie," the man gasped, "I need your help. You know that new young nightclub singer I got? His fiancée insulted the boy's mother, so he called off their wedding. But now the fiancée's father is insulted. He's got the boy hanging by his legs out the hotel window."

Everyone, including the cabbie, craned their necks to see up the shadowy side street. At the back of the hotel alleyway, there was, indeed, a young man dangling upside down from a hotel window, over a dozen floors up. Filomena couldn't see who was holding his legs. But she noticed several other tough-looking men peering out from a nearby window on the same floor.

Costello, oddly unsurprised, sighed heavily. The agent pleaded, "I told the fellas they gotta wait for you before they take a vote to decide if Vic Damone lives or dies!"

Petrina gasped, then said timidly, "He *does* have a beautiful voice."

Costello thought it over. The agent explained, "The kid *had* to take a stand. You just don't insult a man's *mother*!"

Everyone held their breath as Costello silently exited the cab and stood below the window. Without glancing up, he raised his fist, then deliberately put his thumb up.

"The kid lives," he agreed. The agent, relieved but still perspiring, looked up sharply at the men, who, watching from the second window, nodded and stuck their thumbs up.

WHEN PETRINA RELAYED THIS STORY TO LUCY AND AMIE AT THEIR meeting, her rapt audience exhaled a mingled sigh of relief and awe. "I guess everybody's safe, then!" Amie said.

But Filomena replied, "Yes, as long as Mr. Costello is Boss. Even so, Petrina and I have been talking. And we think all of us should start making some changes."

Lucy raised an eyebrow. Petrina explained, "As long as we're connected to any business that's illegal, we can always be betrayed or blackmailed by people like Anastasia. We can't go to the police when we're threatened. And suppose one day somebody like Anastasia takes over Costello's operations and decides to drop *us* out a window as well? So Filomena proposes that, slowly and carefully, we ease out of all businesses that require tribute, and put our money into the same safe havens that legitimate investors do."

"Like what?" Lucy asked skeptically. "The banks? You weren't in this country when they all crashed, Filomena. Lifetime savings were wiped out in the blink of an eye. The same goes for the stock market. That's just legalized gambling."

"But it *is* legal," Petrina pointed out. She took a deep breath. "I have a personal need to do this. My husband—soon to be my 'ex'—has found clever ways to hide all his biggest assets from me, and from Pippa. He's pretending to be poorer than he is, so that he doesn't have to pay as much alimony and child support as he should."

Amie clucked sympathetically. "Did you talk to Domenico, our lawyer?"

"Yes, of course. But my dear husband has thrown down his trump card," Petrina said bitterly, still pained by the betrayal. "Richard's lawyer said that if I try to expose Richard's hidden assets, then he'll petition for sole custody of our daughter. Richard doesn't really want Pippa—because his fiancée *really* doesn't want my girl. But he'll take Pippa away from me if I threaten his money."

"That's ridiculous! *He's* the one who's been having an affair, not you," Lucy exclaimed.

"He's denied the whole affair," Petrina said. "And he says *he* can claim custody on 'moral' grounds; you know why? He says that my family is a 'bad environment' for Pippa, because we are nothing but gangsters, and because she's been traumatized by witnessing Tessa's murder. They can make it all sound even more terrible than it was."

The other women fell silent. "The thing is," Petrina said, "there is some truth to it. Pippa *was* traumatized. She's had nightmares for months. Her schoolwork suffered. She even had to go to a psychiatrist, which only helped a little. If it weren't for Pippa's dance teacher, I don't know what I'd have done. Dance is her salvation. Pippa's teacher believes she can get her a scholarship for next year to an academy to train to be a professional dancer. As for me, I have to earn my own living, because I'll be getting peanuts from Richard. That's the deal. I get Pippa, and he keeps more of his lousy money. This is why I want *my* earnings to be legit, so Pippa can be proud of us, and her legacy."

She nodded to Lucy and Amie. "Don't you want the same for your children? Do you want us all to be beholden to leg breakers forever?"

Thinking of Christopher, Lucy could not ignore the wisdom of this. No matter what high-minded morality you *told* children to abide by, they simply emulated what they saw at home. She said thoughtfully, "But how will we do it?"

Filomena replied, "We ease out of the betting operations at

Amie's bar slowly, cover fewer bookies. We'll have to devise a way to get our big-time card players to move their game elsewhere. Also, since Mayor La Guardia is now investigating 'silent partnerships' in nightclubs and bars, we should sell off our interests in the clubs and sell a few apartment buildings, too, so we can use that money to invest in suburban real estate in Westchester and Connecticut. When this war is over, there will be lots of returning soldiers who'll want to marry their sweethearts, have a family, and own a house."

"President Roosevelt has signed the new 'G.I. Bill' to help veterans get mortgages with low interest and no down payments," Petrina said. "So, when the war ends, we should be able to sell our suburban property portfolio for a nice profit. And yes, we should invest in stocks and banks, too. Things the Bosses won't get a cut of."

"Essentially," Amie said wryly, "we are talking about laundering our own money through real estate and the financial markets. But it's a start."

"We mustn't wait too long," Filomena said steadfastly. "The ultimate power is the ability to walk away, without holding out for 'the last big score,' as they say."

"I noticed you're starting with Amie's and my operations first," Lucy said tartly. "What about Tessa's book, eh, Filomena? You're operating the most dangerous business we've got!"

"And that's exactly why I must go slowly," Filomena replied, "so as not to alert the Bosses too soon. But I *am* phasing it out, a little at a time, being careful about taking on new debtors—only the ones I know can repay quickly. So, one day, Tessa's book will be closed, too."

The finality of all this hit the women at once. Until now, they'd functioned as temporary keepers of their husbands' businesses, holding the fort until the warriors returned. This new step meant facing the distinct possibility that their men would never come back and that this provisional existence might, in fact, be permanent.

Lucy and Amie exchanged uneasy glances. "What will the men say if—I mean, when—they come home and find out we've dismantled their family businesses?" Amie asked, feeling resistance to the idea of life without a husband at her side.

"Well, there's one way to find out, darlin'," Lucy suggested. "You can run this plan by Johnny and see what he says."

Petrina rolled her eyes, but Filomena said, "Go ahead, ask him."

So Amie had Sal drive her up to visit Johnny on Sunday, when the bar was closed. He was sitting on a balcony, surrounded by books, but dozing in the shade. He was still so fragile looking, but she thought his color was a bit better today, so she took a deep breath and told him about Anastasia, and Filomena's plans to change the business.

To her astonishment, Johnny said instantly, "Good. Let her do it. I don't want our sons to end up as bookies and loan sharks, bullied by racketeers and cops. I want our boys to become doctors and lawyers and professors and bankers."

"That's four professions. We only have two sons," Amie teased him.

Johnny smiled, then he advised, "But make sure you sell off the nightclubs and a few apartment buildings first, no matter what Lucy says, so you can invest in stocks and bonds for backup. For our end, wait until after Christmas, to rake in the last of the holiday profits. Then you'll have to do a bunch of things to make sure the Bosses don't mind that we're shutting down the bar. I've got some ideas. When the time comes, I'll tell you exactly how to do it."

***

ONE QUIET SUNDAY, SOMEONE RANG THE DOORBELL, AND THEN, without pause, started pounding on the door. The Godmothers were assembled in the parlor, awaiting their Sunday dinner. The children were playing in the backyard. "Police!" the caller shouted.

"Oh, God!" Amie said, stricken. "What do they want from us?"

A dozen thoughts crossed their minds, but it was Filomena who said, "We'd better answer it." She went to the front door and opened it, but she blocked the doorway and did not invite the men in. Two young, unfamiliar officers were there; perhaps they were new recruits, for their uncertainty made them attempt to be severe.

"We got a complaint from the church," said the bigger one, who was blond, beefy, and stony-faced. "You got a girl named Pippa here?"

Petrina heard this, rose, came to the door, and said, "Why do you ask?"

The other cop, smaller and dark haired, flipped open a pad and recited, "The monsignor at your parish claimed that this girl damaged church property and threatened a holy father there. We have to talk to her."

Petrina was prepared to lie and say that Pippa was not home, but there were audible shrieks from the backyard as the children played. Pippa was indeed there. Dance camp had ended, now that school would soon be starting again. Meanwhile, Pippa's cousins were rejoicing at having her in their midst. It was entirely possible that the cops had already heard the kids and therefore knew where they were. Petrina looked at Filomena, who nodded. They stepped aside to let the police into the parlor.

"Won't you sit down?" Petrina said carefully. "I'll see if my daughter is in." She went to the backyard and found Pippa teaching Gemma to play jacks—flinging a handful of six-pointed, star-like metal clusters called "knucklebones" that were thrown on the ground, then scooped up while bouncing a small ball.

"Pippa, for God's sake," Petrina hissed. "The police are here. They say you did damage at the church and threatened a priest. What's going on?"

Pippa looked startled, then defiant. "I did *not* damage the church," she said distinctly.

"Then why are they here?" Petrina whispered suspiciously.

Pippa stood up and said, "Because that priest is a creep and a liar, that's why."

"What did you *do*?" Petrina exclaimed, shocked.

"Nothing!" Pippa shouted, at which point the bigger cop came to the doorway.

"We'd like a word with you, missy," he said sternly.

Pippa sized him up, then cried, "Go ahead and arrest me, I don't care!" But she shot past him, making a run for the stairs.

The officer reached out and grabbed her arm lightly but firmly. "Come with us," he said firmly, and they all marched back into the parlor.

Under the cover of this hubbub, Lucy murmured to Filomena, "Call Pete the cop. It's his day off, but he'll come. He helped us with Chris. His number is in the little pad in my purse." Filomena nodded and went off.

The smaller policeman consulted his notebook again. "Father Flynt tells us that you destroyed church property on the roof," he stated.

Lucy said, "Isn't he the new priest who joined our parish at Christmastime?"

"Yes, he's been teaching remedial reading this summer," Amie said, troubled.

Pippa said, "Well, he's old and mean and rotten, and Gemma told me he made Vinnie and Paulie cry. That's not very holy, if you ask me."

"Who's Vinnie and Paulie?" asked the dark-haired policeman, baffled.

"Pippa, what's going on here?" Petrina demanded, losing patience now.

But Pippa only burst into tears. "I promised I wouldn't tell!" she shouted.

By now Vinnie, Paulie, and Gemma had come inside, but the boys, upon hearing their names, shrank back and retreated into the dining room, where they scooted under the table and remained there, hidden by the tablecloth.

Filomena, being the youngest of the Godmothers, spoke in a calm, conversational voice to Pippa, like a big sister. "Tell us about that priest. Why did he upset you?"

"He didn't upset *me*," Pippa corrected, swinging her dark ponytail. "He made Vinnie and Paulie come up to the roof and feed his rotten old pigeons. They stink."

"He only does that with boys he likes," Gemma volunteered.

"His 'favorites.' Only *they* are allowed to feed his pigeons," Pippa said with strained patience for the denseness of adults. "He's been trying to get the twins up there for months."

"So, this priest picked Vinnie and Paulie to feed the pigeons?" Amie asked.

"Yeah, he likes them because they're twins," Pippa said ominously. "They didn't wanna go, but he got mad and said God would be 'displeased' if they didn't."

"So, what did *you* do, Pippa?" Petrina asked sternly.

Looking outraged, Pippa exclaimed, "I didn't *break* anything or *damage* anything in the church. I only told that rotten priest that if he didn't cut it out, I'd kill his lousy pigeons. He still wouldn't stop, so I had to do *some*thing," she said scornfully.

"Father Flynt says she broke open all the cages and set the pigeons loose," the dark-haired police officer volunteered. "He also said she threatened to shoot him."

"Pippa, how could you do such a thing?" Petrina gasped.

Lucy had been watching the girl closely now and recognized something she'd seen, from time to time, on the faces of children at the hospital. She said knowingly, "What else did the priest make the twins do, Pippa, besides feed the pigeons?"

"I can't say, it's too *ugly*," Pippa said emphatically, glancing at the policemen.

"Maybe she can tell me, alone," Lucy suggested. "Come with me, Pippa."

The others watched, mystified, as Lucy led the girl into the garden. For some time, Lucy and Pippa sat there, talking, with Pippa occasionally gesturing. Then Lucy patted her shoulder, and Pippa remained behind while Lucy returned to the adults.

"Amic, why don't you take the other kids into the backyard and let Cook give them their supper on the little table out there?" she suggested. "Because *little pitchers have big ears*."

Amie grasped this, took Gemma with her, and dragged her twin sons out from under the dining-room table into the yard, where she left them with Cook.

Lucy turned to the waiting policemen. "Apparently this priest is in the habit of enticing young boys up to that roof and making them pull down their pants and touch themselves," she said bluntly. "Sometimes the priest touches them. Sometimes he makes them touch *him*. Fortunately, this time, it didn't get that far. Pippa was in church and saw the priest talking to the boys after Mass and making them come up to the roof with him. So, she followed, and watched from behind those pigeon coops. She intervened as soon as the priest tried to unbutton their pants." There was a communal gasp.

The bigger cop muttered, "Well, kids make up all kinds of stories. Boys will be boys—"

"Not *our* boys," Amie said sharply, trembling with controlled fury now.

"All Pippa did was turn the pigeons loose," Lucy said reasonably. "I'd say that priest is lucky she didn't push him right off the roof. She was simply defending her little cousins. They're such young lads and couldn't do it themselves."

"What about a gun?" the dark-haired policeman asked. "The priest said Pippa threatened him with a gun. Sorry, we'll have to arrest her."

"No!" Petrina cried out. "She's just a girl. You can't take her to *jail*!" She looked pleadingly at Lucy, who was also thinking of what incarceration had done to Johnny's health.

"I didn't hear a thing about a gun," Lucy fibbed, glaring at the cop. "So it's his word against ours. Frankly, officers, I advise you to tell that priest that if he even *thinks* of pressing charges for his silly pigeon coops and his nervous fantasies, *we* will file a report for his lewd behavior. I am a professional nurse, and my word will carry weight with the law."

The men exchanged a look of uncertainty. Petrina, still terrified of what they'd do, said, "Furthermore, tell the monsignor that if that disgusting priest isn't taken out of our school and our church—and locked away in some monk's cell where he won't be near children ever again—then our lawyer will see that both of those 'holy men' spend the rest of their lives in prison."

"Should I call the sergeant?" the shorter cop asked the other. Now there was a knock on the front door. It was Pete, the policeman they'd called. Lucy quickly summed up the situation.

"Pete," she concluded meaningfully, "I wonder if you will explain to your colleagues that we are a well-respected family in this neighborhood, and that this new priest should consider himself lucky that we are not pressing charges against *him*."

Pete said to the other officers, "Come along, boys, I know these people. No real harm done today. I'll straighten it out with the monsignor. Good day, ladies."

When she closed the door behind them, Amie let out a long sigh of relief.

"Lucy, why shouldn't we press charges?" she demanded indignantly.

"Because," Lucy said calmly, "Pippa apparently *did* have a gun with her. She and Gemma found it at *your* house, Amie, in a hatbox, when they were playing together."

"It's Johnny's gun," Amie said instantly. "The one he got when he was going to shoot the Pericolos. He told me to keep it, in case there was any trouble. It's untraceable, he said."

Filomena spoke up. "Mario said the same thing to me. I keep his at the jewelry shop, in case somebody tries to rob us."

Lucy looked at Petrina. "So Pippa knows how to use a gun?"

"Richard's a huntsman, and, not having a son, he took Pippa to target practice and skeet shooting," Petrina admitted. "She's good. She could have shot that priest's nuts off, if she really wanted to." She added remorsefully, "Poor Pippa. I yelled at her. I should have known she wouldn't do such strange things without a good reason. It hasn't been easy for her, with the divorce. She doesn't trust men anymore. She was very brave, to stand up to that creep."

"Yes! But today she was just too embarrassed in front of those cops to defend *herself* properly," Lucy said. "She's all right now. She only needed for us to believe her."

"What about Vinnie and Paulie, are they all right?" Filomena asked Amie.

Amie said worriedly, "They just told me that all the boys dread being asked to go up to the church roof. That priest has bothered other kids ever since he arrived, but they're all too ashamed to tell the grown-

ups. This was the first time the twins went up there. But they said they're not afraid anymore, because the priest was 'a crybaby' when Pippa said she'd shoot him. The twins were only worried that Pippa might be arrested today, because of them. They told me that we all ought to 'dummy up' about this, so Pippa won't get into trouble."

"Good God," Petrina breathed. "This is *not* the sort of education I had in mind for our children."

"No. But they took care of themselves," Filomena said softly. "At least we know that they can, if they really have to."

26

September 1944

By September, the Godmothers had purchased several houses in the suburbs to fix up and resell, and an apartment building to rent out. Then, in a town called Mamaroneck, Petrina discovered four beach houses that "needed work" but occupied a promising little seaside enclave on a totally private spit of land, so charming that the Godmothers decided to buy these for themselves.

Petrina was supervising the renovations. Three of the houses were rather dilapidated, but the fourth was in better condition and she was able to quickly upgrade it so that she could live there on the weekdays year-round, allowing Pippa to continue her studies at the private girls' school she'd been attending in the suburbs. The town was only two train stops south of Rye, where they'd been living with Richard when they were still a family.

"So Pippa's life won't be disrupted at all by this move," Petrina said triumphantly to the Godmothers, "and I'll have a shorter commute into Manhattan!"

That same month, Filomena gave birth to a happy baby girl whom she named Teresa, in honor of Tessa. Everyone said that the infant looked just like Filomena, and perhaps she did; but when the little one gazed up at her with a contemplative, curious expression, Filomena saw Mario's face looking back at her, and the effect was startling.

"How strange it is to see a reflection of the one you love, and yet this child is a completely new person," she marveled. She was unprepared for the joyful tenderness that little Teresa evoked; her very warmth and scent overwhelmed Filomena with physical love.

At the same time, she felt a fearful anxiety, for this infant had pried open the door to a corner of Filomena's heart that she'd kept resolutely locked, the place where she'd buried her own childhood memories. At first, this depressed her. She did not want to remember how it felt to be abandoned. She whispered fiercely to little Teresa, "Don't worry, no matter what happens, I will *never* give you away." How could a woman abandon her own child? Filomena now realized just how desperate her mother must have been to let go of her that day. So for the first time, she was able to pity her parents, even if she still couldn't quite forgive them.

She also felt, in a profound way, a sharp new kinship with every living creature on earth, especially now, with the world at war, so blindly determined to destroy itself. She ached with sorrow for those beautiful old European cities and every innocent creature caught in the crossfire. Suddenly, Mario's letters were more vital to her than ever, and she wrote back urging him to do whatever he had to do to stay alive.

She was grateful for the company of Petrina and Pippa, who were spending their weekends in the city with Filomena. Petrina took seriously her role of godmother to Teresa, advising Filomena how to care for a baby with such delicate tasks as keeping her ears clean and fingernails trimmed; and how to select the right carriage and crib, the plushest baby bedding and the softest of infant clothes.

Neighbors and merchants sent a shower of baby gifts to Filomena's house. Among these tributes, one item stood out: an exquisitely hand-carved ivory jewelry chest that was also a music box for a little girl. It had a tiny golden carousel pony atop the box, which pivoted to music from the Broadway show *Oklahoma!* The finely-tuned tinkling song "Oh, What a Beautiful Mornin'" rang clearly and sweetly as the pony twirled.

"I wonder who sent this one?" Petrina mused. "The card must have fallen off. Oh, well. Probably a debtor who wants to stay in your good graces! He'll let us know, soon enough."

But nobody took credit for the gift. No one in the family was bothered by this mystery except Filomena, who felt oddly apprehensive. Someone had noticed her child's birth, and Filomena had been raised to worry that good fortune could also invoke the evil eye of jealousy.

That afternoon, when the telephone rang, Petrina picked it up, and her expression instantly became furrowed with worry. "What? Where is she now? Is the doctor with her? All right, I'll be right over." She hung up. "Amie fainted out on the street. She's home. I'll go."

AMIE LAY IN BED, TRYING TO FIGURE OUT WHAT HAD HAPPENED. ONE moment she'd been coming home from the bar, feeling perfectly fine, and then, halfway down the street, she'd started seeing little black specks in front of her, which she tried to bat away, as if they were flies. But then there were so many black specks that it was like a heavy veil descending, and she felt herself slipping, falling into the blackness.

Fortunately, her bartender had just stepped outside for a smoke, and he saw her go down. He shouted to a busboy, and they called Sal to take her home and summon the doctor.

When Petrina arrived, Amie was asleep. The doctor explained the situation, gave Petrina some instructions, and left. Then Lucy came home, so it fell upon Petrina to break the news to her, upstairs in Lucy's apartment so that Amie could not overhear.

"Lucy, the doctor thinks Amie is pregnant," Petrina said forthrightly. "He's done some tests and will know for sure when he gets the results, but—he's pretty sure."

Lucy felt herself mechanically, silently removing her hat and coat. It seemed to take a great effort when she finally spoke. "I think somehow I sensed this for weeks," she said dully. "I just kept pushing it out of my mind. But a pregnant woman has a certain look, even before she starts to show." Petrina said nothing, simply dreading how much Lucy had guessed.

"It's Frankie's child, isn't it? It has to be. Who else could it be?" Lucy said bluntly.

"Amie's been saying all along that Johnny's feeling better. Maybe she and Johnny . . . ," Petrina offered, then trailed off helplessly.

"Not a chance," Lucy retorted ruthlessly. "I went to see Johnny right after Frankie left town. Poor Johnny could barely breathe, much less make love." She surprised herself by getting choked up at the memory of how Johnny had looked so emaciated—his bathrobe seemed to have grown bigger while he grew smaller. Yet the poor guy had been more optimistic than ever, so eager to recover, which made it all the more heartbreaking.

Lemme tell ya something, Luce, he'd said to her. *I've been reading all about life, and now I get it. I finally get it. You can't let the wheels of society grind you into their gunpowder. Soon as I bust out of this joint, there's going to be some changes. I'll teach my boys how to read and learn, too, and I'll get them away from the mugs and the crooks.* But then he'd fallen back on his pillows, exhausted merely by the urge to create a better future.

"For God's sake, I'm not a fool," Lucy said to Petrina now. "I can count the months! The child *has* to be Frankie's." Lucy made a quick calculation. "It must have happened that night the pair of them stayed up in the mountains together, because of the storm. I got this funny feeling that night, but I told myself it was nothing. Turns out, it *was* something."

Her eyes flashed as if she were daring Petrina to contradict her. For months Lucy had been worried sick about Frankie, until Sal finally got word that he was "safe," whatever that meant. Frankie didn't dare say where he was. Sal thought it meant there was hope of finding Chris. Lucy had been racked with guilt about Frankie's heroic departure. Now she understood.

"No wonder that skunk husband of mine ran off to Ireland," she said dryly. "I wonder who he's more afraid of facing back here: the police, or me."

Petrina said firmly, "Frankie's my brother, and he's impetuous sometimes, but he loves *you*. He always has, from the minute you walked into his life. If something stupid happened, well, it happened. That's all there is to it. Now he's risking life and limb out there, out of love for you and Chris. So, forget about Amie. Her foot slipped; she's been too lonely without Johnny. Think of the kids! You're godmother to Amie's twins, and they absolutely adore you."

"Do the children know there's a new babe coming?" Lucy asked sharply.

Petrina shook her head. "We just told them Amie has a touch of flu. I sent the twins and Gemma to Filomena's house for supper. They'll be back in a little while. So if you want to scream and yell, do it now, get it over with. I haven't spoken to Amie, so we don't know anything for sure. But if you're right, try to forgive everybody, will you, Lucy? Because, take it from me, hatred only makes *you* sick inside, and it doesn't change a damned thing."

Oddly enough, Lucy felt some comfort in knowing that even the glamorous, educated Petrina had suffered betrayal at the hands of a husband and was now trying to help her. Not without gratitude, Lucy said, "Oh, shut up and pour me a whiskey."

She watched Petrina's long, fine-boned fingers pouring out two glasses. Petrina was so tall and slender, she made Lucy feel a bit, well, chunky. Glancing down at her own sturdy, stubby fingers, Lucy thought ruefully that you could only be just so sophisticated after you'd spent your days reaching into blood and guts at the hospital. She would like to use these two hands right now to cheerfully choke Frankie. But even in this moment, she knew that

Petrina was right—Frankie *did* love her and Chris, enough to risk his life for them. Lucy still desperately wanted both of them back. *Then* she could wring their necks. She even found herself hoping that she'd find out the baby wasn't Frankie's, after all. Maybe Amie had had an affair with a doctor at the sanitarium. Women like Amie worshipped doctors as saviors.

Petrina, relieved that her task of delivering the bad news was over, patted Lucy's shoulder and said thoughtfully, "I don't know if it's the right time to tell you this. But Filomena and I hired a private detective, to chase down that strange nun who was in the apartment building the day the cops found that stolen stuff in Frankie's office."

Lucy actually felt hopeful of a reprieve for Frankie. "Did you find out anything?"

Petrina said, "Maybe. I'm going to meet with the detective on Friday. Plus, Gloria, the seamstress, called to say she's finished that lacework for me. So I'm going back to talk to her. You come with me, and we'll see what's what."

"All right," Lucy said, feeling suddenly truly exhausted by the conflict of emotions.

Petrina rose and went to the oven, peered inside, then put on some oven mitts and pulled out a casserole dish. "Okay, dinnertime," she announced.

"Thanks, but I think I'll just go to bed," Lucy said in a tired tone. But the scent of the food actually made her hungry. Yes, she certainly did feel like devouring something.

"You must try this," Petrina said, lifting the lid and sniffing rapturously. "It's from a secret recipe for *lasagne Bolognese*. My favorite aunt was from Bologna, did you know? She's the black sheep of the family because she went back there to marry a communist. Anyway, you must eat. You can't go to bed on a stomach that's only got whiskey in it. You might wake in the night and take a knife and fork to Amie instead."

THE NEXT DAY, AMIE CONFESSED TO PETRINA THAT THE CHILD WAS indeed Frankie's, and that it had happened only in a shared moment of grief between her and Frankie, nothing more.

So it fell to Petrina, once again, to tell Lucy, who simply turned away and said nothing.

"God, I wish she'd yelled," Petrina reported back to Filomena. "It's somehow worse, when Lucy is so calm and stoic."

"Give her time," Filomena predicted. She had always sensed that beneath Lucy's stalwart, tough personality, there lurked a sensitive creature so horrified by her own vulnerability that she could not even admit to herself when she'd been hurt. Filomena knew that she and Lucy actually had a lot more in common than most people suspected.

It was precisely three days later when the storm finally broke. The children were in school, and Filomena held her weekly meeting to go over the books. They managed to get through it in a businesslike fashion, until Amie was tactless enough to remind Lucy that Gemma's school was having a parent-teacher night, saying that Lucy should attend even though she was on the late shift at the hospital that evening.

"You go," Lucy said shortly. "You're her godmother. She likes you more than me, anyway, because *you* don't scold her."

"Oh, no," Amie said without thinking. "You're Gemma's mother, it would mean so much more to her if *you* were there in the audience."

"Really?" Lucy snapped. "Well, Amie, you're the expert on motherhood, aren't you? So maybe when you have this baby, *you* can explain to Gemma why I am *not* the mother of her new little brother, eh? Why don't you explain THAT one to my little girl, all right, Amie?"

"It might not be a boy, you know," Petrina said helpfully. Filomena shot her a look of disbelief. Lucy ignored them, her eyes fixed on Amie, who sat with head bowed in a penitent manner that only infuriated Lucy.

"And while you are at it," Lucy said, rising to her feet to tower over Amie and bring her words down on her like a whip, "maybe you can explain it to *me*, too. Maybe you can explain to me how you DARED to sleep with *my* husband, when yours is still alive. Maybe you can explain *why*, out of all the men in New York City, you had to pick *my* husband to throw yourself on. How *could* you?" Lucy demanded, her voice rising to smother the hurt feelings that she harbored, yet despised for making her feel so weak. "I've always trusted you, and I've stood by you, Amie. Damn it, even when—"

"Don't say it!" Amie screamed, rising, trying to flee the room. "It's not only my fault that Frankie slipped up. It's not like we chased after each other. We were both upset, that's all, over Johnny and all. If *you* hadn't lied to him about Chris, he'd never have turned to me—"

With a shriek of outrage, Lucy caught Amie by the arm and forced her back in the chair. Lucy's voice cracked with pain and fury now. "You already have two sons! Wasn't that enough for you? Did you have to go and tempt Frankie with the one thing I couldn't give him?"

"Oh, Lucy, I *am* so sorry, you just don't know how much—" Amie broke in.

Lucy cut her off. "Are you, now, girlie? Well, here's your chance to prove it. When that boy is born, we'll tell everyone he's mine."

"No!" Petrina exclaimed, horrified. "Are you crazy? Not in this house again, I couldn't stand it. No more secrets and lies in this family! Can't you see where it all leads? Lucy, do you want Frankie's son to run away one day, as Mario did, where he might get himself killed? Oh, Filomena, I'm sorry, but it was my fault that Mario left us. I think of this every night, it's hell."

Amie looked up wildly and said, "But Lucy's right, Petrina. Don't you understand? If I tell Johnny the truth about the baby, it will kill *him*."

"*Basta!*" Filomena said finally, rapping the table sharply for silence. "That baby belongs to all of us. We'll figure out what to say to the men when they come home. Right now, we are all we've got. We swore to *stand by one another, no matter what comes*. Those were your words, Lucy. And you, Amie—did you forget so soon?"

Lucy threw up her hands, but Filomena fixed her with a stern gaze and continued, "You can't go back on this oath at the first sign of trouble. Can't you see, this is a test that we must not fail? Lucy, you are just going to have to find a way to forgive Amie. And, Amie, you are going to have to work extra hard to regain Lucy's trust. That means stop using your weaknesses to get what you want. You've always leaned on Lucy; now it's time for *you* to help her. That's all there is to it. We have work to do. We must all be good to one another—at least until this war is over!"

Lucy put her head in her hands to hide the tears that filled her eyes. The effort to swallow her sobs made her throat actually ache.

"Men are just men," Filomena said more quietly. "From now on, we must think of the children first."

THE NEXT DAY, PETRINA INSISTED THAT LUCY COME WITH HER TO the apartment house. Lucy suspected that this was mainly a distraction, to keep her from strangling Amie. But Lucy agreed to go, mostly because she couldn't bear being under the same roof with Amie.

While she was dressing, Lucy caught her own reflection in the mirror and could not help scrutinizing her body, wondering if, in Frankie's eyes, she lacked something that Amie could offer. *Helplessness*, Lucy thought cynically. Men just couldn't resist a delicate, worshipful female. She was grateful when Petrina dragged her away from the house, into the fresh air.

They walked in silence. Autumn made New Yorkers brisk, cheerful, and purposeful. But Lucy was still feeling fatalistic. Sal was the only one who'd had contact with Frankie, still in those cryptic messages.

"What if this whole nun thing is a red herring?" Lucy said finally.

"Phooey," Petrina replied as they reached the building. "Would I steer you wrong?"

"Tell me," Lucy said as she dodged around children on the sidewalk, some on bicycles, some skipping rope, "how much is this private detective costing us, eh?"

"Nothing," Petrina said with a wink as they entered the apartment building.

"Nothing?" Lucy repeated. "How is *that* possible?"

"He's in Filomena's book," Petrina explained. "He likes to bet on the horses. He hasn't been picking them well lately. Filomena said she'd write off his debt if he did us this 'favor.'"

"I hope he's better at detecting criminals than he is at picking horses," Lucy muttered.

"Oh, he is. He's a retired police photographer. He's been staking out Alonza's house for a week, to see who comes and goes. Watch, you'll see."

Petrina knocked on the door of the topmost apartment. Gloria, who was a widow, looked happy to have their company. She laid out the beautiful lace collar that she'd carefully stitched and embroidered. Petrina cooed over it, put it around her own neck, and declared that Pippa would love it. Gloria stood by, blushing with modest pleasure. Petrina paid her for this, and the box of fine lace handkerchiefs she'd ordered, which would make great Christmas gifts.

Lucy fidgeted with unendurable suspense. Finally, when Gloria poured them tea and they sat down at her tiny kitchen table, Petrina reached into her purse.

"Would you take a look at these?" she said casually. "I think one of these women may be that nun you told us about."

Lucy watched, fascinated, as Petrina, like a fortune-teller with tarot cards, dealt out a series of pictures that she'd gotten from the private detective. They were photos of various women, snapped on the fly, while the unsuspecting subjects were shopping or chasing a bus or pausing momentarily at a front door, a candy store, or a coffee shop.

Gloria adjusted her spectacles and studied each photograph. "Oh, goodness, not her," she said, pointing to the picture of Alonza as she was standing in a dressing gown and speaking haughtily to a postman on the front stoop of her house.

Gloria peered at the next picture. "No," she said, shaking her head. Each time she dismissed the next, and the next, Lucy's heart sank, and she mentally chided herself for having any hope at all in this scheme. "That one," Gloria said, suddenly and positively, pointing at a young woman photographed waiting at a train station. "That's her. But what is she doing without her wimple on? I've never seen any nun bareheaded in public, have you?"

"You're sure it's her?" Lucy asked, stunned.

Gloria nodded vigorously. "Oh, yes. You can't tell here, but she had pretty green eyes."

"Then, do us a favor," Petrina said in a serious tone. "Don't tell *anyone* that we've been here talking about this. It's for your own safety. Also, never open the door to people you don't know. And if you see anything suspicious or out of the ordinary, call me right away."

Gloria looked frightened now. "What is it about?"

"This woman is not a nun. She was only pretending to be, because she got paid by very bad men to do so," Petrina explained.

Gloria turned to Lucy with a tremulous look. "Is this what made your husband run away?" she asked. Lucy nodded. Gloria said, with unexpected mettle, "Frankie was a good boy. I've known him all his life. He would never do anything bad. He always looked out for me. I will help you as much as I can."

Lucy wanted to kiss her. Petrina patted the lady's hand. "We'll be in touch," she said. "But remember what I said. Keep your eyes open and your door locked. Stay away from strangers. Just for the next few weeks, if you need any shopping done, or need to go anywhere, don't go alone. Call us, and we will send someone to go with you."

"LORDY, I THOUGHT YOU WERE ABOUT TO PUT HER IN SOME SAFE house in Coney Island," Lucy said after they left. "Maybe we *should* hide her somewhere."

"She'll be all right," Petrina said. "She sleeps with a gun under her bed. She was married to a mortician, so, believe me, she's had all kinds of people come to ask her husband for a favor, and *she* used to tell him which ones to trust. I heard that her husband was once ordered to bury two corpses in one casket: one in a secret drawer beneath the legit one."

"Saints preserve us!" Lucy shuddered. "But who's the girl in the photograph?"

"Alonza's hairdresser," Petrina said triumphantly. "Our detective thinks she's the girlfriend of one of the Pericolo boys, because she visits them. Our man followed her from Alonza's house to the train station. She bought a ticket for Ossining—

where the Sing Sing prison is, where the Pericolo boys are! The P.I. thinks this girl is ferrying messages between Alonza and her sons. Now we find out Little Miss Hairdresser was *here*, just before the cops busted into Frankie's office!"

Lucy said indignantly, "Okay. Let's go have another little chat with Fred."

They found the janitor in the basement, fiddling with the furnace to prepare it for the coming cold weather. When they asked him to go upstairs to Frankie's office, he wiped his hands on a rag and followed them obediently with the key.

"Fred, have you ever seen this woman before?" Lucy asked gently as Petrina laid the photo on Frankie's desk. Fred leaned forward, then picked up the photo to get a closer look.

"She looks like that nun who came here collecting for the war orphans," he said finally, sounding surprised. "But she ain't got her veil on. Is she a sister of the Sister or something?"

"She wasn't really a nun," Petrina said. "This woman dressed up as one, to fool you."

"Why would she do that?" Fred asked, bewildered.

"Fred, darlin', did you see her the day the police raided Frankie's office?" Lucy asked. "We heard she was hanging around in the yard earlier that same day."

Fred scratched his head. "Yeah, it could have been. Sure. That's right! It was around lunchtime. Because the cops busted in that night."

"Did you speak to her?" Petrina asked breathlessly.

"Yeah. She knocked at the office door, looking for Frankie," Fred said. "Said she knew him to be 'generous' with the church. I'd been making phone calls and was about to lock up. She asked if she could use the phone to call her convent. So I said, 'Sure, Sister.' She gave me a medal of the Virgin Mary, said it was blessed. Said I could give it to my wife. I told her my wife was dead, and she said she'd pray for her soul." Fred grew a little misty eyed.

Lucy said, "Did you stay in the office while she made her phone call?"

Fred shook his head, embarrassed. "Nope. I stepped out to give her privacy."

"Why didn't you tell the police about her when they came here?" Lucy asked.

Fred looked shocked. "I didn't even think of it! She's a *nun*." He saw them exchange a look with each other and then said, "I thought she was. Are you sure she ain't?"

"Yes," Petrina said firmly. Lucy explained that the woman was likely a friend of the very men who had "fingered" Frankie and caused the police to come searching that night.

"Oh, holy cow! Holy cow!" Fred said in anguish, over and over. "Please don't tell Frankie's brothers that I screwed up!"

"But you didn't screw up," Petrina said. "Because you're going to keep absolutely quiet about this, until we need you. And then you're going to tell the police exactly what you told us today. And then Frankie will be able to come back and thank you in person." She repeated the same warnings that she'd given the seamstress.

Fred assured them he'd do whatever they asked.

When they went back outside, Lucy felt strangely energized. She was determined now that nobody—not Alonza, nor the police, nor Amie—was going to take her husband away from her. She demanded, "Why don't we just cart our two witnesses to the police right now, so they can make a statement, before Alonza gets to them and they change their tune?"

"If we go to the police, somebody at the station might tip off someone to warn the Pericolos. You never know," Petrina said. "I'll ask Domenico to handle it from here. He'll get our witnesses scheduled properly to make depositions and go before a judge, so they don't waste their breath just talking to cops who might bury it."

Lucy still looked worried, until Petrina said, "We'll have Sal and some of his men watch this place and protect our witnesses. They'll stand by us. They're loyal, you saw that. They love Frankie, and my family's name still carries weight around here. Don't forget, Lucy—it's your family, too."

27

Autumn 1944

One Saturday, Petrina was at the jewelry shop helping Filomena, when Johnny unexpectedly telephoned and asked to speak to Petrina.

"Donna said I'd find you there. Kid, you gotta bust me out," Johnny said. "I've had it with the mountains. I want to see the sea. I want to see my boys."

Petrina said cautiously, "Don't you want to discuss this with Amie?"

"Nah. That's exactly what we'd end up doing, 'discussing' it. She hasn't been up here to see me in a while. Is she all right?"

"Just a touch of flu," Petrina fibbed. "She didn't want you to catch it."

"Oh. Well, anyway, I called you because I need some muscle."

"Johnny, did the doctors say it was okay for you to leave?" she asked.

"To hell with the doctors. They can't keep me here against my will. You're my 'kin,' so you can help sign me out. But come *alone*. Got that? Don't bring Lucy, she'll tell me to listen to the doctors. Amie worries too much, I don't want her clucking over me and making me rest. I've had enough 'rest' for the rest of my life, and I've read every book in this joint, twice. Get me out *now*, or I swear I'll jump out the window."

"Okay, okay, wait for me!" Petrina said hurriedly. She didn't think her brother would kill himself, but he might try to run away on his own. She told Filomena about Johnny's plan.

"Look, I've got to go up there and help him get out," she concluded.

"What are you going to do with him?" Filomena asked worriedly. "Amie's not showing enough for the twins to notice, but Johnny might, if he gets close to her."

"I told him that she has the flu. He said he wants to 'see the sea' so I'll take Johnny to stay at my house in Mamaroneck, until Amie is 'feeling better,'" Petrina said. "Tell her that this is the last time I'll lie to Johnny for her. This will gave Amie a chance to figure out how to tell him about the baby. But she'd better decide soon!"

ON THE DRIVE TO WESTCHESTER, JOHNNY, STILL PALE AND THIN, gazed out the car window as if seeing the world for the first time and finding all of it beautiful. He enthused about the stunning colors of the autumn trees all along the highway. When they reached Mamaroneck, they followed a long, quiet road that snaked down a narrow peninsula and ended at a security gate for the little enclave of four beach houses that the family owned.

Petrina said, "They were built in the 1920s as summer homes. My house didn't need much work, so it's done. Once we've renovated these other three houses, we can rent out or resell them. We've also bought some houses in nearby villages as an investment. And an apartment building in town—it was beautifully built in the 1890s but needs upgrading."

Petrina wanted to settle him into her guest bedroom, but Johnny insisted on looking at all four houses. He was quick to assess which things needed replacing and which were of value and worth fixing. He admired the hardwood floors and generous porches, the mature fruit trees in the gardens, the view of the sea.

"Don't sell *this* house," Johnny said instantly, selecting the last one at the far end. Its generous lawn offered a tranquil, meditative spot with a panoramic view of the sea lapping at a sandy cove below. "This is the home I want for me and Amie and the boys," he said, looking excited. "I've been thinking about it ever since you told me about this real-estate deal. I want Vinnie and Paulie to go to a good school up here. I don't want them knocking around the streets of New York where I grew up."

"Fine. Fix it up and it's yours," Petrina said gently as they returned to her house.

"I can help you with the renovations on the other properties, too," Johnny offered. "You have to be careful with contractors and repairmen. They start a job, then they leave you in the lurch. You need a man like me to kick ass around here."

Petrina smiled tenderly. Johnny looked like a scarecrow, but even scarecrows could keep the scavengers away. "Thanks, brother dear," she said as they went inside. "But the deal is, you're staying put in my house. You sleep when I tell you, and eat when I tell you. Got that? Otherwise I'll throw you in the trunk of my car and drive you straight back to the sanitarium."

"Okay, boss." Johnny set down his suitcase and paused in the hallway before a framed abstract painting, done in splashes of vivid colors. Petrina loved the new modern art, which Richard called her "shaggy stray dogs." This painting was by an artist who'd been in FDR's Federal Art Project and clearly showed the influence of Pablo Picasso and Diego Rivera. It had given her great joy to buy it.

Johnny looked baffled, but all he said was, "Amie says you're getting a divorce."

Petrina winced. The utter devastation of being unwanted by Richard, a man who'd pledged to love her forever, had now subsided into a dull ache, like a bad tooth. And all the legal wrangling was acting like a dentist's sedative, she supposed. "Yes, the deal is, Richard gets to keep most of his money; I get Pippa—and this painting, which he absolutely loathes."

She paused, expecting Johnny to pass judgment on her. But he said simply, "You want me to beat up Richard? I'd do it with my two bare hands. It would be a pleasure."

"No," Petrina said. "He's not worth it. Let Richard die a slow, torturous death. I know that woman he's marrying will make him suffer far more than we can."

Johnny smiled. "Okay. Just do me one more favor. Get the twins to come up here over the weekend. And Amie, if she's up to it. I haven't seen them in a long while. I want the boys to see how beautiful this place is, before all the autumn leaves are gone."

"Sure," Petrina said. "Pippa can take your kids to a hot-dog stand that everybody around here loves."

"AMIE, PETRINA PHONED. JOHNNY'S LEFT THE SANITARIUM," LUCY announced. "She took him to Mamaroneck. He said he wants his sons to come up for the weekend, and you, too, if you're feeling well enough from your 'flu,'" Lucy added sarcastically.

Amie, who had been dealing with morning sickness and was now sitting on the sofa cautiously sipping tea, said fretfully, "Oh, why did Petrina go and get him? Who told him he could come home? Is he cured enough for this?"

"It seems that Johnny has taken matters into his own hands," Lucy said grimly. "You can't put this off forever. So you and I have to make some decisions, right now."

Amie gazed at Lucy, whose expression was still unforgiving. Lucy persisted ruthlessly, "Look. I think you're right about two things: Johnny's in a fragile state, and he's not exactly going to be thrilled to find out you've got a baby coming."

"Johnny's tougher than you think," Amie said defensively. "He can take it." Privately she thought, *But he might just shoot Frankie, if Frankie ever comes back.*

Lucy found herself considering everything quite coldly, and she continued, "But it's not *his* child. It's Frankie's. You said before that you were willing to give the baby up to me. So, that's what I want you and Johnny to do. I don't see any other way to handle it. I'll tell you one thing, Amie. I am *not* going to just sit by and have *you* raising Frankie's son right under his—and my—nose. I swear I'll kill the both of you."

Amie stared at her in horror. She was a little afraid of Lucy these days. Amie hadn't realized how much she'd depended on Lucy's kindness all these years, but now she missed it terribly, and seeing that serpentlike flame behind Lucy's gaze, Amie wondered how she'd ever get back that closeness, which had been so vital to her.

"All right, Lucy," she whispered. "If that's what you want, that's what we'll do."

"Yes," Lucy said bitterly. "That's what I want. Furthermore, you have to go and tell Johnny this weekend. I don't care how sick you feel. You march yourself right up there to that house, with your twins, and tell Johnny exactly what we agreed on. And you'd better stick to our deal, Amie. If Johnny gives you any guff, you just tell him to come and see me about it."

***

VINNIE AND PAULIE WENT RUNNING ACROSS THE LAWN TO GREET their father, who was bundled up on a sunbed admiring the soft blue Long Island Sound in the backyard of the house he'd chosen for himself. Amie didn't come into the yard with them; the twins said that Mama was in the house making dinner with Petrina and would call them all when it was ready.

But then the two boys stopped short and studied their father's gaunt face. They looked uncertain, wary, as if they'd been tricked, and this skinny man had put on their father's clothes and was trying to pass for the robust, healthy papa they'd grown up with.

"Yeah, it's me," Johnny said wryly.

Somebody should have warned them. But maybe it was his fault, refusing to let the twins come visit him more than once among the sick at the sanitarium, fearing that his boys would catch TB in a place so full of the suffering and the dying. Therefore they hadn't seen Johnny's gradual deterioration over time, as Amie had. Now they just stood there, like a pair of stone statues, the kind that people put on pillars in their driveways.

"Don't worry, kids," he said, arms outstretched. "I lost a few pounds but I'm still your old man. I only bend, I don't break. Come closer, I've got a lotta things to tell you."

His sons curled up there like two dogs on the beach blanket that Petrina had spread out at Johnny's feet. Tactfully, she'd gone back to her house to wait for Amie.

"Look, guys," Johnny told his sons. "It's more important to be smart than to be tough. But you can be both, and then you'll be able to handle anything in this world."

They listened politely at first, but as soon as he told them how important it was for them to do better at school, so that they could get into a good prep academy up here, and go on to an important university, and then grow up to become lawyers or doctors or professors, Vinnie and Paulie felt as if they'd somehow been duped into just another lecture about education. Neither of them liked school. What they liked was baseball, and the very way that the ball players moved. They also liked how the local big shots who hung around the taxi stands and the pizza parlors swaggered about in good suits, carrying fat wads of cash held by diamond-and-gold money clips.

Johnny had always told them it wasn't classy to show off. But Vinnie and Paulie didn't have any men at home anymore, and they felt overwhelmed. If they had been bigger, they maybe could have killed the men who shot their grandmother, so that their mother and their aunts and their godmother wouldn't have cried so much. Their cousins Gemma and Pippa had cried a lot that day, too. That was because the twins hadn't been there to shoot the bad guys and protect the family. That must never happen again.

They'd been waiting patiently for Johnny to come back home and tell them how to fight and be the men of the house.

But their father was a shadow of what he had been before, and all he could talk about was books. Kids who read lots of books and studied hard were the ones who got pummeled by playground bullies. Vinnie and Paulie didn't want to hear about the world's great thinkers. They just wanted to grow up strong.

JOHNNY COULD SEE THAT HIS BOYS WERE NOT REALLY LISTENING TO him. Here he was, using his precious breath to share with them the secrets of life, the hidden mysteries of the universe, the rules of the game, the way the larger world worked, and what they must do in order to triumph over it all and not end up just a couple of dupes.

"All right, we'll talk about this again, later," Johnny said finally. "I'll give you some of my books and we'll read them together, okay, sports?"

"Okay," they said glumly, in unison, as the twins so often did. Then Paulie ventured, "But can we play cards first? We know how to play poker now."

"Aw, who taught you that?" Johnny demanded. "You ought to learn to play tennis. Never mind. Go inside now, it's getting colder. I'll be in, too, in a little while."

After they left, he realized that they'd exhausted him. Disheartened him, really, because he knew perfectly well what they were thinking while they were staring at him incredulously with those dark button eyes. Well, it was because they'd been hanging out in the wrong neighborhoods, with the wrong kids.

Now he knew, more than ever, that he had been right to bring them up here. Next fall, they'd enroll in a good prep school, where they'd meet other kids who weren't afraid to study. They'd play good clean sports, too, with real playing fields and nice fresh air. Petrina had warned him that there were bad kids up here, too; but at least Johnny's sons would have a fighting chance in the larger world.

He'd told Amie all this on the telephone. She'd said they should have a talk after dinner, once the kids were in bed. So Johnny returned his attention to the beautiful sea.

The wind shifted now, causing a stir in the trees that made a few leaves shake loose, wafting back and forth, taking their leisurely time to flutter to the ground, making a carpet of orange and red and yellow-gold at his feet, as if to hail the return of a king after his long, triumphant journey.

Johnny closed his eyes and breathed as deeply as he dared. This was what he'd craved all his life, without really knowing it. This little beach was just a cove, but it was *their* cove, private and peaceful. The kind of place where a man could at last hear himself think. He'd buy a boat and take the boys out on the water and go fishing. They'd breathe in this fresh salty sea air every day, not just on brief holidays.

A shaft of warm sunlight fell on him, feeling momentarily like summertime again. How incredible it was to see the wide-open blue sky. You could just sit here all day and watch the sun come up on that side there, and go down on this side here.

"Beautiful," Johnny said. He was just starting to doze when he heard a whisper in his ear, and then felt a new warmth, as if a hand had pressed his shoulder affectionately, making him suddenly feel truly healed and bathed in love.

Johnny turned his head and opened his eyes. "Pop?" he said, surprised.

Amie had finally emerged from the kitchen and was halfway across the lawn, on her way to fetch him for dinner, when she saw Johnny suddenly slump to one side; and as she rushed to him, she heard his last, soft sigh.

28

Early 1945

Everyone said that this new year simply had to be better than the last one. Surely the war couldn't go on much longer, but basic supplies at home—canned goods, gasoline, tires, even shoes—were still in tight supply, and a man named Joe Valachi was turning a tidy profit as a black marketeer.

One bright snowy morning the doorbell rang, and a telegram courier handed Filomena an envelope. Her heart lurched in her chest as she tore open the notice, read the first line, then sagged against the door, oblivious to the cold, with tears in her eyes.

Petrina had followed her, and now caught Filomena by the elbows and led her back inside to the sofa. "What is it? Mario?" Petrina cried in dread.

Filomena stammered, "He's been wounded. I—I—couldn't read the rest."

Petrina snatched up the telegram, which had drifted to the floor. She scanned it quickly, then said, "It's all right. It's a leg wound. They're sending him to a hospital in London. This doesn't say much, but it sounds like he's going to be all right. He needs time to recover, but at least he'll be discharged from his service." She hugged Filomena. "Don't you see? It means he'll be coming home."

The maid had entered the room carrying baby Teresa, so Petrina took the child from her and plopped her in Filomena's lap. The warmth of her little daughter snuggling close against her belly allowed Filomena to let out a sigh of relief, as if life were flooding back into her own body.

"Your papa is coming home!" she whispered. Little Teresa sensed Filomena's joy and clapped her chubby hands, and gave her mother soft, wet kisses. Filomena could not believe how quickly this sweet creature was learning to grow up. When Teresa gave her first real smile, when she started to coo instead of cry, when she first sat up, and then began to crawl, and when each look of enlightenment crossed the child's face as she comprehended the magnitude of every achievement—all this made Filomena's heart expand with pride, love, and yet, the dread of having to one day release this sweet soul out into the noisy, pushy, treacherous world.

When Filomena looked up, she saw that Petrina's elegant brow was furrowed and she seemed preoccupied. "What's on your mind?" Filomena asked.

Petrina hadn't realized how much her face was revealing. Holding out her pinkie finger so that baby Teresa could grab it with her little fist, Petrina said carefully, "Look, I don't know what this means, but Amie says that Strollo has been showing up at her bar in the mornings. He always goes to the same corner table in the shadows, drinking his espresso and reading his newspaper—and other men come to him to talk business. Amie's too terrified to eavesdrop, which is wise. That man has animal instincts, so he'd know if she was spying on him."

Filomena asked thoughtfully, "Is he watching her or the gambling operation?"

Petrina shook her head. "Amie doesn't think he's there to keep an eye on us. He just holds meetings with his men, then leaves. It doesn't take long. Johnny once told me that's what the *capo*s and Bosses do. They hold court in one place for a while, then move on to another place, so that their enemies—and the police—can never be sure where to find them. I told her to just keep on doing business as usual but watch out."

"Good advice," Filomena agreed, then observed, "Amie's been so quiet lately. I thought it was because of Johnny. Does she need any help at the bar?"

"I don't think so. She just misses him so much," Petrina said, adding with emotion, "so do I."

"Me too," Filomena admitted. At the burial ceremony, Johnny had been laid to rest in the mausoleum, right next to his parents. Filomena had kept her gaze averted from the other alcoves allotted for Mario and Frankie when their time came, and she'd caught Lucy doing the same thing. They'd exchanged a brief look of understanding; neither one wanted to think that her husband would be the next brother to be laid to rest here.

The snow was falling lightly today. Petrina, glancing out the window, saw Lucy coming up the front walk and went to the door to let her in. Lucy looked cheery for the first time in weeks, her cheeks flushed from the cold and from excitement, as she paused on the front stoop to stomp the snow off her boots and to wave goodbye to the man who had driven her here.

"Was that our lawyer?" Petrina asked. "Why didn't you invite him in?"

"Domenico's got another appointment," Lucy said breathlessly. "But oh, I'm sorry you weren't at the courthouse today! Lordy, I have to say that he handled it beautifully. Well, after all, we had our star witnesses. You should have seen Fred and Gloria. They did a great job. After they gave their testimony, I just wanted to cheer!"

Lucy had thrown her coat on a peg in the cloakroom and tugged off her boots. Now she hurried into the parlor so that Filomena could hear, too—about Fred the janitor and Gloria the seamstress, who'd appeared before a judge to testify about the strange "nun" in the apartment building on the day that the false evidence against Frankie was planted in his office.

"The fake nun's name is Millie," Lucy said, dropping into a chair. "She gave evidence today, and so did the police. See, this whole thing happened in stages. Before today's hearing, Domenico took depositions from our witnesses, then a judge issued a warrant for Millie's arrest. When the police picked her up, she spilled the beans on Alonza, because the girl didn't want to take all the blame. She said it was Alonza's idea for Millie to dress like a nun and plant that swag. Sergio told her to go to Frankie's office on a Sunday when he wouldn't be there."

"So, then what happened?" Petrina asked, enthralled.

"The police went to Staten Island to arrest Alonza. She didn't go gently. She kicked and screamed like a banshee. The cops told her it would go easier if she confessed, so she did." Lucy paused. "You know Alonza's had a heart condition, ever since she had that attack last year, remember? Well, after they questioned her, she just collapsed at the precinct. She was dead before they even got her to the hospital."

"I shouldn't feel sorry for her, but I do," Filomena said quietly. They were silent awhile longer. Petrina had brought Lucy a cup of English tea, and she gulped it now.

Then Lucy took a deep breath and said, "So the judge reviewed all this today, and the upshot is, he dropped all the charges against Frankie. It means—it means—" To Lucy's own surprise, her voice faltered and she had to gulp for breath.

"It means Frankie can come home now," Petrina said with feeling.

"Yes!" Lucy said tremulously. "Domenico will tell Sal, so he can try to get word to Frankie. The last time they made contact, Frankie told Sal he thought he had a lead on Chris." Lucy stopped talking, choked with emotion, unable to allow herself to voice any more of her hope for the boy's return.

"Wonderful! I'll send a telegram to Mario," Filomena said. She handed little Teresa to Petrina, then rose, removed the crocheted shawl she was wearing, and draped it around Lucy's shoulders, for she was trembling. Lucy looked up, startled and touched by this gesture.

"Thanks, darlin'. Did Gloria make this shawl?" she asked. Filomena nodded. Lucy said, "I'd like to help our witnesses. I talked to them. Fred still wants to stay put in his janitor's apartment; it reminds him of his wife, he won't ever leave it. But Gloria says she 'wouldn't mind' moving into a better apartment. We have a vacancy, but of course the rent is higher than she could possibly pay. I think we should let her have it at her old rate. All right with you?"

"Of course," Petrina said, and Filomena nodded. When baby Teresa cooed her approval, it made Lucy's heart feel so full of hope for the future, for the first real time in months.

A FEW WEEKS LATER, AMIE WENT OUT ALONE, EARLY. SHE HAD GOTten into the habit of going to the first Mass of the day, twice a week. She actually preferred these weekday Masses to the Sunday service, because they were quieter, shorter, restful, and consoling. Most of the time, she was in the company of only a few elderly ladies in their black dresses, scattered among the largely empty pews, silently praying their rosaries. The new young priest, who seemed barely awake himself at this early hour, usually kept his sermons short.

Amie always sat in the back row, praying to Johnny for forgiveness and guidance, as if he were her patron saint. *I'm doing what you asked, Johnny. I'm taking our boys out of the city soon. I plan to enroll them in a prep school near our new house, this autumn. That gives me the summer to find a buyer for our bar. If I pick the right buyer, he can take over all the betting and gambling if he wants to, and that will keep the Bosses happy. You told me I could close up the business after Christmas, and the Godmothers agree, so I'm really going to do it, this year, and I hope you don't mind. I wish you'd send me a sign that it's all okay with you.*

She didn't pray to Johnny about Frankie's baby that she was carrying, which she planned to give up to Lucy. She figured that Johnny's soul either knew about it—in which case nothing had to be said—or he didn't know, and she needn't bother him about it. Surely heaven bestowed magnanimity on the souls who entered it.

Amie left the church in a contemplative mood, walking down the quiet streets. When she approached the bar, she saw that a small light had been left on. But the bar was closed at this hour. She frowned. These days, she worked here only three times a week, to keep a sharp eye on the books. Otherwise she left the daily running of the place to the bartender. But anyone who worked for her knew enough to turn off all the lights before closing up. This one could have been burning all night, driving up the electric bill.

As she drew nearer, she saw that the back door was slightly ajar. It was much too early for even the first of the morning deliveries. Had someone failed to lock up properly last night, too? Maybe it had blown open, then. Or else, one of her employees might have been using the place for something nefarious, or maybe a thief had broken in.

Amie supposed that she should call the police, but the last thing she wanted was cops asking what business she was running in that back office. Maybe the bartender was merely contending with somebody they had to pay off, doing it after hours. She would normally call Sal, but he was driving Petrina back to the suburbs today with some furniture and supplies for the houses, so he wouldn't be available to help just yet. Amie could telephone Filomena, or Lucy at the hospital, and ask them what to do.

But perhaps she still had Johnny on her mind today, and maybe he *had* heard her prayers, because suddenly she recalled the day her husband had asked her to look out for his business—and she'd said that she wasn't as clever as Petrina, or as tough as Lucy, or as brave as Filomena—and Johnny's reply now strengthened her resolve again: *You're smarter and stronger than you think.* She moved forward and peered inside.

It was silent inside the bar. Tentatively she ventured farther in, but then she froze at the sound of men's voices, coming closer now. She ducked quickly into the ladies' room and waited, terrified. Her heart was fluttering in her chest like a caged bird, and she held her breath to keep from gasping in panic. Strange men were walking back and forth right past this door, muttering in tough voices. She could only make out snatches of their conversation as they passed the restrooms again and again:

Does it look secure? Can anyone see? No slip-ups. Did you test it? Yes, I got everything, clear as a bell . . . Nothing beats hearing those wiseguys in their own words . . . best wiretaps yet. Strollo comes here every day, always that table . . . Barman says to give the keys back to him the minute we're done here . . . Some dumb housewife owns this place, believe that? Same family as that old lady who was gunned down in the street around here . . . bet she was selling narcotics.

Amie listened, paralyzed, until she finally heard their footsteps fade away as they walked out and locked the door. Still she waited, just in case they returned. But the silence was unbroken.

She emerged cautiously from the ladies' room, tiptoed to a smaller front window, and peered out one of the slats of the blinds. She saw two strange men in drab-looking suits, who crossed the street and went into a parked white van that remained there, unmoving, yet keeping its engine running.

A few minutes later, she saw her own bartender appear on the street, glance around nervously, then go right up to the passenger side of the van and hold out his hand, while one of the "suits" deposited something there. Was it a payoff? Or the key to the bar that she'd heard them talk about returning? One thing was obvious: here was a traitor, who'd given strangers a chance to enter her place and illegally wiretap it.

"Dumb housewife, indeed," Amie muttered, indignant now. And were they talking about Tessa's murder when they'd made that particularly nasty last remark?

Now she heard the milkman's delivery van arriving at the alleyway, so Amie realized that she couldn't escape out the back door, either, without being seen. The milkman might tell the bartender she'd been inside. The barman would soon enter, to serve espresso, cappuccino, and little sandwiches that were pressed in a machine like a waffle iron. He must not see her yet.

Amie retreated to the ladies' room. She was safe, for the moment. She would wait until the bar officially opened for the hungry morning crowd. She listened to the bartender whistling as he unlocked the front door and arrived for work. She heard him turn on the radio, low, while he prepared for the busy day ahead. She heard him calling out to the deliverymen unloading out back: the milkman, and then the beer man, and the bakery boy who brought the sandwiches. They were all shouting and laughing as they worked. Then, finally, the customers began streaming in.

At last, Amie slipped out of the ladies' room and moved quickly through the bustling throng of hungry people. The barman was too busy to notice her, but she walked right up to him, as if she'd just arrived through the front door.

"Everything all right today?" she asked. She saw him jump, and for a split second, an unmistakable look of guilt crossed his face. It was only a moment, but it told her all she needed to know. "Just checking the books," she said as she headed to the back office. But then she kept going, right out the back door. The truckers were gone.

She knew that Mr. Strollo would show up soon. She hurriedly crossed an alleyway, turned the corner, and ducked down the side street from which he usually came. The street was full of people. She watched every passerby, then finally spotted his familiar figure. Strollo didn't notice her until she walked right up and deliberately collided with him, dropping her purse dramatically on the ground.

"*Scusi,*" she murmured. As he stooped to pick up the purse of the clumsy pregnant lady who had knocked into him, Amie bent her head near his and whispered, "Mr. Strollo, do not go into my bar today. My bartender has let some investigators come in, and I fear they have put a wiretap at your table."

Strollo straightened slowly, his face impassive. His lips barely moved, but she heard him utter the words "*Grazie, ricorderò questa gentilezza,*" before he turned and went in the opposite direction.

WHEN AMIE REACHED HOME, SHE SAW THAT SAL HAD PULLED THE car up to the curb but was sitting there, parked, as if lost in thought. She knocked on the window, and he got out quickly.

"What's the matter?" he asked, concerned. "Do you need my help?"

"Listen, Sal," Amie said breathlessly. "I've been thinking about your offer. Do you still want to buy the bar from me?"

Sal nodded. "Yes, I do."

"Well," Amie said, "I think that's a fine idea. Of course, I'll have to discuss it with the Godmothers. If it's okay with them, then we'll have a deal."

"That's great, *Signora,*" Sal replied.

Then Amie felt obliged to tell him what had happened this morning with the intruders. Sal listened gravely, undeterred from making this deal, as if such things were the price of doing business.

"Could be the narcotics bureau boys," Sal guessed.

"But we don't have anything to do with drugs!" Amie said indignantly.

"Of course not. Perhaps they hope to implicate Strollo. My guess is they caught the bartender dealing in the stuff and got him to cooperate," Sal said. "For all we know, he could have lied and said he was peddling dope for us."

"Then you'd better fire that bartender!" she warned.

Sal said dryly, "Unless Strollo gets to him first. Fine with me."

Now he glanced back worriedly at the house. Amie recalled

that Sal had been sitting in his car here, fretting about something else before she'd arrived.

"What's bothering you, Sal?" Amie asked quickly.

"I lost touch with Frankie," he said quietly. "The last I heard was when he said he thought he had a lead about Chris. Nothing since. So I just sent word to Frankie again, to let him know that the charges against him were dropped and that Mario was being sent to a hospital in London—but I can't even tell if Frankie will get this. We have contacts in Ireland who've been ferrying our messages and helping him, guiding him around, but I'm not hearing much from them, either. I don't know how to tell Lucy this."

Amie saw that Sal—who was unafraid to confront any tough guy on the street—couldn't face Lucy and was now behaving like an undertaker. This defeatist attitude would disturb Lucy even more than the information. "I'll tell her," she volunteered.

She would wait until after dinner, because she knew that Lucy would not eat a bite after such news. She would see that Lucy had a little wine with dinner, too, so that she might have a chance of sleeping tonight. Amie would explain it all and then assure Lucy that in wartime, such silences were not uncommon and didn't always mean the worst . . . and that Frankie would surely be in touch again, very soon, with good news.

29

Spring 1945

Easter came early that year, on the first of April, when the weather could still turn treacherous with the bitter winds of winter's last stand. But the sun was determinedly pushing through, and a few bold squirrels were scampering in the garden, while the first brave birds began to flutter and sing.

Not long after the Easter holiday, on a particularly beautiful day when the sky was streaked with violet and pink and yellow, Amie's baby came into the world.

Amie was furious, because, just as she heard the obstetrician say, "Here comes the head!" they gave her sedation. "Why'd you knock me out?" she murmured in frustration when she awoke. "I made it through the hard part, with all the pain, for God's sake! Where's my baby?"

"Right here," Lucy said. Amie turned her head and saw Lucy cradling a bundled infant who was howling lustily for milk. Amie felt her breasts responding already.

"Easy now, hungry one!" Lucy crooned, rocking the newborn gently. "Give Amie a chance to wake up first."

"Let me see, let me see!" Amie cried out.

The doctor looked up and said in some surprise to Lucy, "Nurse, give the baby to the mother, she's waiting."

Lucy reluctantly handed Frankie's child to Amie, who was trying to prop herself up to see better. "What is it?" she demanded. "Boy or girl?"

"Girl," Lucy said with some satisfaction. She could not help thinking, *Frankie already has one of those*. Then, feeling slightly horrified at her own smallness, she said briskly, "We ought to think of a name for her, so I can put it on her tag."

"Nicole," Amie said immediately, leaning her cheek against the baby's warm little face. "That was my mother's name."

"Fine," Lucy said shortly. She knew that she was being mean to Amie, but she simply could not stop. Lucy had not been herself for weeks now, not since Amie had reported that there was no news from Frankie, and therefore, nothing about Christopher, either. Lucy had gone back to her old habit of working the late shift, so that she wouldn't have to talk to family members, who meant well but only made her feel worse when they tried to reassure her. So she slept by day and roamed the world at night, like a bat.

The doctor said, "Everything looks fine here. I'm exhausted! Nurse, see that this new mother and daughter get to their room and have what they need. I'll check on them before I go home tonight."

"Yes, doctor."

After Lucy got Amie settled in her room, and little Nicole, having been fed and changed, was sleeping contentedly on Amie's chest, Lucy said with false brightness, "Amie, we have to talk."

Despite the fact that Filomena and Petrina had warned Lucy to wait until morning so that they could all be there to help decide what to do, Lucy could not resist the pleasure of sharing this twisting pain in her heart with the woman who had caused it in the first place.

Amie lay back on her pillow, suddenly utterly exhausted after the adrenaline rush that had been fueling her strength throughout her labor. She gazed at her sweet little infant in the pink blanket and whispered to her, "I always wanted a girl."

Yes, here was the very daughter she'd longed for, so that Amie could buy pretty baby dresses, comb her curls, teach her all the things she'd wished her own lost mother had had time to tell her. Amie had even dreamed of the twins' having a little sister to protect. "Look at your soft, curly hair," Amie crooned, for Nicole had not come out of the womb hairless, no, not this pretty little female. Nicole was listening to her mother with a bright, intelligent expression.

"Beautiful girl," Amie whispered.

"Amie!" Lucy said sharply. Reluctantly, Amie turned her gaze toward Lucy, who wore a hard, enigmatic look. The truth was, Lucy didn't really care about having another girl to present to Frankie—if he ever came home to her again. He loved Gemma, but he'd always treated his daughter like a china doll that he didn't want to risk breaking. He'd been much more interested in playing ball with Christopher, and with Amie's twin boys.

Amie sensed all this, and now she said, quite firmly, "I know what I said when Johnny left the sanitarium, but things have changed. You don't want another daughter. You'll never really love this child, knowing it's mine. A baby should stay with her mother. That's what's best for all."

"And Frankie?" Lucy asked bitterly. "It's his child, too, you know. And he *will* be coming back to me, Amie. I *know* he will."

"Well, neither one of you is going to take this baby away from me. Understand?" Amie said with a newfound sharpness. The exhilaration of giving birth had imbued her with a strange, strong clarity, as if the blurry world of her own nearsightedness had finally come into sharp focus. Life had given her this precious gift, to counteract the heartache of losing Johnny and her own mother. She was tired of taking orders from Lucy.

"Is that clear?" Amie persisted. "When Frankie comes back, if you want me to tell him that this is Johnny's child, then that is what I'll do," she offered, feeling that Lucy didn't entirely deserve her generosity but sensing that perhaps this was what Lucy wanted to hear.

Lucy studied her keenly. "Yes," she said after a moment. "Say it's Johnny's child. I don't want Frankie—or anyone else besides the Godmothers—to *ever* know it's his. And there's one more thing. Filomena says you want to move to the suburbs and enroll your boys in school there. That's a good idea. Are you really going to do it?"

"Absolutely!" Amie said enthusiastically, relieved that Lucy had agreed to let her keep Nicole and their feud could finally end. "It's all set. The house Johnny picked out should be ready for me and the children to move into by July. And since we all agree that I should sell the bar to Sal, I've got Domenico working on the paperwork for the sale."

She had told the Godmothers all about what happened with Strollo. "Wasn't Sal clever when he found the wiretaps but left them there?" Amie whispered. "He actually hired a couple of showgirls to sit at Strollo's table and chatter about Broadway shows! He said it would 'bore the dicks stiff.' And it did!"

For, after the "bugs" yielded no fruit to the investigators who'd planted them, one day, mysteriously, the wiretaps vanished—and so did the bartender.

"I don't give a damn about Strollo and that bar of yours!" Lucy snapped. "Listen carefully, Amie. Here are my terms. This summer, you go to Westchester and stay put there. I don't want you hanging around my husband here. So don't come back to the city unless I invite you, on holidays and stuff. I want you to give me your half of the town house, so that you can never come back and live in it. Plus, I want Johnny's name on that birth certificate for Nicole. And if you *ever* try to tell Frankie it's his baby, then so help me God, I'll go to Anastasia, find out where Brunon is buried, and turn you over to the cops. You understand?"

Amie caught her breath, wondering if Lucy had gone a little crazy, holding her misery so tightly that she blamed Amie for everything—even Frankie's disappearance, and Christopher's. If

Lucy was like this now, how would she feel if Chris or her husband never returned? And now, to speak of Brunon, on a special day like this!

Amie glared at her. "You promised you'd never mention him again."

"You keep *your* promise," Lucy said meaningfully, "and I'll keep mine."

"Fine. I'll do it. Now, please tell Filomena I'd like to see her," Amie said stiffly.

Lucy went home and told the others about her agreement with Amie. Petrina sized up Lucy and decided that it was useless to warn her against lying about this baby. Perhaps this was all for the best. Then Lucy told Filomena, "Amie is asking to see you."

"I'll go right now," Filomena responded. "Will you two look after little Teresa for me?"

"Of course," Petrina said soothingly. "Come on, Lucy, let's have a cocktail."

WHEN FILOMENA ARRIVED AT THE HOSPITAL, AMIE SAID ECSTATI-cally, "Here, you can hold the baby. Isn't my daughter beautiful? Her name is Nicole, after my mother."

"She's lovely," Filomena said, accepting the pink bundle with a smile. "You know, she's only seven months younger than my Teresa. I think our daughters are going to be very close friends. Won't that be nice?"

This was just the opening that Amie was hoping for. "Oh, yes! And, Filomena, there is something very important that I need you to do," she said, leaning forward intently. "It's the most important thing I'll ever ask of you, and if you agree, I swear I'll never ask for another favor," she added dramatically.

Filomena said, "I'm listening."

"Will you please do me the honor of being godmother to Ni-cole?" Amie said formally. Then she added in a rush, "You know

I can't ask Lucy, that's for sure! And I think Petrina is just a little too permissive to be a steady influence on my daughter. I want my girl to be strong and calm, like you. I need to know that you will protect Nicole—from Lucy, from anybody—if something happens to me."

Filomena had been gazing at the little one lying quietly in her blankets; this baby seemed to be listening closely to the rise and fall of their voices, as if trying to make out what they were up to. Amie noticed it, too, and smiled.

"She's holding her breath till you say yes," Amie teased. "All the nurses say she's so 'responsive.' She's going to be so smart," she promised. "Not a little mouse like me. Will you do it, Filomena? You're absolutely right; this girl will be close friends with your Teresa, just like Gemma and Pippa are with each other. So, you'll be seeing my Nicole all the time, anyway. Will you be her godmother? *Please* say you will."

"Yes," Filomena said softly, patting Amie's hand.

***

MARIO LAY IN HIS HOSPITAL BED HALF-DOZING, WAITING. IT SEEMED to him that 90 percent of war was waiting—waiting to be assigned to a division, waiting to ship out, waiting to arrive, waiting on line for food, for clothing, for shelter; then waiting to fight, waiting to be discovered in a ditch when you were wounded, waiting to get evacuated out of the war zone, waiting for surgery, even waiting to die. By contrast, the remaining 10 percent of wartime—when the shelling erupted into the utter confusion of combat, which no movie could ever duplicate—went by so breathtakingly fast that your whole life truly flashed before your eyes at the speed of light, just to distract you from the astonishing pain of being wounded.

Now Mario was waiting to be released from this hospital in London, a city he'd never really seen, because his medical unit had arrived in the night—after a tumultuous crossing in a ship that, while routinely defending itself against enemy attacks, had managed to kill some harmless bottlenose dolphins and harbor porpoises along the way. It was the collateral damage that disgusted Mario most.

Lying here now, he missed Filomena. He'd dreamed of her, written to her, even prayed to her, as if she could intercede with God himself. He only wanted to make it home and lay his head in Filomena's lap, not caring if death overtook him after that.

And so, he thought he was dreaming when the doctor, an older man stooped with his own fatigue, came in with a broad smile to tell him that he could finally go home.

"You're a lucky man!" said the doctor. "You've got family here to pick you up."

For one wild moment Mario thought it must be Filomena, as if she could simply take wing and fly across an ocean to escort him home. But then he saw Frankie, of all people, approaching with that familiar walk that commanded respect; yet, even Frankie, despite his usual high energy, looked older, touched with a few threads of premature silver in his hair as the price he'd paid to survive these days.

"Sal told me you were here," Frankie said briskly. "Come on, the doctor says you're done. Let's get the hell out before the military brass change their minds."

You couldn't blame a man for being superstitious these days. What else was there to turn to? Not God, not science, not man nor beast. Only an ancient feeling in your gut that warned against lingering in the places where you'd suffered. Mario reached for his cane, which he still needed after the surgery, and Frankie helped him into his coat. When they reached the sidewalk, the cool, damp air on his face felt like a benediction to Mario.

"I've been to Ireland, and I found Chris. He's coming home with us," Frankie confided in the English cab, an enormous vehicle that careened around London with mad expertise.

"That's great! But how the hell did Chris end up there?" Mario asked.

"Well, that thug from Hell's Kitchen—you know, Eddie—told Chris that *he* was his father, come back from the navy, so Chris believed him, because Lucy always told the kid the same story she told all of us: that Chris's father went missing and was presumed dead. Eddie even said he was working for *us* now, and had a job to pull, and needed Chris's help. Said they were going to Boston but took the kid on a freighter to Ireland instead. He locked Chris in his cabin for most of the trip, and as soon as they got to Ireland, Eddie went to his parents' farm outside of Dublin and dumped the boy there. They made Chris work as an unpaid farmhand. But it was a blessing in disguise, because Eddie took off for Dublin on his own, so he wasn't around Chris much."

Mario absorbed this. "How did you get Chris away from the farm?" he asked.

"I hung around that one-horse town near the farm, waiting for my chance. One day Eddie's parents went out to some county fair to sell livestock, and Chris was left behind on the farm. Chris looked damned glad to see me. Didn't even hesitate when I asked him if he wanted to come back to America with us or stay with Eddie's folk. So now I've got him at an inn here in London. We all have to stay put for just one more night, Mario, and then we've got passage for all three of us to go home."

The cab stopped in front of a rather nondescript tavern with rooms above that served as an inn. "Best I could do, with the war and all," Frankie said. "It's clean enough. Chris had his supper; he's upstairs in the room, resting. Let's get you some chow. They've got a thing here they call bangers and mash. Sausage and potatoes and peas."

The publike atmosphere was warm and comforting. Men were drinking and talking and throwing darts at a target on the wall near the bar. Frankie led the dazed Mario to a table in a far corner. Mario sat with his back to the wall and ordered a pint of pale ale with his supper. The brothers spoke frankly, comparing notes. Frankie told him that he was finally in the clear after the Pericolos had tried to set him up. Then they talked about Johnny.

"Rosamaria wrote to me about him," Mario said quietly. "But it's still hard to believe that he's dead. We didn't even get a chance to say goodbye to him."

"I know." Frankie nodded. "I keep thinking he's still up there in the mountains at that place, reading books, waiting for us to come see him." They both fell silent.

When they were done eating, Frankie searched his pockets. "I've been smoking since I got here," he admitted. "I'm out of cigarettes. There's a little shop across the alleyway that sells them. You go on upstairs and say hello to Chris."

Frankie paid the tab and handed Mario the keys to their room. Mario said, "Does Sal or the family know we're coming home?"

Frankie shook his head. "I didn't want to tempt fate by announcing our plans. Never know who's listening in or reading telegrams these days."

Mario understood. As Frankie rose and headed out, Mario reached down under the table, searching for his cane. It had fallen onto the floor in the darkness, amid the sawdust that made it easier to sweep up any spilled beer or cigarette butts.

And as Frankie went out the door, another man, seated alone at the bar, quietly rose and followed him, out into the dark alleyway.

***

AT HOME IT WAS CLEAR TO EVERYONE IN THE FAMILY THAT THE whole world was changing.

"The President's dead!" Pippa announced importantly one day in spring. She'd heard all about it at school. "Did you hear me? President Franklin Delano Roosevelt is *dead*!" she intoned as if she were a radio announcer.

Soon afterwards, they learned that the Vice President, a man called Harry Truman, who once used to sell hats, had asked the country to pray for him, saying that he felt as if "the moon, the stars, and all the planets" had fallen on him when he was sworn in as the new President.

"That doesn't exactly inspire confidence, does it?" Petrina observed.

And then, the news came that the Germans finally surrendered on the seventh of May, and the war in Europe was over.

"Now we just have to beat the Japanese!" Amie's twins said enthusiastically.

One summery day, while the children were playing in the yard and the Godmothers were gathering at Tessa's table just before dinner, they heard a car pull up and honk its horn.

"Who can that be at the supper hour?" Petrina asked apprehensively. She hoped that nobody had gotten in trouble with the police again.

Filomena went to the parlor window and cautiously peered out from behind a curtain. A taxicab had pulled up to the curb, and the driver had come out to assist a dark-haired serviceman in uniform, who was leaning on a cane as he got out of the car.

The man raised his head, and Filomena saw Mario's face gazing back at her. His curly hair had been cut so short that at first she couldn't believe it was he. He waved and made his way up the front walk.

Filomena hurried down the stone steps to meet him halfway. She flung herself into Mario's arms and kissed his face and his neck. For a moment she was simply weakened by emotion, very much needing the strength of the loving arm he put around her.

"Mario, *caro mio!*" she cried. He smelled of wool and cigars and steamships and taxicabs and other hints of foreign places. His body felt a bit bulkier, more muscular. She pulled away from him, just to gaze into his eyes. His travels had left a palpable aura of strangeness about him, a hint of a wider world of both wonder and yet unimaginable ugliness.

"Is it really you?" she murmured as they kissed. "Or am I only dreaming?"

"It's me, all right," Mario said ruefully. "Goddamn, you can't possibly know how good it is to be home . . . and to see your beautiful face, for real this time."

Filomena said softly, "We got the telegram that you were wounded. I couldn't tell from your letters—how bad is it? Are you in pain?"

"It's not too bad. I will need one, maybe two more surgeries eventually, but they say after that, I should be able to walk better," Mario said in that lovely voice that she had missed so terribly, for so long. He glanced up and saw the other Godmothers standing in the doorway.

"Where's my little daughter?" he demanded. Petrina, who was holding Teresa, now brought the baby to him. Mario, still leaning on his cane, put his face right up to the child, who reached out with her small hands and grabbed his hair with instinctive delight. Mario murmured, "*Dammi un bacio, la mia bambina.*"

"Give your papa a kiss," Filomena said, and Teresa made kissy sounds, turning her face up to him. Mario kissed her, then looked up at the family in the doorway.

"Lucy," he said, "there's another fellow here to see you."

He nodded toward the taxicab, which was still there, as the driver and a lanky young redheaded boy were hauling some duffel bags from the trunk of the car. Mario waved to him, and the redheaded boy looked up slowly, almost uncertainly.

"Is that—Christopher?" Lucy whispered, wanting to rush out and clutch him to her heart, but stopping herself because of the reserved look on the young man's face. "Oh, God. He got so— tall—" Her voice choked off and she could say no more.

"He's all right," Mario said in a low voice. "Chris still had some questions about how you came to be his mother. I told him that as far as I knew, he was always yours, Lucy, because you were the one who really loved and wanted him. Just take it slow with the boy, okay? Don't ask for too much, too soon. He needs some time, to get used to us again and feel safe here."

Mario resumed his normal voice and called out, "Hey, Chris, say hello to this lady who's been worried sick about you ever since you went away." He said it in a meaningful tone, as if he'd already briefed Chris to keep in mind how much Lucy loved him and how painful his absence had been for her. Chris dutifully climbed the stairs and awkwardly held out his hand to Lucy, not knowing how else to express what he himself wasn't even sure of.

Lucy let him shake her hand as she thought, *He's so tall and he's so thin, and he's already grown into a new young man, and yet I still see the same sweet face of that infant that made me want to protect him.* Her heart was aching with sympathy and longing.

But she only smiled at him as she touched his shoulder and said lightly, "Well, now, it's high time you showed up, my laddie! I thought you'd run off and joined the army with Mario." Chris looked startled, then realized that she was teasing him and grinned.

"Come on in, my darlin'," Lucy said, steering him gently inside. The others showered him with affection, which he bashfully appreciated.

Lucy paused, then turned to Mario. "How did you find him?" she asked, half in dread. "And—where's Frankie?"

For she'd noticed that three duffel bags had been brought from the trunk of the car, but only two passengers had come out of the cab.

Mario nodded toward Lucy's town house. Sal was standing on the front stoop, talking to someone whose back was turned. Sal shook hands and walked off down the street. The other man now turned and made his way to Mario and Lucy, cautiously, as if he, too, had been wounded. He looked exhausted, but as soon as he caught her gaze, he gave her a jaunty grin, and suddenly he looked like her Frankie again.

"Hey, Luce!" he called out. "I'm starved. What's for dinner?"

Lucy, overwhelmed, felt herself trembling so hard that she could barely gasp out words of greeting. But as Frankie came closer, she reverted to the usual way she dealt with him when he was being impossible, and she gave him a mild shove. "You bastard! Why didn't you *tell* us you were on your way home?" she exclaimed indignantly, still trembling.

"Because right until the last minute I didn't believe for sure that we'd make it," Frankie said in his practical way, "and I didn't want to stir you all up for nothing."

She saw that he was favoring one side of his chest. "Are you all right? Have you been wounded, too?" Lucy asked worriedly.

"Yeah, but I'm fine." He took her in his arms, felt that she was shivering, and held her close, kissing her lips softly, again and again.

The others rushed back to the front door in amazement, clamoring for Frankie. "Come," Lucy said, steering Frankie gently. "The gang's all here. Pippa and Gemma and the twins—"

"And who are these little ones?" Frankie asked, seeing Teresa and baby Nicole.

Everyone was in the parlor now, all talking at once. Lucy held her breath as the men were introduced to the new additions to the family. Amie, still cradling her daughter, behaved as if she'd convinced herself, too, that this was really Johnny's baby. When Amie looked up, Lucy caught her eye with a brief, silent warning: *Remember what you promised. Stay away from my husband.* Amie gave her a brief nod.

Frankie, weary from his travels, simply accepted Nicole as Johnny's child, and a gentle but sorrowful expression came over him as he thought of his brother. Mario, too, looked touched by the sight of baby Nicole. He smiled as Filomena said, "I am her godmother."

Petrina, after hugging Mario, had been silently watching them all. As everyone else went into the dining room to sit around the big table, she hung back long enough to detain Frankie with a hand on his arm, and she murmured, "Frankie—what happened?

What about that man who took Chris away?"

Frankie lingered momentarily with her in the vestibule, so that the others wouldn't hear, and he said in a low voice, "We will never have to worry about Eddie anymore. He's dead. That's why I was talking to Sal. He's already putting out the word in Hell's Kitchen that Eddie was killed by an Irish local, in retribution for the union man he murdered over here. Eddie had enemies in Ireland, too. He's buried where no one will ever find him."

"Did *you* kill him?" Petrina whispered worriedly.

"No," Frankie said shortly. "Mario did."

Petrina stared at him in utter disbelief. "*Whaat?*"

"When I took Chris to London with me, someone must have seen us at the Irish train station, because Eddie caught up with us in London. The night before Mario and Chris and I were set to sail, Eddie jumped me in this dark alleyway near the tavern we were staying in. He pulled a knife on me. I tried to reason with him. He didn't really want Chris—he said the kid was more trouble than he was worth because of us. But Eddie was convinced that we were behind the Pericolos and all the trouble *they'd* caused him, and Eddie said we 'owed' him something. So, first he asked for money in exchange for Chris. I was ready for this. I said we'd pay. But Eddie was drunk and he got mad—even after he took the money, he just came at me with the knife to 'finish me off' anyway. He got a stab in. I thought I *was* finished."

"But how—"

"Mario had spotted Eddie getting up from the bar to follow me out. So Mario came up behind *him,* and just in time. Snapped his neck. The guy hardly made a sound."

Petrina stifled a cry of dismay.

"Hey, Mario's been at war," Frankie said reasonably. "He learned how to kill, efficiently. What did you think they were teaching him? But he's all right. Chris is all right, too; I told him Eddie was dead, and he didn't even ask how it happened, he just said, 'Good!' Like it was a big relief. So, everybody's all right."

"God!" Petrina gasped, sagging against the doorway in utter dismay.

Frankie put a hand on her arm. "Smile, Petrina, they're all waiting for us. Smile and let everybody be happy tonight. We're all home, and we're all safe and sound."

1957-Present

30

Nicole and Filomena

Mamaroneck, April 1980

My godmother and I had moved into the dining room to have lunch while we continued our talk. Now I fell into a stunned silence as I absorbed all she'd revealed.

Of course, some of this I already knew. My mother, Amie, had kept her promise to Aunt Lucy and never told Frankie that I was his daughter. But when Mom thought I was "old enough to handle it" after my graduation, she'd told *me* the truth about my birth—her affair with Frankie, her "arrangement" with Lucy. I went through various stages of disbelief and outrage.

I remember saying accusingly to Mom, "So *that's* why Aunt Lucy acted as if I were a land mine that she didn't want to get too close to." For, although Aunt Lucy had been kind enough to me at family gatherings, I'd sensed that she didn't really want me around. I almost felt she was a little afraid of me. Now I knew it wasn't my fault that she'd sometimes wished I didn't exist.

"But she loves you," my mother had assured me. "She always sends you a birthday gift. So you must keep this to yourself and not upset Aunt Lucy." In effect, Mom made it impossible for me to discuss it with Uncle Frankie. By this time he and Aunt Lucy had moved to California, which I suspect is why Mom finally told me. "In this family," she concluded, "it's best not to dwell on the past. I always felt that Johnny was looking out for you, just as a father would. He'd tell you, 'Be happy in the present, and make the most of your life.'"

After that bit of news from Mom, I'd stared into the mirror for weeks. I don't look much like my mother; people say I've got her cheekbones and her smile, but she's a blonde, and I have the brown eyes, dark hair, and pale skin of my father's side of the family, just like my brothers, Vinnie and Paulie. And although Uncle Frankie—as I continue to think of him—was always friendly to me, I knew that he had a fearsome temper; I'd heard him shout at Chris, and at his daughter, Gemma, too. Whereas, I'd always believed that Johnny, the benevolent-looking man in the silver-framed photograph atop my mother's piano, was my loving papa who'd died before I was born, so, even now, Johnny still feels like my guardian angel.

It was at this time that I became aware that my godmother truly wanted to help me. I don't think that Mom told Filomena about our "chat," but Filomena must have sensed my distress. She never gave me advice or consolation, but whenever we spoke, she kept the conversation focused on my future, always asking about my plans to go abroad to study, even telling me that she'd consulted a fortune-teller, who'd predicted that my destiny would be fulfilled in France. Strange, how just having an adult treat you as promising can be such a lifeline.

For, soon afterwards, I moved to Paris to do my graduate studies at the Sorbonne, and I fell in love with James, so the shock of the past, as incredible and infuriating as it was, seemed far away now, eclipsed by the dazzling present and the promise of a bright future. I was glad to be a grown-up at last, free of my family and all its entanglements. Perhaps my mother *had* succeeded in teaching me to push difficult memories out of my mind, after all.

But every now and then, I had that fearful sensation that there were other secrets lurking among the shadowy threats that I could only barely glimpse in my peripheral vision.

Now, with this new information I'd just obtained from Godmother Filomena, some pieces of the puzzle were falling into place; yet, they also raised more questions. Knowing what dangers Mom had faced in her life, I realized how much she'd tried to protect me.

"Wow," I said, sitting back in my chair in amazement. "We kids only *sensed* what was going on, but we didn't really know that the Godmothers tangled with big-time gangsters!"

I felt a surge of admiration for those four brave women struggling to get out from under the thumb of such powerful brutes. At the same time I was wondering, with mounting apprehension, if the State Department's background check, which my husband had warned me was imminent, might turn up some of my ancestors' troubled history. Could anyone hold it against me, and could it actually put an end to James's career?

As if reading my thoughts, Filomena said quietly, "Nicole, it was a long time ago—in a different world—and it has nothing to do with you or your husband. It doesn't matter—now."

I nodded hopefully. Surely this was true. Even so, I dreaded going back to tell James about these things that might just cut short all of his plans. Earlier this morning, I'd left a brief message with Mom to let her know that I'd gone to visit my godmother. Now, just as we were finishing lunch, the telephone rang. My husband had some news of his own.

"Well, it looks like that job in Washington is off!" James announced. When I gasped, he explained, "Haven't you heard? President Carter and his men ignored Cyrus Vance's advice—even though he's Secretary of State, for Chrissake—so Carter and his team went ahead and sent in helicopters to try to rescue the American hostages in Iran. What a disaster! Four choppers crashed, and eight servicemen dead!"

"Oh, my God!" I exclaimed, horrified. "Those poor guys. How awful for everybody."

"Yeah, it's bad. Vance warned them. And now he's furious because his rivals schemed the whole thing behind his back. So he resigned! That means my job offer is *kaput,* too."

"Ohh! I'm sorry, babe," I said, but I couldn't help feeling secretly relieved.

"I'm not," James said soberly. "This is no time for us to go to Washington. It looks like the beginning of the end of this administration, and anyway, Vance is out."

After I got off the phone, I told Godmother Filomena what had happened and that the background check wouldn't be necessary, after all. "All right, then. Let's have our coffee," she said briskly, rising from the table with a note of finality.

"But, Godmother, you can't just stop there!" I objected, realizing that by now my own reason for being here had shifted to a much more personal mission. "*I* need to know more! Did you really get out of 'the business' completely like you wanted to?" I had my suspicions, and I wanted validation for these uneasy feelings that lurked in my own memories. "What happened with the mobsters—did they truly leave you alone?"

"Oh, no," she said softly, handing me a tiny china cup of velvety espresso. "It's never *that* easy for a fly to escape a spiderweb. You see, for many years, there were still politicians, police, judges, lawyers willing to look the other way, so that only gave the Bosses more power and made it hard to stand up to them. Even that Mr. Hoover of the FBI wouldn't admit that the mob existed in this way. Many people had their reasons not to rock the boat. But little by little, the times *did* begin to change—and we watched for our opportunity to get out."

"What about when your husbands came home?" I persisted. "Did they like the changes you were making? Did they let you stay in charge?"

Godmother Filomena said musingly, "It's a strange thing, when men return from war. At first, Frankie and Mario behaved as if their authority was a hat or a coat that they'd left hanging on a peg in the closet and could just pick up and wear again. Well, the whole country was like that. Women couldn't get a bank loan and start a business without getting a father or husband to co-sign the loan. Everyone told us to go back into our kitchens and buy washing machines, so that the returning soldiers could get jobs. Pure economics. It had nothing to do with God or biology, as the politicians, doctors, and clergy insisted it was all about."

I couldn't imagine living under such restrictions, just for being female. "Well—what did you Godmothers do about that?" I asked, envisioning the struggle.

"We'd already begun to put our big plans in motion. So now we had to explain to our husbands why we wanted to cut all ties with any of our businesses that allowed the Bosses to extract tribute," she said. "I also felt, after the war, there was new danger in the air, something bad about to happen which would eventually force us to give up the old ways, anyway. Even so, we couldn't just snip those ties with a scissors. We had to keep phasing them out, bit by bit."

"Did Uncle Mario take over your book?" I pursued, fascinated by Tessa's ledger.

Godmother Filomena smiled and shook her head. "No. I stayed in charge of the book. Mario only wanted to run his shop. He didn't mind having me by his side, but he couldn't stand the idea of working with Petrina. I had many talks with him, telling him he must be kinder to her, and I know he forgave her, but he simply would not spend entire days with her. Fortunately, Petrina was ready to put down deeper roots in the suburbs, so she opened her own shop in Mamaroneck, and Mario and I kept the one in Greenwich Village."

Somehow, the mention of Aunt Petrina's jewelry shop in the suburbs was, at last, luring the shadowy memories to emerge from my peripheral vision, as if they finally thought it was safe to come out into the open. I remained very still and silent, so they wouldn't vanish.

Godmother Filomena was saying, "As for Frankie, at first he resisted selling off the rest of the silent partnerships. Lucy was still working at the hospital, so I think she was just relieved not to have to do Frankie's job anymore. But eventually she convinced Frankie to sell, and to invest the money; I think he enjoyed the gambling aspect of the stock market. We were all changing, after that war. Amie and you and your brothers were already living in Mamaroneck, and that's why your mother opened her restaurant up here."

"I remember. It was a big deal for Mom, that year. Let's see. That was in 1957," I said quietly, certain that we were getting closer to something much more important. As always with puzzles, the background pieces were falling into place first. I sensed that the more revealing ones might have something to do with my female cousins, not just me. Filomena's daughter, Teresa, had been my best friend. We'd worshipped our older cousins, especially Petrina's daughter, Pippa, who'd been dancing professionally for years and seemed so glamorous to us.

"In 1957, Teresa and I were twelve years old," I said searchingly. "You and Mom took us to see Pippa in the ballet. Let's see, Pippa would have been twenty-five, right? I hardly recognized her when she came onstage. She looked so beautiful—and scary—in all that dramatic makeup, playing the ghost of a swan princess, dancing by moonlight. And I thought it was so cool, the way men threw roses at her feet and shouted *Brava!* But then we went backstage, and she showed us what her toes looked like. God! Those pink ballet slippers seem so delicate, but her toes were like gnarled tree roots."

"Yes. By then she wanted to find a nice man to share her life with," Godmother Filomena observed. "She told me that the ballet director said, 'Either you dance, or you have kids, but you can't have both.' That's how it was, in those days."

I soldiered on, as if I were setting the stage and knew all the players. "Vinnie and Paulie were just graduating from high school that spring. Lucy's daughter, Gemma, was, um, nineteen. A real knockout—when she walked down the street, men stopped their cars to call out to her, just to see if she'd smile at them. Her brother, Chris, had come back from serving in the navy. He was in some kind of hot water with Uncle Frankie, and he got my brothers involved. In fact," I said finally, "the whole family was in turmoil. Then—I saw something."

I stopped short. It was as if my godmother and I had been groping through a thicket of deliberately buried memory but had finally reached a clearing. "Yes, something happened to us, that year," I said slowly. "I remember the police swarming around. I never told anybody what I saw, because I never really understood *why* it happened. But you know, don't you?"

And suddenly, I felt certain that, all along, I'd been trying to find my way back to this one year in our lives that had somehow determined all of our fates.

Godmother Filomena was sitting very still in her chair, as silent and watchful as a cat. Now she said gently, "What did you see, Nicole?" And I looked her straight in the eye.

"All right, Godmother. You tell me your secrets, and I'll tell you mine."

And that's how she finally spoke about what happened to our family in 1957.

31

The Family

Greenwich Village, May 1957

Nearly a dozen years after the war in Europe ended, Filomena awoke at dawn in her bed in Greenwich Village, gasping from a terrible nightmare. She'd dreamed that her entire family—all the Godmothers and their husbands and children—were living in an enormous penthouse at the top of a building like the Majestic, with large rooms full of beautiful furniture and treasures, overlooking verdant fields, trees, and a lake, like Central Park.

But then came an inhuman screech of airplanes, and seconds later, the bombs fell, destroying all they touched. The penthouse was shattered and everyone tumbled out, falling through the sky, that long way down. Filomena was the first to land on all the rubble, so she saw the others of her family tumbling toward her—but their bodies were in the shapes of numbers, swirling wildly, as if the wind had flung them haphazardly, like a handful of autumn leaves. She stood up and tried to catch them. But a stone-cold hand emerged from the rubble and pulled Filomena aside, and she heard the voice of Rosamaria saying, *It will all fall down. Only the children matter now. You must get them out of here, before it buries them.*

***

ON THAT SAME MORNING IN MAY, LUCY HAD THE EARLY SHIFT AT the hospital, and when she took a break, she found herself worrying about her son, Chris. At twenty-three now, he was cheerful and resilient, yet his misadventures had scarred him; there was no denying it.

When Chris had come back from Ireland, at first, he refused to discuss any of it. But gradually, he'd asked Lucy about his origins, so she told him the truth about his birth. Chris had said in awe, "Eddie's men ordered you to kill me, but you stood up to them? And saved me from the orphanage, too. Why'd you do such a crazy thing?"

"Because you smiled at me, and it was one of the most joyful moments in my life, laddie," she'd said honestly. Then Lucy had burst into tears, and Chris hugged her.

"Don't worry, Ma," he'd whispered, "we're both free now."

But she could tell, from the look on his face, that Chris had learned something about life, which was that nothing was really permanent and that things could change so drastically that you might be left never truly knowing who you really were.

Also, upon his arrival home, Chris hadn't done particularly well scholastically, although he at least managed to graduate from high school. From there, on Frankie and Mario's advice, Chris had gone into the U.S. Navy, even though Lucy wasn't keen on this idea.

"Must I give him up to the dangerous world again?" she'd whispered to Frankie.

"Show that you trust him. Let him go," Frankie advised. "He'll come back."

And he did; Chris returned looking bigger, tougher, with his muscular arms covered in tattoos. Furthermore, he'd found a marketable skill he excelled at, because they'd put him on kitchen duty, cooking for the officers. So, once back in New York, he'd enrolled in a fancy cooking school. That had been Petrina's idea.

Then Chris had gone to work in a couple of popular restaurants. Now he and Gemma shared the downstairs apartment in Lucy's town house, where Amie and Johnny had once lived with their twins. Lucy and Frankie still lived upstairs, able to keep an eye on their kids.

And everything had seemed fine, it truly did, until today, just as Lucy was about to take her lunch break. Gemma telephoned Lucy at the hospital.

"Chris got into trouble, and Daddy is yelling and hitting him!" Gemma reported. "You'd better come help me break it up, before Daddy kills him."

***

EARLY THAT SAME AFTERNOON, PETRINA, SEATED IN THE FRONT ROW among a poshly dressed audience, watched closely as an auctioneer raised his gavel threateningly. "Last call," he warned, "for this excellent Jackson Pollock painting! A great and rare early find, from a star of our twentieth century, shining in the firmament with Picasso and Diego Rivera."

"Sure, everybody says that *now,*" whispered Petrina's escort. "Ever since *Life* magazine picked Pollock as the greatest thing since sliced bread. But *you* were onto him decades ago, when nobody knew nor cared about him!"

"Doug, be quiet," Petrina whispered, pinching his arm.

"Going once . . . ," the auctioneer intoned. "Going twice . . ."

But the painting didn't go just yet. Two other bidders decided to jump in, so now there were three people vying for it—an older lady in furs, a man with a pipe, and a chilly young woman in a severe black suit and veiled hat. They batted around the bids like people playing badminton, Petrina thought in awe. As the price climbed higher and higher, she caught her breath. The room was astir now; even the doormen and security guards had peered in to watch, as if they were all in a casino.

"Lotta money on the floor tonight," the guard commented

sagely.

"Fair warning! Once, twice, three times—sold to the foxy lady!" the auctioneer sang out triumphantly, nodding to the older woman in furs.

Petrina exhaled in relief. It was over. She'd finally sold it. "But now that it's done," she admitted, "I'm sorry to say goodbye to it. That painting got me through some rough times." She remembered her brother Johnny staring at it on her wall at the house in Mamaroneck.

Her handsome escort kissed her. "Let it go," Doug advised. "You won't have any more rough times ahead." He looked at her tenderly, very serious about protecting her.

Petrina hoped he was right. She'd decided to sell this painting because here she was, in her mid-forties, on the brink of massively changing her life, which meant getting rid of things that reminded her of past sorrows. Resolutely, she took Doug's arm and they navigated past others from the audience who were chattering excitedly as they streamed out onto the sidewalk. Several women glanced admiringly at Doug, so tall and striking; then they eyed Petrina enviously, for snagging him.

He was an architect she'd met in Westchester a year ago, tall, lean, with intelligent grey eyes. A friend had recommended him to Petrina because she'd bought more houses to fix up and resell. Doug lived in Westchester but came from an illustrious old family in Virginia, and he had the modest Southern manners of a man confident of his place in the world. His first wife had died of a pulmonary infection and left him without children. He was the kind of man who moved quietly through life, keeping his troubles to himself. But something about Petrina had reawakened his hope.

They'd danced around each other awhile, meeting at the same parties, until finally they began dating and surrendered to the force that seemed to want them to be together. When he'd proposed to her, just last week, he presented her with his grandmother's beautiful sapphire ring. It was sparkling on her hand right now, in the lovely spring sunlight.

"I have to wait here to pick up my check from the auction house," Petrina said.

"I've got to catch the train back to Mamaroneck," Doug said regretfully as he flagged down a cab. "You coming up this weekend?"

She nodded. "I'm just staying overnight here with my family. I'll head out tomorrow morning."

He kissed her again, long, lingering, and delicious. "Love you," he said. Petrina whispered it back to him as he climbed into the taxi.

Now a tall, sandy-haired man was heading purposefully in her direction. He probably wanted to nab the next cab, ahead of the jostling crowd. Petrina thought nothing of it until the man deliberately planted himself in front of her. Then she recognized him.

The first thing her ex-husband said was, "Fine-looking man, your escort," as he gazed in the direction of Doug's retreating cab. "And you—you're glamorous as ever."

"Richard," Petrina said, astounded. "What are *you* doing here?" She didn't add what she was thinking, which was, *You look much older, Stranger.* But he seemed to guess her thoughts, because he smiled ruefully. She knew that, after the war, he'd finally made that move to Boston, where he'd run for office in some primary but lost the nomination. He rarely saw Pippa; he'd attended her performance when she was in Boston, but not much else. Since the divorce, the proud Pippa had wanted little to do with him. So Petrina hadn't seen Richard in years. His face was puffier, his hair thinning a bit, his mouth turned down at the corners.

"Doris and I just moved back to Manhattan," Richard said in a mild tone. "Had to take over the firm, when Dad died." So, he was still married to that homewrecker. But clearly, life had disappointed him, as if he'd realized with a shock that he would never be quite as exalted and admired as he'd been in his dazzling youth, running around winning tennis tournaments.

"One of the partners at my firm is a collector, and he had a brochure for this auction," Richard was saying. "When I saw your painting in it I said, 'Holy God, is *that* up for sale? The one I ridiculed my wife for buying, back in the forties?' Well, Petrina, what did you get today, like, twenty times what you paid for it? I should have known. You always had a good eye."

"True, you never did realize the value of what we had," Petrina agreed pertly. "When you and your lawyer were divvying up our possessions and you chucked that painting into my meager pile, you gave away our most valuable treasure!"

Richard looked at her deeply and said, "It wasn't the painting that was the most valuable treasure. It was you."

Startled, Petrina recovered quickly enough to gently laugh it off. But she thought to herself, *You still don't have it right. The most valuable treasure we ever had was Pippa.* But she didn't say it aloud. Even though Pippa was a young woman now, independent and free, Petrina could still feel the old fear of Richard's threatening to take her daughter away.

***

THAT AFTERNOON, AMIE BROUGHT HER CHILDREN TO GREENWICH Village to stay for the weekend, at Filomena's request. "I'm so glad you came," Filomena said, giving Amie a hug as they entered Tessa's study. Their daughters had already scurried off together. "I wanted to talk to you before the rest of the family gets here," Filomena confided. "It's about Nicole's future."

"Her future?" Amie echoed, dropping into a chair. "She's only twelve. She hasn't even had a date yet! She still thinks of boys as chums. It'll be years before she marries."

"I'm not talking about boys," Filomena said a bit tartly. "My Teresa says that all the teachers are raving about what a remarkable, gifted girl *your* daughter is."

"Yes, Nicole always gets straight A's," Amie muttered. She herself had been a terrible student. So she could not help feeling a swift dart of envy on every parents' night, when all the instructors rhapsodized that her girl was "a delight" in the classroom.

"Nicole's teacher wants her to go to a school for gifted girls next term," Filomena persisted. "Teresa says they've been asking you to do that for years. Why haven't you?"

Amie said defensively, "Frankie didn't send Gemma to college! He says it's a waste of money because daughters only get married and have babies. Why put ideas into Nicole's head? As it is, she reads too much. Two books a week! I try to stop her, but she goes under the bedcovers with a flashlight. She'll end up nearsighted, like me."

Filomena smoothed the palms of her hands on her skirts, as if to iron out all the wrinkles in their lives. "I suppose it's normal for mothers to be jealous of our daughters when they outdo us," she said reflectively. Her own Teresa had a gift for music, just like Mario. And, truth be told, Teresa was closer to her father, being of the same temperament, which sometimes gave Filomena the queer feeling of being an outsider. "But after all, we want our girls to be independent and not to have to rely on men to survive, right?"

Amie was shocked. "I want my daughter to fall in love and marry. Don't you want the same for Teresa?"

"That would be nice—but not if she *has* to depend on a man," Filomena said.

"Is that so? Then why aren't *you* sending *your* daughter to a fancy, expensive school for smart-aleck girls?" Amie demanded, as if she'd just laid down a trump card.

Filomena said quietly, "Teresa's grades aren't quite as good as Nicole's, but yes, she managed to get in, too, and will enroll there next term. But we had a fight this morning. Teresa says she won't go to that school unless Nicole does, too. I'd love for our 'Little Girls' to be there together. I think Nicole would help Teresa learn. What do you say, Amie? Shall we send our two beautiful daughters to this wonderful school?"

Amie said in alarm, "I've got Vinnie heading into pre-law

and Paulie to pre-med. The twins are getting on by the skin of their teeth, thanks to some very good tutors that Petrina found for them. So believe me, it's taking all the money I've got to pay for that!" she said dramatically, exaggerating, and yet convincing herself in the process.

Filomena said crisply, "Then, as Nicole's godmother, let me help pay to send Nicole to the best schools, as high as she can go. I discussed it with Mario, and he is fine with the idea. You mustn't bury this diamond, Amie. Remember when she was born and you asked me to do you this 'last favor,' to be her godmother and protect her? Now do *me* this favor. All right?"

Filomena had placed her hand firmly atop Amie's, as if she would never let go until she extracted this promise. "Oh, all right," Amie said sulkily. "I guess the Little Girls might as well go to the same school. It will save us a fortune in telephone bills!"

***

FROM THEIR HIDING PLACE IN THE PANTRY, TERESA AND NICOLE squeezed each other's hands to avoid shrieking with joy that they'd soon be together at the "gifted" school.

"See, I *told* you—inside this pantry, you can hear *everything* they say in my mother's study," Teresa whispered. She had Filomena's eyes, but her pixie face was framed by straight, dark hair, cut short with bangs, which made her look a bit like Christopher Robin in the Winnie-the-Pooh books. "Aunt Lucy was in there earlier, talking to Mom. She said Chris is in big trouble. He got fired from cooking in that restaurant; know why?"

Nicole shook her head. Teresa whispered gleefully, "Chris was helping some guys use the place to smuggle drugs. The owner caught them and fired them. Uncle Frankie found out, and thrashed Chris and shouted, 'It's Cook's day off, so get your ass in our kitchen and make yourself useful.' That's why Chris is making dinner for us tonight."

At that moment, the door of the pantry opened, and their big cousin Chris stood right there, looking surprised. "Hello! What are *you* two movie stars doing in my kitchen?" he said, amused to find them looking wide-eyed. Teresa and Nicole giggled.

"You hungry, ladies?" he inquired. They nodded, speechless. He was *so* handsome. "Come on out, let's see what I've got," he said.

They followed him in fascination. To be honest, both girls had a little crush on Chris. He was tall and dangerous looking; his strong arms had scary blue tattoos, from being in the navy. He'd come home bearing gifts for them—exotic coins and stamps from the world's big cities that had magical names, like Cairo and Barcelona and Istanbul. But now he'd gotten fired, for acting like a real gangster.

Both girls were normally obedient, studious creatures. So they felt a vicarious thrill around Chris, who wasn't afraid of anything, even breaking the rules. He didn't look at all penitent about getting bawled out by his parents. In fact, he looked quite cheerful as he sauntered over to the oven. The girls watched, enthralled, while he hauled out a big tray of tiny cupcakes with a sticky honey glaze, which smelled heavenly.

"Here, have a honey cake, but don't tell your mothers that I gave you sweets before dinner," he said conspiratorially. "You can eat here. I'm going to take a break." He stepped out to the backyard, lit a cigarette, folded his arms, and sat there smoking contentedly. The girls gobbled up their treats, then scurried up to Teresa's room.

CHRIS WAS HALFWAY THROUGH HIS CIGARETTE WHEN HE HEARD A low whistle from the other side of the garden wall. A moment later, a busboy he knew hopped over the wall. "New shipment coming in tonight," the man said.

Chris shook his head. "Can't do it. My father's onto me. He'd skin me alive."

The busboy, a squat fellow with a round face, looked incredulous. "Know how much you and I could make on this haul alone?" he demanded.

Chris said ruefully, "I don't want to know. I'm out of the business. And, do me a favor? Don't come here again. The Godmothers might sic the dogs on you."

Of course, there were no dogs. There had never been any dogs. But the busboy didn't know that. The Godmothers still had a reputation; that story about Filomena's knife-throwing had been exaggerated into a stiletto she'd plunged into the neck of a debtor. People believed it, because Aunt Filomena's face said she'd do it again if she had to.

The busboy hopped back over the wall with far less cheer. Chris shrugged. Restaurants were good conduits for moving illicit merchandise quickly, hidden amid barrels of fish or produce or beer. When Chris had succumbed to temptation he'd made a tidy profit, until his boss found out, and wouldn't you know it, Frankie once had a silent stake in that very tavern, until he sold it to the current owner. So of course the owner had gone straight to Frankie to demand a payoff for not reporting Chris to the cops. Frankie had paid him, then stormed home, grabbed Chris by his hair—his *hair*, for God's sake—and hauled him to his knees, forcing him to swear to Lucy that he'd never do it again.

Chris intended to keep his promise. Frankie had always been a good father to him, having risked a lot to get him back from Eddie, a beast of a man whose name still made Chris shudder. On the boat home from London, when Frankie had broken the news that Eddie was dead, Chris didn't even ask how or why. He'd only said, *Good*. That devil belonged in hell.

For a long while, Chris had been on good behavior, glad to be home. But now the walls were starting to close in on him. Normal life seemed too slow, too somnolent. A real man had to roll the dice, take risks, if he wanted to make something of himself. Chris had waited all his life to become old enough, like Johnny and Frankie and Mario, who in their heyday had attracted the respect and admiration of men and women alike. Hell, the men in this family had practically *owned* this town when they were his age. Chris was twenty-three already. Time would simply march on without him, if he let it.

WHEN THE FAMILY SAT DOWN TO DINNER THAT EVENING, PETRINA announced her engagement to Doug. Amid everyone's exclamations of joy, Amie boasted, "*I've* already met him! He's so handsome, he looks like that actor from *High Noon*, Gary Cooper."

"Yeah, Doug's a good guy," Petrina said in a warm voice that revealed just how much she cared for him. Filomena found this touching and gave her a hug.

Mario, who was still a bit reserved with Petrina, had been warned by Filomena that something like this was imminent, so, when she nudged him now, he gallantly opened a bottle of champagne. They all clinked to Petrina's happiness. Teresa and Nicole watched, wide-eyed, for the sophisticated Aunt Petrina was blushing like a girl.

"Congratulations, Godmother," Teresa said rather formally.

"Thank you, darling," Petrina said, taking a quick sip.

Frankie glanced around, frowning. "Hey, where are the other kids?" he asked.

"The twins went out to get some 'fresh air,' but Mom told them to be home by eight sharp," Nicole volunteered about her brothers.

"And where are the Big Girls?" Frankie demanded.

"Pippa has a performance tonight, and there's some black-tie gala dinner afterwards, so she invited Gemma to attend," Petrina said, too happy to notice the storm clouds gathering. "So, they won't be eating dinner with us."

Frankie gave Lucy a significant nod. Lucy took this cue. "Petrina, love," she said worriedly, "Pippa's been taking Gemma out dancing at uptown nightclubs with that glamorous crowd of hers. We're concerned. Our lass is only nineteen, you know."

Petrina was insulted by the implication that her hardworking daughter, Pippa, was a bad influence. But she replied lightly, "Oh, the Big Girls are just husband-hunting. I imagine you approve of *that*, Frankie dear."

Teresa said to Nicole, "I hate the way they call Pippa and Gemma the Big Girls. It means, no matter how old we get, they'll always call you and me the Little Girls."

Nicole was glad when her brothers arrived to break the tension. She was proud of them; at eighteen, Vinnie and Paulie were handsome and strong, and, although diligent at school, they were somewhat rebellious looking, in a dashing sort of way. They breezed into the dining room like a gust of fresh air. Frankie eyed them suspiciously as they took their seats.

"Hey," said Vinnie, "who's the big fat guy in the neighborhood? Man, I never saw a guy so fat. He could hardly walk. He waddled like a bear." He leaned from side to side to illustrate.

"That fatso had to be three hundred pounds," Paulie agreed. At the others' baffled look he added, "He was with a man he called Strollo. They were just outside the pool hall."

The adults looked up swiftly at the name of Strollo. Frankie, feeling responsible for disciplining the boys in the absence of Johnny, gave his nephews a sharp look. "What the hell were you two doing down at the pool hall?"

"Aw, c'mon, Uncle Frankie," Vinnie said as Petrina passed him the *antipasto* plate. "We just wanted to unwind after studying for exams."

"Listen, you mugs. You are not going to disgrace the memory of your father by flunking out. So you don't 'unwind' until your exams are done, you got that? And even then"—Frankie pointed a finger at them—"the only pool I want to see you in is a *swimming* pool. I mean it, boys. You won't impress the girls if you can't dive and swim as well as the Harvard crowd. There are plenty of places to practice, with all those country clubs and sailing clubs and beach clubs all up and down the Long Island Sound. Petrina's a member. She'll let you in, right?"

Petrina nodded. The boys looked suitably chastened. "Okay, Uncle Frankie," Paulie said, then he added wickedly, "but we're sleeping over here in the guesthouse tonight. So, can we interest you and Mario and Chris in a friendly little card game?"

"I'm in," Chris said as he carried in a huge dinner platter of roasted beef and potatoes, and string beans dressed with walnuts and vinaigrette. He placed it at the center of the table. "But first, come on, everybody, *buon appetito*."

THE FESTIVITIES LASTED UNTIL MIDNIGHT. EVEN FRANKIE ADMITTED that the meal had been magnificently cooked by Chris, and nobody wanted the celebratory evening to end. Nicole and Teresa sulked when they were sent to bed at ten. Lucy insisted on staying up until Pippa and Gemma returned, so she told the men, "Deal me in." Petrina played, too, but Amie watched, crocheting. Filomena sat back and sipped a fine after-dinner liqueur that she had made herself, from wine and herbs and violets.

Just after midnight, they heard the front door open and then slam shut loudly. Everyone glanced up when Pippa and Gemma burst in the door, flushed with excitement, looking stunning in evening gowns, fur-trimmed wraps, and gloves.

"The return of the prodigal Big Girls," Frankie said disapprovingly.

"How pretty they are. Like two long-stemmed roses," Petrina murmured to Lucy. "My daughter looks like Audrey Hepburn, and yours is like Marilyn Monroe."

"Never mind *us*! Did you hear the big news?" Pippa demanded breathlessly, flinging herself into a chair. "Frank Costello's been shot!" Amid a chorus of questions, she explained, "Well, he was out having dinner at Chandler's Restaurant, and then he made the rounds of the clubs to see his wife and some friends."

"Were *you* there in some club when it happened?" Lucy asked, horrified.

"No," Gemma said excitedly, taking off her evening wrap. "He got shot in the lobby of that fancy building he lives in on Central Park West! We didn't find out till we were driving home and went past the place, and we saw the crowd and the cops out in front. That nice building—you know, what's it called?"

"The Majestic," Filomena said, exchanging a look with Petrina, recalling the man who'd given them free champagne at the Copacabana—and, years later, invited them to his penthouse. She could not imagine bullets flying in that beautiful art deco lobby. But now she understood the dream she'd had this morning. The bombs exploding, the stones of a building just like the Majestic tumbling into rubble. It had already begun.

"Holy cow! Is Costello dead?" Frankie demanded in disbelief.

"I don't know. They took him to Roosevelt Hospital. They say he gave the cabdriver a five-dollar bill for a forty-five-cent fare!" Pippa replied.

"But *who* shot him?" Lucy demanded.

Pippa said significantly, "Nobody knows for sure. But the doorman at the Majestic said the gunman was a fat guy who charged into the lobby and said, 'This one's for you, Frank,' popped him, and just waddled out into some car that was waiting for him. The reporters are already calling the shooter 'the Fat Man' and 'the Waddler.' But Mr. Costello told the police he 'didn't see a thing.' Isn't that odd?"

Vinnie looked at Paulie, who said meaningfully, "The Waddler. Strollo's friend!"

"Does this mean that Strollo wants Costello dead?" Amie said worriedly.

"He wouldn't make a move like that without the backing of somebody bigger. You can bet Vito Genovese is behind it," Frankie muttered, glancing at Mario.

"Why?" Chris asked, intrigued. "Isn't Costello a bigger man around town?"

"Genovese always thought *he* should have succeeded Lucky Luciano, instead of Costello," Frankie explained. "He's never been happy just being Costello's underboss."

Filomena shivered. She'd seen Vito Genovese on the street only once, but that was enough. His hooded eyes had a cold-blooded, calculating stare, as still as a poised snake. It was said that he'd killed a man just so he could marry the dead man's wife.

"It's the narcotics," Mario said quietly. "It's changing things. Some Bosses are getting into it big-time, but Costello wants nothing to do with it. The politicians don't like it, and Costello knows he'd lose political influence. Especially now, with that new act of Congress—the jail penalties for drug trafficking are stiffer than the other rackets."

Frankie, glancing meaningfully at Chris, said, "Right. Which means only the boneheads can't resist the profits. It's not like bootlegging and gambling. Narcotics is a dirtier business. They're even peddling this stuff in playgrounds, to get kids addicted."

"It's terrible, what heroin does to people," Lucy said, troubled. "I've seen addicts in the emergency room. They waste away till they're like nothing human in the end."

"You see?" Amie said to her twin boys. "This is what comes of hanging out at pool halls." Unexpectedly, she turned to Chris. "As for you," she said severely, "I am your godmother, so you must listen. You are handsome and not too dumb. It's time you settle down, find a girl to have children of your own to worry about. You're a good cook, so come work for me, in my restaurant in Mamaroneck. You'll learn everything I know about the business— but if your foot slips once, you're out on your heel."

Lucy gave a start but did not know what to say. Things between her and Amie had gone from an uneasy truce to something familial again, but they were not quite as close as before. Amie had kept her word and moved to Westchester, leaving her city apartment to

Lucy's children. In turn, Lucy had given up the house she owned in Mamaroneck to Amie, who quickly found tenants for it. It worked perfectly because Frankie—unlike his brother Johnny— was a pure city boy and hated the suburbs. Thus, Lucy's family was exposed to Amie only in small doses.

And even when they saw each other on such occasions as Christmas, Lucy had, at first, watched her husband and Amie closely, alert for any sparks flying between them, any covert yearning, any exchange of something complicit, or telltale sign of remembered passion. But there was none. And Frankie was just as amorous with Lucy as he'd always been. It seemed the past was done. Everyone wanted family life to go back to what it had been before the war.

Yet now, the prospect of Amie's taking Lucy's son to the suburbs evoked her old mistrust. But Chris was undeniably skirting serious trouble in the city. Maybe he truly needed to get out.

Chris smiled winningly. "Sure, Godmother Amie," he said. "I could use the dough."

"As for *you*, young lady," Frankie said severely to Gemma, "no more supper parties or nightclubs." When she protested, Frankie said firmly, "*Basta*. These are dangerous times!"

THAT NIGHT, AS FILOMENA AND MARIO WERE CLIMBING INTO BED, she said, "Amie wants our Teresa to spend the summer by the sea with her kids in Mamaroneck. I told her yes. So they'll all go early tomorrow morning. Chris, too, to work in Amie's restaurant."

"I think it's an excellent idea to get the young ones out of the city this summer," Mario agreed, tucking the bedcovers over her as they settled in.

Although she hadn't told him about her dream, Mario knew why she was worried; she had a sixth sense about trouble ahead and was doing everything in her power to protect them all from what may come. Tessa's ledger would be the last to go; the smaller debtors had slowly paid off what they owed because Filomena had reduced their interest percentages. All that remained now was some of the "big fish"—the high rollers, professional bettors, and bookies, whom she'd kept on the books to cover the tribute to the Bosses. She had calculated that in one more year they could close out Tessa's book entirely. But this was possible only because Costello had been reasonable, not asking for more tribute than they could bear.

Now there were ill winds blowing. Filomena said in dismay, "We are so close to getting out. But if Costello is dead, where does that leave *us*?"

Mario took her in his arms and held her close. "It means we just have to swim faster than we thought, to get to 'the other side' that you always speak of," he said tenderly. "Before these Bosses make us drown in their wake."

THE NEXT MORNING, AMIE LEFT EARLY WITH NICOLE, TERESA, Chris, and the twins. After they were gone, Filomena, Mario, and Petrina were finishing their coffee, silently waiting for news, when Pippa lazily wandered into the dining room in a fancy dressing gown, her long, dark hair piled haphazardly in a knot atop her head, grateful for some coffee to sip quietly. When the telephone rang, Mario went to answer it in Tessa's study.

"Pippa and I are heading back to Mamaroneck, too," Petrina told Filomena. "Are you and Mario coming up later on this summer, for Amie's annual Fourth of July barbecue?"

"Of course," Filomena said. "Mario's looking forward to going fishing."

"Tell him our beach has great clams to dig up!" Pippa said, still yawning over her coffee and stretching out her long legs, exhausted from her performance last night. When she heard the newspaper thump on the front stoop, she roused herself to wander out and pick it up, looking for the reviews. Then she came hurrying back right away, waving the paper aloft to show the big *New York Times* headline:

Costello Is Shot Entering Home; Gunman Escapes

Gambler Suffers Superficial Scalp Wound— Attacker Flees in Darkened Car

"Costello's alive!" Pippa announced in disbelief. Filomena breathed a sigh of relief.

But when Mario emerged from the study, he said warningly, "Yes, Costello survived. But Sal says it *was* Genovese and Strollo behind the hit. He says Strollo hired the fat man that Vinnie and Paulie saw at the pool hall. Word is, he's an ex-prizefighter called Gigante."

Filomena and Petrina exchanged a look at the name of the teenage boxer who'd given the Godmothers lessons in self-defense years ago. "It *can't* be him!" Petrina exclaimed. "He's not fat! He was a successful boxer, in great shape!"

"That was years ago. Believe it or not, they say he bulked up for this hit, just so he could slim back down afterwards while in hiding awhile, to avoid ever being ID'd as the 'Fat Man' shooter," Mario said. He looked at them quizzically. "How do you know this Gigante?"

"Oh, just neighborhood chitchat," Petrina mumbled evasively. "Ma knew his mother."

"Well, according to our sources, Costello has agreed to 'retire' and let Genovese take over his role as Boss," Mario continued.

Filomena gasped. "Why should Costello do that?" she asked in dread.

"They missed him once," Mario said. "The next time, they won't miss."

Filomena had been studying his face, and now she asked, "Is that all?"

Mario said carefully, "No, there's something else. One of the Pericolo brothers has finished serving his time in jail, and he's out. They say he's gone to Las Vegas."

Pippa saw her mother go pale. "*Who's* out of jail?" Pippa asked uncertainly.

Petrina, tempted not to tell her, finally said, "The men who killed your grandmother."

"Only *one* man is out. It's Sergio," Mario corrected. "Ruffio died in prison, years ago."

Pippa felt her entire body go cold at the memory of that awful scene. To this day, she could still smell those two killers as they brushed past her; she could even recall the hot, sweet, slightly iron scent of Tessa's spilled blood. All these years, she'd known one thing for sure—that this evil was only hidden and had never entirely gone away.

32

Greenwich Village and Mamaroneck, Late Summer 1957

Months later, on a very sultry evening, Lucy's daughter, Gemma, had a fight with her parents. It really wasn't her fault. Things had already gotten pretty tense around their house that summer. Lucy and Frankie would only tell her that the new Boss was "putting the squeeze on people," which meant they were all being extorted for more money.

Gemma was still not allowed to go out with Pippa at night. And yet, despite such parental protectiveness, Gemma had always felt slightly unwanted, ever since childhood. Vinnie and Paulie got attention because they were twins. Chris, who'd caused them all lots of trouble, was still doted on by Lucy, as if he were her little angel. When Gemma was a child, Lucy had surely loved her, but even then, Lucy was so distracted and preoccupied. Something—or somebody else—was always more important.

As for Gemma's father, Frankie, yes, he'd been affectionate with her, in an absent-minded way; when she was little, he would pick her up and waltz her around the room, saying, "How's my dancing partner today?" But then he'd go off and play baseball with the boys, even though Gemma could bat a ball clear to the end of the park. And now that Gemma had put away her roller skates and was a "young lady" of nineteen, Frankie didn't hug his daughter much anymore; he acted as if she were as dangerous to hold as a stick of dynamite.

"It's because you have breasts now." Pippa was once again the one who had to explain it to her. "Fathers are men, you know. He doesn't want to notice your looks. You're too sexy for your own good. You make all the men lose their heads!"

"I can't help how I look," Gemma objected. When males had started noticing her—and the grown men did, even before the boys at school—Gemma thought it was most peculiar. Her body had always been her private space. To have men suddenly studying her legs, or staring at her chest as if she wore cupcakes there, made her feel slightly sick, to be honest. She lay awake nights worrying about how she was supposed to react to this intense interest. At first, all she could feel was that she wanted to be left alone.

"Don't worry," Pippa had advised. She was twenty-five now, and her dance career had made her a woman of the world. "When you go out of the house, it's just like being onstage. *You* be in charge. Smile, but you don't let them catch your eye. You don't have to let anybody touch you unless you really want to. Don't be afraid. Because if you're not afraid, then you can scare the hell out of them. Most of them are big dreamers; they just like to fantasize about it. Pick a good guy, though, and *you'll* have a good time kissing and being in love."

Shortly afterwards, Gemma's mother had decided it was time to have "the talk" with her. Gemma pretended that Pippa hadn't already enlightened her about sex. Lucy was frank, calm, but acted just like a nurse instructing a patient. Gemma enjoyed this unexpected solidarity with her mother, but by then it seemed too little, too late.

Nowadays, it was the "Little Girls," Nicole and Teresa, who were getting tons of praise for their scholastic abilities. So, since nobody seemed to think that Gemma had much of a future, she had taken matters into her own hands.

Gemma sighed, glanced in her mirror, gave her strawberry-blond curls a final smoothing, and joined her family for dinner.

They were eating at Uncle Mario's house, because Aunt Filomena had cooked tonight, making a delicate sole sautéed to perfection and served with fresh *zucchini* that had been minced and mixed with bread crumbs, then stuffed right back into the big yellow blossoms of the *zucchini* and lightly fried. The chilled Soave wine was crisp and dry.

But by the end of the meal, there was trouble. It began when Filomena said warmly, "Gemma, Petrina phoned to say that Pippa told *her* that you got a new job. Congratulations!"

Gemma gulped. Apparently Pippa had assumed that Gemma had broken the news to her parents by now, since she'd been at this job nearly a week already. Well, she hadn't planned to spill the beans just yet.

Lucy put down her fork and knife and said, "*What?*" with a suspicious glance.

Frankie, as usual, didn't even look at her. He just aimed his remarks at Lucy, which Gemma found insulting. "What the hell does she want a job for?" he demanded. "We give her everything she needs."

"Pippa works," Gemma countered. "She's been a ballet dancer for years."

Too late, she realized that this only made it worse. Her father retorted, "Great! Prancing around in tights, half-dressed for men to stare at, like a common showgirl."

"What sort of job have you got, Gemma?" Mario asked kindly.

"I'm a manicurist," Gemma said, her confidence fading by the minute. "At a fancy hotel. It's a cushy job with great tips, and it can lead to better things, because you meet all kinds of interesting people that way. You know, people who travel—" She stopped.

Pippa had found her this job, because she had lots of "connections" uptown. Pippa had said this work could lead to Gemma's being "discovered," maybe as a model or a movie star. But Gemma didn't want to tell her parents what else Pippa had said, which was, *You could meet a millionaire to marry. Rich men just love having pretty girls holding their hands and playing with their fingers!*

"A manicurist!" Lucy shrieked, ignoring Filomena's cautioning look. "Where did you get a crazy idea like that?"

"Gosh, I don't know, I guess this 'idea' just ran out from behind a bush and grabbed me by the nose, like a head cold," Gemma said sarcastically, feeling stung. Somehow, these plans that meant so much to her had just fallen flat as a pancake when she'd said them aloud in a rush. She felt stupid now, with everybody staring at her.

"Don't get smart with us, young lady," Frankie warned. Gemma bit her tongue. She never understood why getting "smart" was bad for a girl, especially since her parents were so impressed with her studious, obedient little cousins.

Frankie turned to Lucy. "If she were my *son*, I'd belt her. So *you* deal with her!"

As far as Lucy was concerned, having a beautiful daughter was hardship enough—when men old enough to be Gemma's father wolf-whistled as mother and daughter walked down the street, Lucy knew they weren't whistling at her. But she worried about Gemma. A woman who relied solely on her looks was destined for a disastrous end—especially in jobs that encouraged men to ogle and proposition them, like hat-check girls and cocktail waitresses.

So Lucy said sharply, "It's high time you got over yourself, lassie. You want to work? All right, we'll find you *decent* work. I can get you enrolled in a nursing school. They are always short of nurses these days—"

"No!" Gemma cried out, horrified. "You think I want to come home all pale and exhausted, and smelling of disinfectant every night, like you do? You think I want to spend my days cooped up in that crummy hospital with nothing but the sick and the dying all around me? I'd rather *die* myself than be a nurse."

"Don't speak to your mother like that!" Frankie said. "Nurses are beautiful, that's why I fell in love with her. It's a noble calling. I'd be proud if you had a profession like that. But why would anyone take some cheap job if they didn't have to?" He looked truly bewildered.

"Well, I *do* have to!" Gemma shouted. "I'm not talented and artistic like Pippa, and I'm not smart like Teresa and Nicole. But maybe I could have been, if anybody around here ever gave a damn about me when I was little."

"If you *ever* use a word like that again—" Frankie was livid now.

"What, are you threatening to beat me up? You think I'm one of those people you and Sal can push around?" Gemma was past caring now. There were tears streaming down her face, and she felt utterly humiliated. She didn't want to spend her whole life as a manicurist; it was just an entry into the beauty business, which *was* a career. But she certainly wasn't going to say that now, not after the way they'd already trampled on her small dreams of having a life of her own.

So Gemma, clinging to her last shred of self-respect, stood up defiantly. "I'm nineteen years old, I can do what I want. I have a friend who works in a department store, and she and I are going to rent an apartment together uptown. So I'm going to keep this job and live on my own," she cried. "And that's that!"

She fled from the dining room sobbing, going through the corridor that led to her parents' town house. She entered her bedroom, locked the door, and flung herself on the bed.

"CAN YOU BELIEVE THE WAY SHE TALKED TO US?" FRANKIE DEmanded. "Know what Ma and Pop would have done to us if we ever spoke to them that way?"

"Frankie, let it go," Mario said reasonably. "She just wants to try her wings."

"Only angels have wings," Frankie muttered.

Lucy, oddly enough, took no offense at Gemma's outburst. Even the insults struck her like a breath of fresh air, causing Lucy to realize, *I have let my daughter down. All because I knew Frankie wanted a boy, so I treated Gemma as if she were second prize. I wonder why it mattered so much—what Frankie wanted. Why did I never ask—what do I want?*

"Mario," Filomena said tactfully, "will you help me carry the coffee and dessert outside? It's nice and cool there, with the fountain."

Left alone with her husband now, Lucy said thoughtfully, "Frankie. Let Gemma keep that job. The odds are, she'll be bored stiff soon enough. But if we stop her, she'll always imagine it would have been more glamorous."

"Fine," Frankie said in exasperation. "You're the one who was so dead set against it. Gemma can keep the job, but she's not going to live in an apartment uptown. She has to stay put, right here. That's the deal. She can take it or leave it."

"All right," Lucy agreed. Then she surprised herself by saying gently, "You know, darlin', all young girls need to see that their father really wanted them. They can sense when a man wished he'd had a son instead of a daughter. And don't tell me that boys 'pass on the family name.' We're not kings. It's just a dick thing, men wanting sons so they can see a reflection of themselves. But it hurts girls to be unwanted. It hurts a lot."

Frankie, perplexed, muttered, "I never said I wished she'd been a boy. I was really happy the day that Gemma was born."

"Well, someday you should tell *her* that, not just me," Lucy answered, watching Filomena and Mario standing in the garden arm-in-arm. She took Frankie's arm. "Listen, my love," Lucy said, "you and I never really had much time to ourselves after we got married. Why don't we go away, somewhere nice, just the two of us?"

It had actually been Filomena's gentle suggestion; Lucy, startled at first, was touched by this consideration, and she could see the wisdom of it. She added, "Filomena says she'll keep an eye on Gemma for us while we're away."

"Go away? Like where?" Frankie asked, more baffled than ever.

"You always said you wanted to go to California and see the vineyards, maybe even buy one," Lucy suggested.

"California is a *long* way away," Frankie said doubtfully.

"Yes," said Lucy. "That's exactly what I'm thinking."

Frankie grinned and kissed her. "Okay, baby. This time it'll just be 'me and my gal,'" he added, humming the popular tune, holding her close. Lucy sighed deeply.

***

SUMMERTIME IN MAMARONECK WAS DELIGHTFUL. PIPPA STOPPED BY her mother's jewelry store after a day at the beach club, with her younger cousins Teresa and Nicole in tow. Teresa, her pixie face framed by straight, dark bangs, looked more like Filomena every day, and she had Mario's sweet, self-possessed disposition. Amie's daughter, Nicole, bright as a button, had a radiant exuberance and a headful of curly hair the color of a shiny chestnut.

Petrina glanced at the girls from across the gleaming glass counters of her shop, smiling but feeling slightly distracted today. "Pippa, can you help me close up?" Petrina asked. "I am so late for everything. I'm supposed to be at the florist's on the other side of town before *he* closes, to pick out all the arrangements for the wedding."

"You go ahead, Mom," Pippa said. "I'll do it for you. I've closed up before."

Pippa was proud of her mother. Petrina's jewelry store was the talk of the town. She had a real talent for designing unique pieces in gold studded with precious gems, inspired by ancient Roman, Greek, and Egyptian styles, which made their owners feel like royalty.

And Pippa heartily approved of her mother's fiancé, Doug—a

man whose Virginia pedigree was illustrious, and yet, Doug was modest and kind. Aunt Amie was right; Doug *did* look like Gary Cooper, laconic but strong, equally at home in jeans as he was in an elegant dinner jacket, spiffily escorting Petrina to the best parties.

Petrina caught her daughter's gaze and suddenly experienced a strange, poignant feeling of the fleetingness of time. All these girls were growing up. Teresa was so much like Mario, and Nicole reminded her of Johnny and Frankie. As for Pippa, at twenty-five, she'd reached an age of perfection, still wearing her dark hair waist-length, ever the long-legged ballerina.

When I was her age, I was already a mother, with my diploma locked in a cupboard, Petrina thought. That was why she'd urged Pippa to pursue her dreams, have a career, advising, "Men aren't so important. Marriage can wait."

But now that Petrina had found Doug, she believed in married love again and didn't want her daughter to be deprived of it. Pippa's experience of men hardly inspired faith in marriage: the father who'd given her up, the gangsters who ruled the city, and the jaded theater and nightclub set. Love could only be found when two honest, open hearts met. If Pippa got too sophisticated, she might miss it, like a last train home.

"Hey, Pippa, here comes that cop who's in love with you," Nicole announced, gazing out the front window. An athletically built man was strolling slowly by, and he tipped his hat as he passed. Pippa glanced up, then waved genially back at the police detective.

"You can set your clock by George; he always stops for coffee across the street," Petrina observed, peering out. "Hmm. He's here on his day off—just to see if *you're* here today, Pippa."

"George and I are just friends," Pippa assured her. George had been her first admirer here in the suburbs but certainly not her first love. Pippa's very first crush had been a fellow dancer; then she'd fallen for a charming older diplomat who sent flowers to her dressing room. Now she was more seriously involved with a violinist, although she hadn't told her family yet.

So she'd had to let the policeman down gently. "I told George I'd introduce him to my gorgeous cousin Gemma when she's in town this fall for your wedding, Mom," Pippa said. "I even taught George how to ballroom dance. He's good!"

Petrina sighed and hurriedly gathered up her things. "I *am* late. Sure you don't mind finishing up here for me? Business is slow today. The street's been empty nearly all afternoon. Everybody's out soaking up the last rays of summer."

"Fine. Go on, get some nice flowers for your wedding," Pippa said encouragingly.

"Godmother, can I go with you to the florist?" Teresa asked eagerly.

Petrina said, "Sure. What about you, Nicole? Want to come with us?"

"No, thanks. I'll stay here. All the bugs in those greenhouses bite only *me*. They never touch Teresa," Nicole complained. "I like jewelry better. It doesn't bite."

JUST BEFORE CLOSING TIME, A DELIVERYMAN CAME WITH SOME IN-sured packages for the jewelry store, and Pippa, who was expecting him, told Nicole, "Wait for me in the back room, and you can help me record these new arrivals. Then we'll pack up all the jewelry and put everything back in the safe."

Nicole had been gazing at herself in the mirror, admiring a pretty necklace that Pippa had draped around her. "Okay," said Nicole, hopping down from her chair and going.

Pippa signed for the packages, and the deliveryman went off. She locked the front door and turned the sign to CLOSED. Then she opened an empty strongbox and methodically removed the jewelry from the display cases. Her mother had taught her an efficient way to do this, making a U-shaped route around the store. When Pippa was done, she carried the strongbox and the new parcels into the back room.

"Nicole, you've been quiet as a mouse. What have you been up to?" she called out suspiciously. She hoped that Nicole hadn't started reading Petrina's order books. That girl read everything in sight, even the backs of cereal boxes.

"Nicole, let's—" Pippa began, then stopped short, aghast.

A man with a black hat pulled low over his face had grabbed Nicole and was holding her. His left hand was clamped over the girl's mouth; his right hand held a gleaming knife to her throat. Nicole's eyes were big and terrified. Pippa gasped, then tried to speak calmly.

"Let her go," Pippa said, putting down the things she'd been carrying. "The cash register is in the front of the store and it's still full. Help yourself, but leave her alone."

"Thanks, don't mind if I do," the man said, as if she'd offered him chocolates. He kicked over a nearby waste-paper basket. "Empty it," he ordered her, "and put all the jewelry in it. Then go get the money from the cash register, and bring everything back here. The kid stays with me, so don't try anything cute with the neighbors, or *she* gets it," he warned as he put the knife tip closer to Nicole's soft neck. Nicole let out a stifled moan of terror.

The man growled at Pippa, "And make it snappy!"

"Okay, okay," Pippa said, turning swiftly to do what he'd ordered.

She felt herself shaking but fought for self-control. This man sounded as if he'd done time. She knew his type. After all these years, she'd learned to identify exactly what kind of man was trying to pick her up, in bars and supper clubs, even backstage after a performance. Once in a while, some well-suited thug would betray his criminal character with the resentful, chip-on-the-shoulder way he spoke, especially to women.

Her heart was pounding as she went to the front room. She gave a quick glance out the windows, hoping to spot someone to whom she might signal for help. But at this time of year people around here spent the entire day at the beach clubs, or out on their boats, from sunrise straight through to the dinner hour, when they partied under the stars. If only her police friend George had shown up just a little bit later, he could have helped. But he was long gone now.

Pippa hurried to the cash register to pull the money out. Normally she'd have to arrange all the bills in their stacks of fifties and twenties and tens, and she'd put the checks into a red wallet with a deposit slip for the bank. But now she just threw it all into a large felt jewelry sack. Her fingers were shaking so much that she dropped some bills. She stooped to pick them up. She hadn't been this terrified since something very bad had happened to someone she loved, a long time ago.

And then, as Pippa straightened up, that awful memory emerged again, a thing that had taken her years of dance—and psychiatrists and booze and men—to overcome. She took a deep breath, then reached into the drawer beneath the cash register where the checks and extra rolls of coins were stored, and she took what she needed. Then she returned to the back of the shop. The man was waiting, still holding that knife to poor Nicole's throat.

"Put that cash in the waste basket," he snapped at Pippa. He watched her do it, then suddenly demanded, "Where's Mario? Why is his shop in the Village closed today?"

Pippa, surprised, stammered, "I—I don't know." It was a lie. She knew that Mario's leg, which he'd wounded in the war, was still bothering him, and he was going to have another surgery on it again soon, so today he'd gone to see the doctor for some tests ahead of the operation. After that, he and Filomena planned to come up here for the weekend; Filomena had insisted that he get off his feet and spend some time in the country resting before the surgery. But Pippa would never tell this man that Mario was expected up here tonight.

The man eyed her mistrustfully. "I want to have a little talk with Mario. The shopkeepers in the Village said he and his sister have another store here." The man nodded toward the waste basket full of jewelry with a look of scorn. "This is all his loot, isn't it?" he snarled. "Now, speak up. Where is he?"

Pippa's heart was pounding and she felt paralyzed with terror, so lightheaded that she thought she might just faint or die on the spot and get it over with, right now. But poor Nicole was looking at her older cousin as if praying for deliverance.

And then Pippa seemed to hear her grandmother's voice inside her, instructing her with the very words that Gemma had once claimed she heard Tessa say in a dream, long ago, that day they were on roller skates: *Tell Pippa to take care of you all, now that I'm in heaven.*

"Where's Mario?" the man repeated angrily.

Pippa exhaled her fear and straightened her spine. She was, after all, a born performer who'd vanquished an equally paralyzing stage fright. So, feigning a careless shrug, she gave him a brilliant smile. "Oh, he'll be along. C'mon, mister," she purred coaxingly. "Let go of the kid. If you really want to point that silly knife at somebody, aim for a grown-up. Like me."

She wasn't entirely sure that it was sex alone that caused a sadistic glitter in this man's eyes. He said dismissively to the terrified Nicole, "Go into that bathroom, kid, and stay there." He gave the girl a rude shove that sent her sprawling and made her cry out briefly. Then he took off his black scarf and tossed it at Pippa.

"Shut her up," he commanded. Pippa reluctantly tied the gag around Nicole's trembling mouth and murmured, "Just stay quiet, baby. Lie on the floor." Nicole scurried into the tiny washroom and shut the door.

Pippa, still shaking, sat atop the desk to show off her dancer's legs to full perfection, and forced herself to say conversationally, "You look familiar. Ever been to the Copacabana?"

The man gave a snort of derision. "That stuffy old place?" he said defensively.

Pippa was still sizing him up to make sure she was right in

thinking she recognized him. He'd lost some weight—in jail, no doubt. But it was the way he'd talked about Mario that alerted her. "You're one of the Pericolo brothers, aren't you?" Pippa said quietly.

It was her worst nightmare come true—as if she'd been expecting a violent end to her own life at the hands of this frightful specter who'd haunted her entire existence.

At the mention of his name, the man jerked his head up alertly. She quickly resumed her flirtatious tone and said, "Which one are you, anyway, Sergio or Ruffio?"

"Ruffio died," the man said shortly. "In jail, like a pig in a sty, thanks to Mario and his family. How the hell do *you* know me? Who are *you*?" He advanced toward her.

"I wouldn't forget a man like you," Pippa said alluringly. When he gave her the once-over, she knew he was hooked. "I have a little message for you," Pippa murmured, so softly that he had to cock his head closer to hear her. She reached into the pocket of her skirt. With icy calm she said, "My grandma Tessa says hello—and goodbye."

He was so close now that she really couldn't miss. Pippa aimed her pistol—the one she'd stolen from Aunt Amie years ago to wave at that priest, which Petrina had taken away from her and now kept in the drawer beneath the cash register for moments like this, which never happened, but had just happened—and fired it straight at the man's head. She'd always been a good shot, after years of target practice and shooting skeet with her father. But now it took the last drop of her courage to keep her hand steady, her fingers cool and certain.

The shot rang out, and Sergio fell backward with a look of utter surprise. Pippa took aim and shot twice more, to make sure he couldn't get up again. He didn't.

She paused, peering cautiously at him until she was sure that he was dead. Then she let out a gasp and grabbed on to the sides of the desk to steady herself, because her legs suddenly felt like wet noodles. She stumbled to the back door to lock it, just in case this guy had a friend. Then she picked up the telephone, to call George the cop—but something made her telephone her cousin Chris instead. He was just arriving at Aunt Amie's restaurant, not far from here, to prep for the dinner shift, and when she blurted it out quickly, he said he'd come right over.

Pippa opened the bathroom door. Poor Nicole was obediently lying on the floor, the gag tied around her mouth, tears streaming down her face. "It's okay, sweetie," Pippa whispered, removing the gag and tossing it aside. "That bad man is dead. But he doesn't look so good. So, why don't you wait in here until they take him away?"

"No," Nicole said unexpectedly. "I want to see him."

"Trust me, you don't," Pippa said. "It'll haunt you forever."

Nicole looked her straight in the eye. "I have to see for myself that he's really dead."

PETRINA HAD JUST ARRIVED HOME WHEN SHE HEARD THE TELEPHONE ringing. It was Chris, calling from the jewelry store. He told her about the break-in.

"Listen, Pippa shot and killed the man," Chris said without ceremony. "It was Sergio Pericolo. It was self-defense. He was looking for Mario and he threatened Nicole with a knife. Pippa wants to call her police friend George. But I know some garbage contractors from Brooklyn. For a fee—no questions asked—they'll dispose of the body and nobody will ever know. The gun is untraceable, so it could have belonged to anybody, and I can ditch that, too. Pippa said to ask you. What do you want to do, Aunt Petrina?"

Petrina was momentarily tempted. Then she said, "Let Pippa call George. He'll know what to do to protect her. Just make sure you tell her to keep saying that word over and over: *self-defense*. Oh, and tell her not to mention that she knows it's Pericolo. It was

just a guy who broke into the store. Got that? I'll be right over."
She rushed out the door.

When she reached town, Petrina discovered that the street was
now closed off by a police cordon, so she had to park the car a
block away, then run the rest of the way. Just as she got to the
shop, she heard one of the policemen on duty on the sidewalk,
talking to another cop about how George had saved the day.

"Damned good timing—the detective says he was just passing
by on his day off for a cup of coffee, and he saw the thief break in,"
the cop was saying. "So he jumped the guy and ended up shooting
him with the thief's own gun."

"Lucky for the lady who works in that store!" the other officer
said.

Petrina looked up and caught George's glance. They exchanged
a brief nod of understanding, with Petrina's eyes full of thanks.

Then she hurried inside to embrace her daughter.

33

New York City, October 1957

Late one afternoon, near the end of October, Mario went into the hospital to have his surgery. He groused about having to check in on the day before the operation for some prep work, but Filomena soothed him, then left him sleeping there that night.

Lucy and Frankie were away on their first vacation, in California, so that Frankie could inspect some vineyards that he was thinking of buying and the couple could have a little time to themselves. Their daughter, Gemma, who was still living in her parents' town house and taking her meals with Filomena, was not home from work yet, and the rest of the family, even the maid and the cook, were in Mamaroneck preparing for Petrina's wedding this weekend.

And so, for the very first time since she'd arrived here, Filomena found herself completely alone in Greenwich Village. She didn't mind; there was still much to do. Now that their daughter, Teresa, was enrolled in the school in Westchester, Filomena and Mario had decided to move some of their things into the suburban house that they owned, in that private enclave, right next door to Petrina's and Amie's. Filomena had been renting out hers to a film producer, whose lease was up. So she and Mario would now be living there on weekdays during the school year. Amie was very helpful and had promised to drive down here tomorrow with Chris to help Filomena make the move.

So today, Filomena went from room to room, listening to her footsteps echoing as she moved about, checking her list, organizing the items that the moving men would be coming to pick up on Monday. Much of the furniture was covered, and everything else was stored in large, numbered boxes. Tessa's china and silver were carefully wrapped into a locked trunk.

As she entered the dining room, Filomena found herself remembering how she'd felt when she first came into this household; and tonight, she sensed Tessa and Gianni's presence in these silent rooms, as the fiery autumn sunset came slanting in long, burnished rays across the polished floors. She wondered if Tessa knew, somehow, that the threat of those men who had killed her was finally vanquished, thanks to Pippa. She could almost hear Tessa say, *Yes, but at what cost? When will my grandchildren be truly free of the terrors of their elders?*

Filomena had discussed this with the Godmothers. Petrina had said thoughtfully, "But Pippa's not afraid of anything now. She told me she slept through the night, for the first time since Tessa's death. She says she doesn't have to worry about 'men with guns' anymore."

"But how is Nicole handling all this?" Filomena had asked, worried about her sensitive, gifted goddaughter. The incident had made Amie and Nicole become closer, yet secretive.

"She was pale as a ghost when she came home from the jewelry shop," Amie had admitted. "At first she hardly ate or slept at all! But we've spent a lot of time together. She's fine now; she won't talk about it anymore; she says, *It's over.* She's so glad to be back in school with Teresa."

Filomena, not entirely trusting this sunny tale, had looked at Amie keenly and said, "Someday, we should tell Nicole all about this family and how the Pericolos came into our lives, so that she understands what happened in the jewelry store and why she was attacked."

Amie said quickly and protectively, "Someday. If she asks us. But not now. Nicole has put it out of her mind, and that's healthy. She just wants everything to be normal again."

And so, on the surface, at least, life had settled down into something resembling its usual routine. *Surely the danger to this family is finally gone,* Filomena thought fervently, as if in prayer to the ancestral spirits whose presence she sensed.

But now, when she reached the kitchen, something moving in the backyard made her look up sharply. It was not one of her ghosts. It was a real-life man, standing right there in Tessa's garden, with his arms folded across his chest, a cigarette dangling from his lips as he stared aggressively into the window at her. His hair was touched with silver now—he must have been in his mid-fifties—but she recognized those coal-black eyes, with their bushy eyebrows, and the nose that curved down a bit at the end, like the beak of a bird of prey.

"God, it's him!" Filomena murmured. The Lord High Executioner, who'd once run "Murder Inc." out of a candy store in Brooklyn, had recently come up in the world of gangsters. He was now a Boss of one of the Five Families—after the ominous, and convenient, disappearance of the man who'd held that job before him. No body had been found.

Albert Anastasia was not a man to be kept waiting. He unfolded his arms and crooked one finger to beckon her to come. Reluctantly she opened the door and stepped out into Tessa's garden. She felt that this man would always convey the heart of a brute, just by standing there. "How's the family?" he asked brusquely, as if this social nicety were a weapon.

"Fine," Filomena said guardedly, hearing the threat beneath the question.

He was smoking his cigarette reflectively now, as if sizing her up to determine if she could be relied on. "You're not an American. Where you from?" he demanded.

Filomena found herself sticking to her original story—the story she'd told Tessa, who'd repeated it to all the neighbors—of Rosamaria's identity. "From Tropea," she said.

For the first time, Anastasia smiled. Filomena wasn't sure that this improved things at all, but he said, "Tropea? Hah. Me too. Nothing much to miss from there, eh?" he asked, his eyes narrowed, as if this were some sort of interrogation.

Filomena felt as if it were Rosamaria who answered. "The beautiful blue sea. And those perfect red onions, so sweet that people made ice cream with them." He nodded.

She shivered as an autumn wind stirred the trees. He said, "Gettin' chilly. Let's go inside." He followed her indoors, where packing boxes were stacked in every room. Then he said abruptly, "You weren't there that night—when your family asked me to do them a favor."

She waited in dread. He continued, "They didn't need no help doin' the killin'. They only needed the body taken away, so it wouldn't show up again. You gotta know how to cut up a body. You gotta slice the lungs and the stomach just right, so they don't fill up with air and float to the surface, where fishermen can find them."

Filomena felt her own stomach go cold. Somehow she'd always known that, thanks to Amie, this one incident had produced a ghost that would not die easily.

Rather unceremoniously, Anastasia said, "I lost at the track today. Lost big, in fact. They tell me you're the one who covers my bookie's bets."

Filomena caught her breath. Anastasia's name had never been directly on her ledger as a debtor. She had told the remaining bookies not to take on anybody new. But of course, nobody said no to this man, so it was entirely possible they'd taken his bets. She had indeed heard that he'd been losing heavily at the racetrack lately, and that this made him even more ill-tempered than usual, if that was possible.

"So now you can do *me* a favor," Anastasia said, exhaling smoke. "Write off my bet."

"Of course," Filomena said, relieved. "Consider it canceled."

"And—I want to see this loan book everybody says you have. You can give me a nice 'taste' of it for protection, before that cocksucker Genovese gets his grubby fingers on all of it."

Filomena did a quick calculation. She was at a point where she was finally able to think of selling Tessa's book to someone who'd want to take over the managing of the remaining loans. But clearly Anastasia wasn't offering to buy it from her. He wanted a "taste," so, once he saw the ledger, he'd surely ask for a staggering weekly share.

She wished she could just give him Tessa's book and be done with these men. But she still had to pay tribute, via Strollo, to the scary Mr. Genovese, who had taken over Costello's territory. Already, Strollo's Greenwich Village Crew had upped their share. Also, she was still paying 2 percent to Sal, and she had to give Domenico a weekly sum to pay the police. So she simply couldn't afford to keep two Bosses on her ledger.

Anastasia had been watching her face, because now he said, "And don't go crying to Mr. Costello like last time. He comes to *me* for advice now."

"Yes, I understand that Mr. Costello has retired, and Strollo collects for Genovese now," Filomena said, stalling for time. But Anastasia surprised her with his next remark.

"We'll see about that," he answered enigmatically. She wondered if it meant that Costello was plotting a comeback of some sort, to overthrow Genovese and reclaim his territory. But all Anastasia said was, "Let's see the book."

"Certainly, *Signor,* but you see, I don't have it here. It's in a safe at the bank," she said. Gesturing at all the boxes, she added, "I'm moving a few things, so I didn't want to keep the book here while there are movers coming in. It wouldn't be secure, with strangers around."

He must have believed her, because he hadn't yet killed her for telling this lie. He said, "Women! They have no business doing business." Then his gaze fell on one of the packing boxes that lay open, with Teresa's things inside. Right on top was the mysterious musical jewelry box with the little carousel pony atop it. He picked it up, wound it, and watched the pony pivot to the music. "Nice toy, don't you think? Does your daughter, Teresa, like it?"

Filomena tried not to show how she felt about hearing her child's name on this man's lips. Now she knew why she'd always been unsettled about this gift. But all she said was, "She loves it. But we couldn't find a card from the sender. So we were never able to thank him properly."

"All kids should have nice toys, don't you think?" he said, sounding oddly mournful. He replaced the music box, returned to the back door, glanced outside, then stepped out again. "All right, then, bring me the book tomorrow," he said sternly, taking one last drag on his cigarette before throwing it on the patio and not even bothering to crush it out. "Ten o'clock sharp. Meet me at the Park Sheraton Hotel. Just ask at the lobby, they know where to find me."

THE NEXT MORNING WAS A BRIGHT OCTOBER DAY, THE LAST FRIDAY of the month. Filomena took a taxi uptown, because Sal had the car in Mamaroneck to ferry Petrina about as she prepared for the big wedding.

In Manhattan, people were moving briskly, as if in a great hurry to get their work done so they could have fun for the weekend. Halloween was not until next week, but many stores had paper ghosts and witches in their windows, and the society pages of the newspaper were chattering with anticipation about the upcoming masquerade balls of the rich and famous.

When Filomena alighted from the cab at Fifty-Sixth Street and Seventh Avenue, she glanced about apprehensively. She had never been to this hotel before; it was a swanky stopover for movie stars and singers and other big shots.

She saw a sign for the hotel's Mermaid Room, a cocktail bar famous not only for its clientele and piano music but also for its naked mermaids painted on the ceiling. But apparently the mermaids' exposed breasts had bothered First Lady Eleanor Roosevelt when she stayed at the hotel, and her complaint had finally caused the hotel to put bras—which appeared to be made of fishing nets—on its sensuous mermaids.

"I must be nervous, thinking about topless mermaids at a time like this," Filomena muttered to herself after she'd paid the cabbie and allowed the hotel doorman to open the door for her. She marched herself to the front desk, clutching Tessa's book to her chest. She'd wrapped it in brown paper with string, as if making an ordinary delivery from a bookstore.

When she told the clerk at the front desk who she was looking for, he said quickly, "Mr. Anastasia? He's right over there," and he jerked his head, indicating a barbershop across the lobby, just beyond glass doors. "Nice guy," the clerk said reassuringly. "Gives great tips. He spends a lot of money on toys, too. He likes to give toys to kids." Filomena peered in.

The first face she saw was that of Gemma. Yes, here was Lucy's daughter, all right, smiling her prettiest smile, and even in her manicurist's smock, she looked ravishing. Her lips and nails were painted blood-red, her hair coiffed like the actress Marilyn Monroe's.

Gemma had just stepped forward to greet a male customer, who took her hand and kissed it, and then held it for a long time as he spoke to her while eyeing her from head to toe. When the man turned his head, Filomena recognized Anastasia. Behind him stood a big, watchful man, acting like a bodyguard.

The barbers and other men all smiled knowingly at Gemma, as if this sort of exchange between her and Anastasia had happened before. Gemma blushed, pleased and flattered, then nodded and stepped back, busily preparing her little manicure cart so that she would be ready to do this man's fingernails after he got his shave.

Anastasia sat on one of the barber chairs. A barber moved forward briskly with hot towels, to prepare his customer's beard for his usual shave and haircut.

"I'll get some breakfast from the coffee shop," Filomena heard the bodyguard say as he came into the lobby, passed her by, and disappeared out the main door leading to the street.

And so, as Filomena later told the other Godmothers that day, all she could think of just then was that she had to drag Gemma out of there and find her a different job. With her maternal instinct at its most atavistic peak, Filomena determinedly pushed open the glass doors and entered the barbershop.

"Gemma," she said crisply, "come here at once."

Gemma looked startled, then blushed guiltily before tilting her chin up defiantly.

"Oh, hello, Aunt Filomena," she said cheekily.

Anastasia said something in a muffled voice under the towels that swathed his face, and one of the five barbers in attendance assured him, "It's okay, it's just the manicurist's auntie."

"What are you doing here?" Gemma whispered. "Did you follow me?"

"What are *you* doing here?" Filomena hissed. "Do you have any idea who that man is?"

"Of course!" Gemma took Filomena's arm, as if to hastily sweep her out of the shop like the shorn hair that a clean-up man was brooming away. "He's very nice. He *likes* me. He takes me out for drinks sometimes. Did Mom send you here to spy on me? Well, you just tell *her*—"

Gemma never finished her sentence, for, at that moment, two big, burly men in dark suits, hats, and sunglasses burst through the shop's outside door. They barreled past Gemma so forcefully that she inadvertently bumped Filomena's arm and caused her to drop Tessa's book on the floor, right in the midst of all those shorn hairs that hadn't yet been swept up.

The men with the sunglasses halted, pulled out their guns, took expert aim, and blasted away at the figure in the barber's chair. The shots echoed deafeningly, as if everybody were standing inside a big clanging bell that wouldn't stop ringing. Everyone dropped to the floor.

Gemma had shrieked and held on fast to Filomena's arm. Filomena pulled her into a corner and crouched down, trying to cover Gemma when the bullets sprayed.

Anastasia sprang from his chair, clawing off the towels, which made him look like an Egyptian mummy staggering in a horror movie. Instinctively he threw up his arms, ducking to the left and to the right like a prizefighter defending himself. At first he seemed to be handling himself well, fighting on, even as bullets struck his left hand and his right hip; he even tried to lunge forward bullishly at his attackers, as if to strangle them with his bare hands.

But he did not realize that he was lunging toward the mirror, and therefore at only the reflected images of his assassins, who mercilessly fired more shots from behind. Struck in the back and the head, their prey dropped to the floor, his arms splayed out helplessly. Satisfied, the killers raced out of the barbershop. Filomena heard Anastasia emit one last groan, like a wounded dog. She could not help feeling a stab of pity, as she would for any abandoned, dying animal.

By now, everyone—men as well as women—was shouting and calling out for help, even as some remained ducked behind chairs and others rushed out the door. Gemma's little manicure table had taken off on its own, wheeling madly until it hit a wall and came to an unceremonious halt. "Is he dead? Oh, my God, is he dead?" Gemma wept hysterically.

"*Silenzio!*" It was the first sound Filomena had uttered; she hadn't screamed nor cried out, not once. Now she heard police sirens wailing, for the man in the nearby florist shop had called for help. She grabbed Gemma by the shoulders and pulled the shaking girl to her feet.

"I want to get out of here!" Gemma sobbed.

"You listen to me," Filomena murmured in a low but firm voice, with her hand gripping Gemma's arm. "The police are coming. They will want witnesses. But nobody here is going to say they saw a thing, and neither are you. *Do you hear me?* People know you were here today, so you mustn't run away; that would look bad and they'll search for you if you run. So stay, just long enough to tell them only your name and your job, and that you saw nothing. Gemma, tell me you heard me. You did not see a single thing, do you understand?"

"I really *didn't* see it," Gemma said shakily. "You put your arm over my head."

"Fine. You didn't see it, and *I wasn't here,*" Filomena said. "Just catch a cab and meet me at home. Here is money for your cab. Gemma, tell me exactly what you are going to do!" Filomena said sternly, pressing the money into Gemma's hand.

Gemma looked confused and terrified, but when Filomena put the money in her palm, it seemed to awaken the girl to the importance of the situation; it reminded her of, years ago, when she was a child and got money from Grandmother Tessa for Christmas. *Toys are for babies,* Tessa had said. *But money is a serious gift.*

Filomena was relieved to see a sign of comprehension cross Gemma's face; for a moment, she looked like her father, Frankie. "Say it," Filomena commanded.

"I saw nothing, and you weren't here," Gemma said in a sturdy voice just like Lucy's.

"And then?" Filomena pressed.

"I take a cab," Gemma said, "and I come home to you."

"Good." Filomena turned to go. She paused only once on her way out of that barbershop. She'd remembered Tessa's book, looked around wildly for it, and then spied it on the floor, where it had slid from her arm when Gemma involuntarily bumped it. Filomena surreptitiously picked it up, put it in her big handbag, and walked out onto the avenue.

There were throngs of people crowding around now, with tourists and onlookers trying to peer in, for in New York City, bad news travels fast. But nobody paid any attention to the modest-looking woman who moved down the streets with her head deliberately bowed, so that her face would not be remembered.

Once she was safely inside her house in Greenwich Village with the door locked, she took a little glass of brandy, which she drank more quickly than she'd ever drunk anything in her entire life. Thus fortified, Filomena remembered to remove the book from her handbag. Only then did she notice that the wrapper had been torn away at the corners, from being kicked around, and Tessa's book was now stained with blood.

THAT AFTERNOON, FILOMENA KNEW EXACTLY WHAT SHE HAD TO DO. Now that Anastasia was out of the picture and there was only one Boss to answer to, the way was clear for her to make the boldest move she could think of. But it had to be done quickly, before some other seismic event changed the landscape yet again.

"It's now or never," she told herself firmly. First she telephoned the hospital to make sure that Mario's surgery had gone well. Mario was still feeling the effects of a sedative and couldn't talk much but assured her that he was fine. Chris, who was with him now, told her that Amie had left the hospital and taken a subway and was on her way downtown. Chris would wait for the doctor to discharge Mario, then drive him to Greenwich Village.

So Filomena woke Gemma, who'd made it home and had shakily drunk the red wine Filomena had given her, then gone to lie down in Filomena's spare bedroom.

"Come, Gemma," Filomena said gently now. "You are leaving this city today."

Gemma sat up with a start at Filomena's touch. "I keep seeing him lying there, in a pool of blood!" she whispered, trembling.

Filomena handed her a cup of tea and said, "Yes, that is the fate of gangsters. But tonight, we put it all behind us. We are going to Godmother Amie's house in Mamaroneck to rehearse for Petrina's wedding. You have your dress? Good. Pack it with tissue paper, and pack enough of your things so that you can stay in Westchester for a long time. Just do as I say, and you'll be fine."

"Okay," Gemma said meekly. When the doorbell rang, she clutched Filomena's hand.

"It's just Amie," Filomena said, and went to let her in. She pulled Amie aside for a consultation, then turned to Gemma with a slip of paper and said, "If Amie and I aren't back here within the hour, call Chris and Mario at this hospital number—and tell them I went to see Strollo at this address."

Gemma asked fearfully, "Why are you going to see that man Strollo?"

"To make us all safe." Filomena put on her hat and took up her big handbag.

"Maybe you should wait for the men to come, so they can go with you," Gemma urged.

Filomena shook her head. "No, all I need is Amie."

As they stepped out, Amie said, "Are you sure you want to play it this way?"

"It's the only way," Filomena replied steadfastly.

THE SOCIAL CLUB, AS IT WAS CALLED, WAS REALLY A NONDESCRIPT storefront with the windows permanently covered in blinds so that nobody could see inside, ever. It looked as if it were out of business. But Filomena had telephoned ahead, to ask permission to see Strollo. So when she knocked on the door, a man peered out through a peephole, unlocked the door, and permitted her and Amie to enter, before he locked it again.

The room had only an espresso bar, several simple card tables ringed with folding chairs, a jukebox, and a back room marked

Private.

Strollo sat at a table in the farthest corner, drinking his espresso and reading his newspaper. There were other men playing cards at the opposite side of the room.

As Filomena passed the card players, she overheard one of them say in an aggrieved tone, "They put Albert in a body bag and got two city workers to haul him to the sidewalk, like a sack of garbage. Where is the respect?" And she knew they were talking about Anastasia.

Amie heard it, too, and exchanged a quick look of comprehension with her.

Filomena stiffened her spine as she approached Strollo. He glanced up at her over his newspaper, then lowered it warily, revealing that "tall" head with its high forehead, and inscrutable eyes that had such a distant look. "Yes?" Strollo said.

"May we sit?" she asked.

He recovered his manners. "Of course."

Filomena and Amie sat down. "Today is not a day for small talk," Filomena said in a low voice, "so, *con il vostro permesso,* we will go straight to the business at hand."

He nodded. It was Amie's turn to speak, so she said resolutely, "Years ago, you conducted business in my tavern, but one day, some men planted a microphone at your table to trap you. But a pregnant lady stopped you on the street and warned you not to go inside that day. I am that lady."

Strollo looked at her more respectfully now and said, "Yes. That, I remember."

Amie had memorized what Strollo said to her back then, and Filomena had explained its significance. Now, Amie recited it, word for word. "You said, *Grazie, ricorderò questa gentilezza.* In all this time, I never needed your favor in return, until now. This is why we are here today. We need *una gentilezza* from you." Strollo raised his eyebrows but said nothing.

Filomena spoke now. She said, "Our family is going out of the business."

"Yes, I've heard that you've been having a fire sale," he commented. "'Everything must go,' as they say. Do you think this is wise?"

Filomena nodded. "We are modest people, and we have worked hard, but we are older now and must retire. It's important to retire in time, before one starts to make mistakes," she said boldly. "All we ask is that our family be left alone to live in peace."

Strollo spread his hands. "I'm not God," he said.

"But we are all his angels, even if we are his fallen ones," Filomena said. He allowed himself a wry smile. "Would the Bosses leave us in peace if you asked them to?" she inquired.

He shrugged. "Sure. If I ask. But," he said slyly, "as I understand it, you still have some money left on your book. Which means it should keep coming *our* way."

"That is why I am here," Filomena said. "You speak of my book. Another man wanted to buy my book. But as you must know, he is now dead."

Strollo remained sphinxlike. Filomena knew perfectly well that he could be in league with the very men who'd killed Albert Anastasia. She was treading in dangerous territory, even just mentioning it.

Now she pulled out the book and laid it on the table. She had not cleaned off the blood. Strollo saw this, and although his eyes reflected instant recognition, he said nothing.

"But I will *give* this book to you," Filomena said, "so that you can give the Bosses the last of what they need from us, in exchange for my family's peace."

Amie watched all this in awe. Filomena could have simply tried to sell him the entire book, so that she could make one last profit. Instead, the path Filomena had chosen meant that she was, in effect, exchanging all the remaining income in her book for her ticket out, which had much more value to her. It was the consummate roll of the dice, proving that Filomena had really meant what she'd said, years ago, when she'd first convinced the Godmothers of her plan to get away from the Bosses: *The ultimate power is the ability to walk away, without holding out for "the last big score."*

Strollo studied her. "I knew Gianni and Tessa. They were good people." He paused. "All right. This will be acceptable to us."

Filomena said, "Thank you."

In one deft move, Strollo folded his newspaper around the ledger and then laid the parcel on an empty chair beside him. He had not once opened Tessa's book, but he knew what was in its pages. Now he took a cigar from his pocket but politely did not light it, waiting for Filomena and Amie as they rose to go.

"*In bocca al lupo*," he said suddenly.

"*Crepi il lupo!*" Filomena replied.

When they were back out on the street Amie whispered, "What was all that?"

"It's a hunter's expression for luck, when you are both in a dangerous situation and pass each other in the woods. Like actors when they say 'Break a leg.' He said, *In the mouth of the wolf*," Filomena explained. "And I said, *May the wolf die*."

34

New York City and Apalachin, New York, November 14, 1957

November arrived with a brisk wind and darker afternoons that caused the city streetlamps to glow as early as four o'clock in the afternoon. But the weather was unusually mild for this time of year.

"Hey, guys," Chris said to the twins, one soft, cloudy morning, "you want to help me out? I'm cooking for a private party tonight, in upstate New York."

They were in the kitchen of the downstairs apartment in the Greenwich Village town house where the twins had grown up with Amie and Johnny. Chris now shared this apartment with his sister, Gemma. Vinnie and Paulie had come to town for a classmate's birthday party last night, then stayed over with their cousin Chris.

"I thought this was your day off," Vinnie said. "That's what Mom said. You moonlighting for somebody else?"

"Nah. This is just a one-off," Chris explained. "I owe a favor to a guy who runs a catering company. If you help me load and unload the truck, and assist me in the kitchen, there's good money in it for both of you."

"Sure, we could use the moola," Vinnie agreed. Both twins were short of funds, since their mother, Amie, kept them on a tight budget. The other kids at the academy got much better allowances, which gave them more spending money for date nights. You couldn't ask a girl out without ready cash, and the holiday season meant lots of parties.

"Okay, let's get all this food into the coolers," Chris instructed. "Pack it well in the ice, we can't let anything spoil. Believe me, we're cooking for some very important people who will *not* take it well if you ruin the meals at their big shindig."

"Look at all that meat!" Paulie marveled as they hoisted the boxes. "Are you cooking for an army or something? What *is* all this?"

Chris took a pencil from behind his ear and consulted his list. "Two hundred seven pounds of steak, twenty pounds of veal cutlets, and fifteen pounds of cold cuts," he said as he ticked them off. This was going to be a spectacular dinner with many guests.

Vinnie and Paulie obediently carried the heavy sacks of food, trotting back and forth to a truck parked in front of the house.

"Here's the address, and a map," Chris said. "Paulie, put that in the car, too."

"Hell, that's a crummy map. I got a better one," Paulie said.

"Fine. Copy the directions onto it, and let's get going," Chris said.

When they were ready, Chris took off his apron and shouted upstairs, "Hey, Ma, I'm going to cook for a private party upstate. I'll see you in Westchester." And before Lucy could answer, Chris and the twins had hopped into the truck and roared off.

Lucy and Filomena were upstairs drinking tea. Filomena had returned from an appointment at the bank, and she'd found Lucy poring over car catalogs. Lucy had explained, "Frankie taught me how to drive while we were in California. Now all I need is a car. I think this is a nice model—pine green, with cream-colored leather seats."

Frankie and Mario were in Westchester, having been invited to go fishing with Petrina's new husband, Doug. Lucy and Filomena would meet up with their husbands tomorrow. They were looking forward to seeing Petrina, who'd just returned from her honeymoon in Bermuda.

"Petrina was a gorgeous bride, in that pale blue gown with all that elegant beading on it—thanks to our resident seamstress, Gloria," Lucy observed. "Why, Petrina looked ten years younger, coming down that aisle!"

"So do *you*, after your California trip," Filomena replied with a smile. "You and Frankie came back looking like a pair of honeymooners yourself!" Lucy blushed.

When Chris called up to them, Lucy glanced out the window and saw him and the twins mysteriously loading up a strange truck. "What's *this* all about, then?" she said suspiciously to Filomena. "They're up to some shenanigans, no doubt." She hurried down to confront Chris, but by the time she got outside, the young men were gone.

An hour later, a soda delivery van neatly pulled up in its place. The driver was a short, stocky young man who knocked on the back door at the kitchen and asked for Chris. When Lucy told him that Chris had departed for the weekend, the man looked aghast.

"Holy cow!" he exclaimed. "I was supposed to unload all this stuff so Chris could take it with him. He's *got* to have it. If he doesn't, we'll both catch hell."

"So why don't you just drive up there?" Lucy said reasonably.

"Drive all the way upstate? I gotta work here in the city all weekend."

Filomena had followed Lucy into the kitchen and now she noticed a folder there. "Chris left this map on the countertop," she offered. Lucy peered over her shoulder, saying, "What's the name of this town they circled? Appa—what?"

"Apalachin," the man said, pronouncing it *Apple-lake-in*.

"Oh, dear God!" Filomena gasped. "Not *that* place!"

The man nodded and said darkly, "All the big shots will be there. And they ain't gonna be too happy if they don't get their cream soda and root beer."

Lucy was truly worried now. "What kind of trouble is Chris in?"

"The kind you can get your head blown off for," the man said inelegantly.

Filomena pulled Lucy aside and said in a low tone, "Mario told me the Bosses are holding a special conference there and it's very tricky—Genovese wants to be recognized as the head of Costello's family, and Carlo Gambino wants to take Anastasia's place. The Bosses will take a vote. Nobody can afford to make a false move. Our boys mustn't be *there*."

"Oh, Lordy! Then we *have* to do something," Lucy said urgently. "Chris just can't get into trouble again. Frankie will kill him."

They returned to the stocky young man in the doorway. He said coaxingly, "All you have to do is deliver these goods. You got a truck?" he asked doubtfully.

"We do *not*," Lucy said, annoyed. "You'll have to let us borrow your van."

"Aw, nuts," the man grumbled, handing her the keys. "This just ain't my day."

APPROXIMATELY FOUR HOURS AFTER THEY'D LEFT THE CITY, VINNIE and Paulie managed to get Chris to tell them what this "shindig" was all about. Just running through the guest list was enough to give them a serious pause.

"Joe Profaci, Tommy 'Three-Finger' Lucchese, Don Carlo Gambino and his *capo* 'Big Paul' Castellano, Don Vito Genovese—"

"We're cooking for *all* the Big Bosses of New York?" Paulie asked in disbelief.

Chris grinned. "And their *capo*s. And a Boss from Florida—Santo Trafficante Jr.—and hotshots from Pittsburgh, Philly,

Cleveland, Los Angeles, Colorado, Massachusetts."

"Didn't they just have a big convention like that last year?" Vinnie asked. "I thought they only do these 'barbecues' every five, ten years."

Chris smiled enigmatically. "That's right. But this is no ordinary year. The new Bosses want to make sure that nobody tries to take revenge on them for the shootings of Costello and Anastasia. But keep your mouths shut about it. They got other items on the agenda, too—things that you don't want to know about."

Vinnie and Paulie exchanged a doubtful look. Hadn't they all been warned about the new rackets, like heroin? "How'd you get roped into this?" Vinnie asked dubiously.

"I told you. I used to work for this caterer, and I owe him a favor," Chris said. "When you owe a guy a favor, it's better to get it over with quick. Besides, there's good money here for all of us. Relax, guys."

Vinnie nervously turned on the radio, which was playing "That'll Be the Day" by a great new group, Buddy Holly's Crickets.

Chris knew that the Godmothers would definitely not approve of this jaunt, yet it couldn't be helped. A man had to keep several irons in the fire just in case things didn't pan out, such as working in Godmother Amie's suburban restaurant. Oh, it looked promising, for profits; Amie's combination of authentic French and Italian cooking was attractive to the United Nations diplomats and Manhattan theater folk who lived in those elegant suburbs.

But Chris wasn't at all sure that he was cut out for spending the rest of his life in the cautious atmosphere of these quiet towns. He was feeling restless already.

"Damn, where *are* we? I just saw some cows in that field. We must be almost to Pennsylvania by now," Vinnie complained a short while later, with a city-boy horror of rural life. It was not lost on him that the radio was now playing "Jailhouse Rock." "I bet the mobsters come all the way up to the boondocks here because they know the cops and the Feds—and anybody in their right mind—would never look for them here. The whole place gives me the jitters."

He'd been gazing apprehensively at the scenery; this far north, the air was cooler, and the trees were bare of their autumn leaves, looking like angry skeletons bracing for months of winter ahead.

"Shut up," Paulie advised. He was actually in awe of the countryside. There were big red barns and yellow tractors in the wide-open fields, where corn and grain grew. There were fruit trees, and even grapevines, and chicken coops, and old grey horses pulling carts. Food came from old-fashioned places like this, then got packed onto trucks or loaded onto boats that floated down the river. It made the city seem artificial, like a strange dream they'd left behind. Did the mobsters come up here to escape the rat race, to be reminded of the old country?

Finally, they turned off the main highway, taking a country road that led them to a verdant, secluded estate that resembled an English manor house on a hill.

"Looks like the country digs of the Prince of Wales or something," Paulie observed of the rolling green lawns and mature trees. "Whose set-up is this? Must be a hundred acres."

"A hundred *thirty* acres. Belongs to Joe the Barber. The Boss of a Pennsylvania crime family," Chris said. "Used to be a bootlegger. Runs a beer and soda company."

"Well, we must be in the right place. Look at all those Caddys and whitewalls!" Vinnie marveled, for, as they drew nearer, they saw that the estate was ringed with beautiful luxury cars parked neatly in a row, like an outdoor showroom for the world's most expensive autos.

Chris slowed the truck for a guard at the gate, gave the name of his caterer, and was waved through. "Come on, boys," Chris said as he pulled his truck to a back entrance where he'd been told he could get to the kitchen. "Time to unload."

FILOMENA SPENT THE FIRST FEW HOURS OF THIS TRIP HOLDING ON TO the rims of her seat and silently praying to the Madonna to keep her alive through this perilous journey. It wasn't the mobsters that she feared; it was Lucy's driving that threatened life and limb.

"This van *is* a wee bit different than driving a car," Lucy had admitted from the moment they'd lurched away from the curb, to the sound of soda and beer bottles clinking ominously on their pallets. Filomena held her breath and considered it a miracle that they survived all the careening and swerving through the city, where she crossed herself more than once at what looked like an imminent crash.

But Lucy stuck her chin out in determination and hunkered down behind the wheel, grimly steering out of town and along the busy highway for hours. Once they were in the countryside, things settled down—somewhat—and Filomena began to breathe easier.

Lucy said cheerfully, "Well, after this trip, it's a cinch I'll get my driver's license."

At Filomena's shocked look, Lucy said hastily, "There wasn't time to do it when I got back from California. I've been so busy. Did I tell you I just got a promotion at the hospital?"

Filomena congratulated her, having already admired the heroic way that Lucy, with her sturdy arms and capable hands, manipulated the steering wheel and car levers to make this beast of a machine obey her commands. It was easy to imagine the competent Lucy at work at the hospital, dealing with blood and flesh with the same combination of athletic physical strength and quick, intelligent brain work.

Lucy caught her glance and said abashedly, "I'm just a brute of a girl, eh? I'm not educated or elegant—like Petrina, and she, so tall and fine, with those delicate bones of hers, those lovely long legs and fingers. Ever seen the size of her wrists? You're a bit like that, too."

"But Frankie once told me that you're *unica—una ragazza bellissima acqua e sapone*," Filomena said. "A rare 'soap and water' beauty."

Lucy smiled. Frankie *did* still adore her. She knew that now.

Filomena glanced at the map. "You turn off the road here."

Lucy followed her directions and pulled up to the gate of an impressive manor house. When they saw a guard there, Lucy slowed down and opened her window.

Asked for their names, she said only, "Sally and Jane. We're with the caterers. We've got their soda. See? The company name is on the side of this buggy."

"You think I wouldn't recognize one of the Boss's delivery vans?" the guard said. "Go through. Kitchen entrance is in the back."

As they drove around the house, they spotted many well-dressed but heavyset men, accompanied by younger sidekicks, all streaming toward the front door, talking and laughing in rich, deep male voices.

"Not a woman in sight," Lucy observed. "We'll stick out a mile. We'd better keep a low profile." She pointed to Chris's parked truck. "He's here," she said triumphantly.

She stopped and they got out. They marched to what was clearly the kitchen door, where aproned workers were moving to and fro amid the clatter of dishes. Inside the kitchen, there were appetizing scents wafting from various stovetops: men were sautéing steaks and veal cutlets; in another corner, sausages and onions sizzled in their enormous frying pans.

Filomena spotted the twins, wearing long aprons like the others, resembling butchers. Chris, busy at a huge oven, had paused to speak to a spiffy, authoritative young man in a well-tailored blue suit who'd entered from the main house and seemed to be assessing their progress. The other workers were immediately deferential to this young man, but Lucy heard Chris say to him, "Hey, where the hell is the fish?"

The blue-suited man looked worried. "It should have been here by now. Pop will have my hide if that fish don't show up. I'd better check on this myself. I need a car."

"Take my truck," Chris said, handing him the keys. "It's got plenty of ice and coolers. If you find the fish, better haul it over here yourself." The well-dressed man took the keys.

"Hi, ladies," the man said on his way out, looking nonplussed at their presence.

That made Chris look up, astonished to recognize his mother and aunt. "What are *you* two doing here?" he asked, looking annoyed.

Lucy said, "You forgot the soda, you idiot. Why'd you bring Vinnie and Paulie up here? Are you crazy? Amie will be furious, and she'll tell Frankie what you did."

"You *can't* tell them we were here!" Vinnie spoke up in pure panic.

"Saints above, do you hooligans have any idea what's going on in this place?" Lucy hissed at Chris. "You're in the belly of the beast, with the country's biggest criminals!"

"Which is why this is no place for women," Chris said urgently, pulling her aside. "You must go home, Ma. Take Vinnie and Paulie if you have to."

"I'm not leaving without you, young fella," Lucy insisted, "even if I have to drag you by your nose." To prove she meant it, she reached out to tweak it, but Chris ducked.

"I'm not your little boy anymore!" he said severely. "And you will *not* embarrass me in front of this crew. What good would my rep be if word got out that my mama showed up at Apalachin to drag me back home?"

At that moment, they all heard a shrill whistle. Everyone paused. Within seconds, they heard a stampede of running feet in the house, loud voices shouting, and the slamming of doors. Then a kitchen worker burst into the room, looking terrified.

"It's a raid!" he cried out, looking stricken. "A police raid!"

"We'd better get the hell out, Chris," Paulie pleaded.

"Relax!" Chris said, waving a spatula. "The cops are probably harassing them about all the parked cars, just to get a payoff. You think I can just leave this cooking?"

Filomena had gone to the doorway and looked out. "The guests are all running into the woods in their wing-tipped shoes," she reported. Chris peered out and saw that, indeed, most of these well-dressed big shots had fled the house in an ungainly way, their coats flapping, making them look like a flock of startled crows. Furthermore, there were police cars everywhere, with cops stopping anyone they spotted trying to drive off.

Lucy snapped, "You thickhead! *Nobody's* staying for dinner. And neither are we."

Vinnie and Paulie had gone pale with terror, but even now they didn't want to leave their older cousin in the lurch. "Chris, what do you want us to do?" they asked, looking at him so trustfully that Chris suddenly realized the foolish jeopardy he'd put his younger cousins into. If they got arrested in this roundup, they'd be tagged for life as criminals, and they could surely kiss goodbye any dreams of university admission and a respectable profession after that. It was a betrayal of the whole family, bringing them here in the first place. And what kind of man didn't protect his own family?

"Let's scram," Chris said hastily. Vinnie and Paulie dropped everything, turned off the stoves, and helped him shut off the ovens and rapidly put the food away. "Maybe *we* should head for the woods, too," Chris said, peering out apprehensively.

"No. It will make us look guilty if we run," Filomena warned. "But you gave away your truck. So we'll have to put you boys in the soda van. *Andiamo!*"

When Filomena climbed in front and Lucy slid behind the wheel, Chris said in disbelief, "Ma, you can't drive this thing!"

"And how on God's green earth do you think we got here?" Lucy said crisply.

Filomena said quickly, "You boys can't be seen by the police. They'll mistake you for a bunch of mobsters. Climb in back, and duck down behind the soda pallets."

"Key-hrist!" Vinnie moaned as they obeyed and shut the door.

Lucy put her foot down on the accelerator and took off. But they didn't get very far. At the bottom of the drive, the cars were barely inching forward, being forced to stop at a police cordon. "Holy Mother of God. It's not just cops here," Lucy said tensely. "There's also state troopers. And some grim-looking men in suits."

"G-men!" Chris said in a muffled voice. "FBI or the narcotics bureau!"

"They're checking every car and writing things down on a list," Filomena reported.

Lucy saw the drivers being forced to hand over something she didn't have. "They're asking for driver's licenses," she said in a small voice. "I haven't got one."

"Great, we're all going to jail," Paulie muttered.

"Get down, you fools!" Lucy snapped. She moved the van forward at the excruciating snail's pace allowed. Inch by inch, they made their way to the front of the line. Lucy could just imagine the headlines tomorrow, with her name in the story. The hospital would fire her on the spot. But now it was her turn to face the young cop.

Steeling herself, she rolled down her window and said sweetly, "Hello there, young man. Goodness, what a holy fuss today! We're just the caterers. We have to get ourselves back to the city, or our employer will be *so* mad at us."

As the policeman peered in at them, he looked surprised to see two women, about his mother's age. He glanced questioningly at an older cop, who walked over to the soda van.

"Whaddaya got here?" the older man asked sharply.

"Only a couple of lady cooks," the young officer said. The older cop peered in appraisingly, seeing two middle-aged matrons with crates of soda stacked behind them.

Lucy silently prayed to all the saints and angels she could think of, then vowed, *Mother Mary, get us out of here and I'll make a novena every week for a whole year.*

"Okay, let 'em go," the older officer said, "we got bigger fish to fry."

Lucy drove through the gate, forcing herself to go at a normal pace, worried that the older one might find out that the first cop hadn't asked for her license. But apparently she and Filomena looked so insignificant that they weren't even worth noting. Lucy held her breath until she was finally away from the police cordon and onto the main country road.

She accelerated again and did not slow down until Chris said, "Stop, I'm getting carsick back here. I have to sit up front, or else I'll puke."

"He will, too," Lucy said. "Boats don't bother him, but backseats do. He was always that way." She pulled to the side of the road, which had thick woodlands on both sides. "Fine, you drive, laddie, I'm exhausted, and me nerves are shot," she declared.

Chris hopped out, and she slid over for him. But just as Chris had settled in at the steering wheel, a man in a three-piece suit and fedora, with a camel-hair coat flung over his shoulders, came walking calmly out of the woods. He raised his left hand with his thumb up. If a king were hitchhiking, this is how he would do it.

"See what you've done?" Lucy hissed. "This guy thinks we stopped for *him*."

"I've never seen a hitchhiker dressed like *that*," Chris observed. For the man had an unmistakable aura that indicated that he was clearly one of the gangster guests.

"It will surely be more dangerous to refuse him this favor than it would be to pick him up," Filomena murmured astutely. The man approached the driver's side, and Chris reluctantly lowered his window partway, to hear what he had to say.

"Pardon me," the man said in a deep, low voice. "My car broke down while I was visiting a sick friend. Had to leave it with him, for now. I'm heading to New York City. Can you give me a lift?"

Chris thought that there was something familiar about this

guy. He had neatly combed hair above a high forehead and alert, slightly squinted eyes. He had a small cleft parting his chin. Chris said cautiously, "Sure. Ma, you ladies sit in the back."

"No, no," said the man, peering into the van with a quick, assessing look, "don't disturb the ladies. I can sit back there with these two fine boys. Twins, are you?" he asked, as if mentally assessing their age and reliability. But he glanced doubtfully at all the soda pallets and fold-down benches.

"It's okay," Lucy said hastily, comprehending that Chris was somehow trying to protect them all. "You ride up front. We'll sit in the back with our kids."

The man tipped his hat to her. "Much obliged," he said in a debonair way.

He settled in beside Chris. As they drove off, the hitchhiker glanced all around, peering out the windows, looking to see who was in every car they passed. He took out a fine linen handkerchief to wipe his perspiring brow.

They took off without another word. The radio was playing Johnny Mathis singing "Chances Are." At one point, a state trooper's car went rushing by in the other direction, its lights flashing, and Chris saw his tense passenger flinch before finally exhaling with relief as it passed them by.

The man sat rigidly for about a half hour, then he appeared to relax and doze. Chris had seen men in the navy do this, from pure exhaustion, but also as a kind of defense mechanism, to ward off having to talk to a stranger. But men in war, even when asleep, always kept "one eye open," as if their bodies were forever on alert.

After a while, the radio was playing a Pat Boone song, which Chris despised. He reached out to search for something better. As he adjusted the tuning, he glanced down and saw his passenger's right hand, which was missing its thumb and forefinger. Just two stumps in their place. Chris glanced away hastily, but this did not escape the notice of the hitchhiker, who, without moving, had opened his eyes and was watching him carefully.

"You know who I am?" the man said quietly.

"Yes," Chris said. After a pause he added, "But I never saw you today."

"Good." The man jerked his head toward the back of the soda van, where the others were murmuring in subdued conversations of their own. "What about them?" he asked. "Are they smart enough to keep quiet about what they've seen up here?"

Chris heard the stern, implicit threat. "Of course," he said. "I'll see to it."

The man nodded. "This all you do, deliver soda?" he asked. "Who's your boss?"

"My aunt back in Westchester," Chris said carefully. "I cook in her restaurant."

"That right?" his passenger said. He wore a casual expression but was still watching very keenly and listening very closely. "It's good to have a profession. Something you can do well. A lot of kids today, they see the big men around town who make it look easy, and they think, *Hell,* that's *the ticket! I want* that *guy's life!* They never get wise to the fact that if you want the big boys' 'ups,' you also gotta take the big 'downs.'"

Chris said, "I guess that's fair, to take the bad with the good."

"There's nothing fair about the jungle," the man shot back, a bit agitated now. "It's full of animals that will tear your head off. If that's where you were born and you got no skills, then you can't help it. Best I could do as a kid was work in a machine shop. So, of course I got hurt. Then I had to look for something else to do. I washed windows. There's no easy way, kid. Especially now. The old days are gone. You can't even trust the cops and the government no more," he said, sounding disgusted. "And it's only gonna get uglier."

Now Chris was certain that he knew who his passenger was—a man who'd turned window-washing into the kind of enterprise where if you didn't let him wash your windows, they'd get broken. And if you still didn't pay up, *you'd* get broken.

The man's gaze was darting vigilantly out the window, as if he'd spent a lifetime glancing over his shoulder to see who was gaining on him. He looked exhausted.

CHRIS DROPPED OFF HIS HITCHHIKER IN MIDTOWN, AS INSTRUCTED.

"Thanks, kid," the man said briskly. "I owe you one."

Chris nodded and drove on. His other passengers had dozed off and didn't rouse themselves until he pulled up to the house in Greenwich Village.

"You'd better call Godmother Amie and say you're on the way to Mamaroneck," Chris advised them. "Then all of you should catch the next train there and stay put until Thanksgiving weekend. Just lay low, you understand? It may get rough here in town."

"What about you?" Lucy demanded. "Aren't you spending the holiday with us? Frankie is already up there, waiting for you."

"Don't worry, Ma. I'll be there, but first I have to make some calls about getting my truck back and returning this van," Chris said. He tilted his head to address the twins with a warning stare. "Now, listen. Not a word about where we've been. You understand me, guys?"

"Who the hell *was* that man we picked up, anyway?" Paulie demanded.

Chris drew a deep breath. "He's the Big Boss of his own crime family. He's got his hand in the garment district, trucking, unions . . . and kosher chickens. To name a few. You just met Tommy 'Three-Finger' Lucchese."

"God! Does he really only have three fingers?" Lucy asked, aghast.

Filomena said quietly, "He's an old friend of Lucky Luciano and Frank Costello."

"Whoa. He's the real deal!" Paulie said, suitably chastened.

"What were you guys talking about so much?" Vinnie asked curiously.

"The future," Chris said soberly, thinking of how absurd and undignified those big gangsters had looked running into the woods. Why had he ever imagined that their life was something to aspire to? With a wry grin, Chris added, "He says it's not a great time to be a racketeer. And I figure, *he* ought to know the score. See ya later, folks."

As the others went inside, Lucy murmured to Filomena, "I never thought I'd say this, but I thank my saints and angels for planting Mr. Lucchese in our path! And I'm going to light a candle to Mother Mary, because this crazy day just may have been the only way to save my son from a life of crime."

35

Mamaroneck, Thanksgiving 1957

Always listen to your godmothers," Amie told the young ones as they gathered at Filomena's house by the sea. The dining room's big windows overlooked the drowsy Long Island Sound as its pewter-colored waves softly rolled onto a little beach in the cove below. Mute swans and bufflehead ducks floated serenely at the inlets, unperturbed by the gentle swells of the tides. The dappled, glowing autumn sunlight streamed inside as the entire family took their seats around the big table.

"You should especially listen to *this* godmother," Mario continued, pulling a chair out for Filomena to sit upon. "She practically predicted the Apalachin Conference," he announced, holding up a newspaper headline that screamed:

Feds Nab Over Sixty Mobsters In Apalachin Meeting

"What's Apple—Appa—?" Teresa asked, then gave up on pronouncing the word.

"App-eh-*lay*-kin," Mario said as Amie passed around the first-course platter of pumpkin ravioli made with sage butter and Parmesan. "More than sixty big-time mobsters and their henchmen were arrested, it says," Mario reported. "They even nabbed Vito

Genovese! And Profaci, and some Bonanno people, too. This is some crackdown. There's a whole list here." He paused. "Naturally, the papers didn't spell all their names right."

He scanned the article further. "Apparently the upstate police took the names and license numbers of all the men who showed up there. What a rogue's gallery!" Mario said, tossing the newspaper aside. "Everybody who's anybody in the rackets was there."

By now Vinnie and Paulie could not resist elbowing each other, then snickering, and they had to put their heads down to stop. Lucy gave them a quick warning look.

"If you ask me," said Pippa, "it was just plain stupid for all the Bosses to park their big swanky cars around some old farmhouse. So conspicuous, among the cows!"

"My friend George says that it was a state trooper who first got wise to the gangsters, because he noticed that the 'host' of the party had booked a whole lot of motel rooms for his guests," Gemma volunteered.

Frankie sighed. "Your 'friend George' says so, eh? Never thought my daughter would fall for a cop. That guy danced almost every dance with you at Petrina's wedding."

"George *happens* to be a detective," Gemma said stoutly. "And a good dancer!"

"I take one vacation in my life, and this is what comes of it," said Frankie, undeterred.

"Maybe it wasn't just a bright-eyed trooper who figured out that the mobsters were up there," Petrina suggested slyly. "Maybe someone tipped him off. Possibly to spoil it for Genovese, who wants to be crowned king of New York."

"Well, now there will be hell to pay," Mario said soberly. "The narcotics bureau is on it, and Hoover and the FBI are getting into the act. There's talk of a Senate hearing, too. Sounds like the beginning of the end of things."

"Makes Costello look real smart. He got out just in time," Amie observed.

"So did we. So now it's none of *our* business," Filomena said firmly. "Anymore."

"*Salute!* Now, where the hell is that turkey?" Frankie demanded. "I'm hungry."

As Chris appeared carrying a big roasted turkey on a platter, Pippa said, "Uncle Frankie, pour some more champagne. Uncle Mario says he wants to make the toast this year."

Frankie obligingly popped open another bottle and poured the lively golden wine into the tall glasses. Everyone turned expectantly to Mario, who smiled tenderly at Filomena and said, "I raise my glass today to my beautiful, wise wife."

Everyone else lifted their glasses and clinked, smiling at Filomena. She noticed that for the first time, she had stopped seeing numbers for her family members. Only their happy faces now. *Perhaps this means they are finally safe,* she thought.

"*Salute!*" said Petrina's new husband, Doug, who'd been listening quietly.

"*Salute!*" the others chorused, laughing and drinking.

"*Cent'anni!*" Frankie said, kissing Lucy.

"What's that mean?" Doug inquired.

Petrina explained, "'A hundred years.' As in, 'May you live a hundred years.'"

But Filomena thought elders shouldn't toast themselves. Gazing tenderly at all the younger faces smiling at her, she just lifted her glass and said softly, "*Ai bambini.*"

Pippa, Gemma, Chris, Vinnie, and Paulie all glanced at one another guiltily. This was not lost on Teresa and Nicole, who exchanged a look, vowing to find out why.

But the adults only clinked their glasses and agreed, "To the young ones!"

Nicole

Mamaroneck, 2019

After I went to see Godmother Filomena, I wrote down all that she'd told me that day, just so I wouldn't forget anything; our discussion was so cathartic to me, and I wanted to keep all the details straight in my mind. But then I put it away for years, to honor her request: *At least wait until I die*, she'd said.

I didn't think much more about it, until many years later, when I was up in the attic going through my notebooks. And then my cousin Teresa called to say that her mother was very ill. I knew I had to go back, right away.

It was early September, still summer by the calendar, a warm day with a sky of dazzling blue. When I arrived at my godmother's house, Teresa was waiting on the porch overlooking the sea, where sailboats dotted the view. "Can I go see her?" I asked.

Teresa shook her head. "Not yet. The doctor is with her. Mom threw me out."

I sat down beside her on the porch glider. "How is she?" I asked, impressed that Filomena, now in her mid-nineties, was still feisty enough to boss everybody around.

But Teresa just shook her head. All our uncles and the other

Godmothers were gone now. After Frankie's death, Aunt Lucy had moved back here, so she and my mother, Amie, became closer again in their final years together. Filomena was the last to survive.

Teresa gazed at me with those big, luminous eyes and said, "Remember when we hid in the pantry and eavesdropped on my mother?"

"Yes," I said fondly. We sat in silence awhile, then spoke about our cousins. The fearless Pippa had married her violinist suitor, and they owned a dance and music academy; Gemma, who'd been a sought-after fashion model in the early sixties, had married a photographer and started up a series of beauty spas. As for my twin brothers, Vinnie did become a lawyer, always insisting on looking at any contracts that we were about to sign; and Paulie, "the doctor in the house," never failed to make a house call no matter how late at night it was, right up until the day he retired to Florida. And our "wild" cousin Chris owned several restaurants, always keeping a special table for our family, which had grown with all of our marriages.

Then we discussed our own work. Teresa was a concert pianist, and I was on sabbatical from teaching journalism at Columbia University. When she asked what I planned to do with my time off, I confessed, "I'm thinking of writing a book about the Godmothers."

Teresa said reflectively, "You should, Nicole. It's astonishing that they tangled with all those gangsters and lived to tell the tale. Mom and I discussed those Bosses just last week."

"Whatever happened to them all?" I asked.

"She told me that Lucky Luciano was deported to Italy and died there, just before drug agents were about to arrest him. Costello lived into his old age and raised prizewinning flowers in his garden; he died at home, which, for a mobster, is pretty good. The guy who ousted him, Genovese, went to prison on a stiff narcotics charge soon after he took over Costello's operations, so Genovese

died in jail. And Gigante, the ex-boxer who shot Costello, eventually became Boss of Costello's 'Family'; but Gigante started wandering onto the streets in his bathrobe, half-crazy, or pretending
to be to elude the cops—yet, he died in jail, too."

"And Strollo?" I asked, intrigued. "What became of him?"

"They say that Genovese believed Strollo set him up with the
drug arrest, so Genovese may have ordered a hit on Strollo—
because, one day in the early 1960s, Strollo left his house and
was never seen again. Just disappeared. His remains were never
found. But some say that Strollo faked his own death, to avoid
being killed."

I shuddered. "Well, I guess we're lucky, to be living in less dangerous times."

Teresa grinned. "That's just what I told Mom. But she gave me
an odd look and said, 'Think so?' Then she talked about all the
shady mortgage deals and predatory loans that crashed the econ-
omy not so long ago, and scandals about the high-and-mighty
laundering and sheltering their money in offshore havens, and
sharky payday loans, and students saddled with college debt, and
pharmaceutical companies pushing addictive painkillers more
powerful than heroin. And she said, 'Sounds like racketeering and
extortion to me, my dear.'"

"She's right," I admitted.

"You know what Mama showed me, just yesterday?" Teresa
whispered in awe. "A million dollars' worth of gold coins she'd
kept squirreled away in a row of shoeboxes! A whole row of them,
beneath the real shoeboxes, in a secret storage area under the
floorboards of her closets. Been there for years; she never spent
any of it. I asked her why, and she said, 'In case any of you run
into trouble.' She was so determined that none of us be saddled
with debt."

The doctor emerged from the house, and he said we could see
Filomena now. When the telephone rang, Teresa said softly, "You
go ahead. I'll be in shortly."

Filomena's bedroom had big bay windows. She lay dozing, propped up on many pillows, as if she'd been gazing out at the view. The sun was casting gentle, warm rays of light across her bed. On her night table were reading glasses and a peculiar, sculpted stone hand that, as long as I could remember, had always held her blue rosary beads.

She was so quiet that I considered tiptoeing out, but then, suddenly, she spoke.

"Dammi la mano. Per favore. La tua mano!" she said plaintively, stretching out her open right hand. The gesture was so imploring that I did as she asked and put my hand in hers. She opened her eyes but didn't really recognize me, for she was looking beyond, to the sea. Yet at my touch, she seemed calmer, and a gentle, surprised smile spread across her soft cheeks with such undisguised delight that she looked just like a little girl.

"Mi ami?" she asked in a childlike voice. *"Sei tornato per me—è vero? Andiamo a casa ora?"* She cocked her head expectantly, waiting for the answer. I'd studied many languages in the good schools that she'd insisted on sending her little goddaughter to. So I understood that she was asking if someone who loved her had finally come back to take her home.

"Si, si! Ti amo," I murmured.

Teresa entered quietly now and motioned for me to stay put. Filomena didn't really see either of us. She just sighed contentedly and squeezed my hand in response. *"Resta con me."*

Stay with me. So I did as she asked, and I stayed with my godmother, holding her hand, until the doctor finally told me that it was time to let her go.

THE END

Acknowledgments

TK